Ellery Queen's
LOST MEN

Edited by Eleanor Sullivan

Here is another feast for mystery lovers – an anthology of stories about men who have disappeared and cannot be tracked down; men who lose touch with their past, their family or friends, either intentionally or through circumstances beyond their control. In every case, the circumstances are intriguing – whether the setting is a baseball stadium, the subway, a foreign hotel, a chemistry lab. And there is Graham Greene's lost Harry Lime, in *The Third Man*.

Also in Large Print

Ellery Queen's
LOST LADIES

Ellery Queen's

Lost
Men

Edited by
ELEANOR SULLIVAN

John Curley & Associates, Inc.
South Yarmouth, Ma.

Library of Congress Cataloging in Publication Data
Main entry under title:

Ellery Queen's Lost men.

1. Detective and mystery stories, American.
2. Detective and mystery stories, English.   3. Large
type books.   I. Sullivan, Eleanor.   II. Lost men.
[PS648.D4E3858   1985]   813'.0876'08   84–23775
ISBN 0–89340–885–9 (lg. print)

Published in Large Print by arrangement with Davis Publications Inc.

Distributed in the U.K. and Commonwealth by Magna Print Books.

Printed in Great Britain

COPYRIGHT NOTICES AND ACKNOWLEDGMENTS
Grateful acknowledgment is hereby made for permission to reprint the following:

This Was Willi's Day by Aaron Marc Stein; copyright © 1956 by Mercury Publications, Inc.; reprinted by permission of the author.
The Man in the Barn by Katherine Rambeau; © 1969 by Katherine Rambeau; reprinted by permission of the author.

Contents

Introduction   1

This Was Willi's Day   5
Aaron Marc Stein

The Man in the Barn   48
Katherine Rambeau

The Vanishing Man   62
Jacques Futrelle

The Adventure of the Missing Prince   92
Robert L. Fish

Woman Trouble   109
Florence V. Mayberry

Death of a Harvard Man   138
Richard M. Gordon

The Man Who Came Back   144
Edna Ferber

The Wrong Fox   164
Michael Gilbert

The Number 12 Jinx   210
Jon L. Breen

Silk Hat 233
Katharine Brush

Only One Way To Go 240
Robert Edward Eckels

A Test of Identity 277
Michael Innes

The Blessington Method 284
Stanley Ellin

Thirteen 309
Edward D. Hoch

The One Real Horror 318
John Dickson Carr

Off the Face of the Earth 350
Clayton Rawson

The Return of Backshaw 394
L. J. Beeston

The Blind Spot 410
Barry Perowne

The Third Man 434
Graham Greene

Ellery Queen's
LOST MEN

INTRODUCTION

The alumni reports of many colleges include a section listing Lost Men – class members who can no longer be reached, who have disappeared without leaving a forwarding address and have been impossible to track down.

There are stories in this new Ellery Queen collection about just such men, men who lose touch with their past, with their families and friends, either intentionally or for reasons beyond their control. In either case – and in every case – the circumstances are intriguing, whether the setting is the New York subway, the London Underground, a baseball stadium, a chemistry lab, a street in Reno, a hotel in Switzerland, or a military academy in South America.

Or, yes, the sewers of post-World War II Vienna – for would a collection of stories about lost men be complete without Graham Greene's Harry Lime? Or Clayton Rawson's Great Merlini, Stanley Ellin's Mr. Treadwell, Aaron Marc Stein's Willi, L. J. Beeston's

1

Backshaw, Barry Perowne's Annixter, Youngman Carter's Adam Makepeace?

What causes these men to defect or fade away or cease to be? The call of a muse? The sound of a different drummer? The lemming instinct? What makes them different from those of us who insist on keeping in touch, who perhaps even like Angie in Florence V. Mayberry's poignant story insist on hanging around no matter how often we're told to get lost? Perhaps they're simply antisocial, with a natural inclination to be reclusive or vagrant. They may have fallen in with bad company or be ashamed of something that they have done or that has happened to them. – It is sometimes hard to sort out guilt we deserve to feel from that we don't. Maybe they're hated or hunted or have perpetrated, or been victim of, a crime. (Where are you, Judge Crater?) Or it may simply be a sleight matter of magic – especially if Clayton Rawson's Great Merlini is in any way involved.

"Men," Plutarch wrote, "being once lost, cannot easily be recovered." But he didn't know Edna Ferber's Ted and Birdie. Or others in this book.

Consider Emily Dickinson's inspiriting:

> "Here a star, and there a star,
> Some lose their way.

2

Here a mist, and there a mist:
Afterwards – day!"

There are other tales in this collection that reflect further literary musings. Such as George Robert Sims: "'Lor, but women's rum cattle to deal with, the first man found that to his cost/And I reckon it's just through a woman the last man on earth'll be lost."

On that rum note, we leave you to your reading, much of it sparked and informed by the imagination and wit of our best Golden Age mystery writers. We dedicate the collection to Jacques Futrelle, one of the greatest of these, who himself was lost at sea aboard *The Titanic*.

AARON MARC STEIN
This Was Willi's Day

It was his dream that gave Willi joy – a dream of going and a dream of coming. He did try to picture to himself the things that might lie between, but that part of it never had more body than did the shadows on a movie screen. Always he reverted to the beginning of the dream and then to its end; for in them Willi could make every smallest detail come clear and hard and solid.

He would walk across the bridge toward the Bahnhof but he wouldn't go straight to the station. He would pause a moment at the end of the bridge where they had the pens for the ducks and the swans.

Ten francs for the maintenance of the waterfowl. Willi would drop it in the box and each time he had gone that far into the dream he would deliberately pause – to wrestle again with the one little problem which always stood alone in the whole big dream as the only thing Willi hadn't managed to lick. He could see the waterfowl when they would come around hours later. By then

5

Willi would be well away, flying over Paris perhaps with the Eiffel Tower insignificant at his feet, or maybe already out over the Atlantic in the great plane that had risen above the clouds.

Willi would glimpse himself as, with superb boredom, he looked down on the tops of the clouds; but at this stage he would never allow himself more than the briefest glimpse, because that was part of what lay ahead; and Willi wasn't such a fool that he would leapfrog one of the best parts of the whole dream. Firmly Willi would force himself back to Lucerne to stand invisible beside the man who smelled faintly of fish. The man would open the box and take out of it the scattering of small coins and among the little coins he would find Willi's ten francs.

That was the problem. Willi could see the man look at the ten francs, finger it to convince himself that it was real, shrug it off as the ten francs of one of those Americans who never did learn to add up properly in Swiss money. That was it. The man would never know that it was Willi's ten francs and Willi wanted very much that everyone in Lucerne should know – the doorman at the Schweizerhof who used to move him on before Willi became smart enough to know

6

it was no good loitering out front and trying to see into the lobby; the doorman at the Palace who had the long nose and knew so well how to look down it; the ticket takers at the Kursaal who so often spotted last week's ticket when Willi tried to use it to get past the door this week.

An anonymous contribution – the words had a fine rich sound and on their fine richness Willi could dream himself away from the end of the bridge, dream himself into the Bahnhof, dream himself aboard a first-class carriage on the Zurich train. The rest was paradise. He knew that first-class carriage – knew it so well that in the dream he could even build for himself the exact feel of the seat cushion under his buttocks.

The Zurich train was really the best part of the dream. When Willi took the trains he never rode anything but first class – at least, he rode nothing else until the ticket taker would come through. Then Willi always left his seat and wandered casually off, as though he wanted to stretch his legs. Nobody had to know that he was stretching them as far as second class, where he belonged. This part of the dream, however, he could make completely real for himself. On that dream-journey he wouldn't get up to stretch his legs. Screening a superb yawn, he would flip his first-class ticket at the ticket taker.

It was after Zurich that the dream became shadowy. He knew just which plane it would be. He had all the brochures on the luxury flights and he had pored over the pictures long enough. He would sit in a cocktail bar as he flew over the Atlantic and he would be buying the drinks.

"Ask all these people what they like," he would tell the steward. "I'm buying."

It was good, but still it wasn't like feeling the seat cushion in the first-class carriage on the Zurich train. He couldn't begin to imagine what people would order to drink. Champagne? One would think that champagne would be the obvious choice, but on those luxury flights they served free champagne – it said so right there in the brochures. They served free champagne but they had a bar where Willi could buy other drinks as well. Willi, the big spender, would have to be in the bar, of course; but Willi wished he knew what one should drink there. It would have to be something so fabulous that one would be disdaining champagne for it and what was more fabulous than champagne? Willi didn't know. He promised himself that when the time came he would know. Somehow he would find out, because

8

on that plane he wouldn't be this Willi who was a nobody. He would be the dream Willi – in the dream Willi with the money in his pocket and the knowledge in his head.

He always wanted to loiter here in the splendors of the sky. He always wanted to loiter in the magnificence of New York, but that was the part of the dream he could never keep from running thin. There would be Willi on the Empire State Building. Attendants, so splendidly uniformed that they made the doorman at the Schweizerhof look like a luggage porter, would bow to him from the elevator. They would greet him by name. They would click their heels. That he could imagine. He could also imagine himself in a pale-yellow dinner jacket. He had seen such a dinner jacket going into the Kursaal on the night of a gala.

It would be in just such a dinner jacket that Willi would go to the Radio City Music Hall. Week after week throughout the season he would sit in his private box and throughout the vast theater – so vast that you could put ten Kursaals into it and lose them all – people would turn their opera glasses on Willi because Willi would be so rich and so important that he would have a season's box at the greatest theater in all the world.

It wasn't that he couldn't imagine it. It

9

was just that he couldn't make it come solid and real the way he could the first-class cushion and the way it would feel under what would then be his first-class bottom.

Despite his wanting to take it slowly, to savor every rich detail of it, his mind was always scampering away from this shadowy part of the dream, reaching for the part of it that would come solid again, the return. He would land at Zurich and the huge Cadillac would be waiting for him at the airport. He would sweep into Lucerne in the Cadillac and he would pull up at the Schweizerhof.

He would hear the whispers.

"Look at him. They say he was once a Luzerner himself. Look at him!"

Willi looked and he felt good about what he saw. The mirror was cracked and spotted, but it served him well enough. He approved of the ruddy tan of his skin. It was the healthy, outdoor, mountain-sun look. That was essential. He approved of his dark-brown eyes. Blue eyes, when they looked at a woman, always had something of hard boldness in them. Brown eyes smoldered. Willi liked to make his eyes smolder. It was an effect. He could turn it on and off at will. He rubbed his hand over his short cropped hair. The dream Willi would wear his hair longer and there would be a wave in it, but that would be later. Now it was right for it to be short. It gave him that boyish look and it was the boyish look that caught their eye every time.

It was the same way with neckties. The dream Willi would wear a necktie. It would be hand-painted and imported from Italy. It would cost a hundred Swiss francs, but that was also for later. Willi didn't have a hundred francs. He didn't even have three francs for a boat hire – not even three francs could he spare! – and anyhow neckties got you nowhere. If your throat was a good brown color and it came down straight and strong into your chest and you had good chest muscles to show, it went better without a necktie. The white shirt open halfway down the chest – that was boyish, too. It was boyish and it was sexy, a combination on which Willi was staking his whole future. He approved of the white shirt. He had washed it himself and he had starched it and pressed it and it had been worth all the trouble.

Willi slammed out of his room without another look at its dingy meanness. He hurried along through the back streets. When he came past the Bahnhof he was still hurrying. That stretch between the station and the piers where the lake steamers tied up he knew too well. There were always plenty of them there. They would be waiting to go up the lake – to the Pilatus and the Bergenstock and the Stanzerhorn. They would be buying chocolate at the stands by the piers and they would be buying the big, expensive Italian cherries, the big, expensive Italian apricots – as if francs grew on the trees. It was no good wasting his time here.

Willi hurried past them and crossed the bridge. Going back along the more fashionable side of the lake he slowed down to a saunter. This stretch of lakefront was for him – the big shops where they sold the fabulous watches the tourists bought, the place where they had the Italian sweaters and the French neckties and the English shoes, the Schweizerhof, the Palace, the Kursaal. He looked at the expanses of lawn and the stretch of park that lay between the hotels and the lakefront and he deplored their beauty. It would suit his scheme so much better if these very best hotels were right down at the water's edge. It was one of those injustices – part of the great conspiracy that Willi had to fight – that put the deluxe hotels back from the water a little way and made those actually on the river, with their balconies overhanging the water, merely the good ones.

Slowly Willi pushed on, following the lake

to the end of the town. He wished he had a watch. That was one of the measures of his ignominy – a Swiss who didn't even own a watch. Besides, it was inconvenient. Paul owned a watch and lived by his watch. Promptly when Paul's watch said 12:30, Paul went to lunch. Willi had heard the clock in the church of the Jesuits strike noon, but now it was not going to strike again before one o'clock and that would be too late. If Willi waited till he heard the clock strike one, he would have too little time before Paul would have finished his lunch.

Coming around the bend, he squinted at the stretch of shore where Paul kept his boat. The boat wasn't there. Willi had to know the exact time. If Paul hadn't brought the boat in yet, then it would be fatal for Willi to loiter here – Paul was so mean about the damn boat.

Willi accosted a man and asked him the time. The man pushed his sleeve back and looked down at his wrist. The man had a watch and Willi silently reminded himself that a watch like this would be one of the things he was going to have – gold, self-winding, and it showed the date as well as the time. Willi knew just how many francs a watch like that cost down the street at Bucherer. It was one of those large sums

13

Willi liked thinking about. He was thinking about all those francs and they filled his mind so satisfyingly that he almost didn't hear when the man told him it was 12:35. Willi scowled at the shore where Paul should have had his boat tied up.

Then Willi saw it. It had been pulled up out of the water and was now lying bottom-up on the grass. Willi started toward it. He began cursing. That fool, Paul, had been painting it again. That was why he had it out of the water. With the paint wet on the boards and on the seats, it would be in no condition for Willi to use it.

Not that he cared about Paul's paint, but he had to care about his own shoes and his pants. They were the only halfway decent shoes he owned and his only untorn pair of pants. He couldn't let them get smeared with paint. He might have known that Paul would choose one of the days of a Kursaal *festnacht* for painting his crazy boat. With only two nights each week at the Kursaal in which to operate, and only a limited number of weeks in the whole season, Willi had no time to lose. And there was his feeling. He'd had the feeling ever since he woke up that morning. This was going to be his day – Willi's day.

He stood over the boat and cursed the wet paint. He didn't have to touch it to know how

14

wet it was. It glistened wetly and he could smell it. More out of angry vandalism than with any real hope, he leaned over and grabbed the newly painted boat to heave it over on its keel.

The boat came over and he grinned. Paul hadn't yet painted the seats or the floorboards and he hadn't touched up the oars. Willi dragged the boat across the grass and down to the water. He was getting paint on his hands, but hands didn't matter. He was very careful of his shoes and his pants and his shirt. The boat left smears of paint on the grass and Willi did have a passing thought for what he was doing to the paint on the boat's bottom. There would be grass stuck in it, and the gravel at the water's edge would grind against it and turn the boat into a pretty mess, but Willi had no regrets. Paul had it coming to him for being so mean about his boat. It didn't hurt the boat any if Willi used it for an hour twice a week. It wasn't as though Willi ever wanted it when Paul would be needing it. Paul had a watch and, when the watch said 12:30, Paul had to have his lunch.

Willi floated the boat and stepped into it. He was most careful to avoid getting paint on his pants or shoes. Quickly he drove the boat out into the current. The green water ran fast toward the Bahnhof bridge, but Willi was impatient. He rowed hard, putting all the weight of his back behind the oars. It might have been wiser if he had saved himself for the long pull back when he would need all his wind and muscle to row the boat against the current, but Willi had a stout heart. He would have more than enough strength left in him for pulling the boat back, and his stout heart kept telling him that this was his day – his day of destiny.

Willi, impatient for his destiny, didn't spare himself. He shot the boat under the bridge into the river. Here, narrowly channeled between the stone-faced banks, the green water carried him along with a rush. The waterfowl rode the current, ruddering themselves toward the railings at Unter Der Egg, gathering, as they always did at mealtimes, in the shadow of the hotel terrace.

Willi stopped rowing. Now he used his oars only to hold the boat steady against the current. For a couple of moments he watched the swans and the ducks. They were working as he did, maneuvering into position under the terrace, holding themselves there against the rush of the water.

Up on the terrace the linen and china gleamed in the sun. The crystal and the silver flashed light. Willi concentrated on the tables under which the waterfowl clustered most thickly. A family with children. Willi passed them up. Children were no good to him. At the next table a young couple had wine in their glasses. A pity it had to be a couple. Then there was an old couple. Willi made a mental note of the old couple. Matched up against the feeling he'd had all morning, an old couple wasn't much, but he just might be wrong and he had had pretty good luck with some old pairs on other days. A meal, a tip – it wasn't much but it did help and there had been that one old couple who told him they had a son like him back home. They had bought Willi a watch. It hadn't been a very good watch but he had been regretful when he had to sell it. He would like to have kept it, not for long but just till the time when he would have the watch he meant to have.

The ducks and the swans could have the old couple for the moment. Willi focused on the champagne bucket at the far end of the terrace. There was a waiter in the way and he couldn't see the table, but he prayed that it wouldn't be another couple. He was having that feeling again, the same feeling he'd had all morning. Something was telling him this would be it. He let the current carry him the length of the terrace. The waiter moved and Willi saw her hair. He winced. It was yellow hair and, just looking at it, Willi knew that it would feel like straw under his hand. It reminded him of the mattress on the cot back in his room, the way the rotting fabric would crack and the grayish-yellow straw would come bursting out of it.

Willi put his mattress out of his mind and concentrated on looking boyish. Deftly he brought the boat in toward the terrace, scattering the ducks and swans before him.

He came in under the table and held the boat there. The woman had a piece of roll in her hand and she waved it at Willi angrily.

"Go away!" she shouted. "You've scared them. Go away!"

Willi held fast and grinned at her.

"Raus!" she screamed in what she obviously believed to be German.

Willi laughed. He never looked more boyish than when he was laughing. Her rings flashed in the sun. His feeling had been so right. Diamonds and champagne and not at the Schweizerhof or the Palace, but here at this merely good hotel. Willi knew the type.

She would have it – maybe even more than the women at the Palace and the Schweizerhof. This kind was careful. This

18

kind let it pile up in the banks. Now that Willi was holding the boat still, the swans and the ducks came edging back. The waterfowl gathered thick along the sides of the boat. One of the swans actually brushed the boat and some of the fresh paint came off green on the swan's white plumage. Willi saw it and laughed some more.

She tossed the bit of roll. Willi was ready. As adroitly as any of the waterfowl he shot into position for it and, having the advantage in height over even the long-necked swans, Willi caught the morsel of bread between his fine white teeth. He tossed it back into his mouth and he grinned at her as he chewed it up.

She laughed. They always laughed, but she did more. She took up her knife and, breaking off another bit of roll, spread it with *pâté de foie gras*. This time it was easy. She threw it at him and it was no trick at all catching it in his mouth. They always threw stuff to him, but Willi had never known one that could throw so accurately. It pleased him that she should have such a good throwing arm. Other times it had been butter on the roll and not *foie gras* and a clumsy pitch had once or twice hit Willi's shirt. That meant washing the shirt and getting it dry and pressed before evening and Willi hated washing his shirt. He had only the one presentable one.

The clock in the church of the Jesuits struck one. He couldn't stay but a minute more. The pull back up the river against the swift current took time and it would be fatal if he didn't have the boat back before Paul finished his lunch and returned to the lake. But for one like this he was ready to push his time to the limit.

She kept it going, spreading *foie gras* on the bits of roll and throwing them to him to catch. He never missed and all the time she laughed harder. She laughed and she drank her champagne. She was a little tight. Willi could see that but he took comfort from the steady accuracy of her throwing. He told himself that she couldn't be so drunk that she would forget him by evening. Laughing harder than ever, she picked up her wine glass. With a wide sweep of her arm she splashed champagne at him. He played along and managed to catch a few drops of the wine in his mouth, but more of it soaked his shirt. He shivered. It reminded him of the time Paul had caught him with the boat and had pitched him into the icy water of the lake. Paul with his damn muscles and damn money. Climbing mountains every weekend, pulling the boat around all the time, always

20

making himself more and more powerful,
and always eating – the way that Paul ate!
Willi glanced toward the church. He had
more than stretched his time. Bending his
back to the oars he pulled away.

"I'm sorry!" she shouted. "Come back!
Don't you want some of my cake?"

He turned to grin at her, but he didn't go
back. His time had more than run out. He
leaned hard on the oars and fought the
current. He knew this river as well as the
waterfowl knew it. He knew each place where
a jut of the bank channeled the current off
and offered a stretch of relatively quieter
water. He took advantage of every one of
those stretches, working against the current
where he must, dodging it where he could.
He made it under the Bahnhof bridge but
here he could see the clock in the Bucherer
shop window. There wasn't a hope. He had
waited too long, Paul would be at the
mooring. He knew just how Paul would look,
his big fists clenched.

Willi told himself he was being a fool.
Here he was trying to get the boat back to the
mooring, trying to tie it up and be away
before Paul came back from his lunch, as
though he could do that today and Paul not
know the boat had been used. Willi looked
down at his hands and saw the paint under

his fingernails. He could imagine what the boat's bottom would look like by now. Paul could never be deceived today.

"The hell with Paul and his boat."

Quickly he backed the boat around into the current. He was laughing again as he rested on the oars and let the water carry him under the bridge and into the river. Skillfully he steered the boat to the bank in front of the market. He caught hold of one of the stakes by the landing steps and made the boat fast. He told himself what a good fellow he was. Anyone else would have turned the boat adrift and let that fool, Paul, go chasing it down the river. It was not as if he were going to need Paul or the boat again. His feeling had been so right. This was his day.

He left the boat and took off on a dead run. He knew Paul. Paul would already be down to the lake and have found the boat missing. Paul would be coming this way, heading down the river looking for Willi. Willi ran all the way back to his lodgings.

There he looked at himself in the mirror. He examined his shirt. The champagne had dried and there was no stain. He wanted to take it off and hang it up so that he could have it fresh for the evening. The good shirt and the good pants and the good shoes – he couldn't waste them by wearing them while he was waiting. He looked at his hands. They were green with paint. That was all right. Hands could be washed but he didn't dare take his shirt off. He couldn't be sure that some of the green mightn't come off on his shirt or his pants. He went to the cracked washstand and started working on his hands.

It wasn't easy getting the paint off. With turpentine it would have been no problem, but he didn't have any turpentine. Some of the paint came off with soap and water, but a lot of it remained. He dug it out from under his fingernails and he scrubbed at his hands as hard as he could. Then he thought of the emery board he used when he did his nails. With that he tenderly buffed the skin of his palms and his fingers. It took him a long time and when he finally gave up, his hands were hot and all but scraped raw.

There were still bits of green stuck in the creases of his skin, but there was nothing he could do about those and they didn't show unless you looked for them. Willi remembered that there had been one of them early in the summer who had told his fortune. She had read his palm. If this one wanted to read his palm, she would see the paint, but there couldn't be another like that one. It was the one who had taken him to Interlaken so he could show her the

Jungfraujoch. A whole week it had been, and then he had lived a whole month on her tip and now almost another month on what he'd managed to pilfer. She'd given him the money to pay and she'd never asked for change, but he had always given her change – that is, a little change. Americans were like that – so smart about money except that they could never count in any money that wasn't their own American dollars.

Willi changed into a shirt and pants that didn't matter. He took off his shoes and lay down on the cot. He drifted into his daydream. Leaving Lucerne – the ten francs in the box for the waterfowl. Ten francs would more than pay them back for the bits of bread he had deprived them of, and if it hadn't been for Willi there would have been no butter or *foie gras* anyhow.

His thoughts went back to Interlaken and that wonderful week, and a nasty fear caught at him. Everything had gone so well with that one and then suddenly she'd had a letter from her husband. They never wore their wedding rings and while he had been wasting all that good time on her he could have been missing out on just the right one.

Like this one today. He had looked most particularly. There were the diamonds but no wedding ring, as though that meant

24

anything. He remembered the hole in the mattress and now he deliberately turned to look at the straw. He grinned at it. No need to be anxious about this one, he thought happily. Who would have this one? With hair like that?"

"I'll have her," he promised himself. The dollars - all those beautiful green dollars. The thought never entered his mind that there might already have been another like him, another lad ready, even eager, to shut his eyes to the hair, to all the big and little things that were wrong with the way she looked. It wasn't that he had any delusion he might be the only man in the world who wanted the dollars. His was another delusion. It just never occurred to him that there could be another anywhere in the world who would go about it so cleverly, who would have every word and every move so carefully planned.

He tried the dream with her in it, skipping the part where she would leave it. For his dream of coming and going, he was always alone - alone with the beautiful dollars.

Paul came slamming into the room. "This time I'm going to kill you. I'm going to wring your dirty, useless neck."

Willi yawned. "Hello," he said. "What bug is biting you now?"

"Didn't I tell you to leave my boat alone?"

25

"Who wants any part of your stinking boat?"

"You didn't put it in the water?"

"Was it out of the water?"

"You know it was out of the water. You know I painted it this morning. You know what a mess you made of it."

"Me? I wouldn't do a dirty trick like that. Are you crazy? Somebody plays you a trick like that and right away you go looking for your friends. Why don't you go looking for somebody who has a grudge against you? What makes you think your friends would do a thing like that to you?"

"The mark of your hands is right there in the paint."

"My hands? You know my fingerprints, I suppose? You're a Sherlock Holmes now, I suppose?"

"Let me see your hands."

Willi put his hands behind his back and lay on them. "You want to compare the fingerprints, maybe? Go away. You're bothering me."

Paul slapped him. It was a heavy, backhanded slap and Paul's knuckles raked across Willi's mouth. Willi tasted blood.

"Show me your hands."

"Get out of my room. I'll count to ten and then I'll call the police."

Paul caught him by the arm and twisted. Willi screamed. He tried to fight it but the pain flipped him over on his face. He had his hand tightly clenched. Paul tried to open it. He picked up Willi's shoe and smashed the edge of the heel on Willi's knuckles. Willi's hand opened.

"Why don't you call the police? You don't count that slow. Call them. I'll show them your hands."

"Leave me alone."

Paul jerked Willi to his feet and slapped him again. Now Willi felt the blood run warm down his chin. He put up his hands and fought. He didn't want to fight, but he was desperate. He was thinking only of his face. He had to protect his face.

He would never have been any match for Paul but he did try to hold him off. With two good hands he might have protected his face, but one hand was all but useless. It throbbed, and when he tried to close it in a fist the pain made him dizzy. He forced himself to shake the dizziness off but still the hand wouldn't close. He fought one-handed but he didn't really fight. He just kept the one hand up as a guard while he ducked and dodged. He tried to kick but it wasn't any good. Paul was ready for that and anyhow Willi had no shoes on.

27

Paul's fist came through Willi's guard and smashed into Willi's face. It struck once and it struck again. Willi went down. Paul waited for him to get up and Willi could have done it, but he stayed down. He hoped that it might still be all right, that his eye wasn't going to puff. Paul jerked him to his feet and held him upright, waiting for him to take up his own weight, waiting for him to put his hands up.

Willi let his hands hang. He dangled limp in Paul's grasp. Paul slapped him, trying to make him fight. Willi wouldn't be drawn. He just rolled his head with the slaps, hoping they wouldn't mark him too much. He knew his eye was swelling, but still he hoped.

Paul let him drop and, standing over Willi, kicked him hard. Willi lay with his head buried in his arms and hated Paul, hated him and despised him. Had he been Paul and Paul Willi, he would have kicked Paul. It wouldn't have been this harmless kick in the buttocks. He knew exactly where he would have kicked Paul.

Willi lay with his head buried in his hands and listened. He heard Paul stamp out of the room and clatter down the stairs. When the downstairs door slammed, Willi moved. He pulled himself to his feet and stumbled to his mirror. His lips were cut and bleeding, but the worst of it was his eye. His eye was hopeless. It would be a week or more before he could show that eye.

He knew it wasn't any use, but he had to try. He soaked a towel in cold water and pressed it to the eye. His hand was throbbing maddeningly. There was blood on his shirt. He thought it was a good thing that it hadn't been his better shirt and then, bitterly, that it didn't really matter any more. He took off the bloodstained shirt and soaked it in cold water, then wrapped the wet shirt around his hand. He worked on his face and his hand all the rest of the day, keeping the compresses cold. The pain ebbed but he didn't care about that. Every time he changed the compress, he looked at himself in the mirror and felt a pain that wouldn't ebb. She would have been the one. He knew it now with the most absolute certainty, and now there had to be this to wreck his hopes. He'd never have another chance. He knew that also with absolute certainty.

From hour to hour he listened to the church clock strike. He heard six and he was still at it. Seven. Eight. At eight, he gave up. He had lost. Eight-thirty was the time for the Kursaal. He should already have been on his way. He studied himself in the mirror for the last time and he couldn't bear it. He threw

29

the towel and the wet shirt into the basin and ran away blindly.

He ran till his wind gave out. Then he slowed down to a walk, but he walked as he had run, steadily, aimlessly, mechanically, letting his feet carry him wherever they would.

When he came to the Kursaal he stopped. He circled the building, looking in through the windows, trying to catch sight of her. The yodelers were on. Then he saw her. She wasn't at a table with a drink like the other tourists. She was wandering about, carrying her drink in her hand, as if she were looking for someone.

"She's looking for me," Willi muttered bitterly.

He could see her very clearly under the Kursaal lights. Those lights were kinder than the sun had been. Even her hair didn't look too bad – it might almost have been real hair. Willi dismissed her hair. He looked hard at her mink stole – pastel, soft, expensive. He forgot about his cut lip and bit hard on it. The pain reminded him, but he bit again, tasting the blood once more on his tongue.

She left the room. Thinking about her mink, Willi shivered. It was the first he realized that he had come out without even putting a shirt on. He turned away and walked down the path to the edge of the lake. He stood there looking at the water. Then he heard her voice at his shoulder, but he didn't turn his head.

"Hello," she said. "Or don't you speak English?"

Willi turned to speak to her. "I've had a misfortune," he said. "You must excuse me."

She laughed. "Aren't you cold without a shirt?" she asked.

An idea began to bloom in Willi's mind. He didn't wait for it to finish shaping itself. He stepped full into the light so that she could see him. The hell with his eye. He knew how good he looked with his shirt off and now he had nothing to lose. He chose the English words carefully.

"I can't afford to be cold," he said. "I haven't a shirt."

"Oh." She took a step away from him. She looked puzzled and uncertain.

"You don't know me?" Willi asked. "You don't remember?"

"Should I know you?"

She didn't have any idea who he was. He could see that she was simply looking for a man, any man.

"I enjoyed the *foie gras*," he said. "I hope

31

you didn't think I was rude not waiting for the cake."

She blinked and then started laughing. "My duck," she said. "You're my duck from lunchtime."

Willi clicked his heels sharply and bowed.

"Yes," he said. "Your duck."

"But what's happened to you? Have you been in a fight?"

Sighing, Willi nodded. "Robbers," he said. "Four of them." Now the idea had flowered and he didn't have to stop to examine it. He knew it was good. This was his day, wasn't it? "I fought them as well as I could," he said, showing her the hand Paul had smashed with the shoe. "But four of them. They beat me unconscious and when I came to they were gone and had taken everything – my money, my watch, my coat, even my tie and my shirt and my shoes."

He went on and on about the shoes. The robbers had taken his and had left him these terrible things. They had even taken his trousers. One of them had been his size and while he was unconscious they had stripped him and changed clothes with him.

She took charge. Tenderly she helped him to her car. Willi hadn't dreamed of a Cadillac at this early stage. The Cadillac was to have come later. She took him to a doctor and

Willi noticed that doctors were much gentler when there was money about. He looked much better when the doctor had finished with him. The bits of neat white tape against the bronzed skin weren't a bad effect at all.

After that it was clothes. Willi didn't even have to guide her. There was only one shop that kept open that late in the evening, the place that had the stuff that caught the tourist trade. She did the choosing. The English shoes, the Daks trousers, the French shirt, the Italian silk necktie, the beautiful tweed jacket. She even wanted to buy him a nylon undershirt but he wouldn't have that. He never wore an undershirt, he said. Besides, he always gave them change. It was good policy not to seem greedy. Not taking an undershirt was like giving her change. She even thought of the sunglasses.

"Like a Hollywood star," she said.

"But you mustn't," Willi said. "I don't know when I can ever pay you back."

"I want to dance," she said, and she bought him a beautiful billfold. She put five hundred francs into the billfold and slipped it into the pocket of the beautiful tweed jacket.

Willi took her back to the Kursaal. They did the rhumba and they even did the Charleston. Willi couldn't be bothered by the fact that the rhumba made him hurt in the place where Paul had kicked him and that the Charleston made him hurt a lot worse. They had champagne but they didn't drink much of it. Willi tried to make her drunk, but then it occurred to him that she was trying to make him drunk and he stopped worrying. She was going to be too easy, but still he was careful. He ate but he didn't drink much and, watching her, he saw that she neither ate nor drank. She was just pretending that the wine was making her gay.

They danced till the Kursaal closed and then she said she wasn't going to let him go home alone. He was hurt and she was going to go with him and take care of him. He told her that they couldn't go to his place. He reminded her of the robbers. They had wrecked his place. They went back to her hotel and she packed a bag and then they drove over to another hotel. Willi registered them as Mr. and Mrs. It was her idea.

"I don't have to seduce her," Willi told himself gleefully. "She's seducing me."

First thing the next morning they were married and she bought him a wedding present – a gold watch, self-winding, that told the date as well as the time. Willi drove the Cadillac and it was well that the place where Paul had kicked him did hurt as he sat behind the wheel. It was as good as pinching himself. He wasn't dreaming.

It was funny. He'd had it all so completely worked out – every last detail and how he would manage it when he had the big chance. Now it was happening and he wasn't managing anything. She was having all the ideas and she acted as though she had not the slightest notion that they were actually Willi's ideas. He wondered if it could be that he had her hypnotized, that he was making her do everything he wanted her to do without even knowing he was doing it. He remembered that he had heard somewhere that certain exceptionally strong minds could do miraculous things. Willi watched his destiny shape itself and he hadn't the least doubt of the extraordinary strength of his mind.

The way he had always planned it himself, it would have been a slow and careful campaign, taken move by move in a calculated sequence. He had never dreamed of a woman like this one, a woman who would rush him off his feet, who would make the moves even before he had begun to prepare her for them, who, if anything, seemed to be preparing him.

All of it happened on that very first day

– even the will. In his own planning it had always been a matter of weeks, even of months, before he could let himself so much as begin to lay the groundwork for a will. Now it was happening in such rapid sequence that it made Willi dizzy. The two-ring ceremony, buying him the watch, rushing him around to the American consulate.

At first, the consulate baffled Willi. He had never dreamed so splendidly. The way she was received at the consulate dazzled him. She was known, she was important. They treated her with deference. Willi never opened his mouth. He just listened, trying to take it in, trying to make himself believe that it could really be this magnificent.

She was emphatic. She was definite, dictatorial. She had come to make a will. She wanted it made at the consulate. She wanted it so firmly a matter of record that there could never be any nonsense about it.

"That family of mine," she said. "You know what they're like."

They knew what her family was like. She began dictating. Willi tried to hold the amounts in his head, but they got away from him. This charity, that charity, and everything in five figures – dollars, at that, not francs.

"The residue of my estate to my beloved husband, Willi."

"Your brothers?"

"My brothers can go scratch."

There had to be four copies – one for her, one to be kept on file at the consulate, one to be sent to her lawyers in New York, one to her eldest brother.

"They might as well know right away where they stand," she said.

Willi was angry with himself. Wasn't this exactly the way he'd always wanted it? Wasn't it better than he'd ever dared to hope? Was this a time to have any anxieties or misgivings? He worked hard at putting every disquieting thought out of his mind. So he hadn't figured on anything so conspicuous as the consulate. What of that? He hadn't dreamed that it would be anything like this much money either.

It made no difference. He would have to wait, of course, but then he had always planned on being patient. He had never thought that he would get this far and then become reckless. Nothing was changed.

He didn't allow himself to think it, but he knew what his real trouble was. It was the next step, the step he had always skipped over in his dreaming. There had always been all this, and then there had been the departure – the ten francs in the box for the waterfowl, the first-class ticket to Zurich, the luxury plane across the Atlantic. In that part of it Willi was always alone and he had always known what he would have to do in between; but he had always let that part of it go with the assurance that when the time came he would know how to act.

Now the time had come.

It was no good telling himself that it wouldn't be safe to do it so soon. She had hurried him this far and now it wasn't too soon to begin the job of planning it. For this part he would need the best plan he had ever made, and he didn't feel ready to start thinking about that.

She was his princess and he was her duck. They spent the rest of the first day hilariously and extravagantly. Willi almost began to wish that she wasn't so terrible-looking, but he resolutely put that thought away. She wasn't going to make Willi go soft.

He didn't put off thinking about it for long. The very next morning he began, but even then it started because she helped him. She was sick in the morning, green in the face with sickness. Even though the look of her disgusted him, Willi carefully did all the correct things. He was her devoted duck. He

38

was frantic with worry. He wanted to get a doctor.

She wouldn't have a doctor. She had been this way before – it would pass. He was to leave her alone. Willi would have been glad to leave her alone but he had to do the correct thing. She would have none of it. Sharply she ordered him out of the bathroom. He withdrew with dignity. He sat in the bedroom and waited, listening to her being sick the other side of the bathroom door.

His normally cheerful turn of mind took hold of him. She knew what this was and she wanted no doctor. He thought of some incurable illnesses. He almost let himself hope that she would take care of this part of it for him, too. He wouldn't even plan his next move.

The jewelry she had worn the night before lay on her dressing table, the diamonds blazing in the morning sun. Willi strolled over and picked up a ring. He tried to guess what it might be worth. He tossed it in the air just as though it were another bit of bread, and like a bit of bread he caught it in his mouth. The big stone was cold against his tongue. He liked it. It seemed to him that it tasted like money. He was enjoying the thought that he didn't have to practice up on that trick any more. It had served.

He spat the ring out into his palm, carefully dried it off, and returned it to the dressing table. Her bag lay with the jewelry. He listened a moment. She was still at it behind the bathroom door. He picked up her bag, opened it, idly explored through it. He came on a picture and looked at it with mild curiosity. It was a man, big, athletic, handsome. One of her brothers? He wondered. Not likely, the way she had talked about them at the consulate. He put the picture back and pulled out a letter. It was postmarked Venice and dated less than a week back. Willi read the letter.

"Sorry, my dear, but you did know I was married ... never a possibility of divorce ... my wife's religious feelings in the matter ... sorry ... are you certain there is no mistake ... doctors are wrong sometimes ... believe me, I am sorry."

Folding the letter, Willie returned it to her bag. He closed the bag and arranged everything as it had been on the dressing table. He could still hear her behind the bathroom door, but now Willi was finished with any cheerful thoughts about incurable diseases. So that was what was wrong with her! It was all right. It made no difference except for driving all the foolishness out of his head.

She'd had her own plan and her plan had called for haste. Now she had a father for her brat. She had what she wanted. Now Willi was taking over. She had been smart, but she'd picked the wrong man. She should never have been smart with Willi. She had walked straight into his trap. Now *he* could plan it, and he would enjoy planning it. It was only what she had coming to her – thinking she could use Willi! She'd find out who was using whom.

Now that he had begun thinking about it properly, the whole plan came into his head in one solid piece. It was as though it had always been there, just waiting for the moment when he would need it. It had always been there – just as the mountains had always been there. All he needed was patience. He couldn't miss, but he mustn't rush. When it happened, it had to be right. There mustn't be too many questions. It mustn't come too soon after the making of the will. Of course, he couldn't wait too long. It would have to happen before the brat came – that was certainly the outside limit. Willi was no fool. He could visualize another scene like the one the morning before.

"And the residue all to my child, Frederico."

The letter had been signed – *Yours always, Frederico.*

Before the birth of the brat certainly, and enough before so that his taking her up the mountain wouldn't look odd. A month or two would be enough to wait, and while he waited they were to be seen together, always laughing, always happy, always – the way she would say it – living it up. He could wait that long to make it look good.

For a stake like this he could wait as long as he had to.

When she finally came out of the bathroom, he was gentle and solicitous. He was every inch her duck. She didn't want to talk about it, so he didn't talk about it. She wanted to be gay, so he was gay.

They were at lunch when she herself suggested the mountain. It was like all her other suggestions, a command. She was still rushing him, Willi thought wryly, but this she couldn't rush. He was going to wait till the time was right, but meanwhile he could start her training. There had been the hour before lunch during which he had come to feel that waiting for the right time wasn't going to be too bad. She had taken him shopping, but this was not like the emergency shopping of the first evening.

That sort of thing wasn't good enough for her husband. Now it was measurements. Willi had been measured for suits, for shirts, for shoes. For Willi everything had to be made to order.

"This is just to fill in," she said airily. "This stuff will do till we go to London or Rome, where we can have the right sort of clothes made for you."

In all Willi's dreaming he had imagined grand gestures – but he had never imagined anything so grand as ordering half a dozen thousand-franc suits of clothes and telling the tailor that, of course, a Lucerne tailor couldn't be really first-rate, but that these feeble thousand-franc efforts would have to do for the journey to London or Rome. Willi had begun to think that the time he would have to wait would indeed not be wasted. He could use it for training her, but he could also permit her to train him. She would teach him how to spend money. For the first time in his life Willi was ready to believe spending money was an art in which he still had something to learn.

She left it to him to choose the mountain and he selected the Stanzerhorn. They were going to concentrate on the less frequented peaks. It was to be the honeymoon celebration. The duck would take his princess to the places where they could be alone with the mountains and the snow and the sky, far away from people. There would always be a mountain railway, of course, and it would supply him all the people he would need. When the time came, the people could testify to the affection and light-hearted gaiety of the newly married couple.

They rode the cable railway up the long slope to the foot of the mountain and they were as gay as a pair of children on a school holiday. They had bought some of the fine Italian cherries at the stand by the boat landing, and all the way up on the train they amused themselves eating cherries. She would toss them in the air for him to catch in his mouth. Some he would catch and eat, but most he would catch by the stem, and then she would lean across to bite the fruit that dangled over his chin. It was a pleasure watching them. Everybody watched.

At the top of the railway they disdained the level path that led to the hotel and struck out over the rough, steep track that led to the summit. Here Willi became protective. At least, he made a try. He took her arm. He made a great show of guiding her over the difficult footing. She was going to have to learn to depend on him, to go along the most dangerous slopes secure in her confidence that Willi would take care of her. She was to learn to depend on Willi's strong right arm, to expect that it would always be ready to reach out and snatch her safely back from death. Little by little he planned to teach her. She would learn to be foolhardy in the mountains, to depend on Willi and to trust him.

He took her arm, but, laughing at him, she pulled away and went nimbly up the rocky trail with Willi in pursuit. She took those very chances he had planned on teaching her to take. Willi followed, telling himself that he might have known that here, too, she would be competent.

He hadn't forgotten the accuracy of her throwing arm, but that was all right. He wouldn't have to lead her to the dangerous places: he could let her lead him.

At the summit Willi caught her in his arms and kissed her. A man and a woman were leaning on the iron railing, looking down with shuddering delight at the sheer tumble of rocks that dropped with frightening grandeur to the velvety patch of jade that was the broad valley far below.

Willi hadn't expected her to respond to his embrace as whole-heartedly as she did. They might have been alone in their hotel bedroom, she came to him with that much abandon. Tittering, the other couple started down the path from the summit, leaving Willi alone with his princess.

He led her over to the rail and together they looked down the dizzying mountainside.

A few feet below them, in a crack in the rocks, there grew one solitary spray of edelweiss.

"I must get it for you," Willi said.

"You can't get down there."

"Watch me."

Willi knew what he was doing. He gave her his stick to hold for him. Confidently he climbed over the rail. Taking a firm grip on the steel stanchion that supported it, he lowered himself till he dangled by one hand from the base of the stanchion. There was a small rock projection where he could plant his feet. He couldn't have been safer in bed. He had the stanchion firmly gripped with his good hand, and his feet were well planted. The hand Paul had battered was still not too good, but it was good enough for plucking a bit of edelweiss from the cranny in the rocks and he was not depending on the injured hand for his hold. He swung his body wide, reaching for the little flower.

It wasn't a dangerous swing but he made it look dangerous. From watching him take such chances she was going to learn to take them with him until the time would be right.

The blinding pain in his good hand jerked his body stiff. His feet slid away from the ledge where he had planted them. His head snapped up and he looked straight at her. He half expected he would see Paul standing beside her, but she was quite alone. In that rigid second he watched her raise his stick and with an easy, practised swing smash it down on his hand a second time.

The hand gave way and Willi slammed downward, bouncing from rock to rock.

That was her plan all along, Willi thought. I had to give mine time. She didn't. She never wanted me. She wanted a father for her brat and she made sure there would be no doubt of it. The consul knows. Her brothers will know. She has the marriage license, and if any questions are asked no one will think she could have planned to kill her husband – not a husband for whom she ordered all those new suits and shirts and ties.

Willi's last thought was the bitterest of all. She could cancel all the orders now. There was nothing to stop her. It would suit her plan to cancel them. He had thought that he needed time to build up evidence of his love and devotion. She had built faster than he had – much faster.

KATHERINE RAMBEAU
The Man in the Barn

He thought he saw Katje waiting in the long shadows as he limped down the Pike. Faithful Katje would be looking for him, her anxious eyes searching the road, wispy curls around her face flattened in the chill wind of early November. He tried to shout, but the wind carried the sound away, and he thought he saw her shiver and turn to enter the old farmhouse.

Perhaps she doesn't recognize me, he thought. Grimy, tattered, and stained.

Katje was wearing a new dress, blue as always. Funny how Katje always managed to be beautiful, whatever the fashion. She had an eye for style, but she herself was always the same.

But I'm not the same. The exhilaration that had carried him through the fighting, the shock and the pain, the confusion – all these and much more were gone. Even after he fell on Chatterton Hill, Cornelius could for a while follow the progress of the battle; but gradually as his fever rose, reality had

48

receded, and he had seen only shadows passing by.

Sometime after the battle was over – hours or days, he couldn't be sure – he got to his feet and walked away, overlooked by the British. He walked north from White Plains. Toward home. To Katje.

It was best, he decided, not to stay too close to the river, for the enemy patrols were active. More than once he had ducked low or sought cover because of the sound of footsteps or of voices murmuring in caution as a patrol beat the brush looking for stragglers.

It was difficult in the daytime to identify friends, and impossible at night. Several times he heard the familiar rhythms of the speech of his own people, but he hesitated to come forward, for in these days even families were divided by loyalties.

Cornelius fought off the faintness, the mind-dimming weariness which had forced him to rest frequently, and tried to push forward to Katje as fast as he could without showing himself to the enemy. His first impulse on regaining consciousness had been to look for his brigade, but he could find none of his comrades still alive in the vicinity, and it had already become apparent that his condition would prevent his being of any further use as a soldier even if he should come upon them.

There was an urgency, almost a panic, in him to hurry to Katje.

"You must listen to me, Katje," he had insisted. "If I don't come back, you'll need –"

"You mustn't talk like that. You will come back."

"But if I don't, Katje –"

"Don't talk about it," she had said firmly.

"But the money, Katje. If the British –"

"If the British come and I don't know where it is, they won't get it." Katje was always calm. Reasonable. Frustrating.

Cornelius had kissed her warmly and gone away with the secret of the hiding place. Nor had he mentioned it in his letters, for Katje would have to ask Hendrik to read them to her, and as Cornelius knew so well Hendrik was an old gossip and, some said, a Loyalist.

Now, however, the matter was vital, and he must hurry, for now that Brooklyn had been evacuated and the battle at White Plains had gone to the British, Cornelius feared that they might push north and so menace the van der Laan farm.

He did not, however, hear or see any signs of determined British pursuit to the north as he traveled toward Fishkill, and by the time he reached the village, late at night, he had regained enough confidence to walk along the road. He was not in uniform. He had never had a uniform, but he still retained his gun. He had no bullets, but the gun was still useful, for he could lean on it. He had to lean on it or fall. The warm coat that clever Katje had made for him was torn and stained.

"But I don't need it, Katje," he had said.

"But you do. And anyway, take it to please me." Katje could do anything. She had woven the cloth, too, of yarn she had spun and dyed herself. "I tried to match the dishes."

"Why the dishes?" Silly question, of course. The yarn was blue for the same reason the dishes were blue. Katje adored blue. Cornelius had been to some trouble to obtain the dishes, and she had been delighted. She had cried, he remembered, when the first one shattered. She hadn't accepted it with her usual aplomb.

Katje would grieve, also, for the stains on his handsome coat, but even more for the wound, now reopened, which had caused them.

Along the main street in Fishkill were his friends, stacked, horrible. His good friends once – now the dead from White Plains.

51

Churches stood at both ends of the monstrous catafalque, like two unlit candles. In the moonlight as he passed close by, Cornelius could recognize a contorted face here, a familiar garment there.

Weak, almost delirious from his own wound, Cornelius became sick from the stench; he almost fell there. But the horror of the thought that he would, in such event, inevitably become a part of this wall of the dead overcame all other considerations, and he struggled to hobble on. Would he never get to the end of this ghastly mortuary?

Soon the fresh air on the open road revived him, and he found travel easier the next day as the thought of Katje getting nearer and nearer drew him up the Pike toward home. His tenderness for her and the feeling, almost a compulsion, that he must make her listen to him, that he must reveal the hiding place of the money to her, that he must tell her how to escape danger, where to go for help – all this drove him the last few hundred feet up the lane from the Pike.

Cornelius hoped to spy Katje in the window, but he could not bear the thought of having her see him this way. He would slip into the barn, rest until dark, chip the ice off the wash basin by the lean-to, and wash away the stains of White Plains. Then he would knock at the door . . .

Katherine van der Laan had become chilled outside and now stood at the window gazing fearfully up the lane. She ignored the cold draft which blew through the shrunken window frame, stirring the loose chips of blistered paint. In the failing light she could see the glint of automobiles speeding along the highway at the other end of the lane.

For an instant Kathy thought she saw him again, the man on the highway. An indistinct figure with a halting gait, he paid no attention to the cars which came so near to him. Once more, for one of those breathless, frightened moments which she had never been able to explain, she thought she saw him turn into the lane, walk up it, and then vanish into the barn.

Kathy had long ago given up trying to find out who he was. She had mentioned him to Dad one evening as they sat on the stoop.

"Who is that man, Daddy?"

"What man, Kathy?"

"That man who comes down the road every afternoon. He goes into the barn – that is, I think he does."

"Where is he now?"

"I told you. He just went into the barn."

And Dad had immediately gone to the barn and searched, but the door was still fastened on the outside, the old padlock protesting as his strong fingers forced the key to turn.

"It's probably somebody's hired hand cutting through the orchard on his way home." Dad was unperturbed. But as the other farms hereabout had gradually been swallowed up into shopping centers, tracts of small houses, and here and there a large factory, and as the road had been paved, then widened and paved again, every reasonable explanation for such a man to pass that way every day had vanished. Kathy had long since given up seeking reasons.

Kathy had never been able to shake off her dread of him, however, and since her return from New York to take care of Dad, she had seen him more than once – or at least she thought she had seen him, and always with a chill of apprehension.

Forcing her thoughts to what was real and present in her life, Kathy resisted the impulse to run out to the barn to see if Dad was there. As for the mystery man, she was not sure, not *really* sure, she told herself, that there had been anyone at all.

She drew the curtains and turned on a lamp. It wasn't quite dark, but this small extravagance and the fire in the grate helped to shut out the bareness and the sadness Kathy had always felt there on the farm in the fall, once the cheerful maples had dropped their leaves.

She decided she would feel more secure if they had supper now. Dad would be in shortly. If she hurried, she could prepare a tray before dark and take in a small percolater to plug in later, so that they need not leave the warm little library until bedtime. *Such a dull supper. What for dessert?*

"Not instant pudding," Dad would say.

"You love it," she would reply, knowing it wasn't true. Dad hated everything symbolic of Kathy's necessary little economies of money and time.

Kathy spooned the pudding into small blue bowls as she glanced out the kitchen window toward the barn. It was dark now. The massive old barn no longer looked quaint and benevolent, as it did in the daytime when the sun deepened the soft yellow of the rough stone walls, tied securely to the earth with thick cords of vine.

Dad must be out there in the barn.

"All the Corneliuses have died in the barn," Grandmother had said, and the circle of small cousins stemming elderberries had shivered appropriately.

According to Grandmother, van der Laans

had tended to marry van der Laans, distant cousins of what had once been a large family, now dispersed this last generation or so.

"What about the first Cornelius, Grandma? Did he die in the barn, too?"

"All the Corneliuses," she had repeated with impressive finality.

Kathy felt troubled. Dad was getting absent-minded and careless, and each day Kathy dreaded more and more to leave him and go to work.

"Promise me, Dad, you won't tear up the floorboards today?"

"Oh, Kathy, you know I have some sense."

"I know I caught you taking down the lean-to last week."

"Well, the money has to be somewhere."

And with a sigh Kathy would pull on her old blue coat and walk out the door to the foot of the lane, where her ride to work was waiting.

All these years Dad had persisted in looking for the money. It had been a joke when he was a boy – all the van der Laan children had, in their turn, searched for the legendary money. But as Dad had seen his pleasant world slipping away, as he watched Kathy leave him every morning for her tiresome job in Poughkeepsie, to return much too tired at night, he had become obsessed with the idea of finding Cornelius' hoard of gold, thus retrieving the family fortune for Kathy's sake.

Cornelius' money had never been found. Although each generation had dutifully hunted for it, the loss of it had never been considered a serious inconvenience until now. The first Katherine had been young and lovely when Cornelius died. Placid and agreeable, she had been much sought after, and she married soon and well again, and yet a third time. Her children, however, were van der Laans. There had always been another capable Cornelius and a pretty Katherine, too, the variations on the pet name changing with the styles of the dresses they wore. Kathy's grandmother had been a Kate, and she, like all the Katherines, had had a fondness for blue.

Kathy stroked the old blue bowl. There were so many traditions, so many ties. *So many lies.* Kathy's mind returned inevitably to the legend of the money.

"Why are you so sure there *is* any money, Dad?" It seemed they never talked about anything else these days. "Surely Katje would have known where it was," she would say. "Maybe she found it. Perhaps it wasn't very much after all."

Dad would wave the faded account book. "According to this," he would say, "the day before he left with the brigade, Cornelius sold a lot of cattle and grain to General Washington's army. The entry is blurred, but we can be almost sure they paid for them in coin."

"Maybe the cattle and grain were confiscated. Or maybe he gave it to them."

Dad would snort. "Cornelius van der Laan was a shrewd businessman, a prosperous farmer, and he had a family to support. He might very well have been persuaded to leave to fight for them, but nobody could ever have induced him to leave them in want. Not likely!"

Dad was always so sure that the early Cornelius had been just like himself before – before he had become so changed, so confused.

Together Kathy and Dad had once dug up the garden, and many times they had searched the chimney for secret compartments or loose stones – he in hope, she trying to temper his excitement to save his heart.

Kathy carried the tray into the parlor, the dishes rattling. *I'm unnerved. Truly, I am frightened. But why tonight?* After all, she had

58

seen him many times, the mystery man. But why didn't her father come in?

She set the tray on the table before the fire and walked firmly to the closet. Pulling on her old blue coat, thrusting a flashlight into one pocket, Kathy walked out the door and pulled it shut behind her. Pausing on the stoop, she purposefully left the protection of Cornelius' old house and walked down the lane toward the barn.

The door was unlocked, and as she swung it aside and played the beam around the barn, looking for Dad, Kathy saw the man. He was kneeling, this stranger she had feared so long, kneeling in front of the first stall. She wanted to run, but could not.

But then the man lifted his head, and Kathy saw it was Dad. In the glare of the flashlight he seemed so happy, so young. Where did he find those awful clothes? I can't leave him alone a minute. She was amused. Irritated. Relieved.

How confusing, she thought, fear can be. And she saw him start to rise . . .

Warmed by the thought that he would very soon be in Katje's arms, Cornelius van der Laan crept into the cold stone barn. Still concerned, as he had been ever since he left his family so suddenly in early summer – so very, very long ago – he went immediately to the first stall, where he had kept the sleek horse on which he had ridden away to the slaughter at White Plains.

There was someone there before him. Cornelius did not, however, find violent interference necessary this time, as he had so many times in the past. The old man in the stall had dropped the pick and collapsed beside the hole he had made in the earth.

Cornelius paused beside the body and took the bayonet which hung at his own waist. He stooped to push aside more debris to reassure himself that the iron kettle in which he had hidden his coins was still undisturbed. It would have been wise to move it long ago, but the pot was very large, very heavy, almost full of gold and silver, and firmly imbedded. It was easier to defend than to move.

Cornelius, probing in the earth, had just revealed the lid of the massive kettle when he heard the sound of the barn door swinging open. He turned, gripping the bayonet.

But it was Katje standing there in the doorway, the blue of her coat soft in the dim light from the lantern she held in her hand, its beam illuminating the hole in the ground before him. He smiled and tried to rise, but the bayonet fell from his grasp, and as he had done every night since that first gray dusk in November 1776, Cornelius van der Laan fell, but now for the last time, into the cold deep sleep of death.

JACQUES FUTRELLE
The Vanishing Man

Charles Duer Carroll paused at the curb in front of a downtown office building and stared across the busy street. There was a feverish restlessness in his merciless gray eyes, an unpleasant frown on his brow. Carroll was a remarkable-looking man. He was young – only thirty – and physically every line of his body expressed power; he had been a famous athlete in college. He had an indomitable, uncompromising jaw, a square aggressive chin, thin lips – avaricious, perhaps – and a slightly hooked nose. In general his appearance was that of a keenly alert man who is never surprised, who chooses his way and pursues it without haste, without mercy – and without mistakes.

Despite his youth – perhaps, because of it – Carroll was the president and active head of the great brokerage concern, the Carroll, Swayne, McPartland Company, with general offices on the fourth floor of the huge ornate building behind him. He held that responsible position by right of being the grandson of its founder, old Nick Carroll. At the time of his retirement from active business the previous year, the old man had banged his desk with a lusty fist and so declared it – Charlie Carroll was to be his successor. There had been objections from the Board of Directors, violent protests even, but the old man owned five thousand and one of the ten thousand shares of the company. Charles was made president.

Financially, the young man was interested in the company only to the extent of owning twenty-five shares, this being a gift from old Nick and a necessary qualification of any office holder. Beyond this rather meager interest – meager in comparison with the holdings of other officers and stockholders in the company – young Carroll had only his salary of ten thousand dollars a year, nothing else; he had been exalted to this from a salary of eighteen hundred a year and a clerk's desk.

Thus it came about that a pauper, from the viewpoint of financial circles, directed the affairs of a company whose business ran into tens of millions annually. When young Carroll felt that he needed advice, he did not hesitate to go straight to the fountainhead, old Nick himself. And when he asked for advice he took it. At other times he sailed his own course, and sailed it as he pleased, leaving accrued profits to inform the stockholders of his actions. At such times old Nick would rub his skinny hands together and smile.

For months after young Carroll assumed the reins of government there had been fear in the conservative hearts of officers and stockholders of a misstep and a consequent wreck of company affairs; all except old Nick. This apprehension was finally dissipated, but it left a residue of rankling envy. Not one in authority would have said it was not for the best interests of the firm that old Nick had infused the staid old company with this young blood. But half a dozen could have enumerated a thousand reasons why a youth of thirty should not hold the position of president.

Be that as it may, Charles Duer Carroll, the pauper, was president of the company, and he had brought into it new vigor and vitality, and a surly, curt, merciless method that had enabled him to achieve astonishing things. And this was the young man who stood at the curb glaring across the busy street. At last he dropped his half-smoked cigar on the pavement and ground it to shreds with a vigorous heel; then he turned and stared up at the building. He could see a window of his office in the corner straight above him, and in that office work called. But he wasn't thinking of work, he was thinking of –

He snapped his fingers impatiently and entered the building. An elevator whirled him up to the fourth floor. A moment later he entered the large outer office of the company. The frown was still on his brow, the steeliness still in his gray eyes. Several clerks nodded respectfully as he entered, but there was no greeting in return, not even his usual curt time of day. He strode straight across the room to his private office and banged the door behind him.

Over in a corner of the outer office Gordon Swayne, secretary and treasurer, was dictating letters. He glanced around at the sudden noise which had disturbed him.

"Who did that?" he demanded of his stenographer.

"It was Mr. Carroll, sir."

"Oh!" And Mr. Swayne resumed his dictation.

For more than an hour he continued dictating; then a letter which required the attention of President Carroll came to hand and he rose and went into the private office. He came out after a moment and spoke to his stenographer.

"Didn't Mr. Carroll go into his office this morning?"

"Yes, sir."

Swayne glanced around the office inquiringly.

"Did you see him come out?"

"No, sir."

Swayne laid the letter aside for the moment and continued with the other correspondence. From time to time he glanced impatiently at the clock, then to the door from the hallway. At ten minutes past eleven he had finished dictating and, worried, he went over and spoke to a bookkeeper near the door.

"Did you see Mr. Carroll go out?" he asked. "And do you know where he went?"

"He hasn't gone out, sir," replied the bookkeeper. "I saw him go into his office a couple of hours ago."

Swayne turned and started to the private office with the evident intention of leaving the letter on the president's desk. The door of the room was still closed, and he was reaching out his hand to open it when it was opened from within and Carroll started out.

"Well, what is it?" Carroll demanded curtly.

"I – er – here's something I wanted to ask you about," Swayne explained.

66

Carroll glanced at the letter.

"You should have called this to my attention two hours ago."

Swayne's face flushed.

"I tried to call it to your attention two hours ago," he explained, "but you were not in your private office."

"I've been in my office all morning." Carroll glared at Swayne. "Wire immediately that we'll accept."

The two men stood looking straight into each other's eyes for an instant. Swayne's face showed not only anger but bewilderment; whatever Carroll felt was not evident. There was more color in his face than usual, but he was somewhat red of face when he came out of the private office.

That afternoon Carroll had a neat placard placed on the door of his private office. It read:

DO NOT ENTER THIS ROOM WITHOUT KNOCKING. IF MR. CARROLL DOES NOT ANSWER IT MUST BE UNDERSTOOD THAT HE IS NOT TO BE DISTURBED UNDER ANY CIRCUMSTANCES.

Swayne read it and wondered, feeling somehow that it was a direct rebuke to him;

67

the clerks read it and wondered and commented on it varyingly; the office boys read it and added their opinions. On the following day the incident was repeated with slight variations. Swayne saw Carroll arrive, pass through the outer office, and go into the private office, closing the door behind him. Half an hour later Swayne spoke to the bookkeeper, Black, to whom he had spoken the day before.

"Please give this to Mr. Carroll."

The bookkeeper took the paper, crossed the office, and rapped on Carroll's door. He returned to Swayne.

"Mr. Carroll doesn't answer, sir."

"You know he's in there, don't you?" asked Swayne blandly.

"I saw him go in a while ago, sir, but I didn't open the door because of the sign on it."

"Oh, that's of no consequence," exclaimed Swayne impatiently. "This is a matter of importance. Take it in to him whether he answers or not."

Again the bookkeeper knocked on the door and again he returned.

"Mr. Carroll wasn't in there, sir," he explained, "and I had to leave the paper on his desk."

"I thought you said you saw him go in."

"I did, sir."

"Then if he hasn't come out, he must still be in there," insisted Swayne. "Are you sure he isn't in there?"

"Yes, sir, positive," replied the bewildered bookkeeper.

"We'll go in there together and see if he isn't to be found."

"But, sir, I –"

"Come along," directed Swayne.

The bookkeeper followed Swayne, wondering what it was all about. Swayne rapped on the door. There was no answer and he pushed open the door. Carroll was sitting at his desk going over the morning mail. Apparently he was not aware that the door had been opened, and Swayne started to close it as he and the bookkeeper backed out.

"You are mistaken, Black, as you see," Swayne remarked casually.

"Come in, Mr. Swayne, and you too, Black," called Carroll.

Swayne warned the bookkeeper to silence with one quick, comprehensive look, then reopened the door; they entered the private office, Swayne closing the door behind them. He faced his superior calmly; the bookkeeper twiddled his fingers nervously.

"Since when is it customary for employees

69

to disobey my orders?" demanded Carroll coldly.

"Mr. Black told me you were not here and I came to see for myself," Swayne replied with a singular emphasis on each word.

"You see he was mistaken," said Carroll with equal emphasis. "Mr. Black, we shall not require your services any longer. Mr. Swayne will give you a check for what is due you. And you, Mr. Swayne, understand that if my orders are not obeyed to the letter in this office, I shall be compelled to make other changes. From this time forward the door will be locked when I am in my office. That is all."

"But I was obeying orders when –" Black began.

"I put my order on the door for you to obey," interrupted Carroll. "Write him a check, Mr. Swayne."

The two men went out. Carroll had been seated at his desk, but the door had no sooner closed than they heard the lock snap inside.

"What does it mean, Black?" Swayne asked the bookkeeper.

"I don't know, sir. Mr. Carroll certainly was not in that room when I first went in there. And as for discharging me –"

"You are not discharged," Swayne said impatiently. "You are just going to take a vacation for a couple of weeks at full salary. Meanwhile, have luncheon with me today."

Professor Augustus S. F. X. Van Dusen – The Thinking Machine – straightened up in his chair suddenly and turned his squinting, belligerent eyes full on his two visitors.

"Never mind your personal opinions or prejudices, Mr. Swayne," he said sharply. "If you want me to help you in this matter, I must insist that you tell me the facts, and only the facts. And I don't want them colored by any ill feeling you may have for Mr. Carroll. I can readily understand the cause of your ill feeling. You are his senior in the office and he was promoted over your head to be the company's president. Now tell me the facts – only the facts, please."

Swayne's face flushed and it was with an effort that he controlled himself. Once he looked toward Black, who had been a silent witness to this remarkable interview.

"Well, after those first two incidents," Swayne went on at last, "the door of Mr. Carroll's private office was always locked on the inside the moment he was left alone. I am not a fool, Professor Van Dusen. It is reasonable to suppose that if Mr. Carroll disappeared from that room twice when the door was left unlocked, he is gone from it

71

practically all the time the door is locked, and I think –"

"Your opinion again," interrupted The Thinking Machine.

"If he isn't gone from the room, why does he keep the door locked?"

"Perhaps," and the crabbed little scientist regarded the financier coldly, "perhaps it's really because he is busy and doesn't want to be interrupted. I'm that way myself sometimes."

"But it is necessary for us to interrupt him. He gets very angry with us when we don't. None of us knows what to do, and it's getting more and more difficult to carry on. And where does he go? And why does he go? But the big question is *how* does he go?"

"If I am to diagnose this case," remarked the little scientist almost pleasantly, "I should say it's a severe case of idle curiosity complicated with prejudice and suspicion." Suddenly his tone, his whole manner changed. "Has the conduct of the company's business been all it should be since Mr. Carroll has been in charge?"

"Well, yes," admitted Swayne.

"He has made money for the company?"

"Yes."

"Nothing has been stolen?" the scientist went on.

72

Swayne shook his head.

"Everything with the company is all right," he said.

The Thinking Machine rose impatiently.

"If anything had been wrong you would have gone to the police. Since nothing is wrong you come to me. I don't mind giving assistance when it is for constructive purposes, but my time is valuable to the world of science, Mr. Swayne, and I cannot be disturbed by such a trivial affair as this. If anything goes wrong, if anything extraordinary happens, you may call again. Good day."

Swayne's face was crimson with anger at his abrupt dismissal. But at the door he turned back.

"Could you possibly tell us how Mr. Carroll disappeared from his office on the two occasions when we know he did disappear?"

"You saw him go in one door, he went out another, I suppose," the scientist replied.

"There is only one other door in Carroll's office," retorted Swayne with something like triumph in his voice, "and that door has been nailed up for years! Besides, it is blocked in his office by his desk and blocked in the stockholders' meeting room, to which it leads, by a long and very heavy couch. He

73

could not possibly go through that door! The offices are fifty feet from the ground, so he couldn't jump from a window. And, I may add, there is no fire escape at his window. Now, how *does* he get out?"

Swayne had raised his voice stridently. The Thinking Machine regarded him a moment, then opened the door to the street.

"I don't know if you know it," he said at last calmly, "but you are almost convincing me that something is wrong at your office – and that *you* are responsible for it. Good day."

The steel-gray eyes of Charles Duer Carroll were blazing as he flung open the outside door from the hallway and entered the general offices of the Carroll, Swayne, McPartland Company. He strode to his private office without a look or word for his subordinates, then wheeled at the door and called:

"Mr. Swayne!"

The secretary and treasurer started a little at the imperative tone, and Carroll motioned for him to come into the private office. The door closed and the clerks outside heard the lock click. Inside Swayne stood waiting the president's pleasure. He sensed a vague physical danger.

"Sit down!" commanded Carroll. The secretary sat down. "You are the secretary and treasurer of this company, are you not?" Carroll asked brutally.

"Certainly. Why?"

"Then you know, or are supposed to know, exactly what securities this company holds in trust for its customers to protect margins?"

"Certainly I know," Swayne answered after a moment.

"You know that in the three million dollars' worth of securities in our vaults, and in the safety-deposit vaults all over the city, there is one lot of four hundred thousand dollars' worth of United States bonds that include the numbers 0043917 to 0044120?"

Swayne paused to consider the matter carefully. He wondered if this was a trap of some sort, but he couldn't decide.

"Do you or do you not know that this consignment of bonds includes those numbers?" Carroll urged hotly.

"Yes," was the reply. "I know that those numbers are included in the Mason-Sackett Trust lot. Also, I know that I myself locked them in our vaults here."

Carroll turned savagely in his chair.

"If you know that, then what does this

75

mean?" and he flung down a sheet of paper on the desk.

Swayne, with a vague sense of terror he could not fathom at the moment, picked up the paper and glanced over it. It was an affidavit signed by E. C. Manners and Company, brokers, and dated the day before. It was the usual form, and attested with innumerable reiterations that United States government bonds, numbers 0043917 to 0043940 inclusive, were in the possession of E. C. Manners and Company, having been bought in the open market three days before.

Swayne stared unbelievingly at the affidavit and slowly, slowly, the color deserted his face until it was chalk-white. He raised his eyes from the affidavit to Carroll and lowered them under the baleful glare they met. When he raised them the second time there was mystification, wonder, utter helplessness in them.

"Well?" blazed Carroll.

Swayne started to his feet.

"Just a moment, Mr. Swayne," warned the president in a voice that had become suddenly and strangely quiet. "You had better stay here while we look into this." He rose, went to the door, and spoke to a clerk.

"Please bring all the securities of all kinds now in our vaults," he directed, "and send messengers to bring the ones in safety-deposit vaults elsewhere. Bring them all to me personally – not to Mr. Swayne."

He closed the door and turned back to the secretary. The color surged into Swayne's face, and he stood closing and unclosing his hands spasmodically. After a while he spoke and his voice was steady and quiet.

"Am I to understand that you accuse me of – of stealing those bonds?"

"The bonds are missing," was the reply. "They were in your care. Whether they were misappropriated or lost, the result is the same. Those bonds were intrusted to us to protect our customers. We are responsible for them; you are responsible to the firm."

Swayne dropped back into a chair. He was utterly at a loss for words. Carroll busied himself until, at last, there came a respectful rap on the door. He unlocked it, and the clerk entered with the securities.

"Is this all of them?" asked Carroll.

"All, sir, except about six hundred thousand dollars' worth in a safety-deposit vault farther uptown. A messenger is on his way with them now."

Carroll dismissed the clerk with a curt nod and spilled the securities on a table. Then he spoke to Swayne again. There was a singular softening of his tone.

"Really, I'm very sorry, Mr. Swayne," he said gently. "I trusted you implicitly, and I daresay every stockholder in the company did. Now, whether you are at fault or not remains to be seen. We must recognize the fact that if those bonds are missing, as the affidavit asserts, other bonds may also be missing. The entire lot will have to be verified. I shall do that personally.

"Please don't misunderstand me," Carroll went on. "You are not a prisoner. This doesn't concern the police – as yet. It would not be safe even for our office force to know what has happened. It might precipitate disaster. Meanwhile, go on about your duties as if nothing had happened."

"My God, Charlie, you don't believe I stole those securities, do you?" Swayne burst out as he rose to his feet.

"That's the first time you have called me that since I have been president of this company," Carroll remarked irrelevantly. "I want to like you, Gordon. I've always wanted to be friends, but of late you have seemed deliberately to antagonize me. This is a disagreeable duty," and he indicated the securities on the table. "I must not be interrupted until I have checked them thoroughly. It is as necessary to you as to me. Now, go on about your work."

For an hour, perhaps, Swayne sat at his desk gazing across the office. Half a dozen questions were asked; he didn't answer. Slowly there came a change in his manner; a strong determination seized upon him and at last it brought him to his feet. For only an instant he hesitated over the idea that had come to him, then he went over and spoke to the girl at the switchboard.

"I want to talk to this number on my private wire," he told her.

He put down a slip of paper with a number on it, and within a few minutes he was speaking to The Thinking Machine.

"This is Gordon Swayne, Professor. Something has happened. I don't quite know what, but you told me if something did happen, something extraordinary, I was to call on you. Could you, sir, come to this office?"

"What happened?" asked The Thinking Man irritably.

"I'm afraid it's a huge defalcation," Swayne told him. "Carroll has locked himself in his office – the room from which he disappeared previously – with millions of dollars' worth of securities he succeeded in getting hold of by a trick. And I believe as firmly as I believe I'm living that he has run away with them. It's the only way I can account for his strange actions. He went into the room an hour ago. I'd stake my life he isn't there now!"

"Why don't you knock on the door and ask to see him?"

"Please, sir, I beg of you to come at once. You will be completely baffled by what is going on here."

"Young man, I am never completely baffled. I'll be there immediately. And don't do anything absurd until I get there. And don't call the police. You are probably still suffering from the complaint I diagnosed for you. Goodbye."

Swayne forced himself to be calm. He glanced at the clock and sat down to wait. The minutes went by; then suddenly he rose, crossed the outer office, and rapped on the door of the private office. There was no response from inside. He tried the door. It was locked. Just then the door from the outside hall opened and The Thinking Machine entered. Swayne hastened to invite him to sit down, and in a voice almost inaudible from sheer excitement related the incidents of the morning in detail.

"I believe – I *know* – Carroll has stolen those securities," Swayne burst out at last, "and he is trying to cover up by accusing me."

For several minutes The Thinking Machine sat silently squinting upward with slender fingers tip to tip; then he stood up and adjusted his glasses.

"Where is the Directors' Room?" he asked. "Since the door to the private office is locked, I'll examine the other room."

Swayne rose and led the way. The door to the meeting room was only a few feet from the locked door to the private office. The scientist stopped as he passed it and read the placard, then followed Swayne.

There was nothing unusual in the Directors' Room; just a large table in the center, with comfortable chairs around it, and across a door – evidently the nailed-up one leading into Carroll's office – was a large and very heavy couch. Two windows faced a side street and one was open. A door directly across from the windows evidently opened into the hallway.

"Is this room ever used for anything except the directors' and stockholders' meetings?" The Thinking Machine wanted to know.

"No, never," answered Swayne.

"Why is this window open?"

"The cleaning woman may have

accidentally left it open when she cleaned the room this morning."

"Does that door there," and he indicated it, "lead into the hallway?"

"Yes, but it is kept locked. The directors come here through the outer office and go out that way."

The Thinking Machine glanced at the open window, then turned and crossed the room. He opened the outside door and looked into the hallway.

"Did you say this door is always kept locked?" he asked Swayne.

"Always, sir."

"Did the cleaning woman accidentally leave it unlocked?"

"I – I don't know," stammered Swayne. "Was it unlocked?"

The scientist inspected the hallway. Stairs to the floors below were opposite. He came back into the meeting room, and Swayne carefully locked the door. He also closed the open window. While he was doing it The Thinking Machine went to the outer door.

"I'll take another look at the hallway," he said.

The look was just a glance. He came back in and closed the door. And Swayne led the way back to the outer office.

Once again as he passed, the scientist

stopped and read the placard. Swayne waited.

"What do you make of it, Professor?" he asked at last.

The professor looked at his watch, checked it with the office clock.

"We will wait for half an hour," he said. "Then if Mr. Carroll does not answer a knock, I advise you to break the lock."

The minutes ticked by. Swayne fidgeted and occasionally fussed with some papers on his desk, while the scientist sat calm, unruffled, glancing every now and then at the clock. The bustling activity of the office slowed.

"The exchange has closed now."

"Yes," said Swayne. "More than ten minutes ago."

"You will knock on Mr. Carroll's door, Mr. Swayne, and this time if he doesn't answer we will find out why."

Swayne promptly rose and crossed the room, the little scientist at his heels. He paused an instant at Carroll's door.

"Well, knock!" commanded the scientist irritably.

Swayne knocked, then rapped a little more insistently. After a moment he heard the key being turned in the lock. He drew back just as the door swung open and Carroll, in person, stood in the doorway.

"I demand those securities!" Swayne burst out furiously. "Where are they?"

"Right here." Carroll indicated his desk. "All of them. I have checked everything and nothing is missing. Now will you please lock them up again?" Then he added, "You are a childish idiot, Gordon, for suspecting me. Come, let's be friends again."

"But how –?" Swayne began in astonishment. "The affidavit –"

"Oh, that!" And Carroll dismissed such a trivial thing with a shrug. His eyes fell on the scientist. "And who is this gentleman?" he asked affably.

"He is Professor Van Dusen, scientist, and logician."

"Oh, The Thinking Machine! I have heard about you, Professor, from a newspaperman I know, Hutchinson Hatch. What can I do for you, sir?"

"You can answer one question – at my house. Any time you like. Good day."

The explanation of the problem of the vanishing man, as The Thinking Machine stated it, was ludicrously simple. After Carroll had returned the securities intact, thus putting an end to Swayne's suspicions

84

that he had stolen them, the secretary had stalked out of the office still very angry. Now, he sat gloomily in The Thinking Machine's reception room.

"You see, Mr. Swayne, my first diagnosis fits the case," the little scientist pointed out. "Curiosity with complications. In this instance you could not, or would not, see anything but the obvious, in the set and inflexible way you men of business have. A little imagination would have helped you, imagination coupled with a knowledge of the rudimentary rules of logic; just as it helped Mr. Carroll. Logic doesn't make mistakes; it is as infallible as that two and two make four not *some*time but *all* the time.

"I knew from your first statement of this case that Mr. Carroll was a comparatively poor man, even though he is the head of a great company. In ninety-nine cases out of a hundred every man, personally, wants to be rich. We will credit Mr. Carroll with such an ambition. He had increased the earnings of his company but, evidently, not his own. He decided to do so.

"In the stock market – and I know just enough about the market to know that money begets money – it is possible to make or lose millions in an hour. All Mr. Carroll had to do was to get the firm's millions of dollars' worth of securities in his possession for just an hour to make a fortune in the open market. Am I right?"

"Yes," admitted Swayne.

"And that is precisely what he did. By a trick. That affidavit which he wrote himself and you took at its face value – he got them together in a way that did not arouse even your suspicions of the truth. We must infer that he made money by the use of the securities or he would not have had them to return to the company. That was what I thought might have happened if he did not open his door after the exchange closed – that he had lost them. I suggested waiting that half hour to give him a chance to get back to his office with the securities – if he had them. Of course, in using the company's money to make money for himself, he technically committed a crime, but –"

"Then he himself was the criminal when he accused me of stealing those government bonds!"

"By accusing you of appropriating or misplacing those bonds," the scientist pointed out, "he did the thing necessary for the success of his plan. He distracted your attention, confused you, and gave himself, even to you, the best possible excuse for getting all the securities together without your suspecting his real purpose. Mr. Carroll is a very remarkable, a very resourceful young man. He has what our mutual friend, Mr. Hatch, would say, a head on him. Now, if he is as honest as I think he is, he will confess his technical crime to the directors, and they'll be a lot of old biddies if they don't absolve him."

"But how – how did he get out of his private office to use those securities in a market transaction? Can you answer me that?"

"It was simple enough," was the reply. "Since there was no other way out except through the window, he must have left through that window."

"But that's impossible!" Swayne exclaimed.

"Nothing is impossible," snapped the scientist. "Please don't say that. It annoys me exceedingly. It is not impossible to climb out of a window, stand on the sill, then inch along a narrow ledge –"

"Ledge? What ledge?" interrupted Swayne.

"Logic told me, Mr. Swayne, that Mr. Carroll left his room by the window, inched his way to another window, and then climbed through that second window into another room. To do this there had to be a ledge –"

"But you didn't even look out of the windows!" interrupted Swayne again.

The Thinking Machine clucked peevishly.

"I didn't have to look out of the windows. I didn't have to *see* the ledge to know that it had to exist. Logic, man! – inexorable, indisputable logic!" The Thinking Machine almost smiled, then went on:

"Please remember, too, that Mr. Carroll was a famous college athlete. He has the strength and steady nerve to accomplish the feat I give him credit for. And since the room he entered by the second window was not occupied – I don't have to remind you that we found the window in the Directors' Room open – he could pass through that room without being observed, and go out through the door leading into the hallway – which, also, need I remind you, was open. The door to the hallway led directly to the stairs. He took a chance of being seen in the corridor, but a little chance like that would not deter Mr. Carroll. It was, therefore, not impossible for Mr. Carroll to leave his office and the building, and stay away for hours with the door locked behind him to discourage curiosity seekers."

"But how did he get back into the meeting room with the securities? I locked that door to the hallway –"

"And I *unlocked* it when I pretended to look into the hallway again. There is really no problem about this affair. There seems to be only a little matter of how much the transaction netted Mr. Carroll."

An hour later the Board of Directors of the Carroll, Swayne, McPartland Company met in the room adjoining Carroll's private office. The call had been issued by the secretary without consulting President Carroll. When all were assembled, the secretary stated the case briefly, but with evident rancor. Carroll listened until he had finished, then stood up.

"I am glad the directors have met here and now," he said. "I admit that I have committed a technical crime. By that crime I have made more than two million dollars. This company is old, it is conservative. If this affair becomes known in financial circles, I realize it will hurt us. You have your securities again, intact. I have made a fortune, and I had intended to offer the company one half of it. Gentlemen, will you accept it?"

There was a long argument among the directors, but finally acquiescence.

"And now," Carroll said, "I wish to tender my resignation as president of Carroll, Swayne, McPartland."

"Resignation?" echoed old Nick Carroll. "What do you mean, resignation? You young scoundrel, if you ever again mention resigning, I'll – why, confound it, we'll fire you! A man who can think of what you did and carry it out – why, Charlie, you're a wonder! And you'll stay right here. That's orders!" He banged the table with a lusty fist . . .

After the meeting Charles Duer Carroll called on The Thinking Machine at his house. The scientist received him in his laboratory.

"You said you wanted to ask me one question, Professor. I'm curious to know what it is," said Carroll.

"You went in and out of your office through the window, of course." It was not a question.

"How did you guess, Professor?"

"I didn't guess, I knew," the professor stated flatly. "With the door to the outer office locked on the inside and the only other door nailed up, the window was the only possible way you could get out."

"It took me some time to think of it," Carroll admitted. "But one morning I was standing on the sidewalk below and just happened to look up at my office window. For the first time I noticed the ledge just underneath it. But it took days of careful planning and many practice attempts at swinging myself in and out of those windows before I tried it with the securities. I had to be sure that the window in the meeting room was left open and the hallway door unlocked. I knew the company's integrity had to be preserved at all costs, and I couldn't take anyone into my confidence."

"Here is my question, Mr. Carroll. Suppose – just suppose – you had found the hallway door in the meeting room locked when you came back that day with the securities? What would you have done?"

"I'd have bluffed my way through the outer office with a great deal of noise to confuse everybody, and I had the key to the locked private office safely in my pocket."

"Good!" It was the nearest thing to a compliment The Thinking Machine had ever uttered.

ROBERT L. FISH

The Adventure of the Missing Prince

It was a bright Thursday morning in May, in the year of '48. I had come into the breakfast room of our quarters at 221B Bagel Street to find my friend Mr. Schlock Homes in the process of lighting his after-breakfast hookah, a gift from the Sultan of Swat, the former Bey Beruit.

After exchanging our usual morning courtesies, I sat down to eat, selecting one of the journals from a pile by the desk, and perusing it intently as I attacked my first kipper. A moment later my thoughts were disrupted.

"I should not even think of the tweed, my dear Watney," Homes remarked, a mischievous smile lighting his face.

"On the contrary," I replied absently, and then looked up in startled amazement. "Really, Homes! I fail to see –"

"Precisely, Watney," my friend interjected. "And yet it is neither mind-reading nor legerdemain. You have a set

92

method of attacking your *Daily Times*. You begin by reading the headlines of the extreme right-hand article; your eye then travels to the left-hand article, and you finally concentrate on the centre article. The right-hand article in today's *Times* deals with a red-petrol case, which held no interest for you. On the left you found a column-head concerning a state visit of an African potentate and his retinue who are here for conferences and to enjoy the theatre season. When this proved of no interest to you, you continued to the centre. Here you read that a stock merger was to be effected, and your eyebrows lifted in interest. As you continued further into the article, a smile appeared upon your face. Obviously the merger will affect your holdings, small as they are, and you wondered at this point if you might afford some small extravagance. Your eye then travelled speculatively to the wardrobe chest. I recall that a few days ago we paused at a window in Regent Street and you commented upon a tweed suit you saw displayed there. Therefore my remark."

"It does seem simple after you explain it," I admitted, my original annoyance abating a bit. "Actually, however, this is the *Herald Press* in my hand, and I have been reading, with pleasure, I admit, an article on the advantages of passing one's holidays on our lovely English rivers. I had more or less decided on the Tweed, and was wondering if my wardrobe still contained the straw floater I won on Boat Race night in '14, when you spoke."

Homes hid his chagrin by returning to his hookah.

"Incidentally," I added smugly, "I see that you have another case coming up, which should be a lucrative one. The person coming to see you should be here very soon, if he is not already overdue."

"Excellent, Watney! You are improving! It would be interesting to learn the reasons for your statement."

I shifted in my seat, imitating the pedantic tones of my colleague. "You have preceded me to breakfast, which indicates to me that you have an appointment, obviously an early one. Your selection of costume informs me that the person is an important one, since you often receive your brother Criscroft and others in your dressing-gown. Hence a lucrative case."

"But why a case at all, my dear Watney?" asked Homes, his eyes twinkling. "Certainly in our many adventures we have made sufficient acquaintances, many of high rank, so that one might be calling for no reason other than to extend his regards."

"That was the simplest of all deductions," I answered dryly. "To be frank, your good humor this morning is a welcome change from the irritability which has had you in its grip for the past week. Only a new case could have wrought this change in your behaviour."

Homes laughed aloud in pure enjoyment. "Actually," he said, copying my tones with a faithfulness that was characteristic of his great histrionic ability. "I had a dentist's appointment this morning, and dressed accordingly. Then, one half-hour ago, I received a telegram cancelling it, as my dentist himself has been taken severely with toothache. Hence, as you say, my good humour."

To hide my chagrin, I ate another kipper. Homes arose and laid his arm in a kindly fashion across my shoulders. "At least, Watney," he said, smiling in a friendly style, "we are free of other appointments today. Possibly we can spend the afternoon at the concert hall. Joshua Lowfitz and his Trumpeters are doing the Waltz of Jericho, and I understand their performance brings the house down."

"I should like that, Homes," I said, rising

to my feet. But our plans for a musical afternoon were not to be realized, for at that moment there came the sound of a carriage-wheel scraping against the kerb, and we looked out of the window to see a heavily veiled woman descend and enter our doorway.

As we waited for her arrival, Homes stared in frowning concentration at the coat-of-arms emblazoned on the carriage below. A moment later our page ushered in our visitor, who was followed by a liveried footman carrying a small bundle.

"Mr. Schlock Homes?" The voice was musical, but taut with suppressed emotion.

Homes bowed slightly, moving his hand in a gentlemanly gesture toward a chair. The veiled woman seated herself on the very edge as she spoke.

"Mr. Homes, believe me when I say that the secrecy of any of your past endeavors is as nothing to the confidential nature of the case which I now bring you. Because of the eminent position of the family which I represent, even the little information I am able to give you must be treated with the utmost circumspection."

She paused as if seeking further words, and then with a muffled sob she fumbled in her reticule and withdrew an envelope which she handed to Homes.

He withdrew from the envelope a wrinkled sheet of paper, perused it quickly, his eyes glittering with excitement. I passed to his side and read the message over his shoulder. It was printed in crudely formed letters, and read:

"No sens lookin under the bed or wistlin. We got him. If you wanna see him agin put eleven millun quid in a shu-box. Give it to the cooks boy he nose wat to do with it. Dont tell the busies or you wont never see him no more.

(sined) The Gang

"Ps. if you cant raise that much you kin put in less but dont go under five quid or you really wont see him no more.

"Pss. Better put in some toffies to, it can do no harm."

Homes was breathing heavily with excitement as he finished the note. He folded the wrinkled paper carefully, and laid it upon the desk before turning back to our distrait visitor.

"Can you give me a description of the little fellow?" he asked softly.

There was another muffled sob from

97

behind the veil. "He is about eight years old," she said, "with long silky hair, black eyes, and the cutest pointed ears! And his nose is long and square and all speckled."

"And the family wants him back?" I asked in amazement.

"Desperately," she said simply. She turned back to Homes. "When he was taken, they also took his little blanket. However, I brought with me the little blanket that was his father's when he was small. I did not know if it would help, but they are identical, and I felt I should bring anything that might prove to be of use."

She took the bundle from the footman behind her and placed it in Homes's hands. His eyes lit up as he saw the word *Rex* embroidered in gold thread in one corner.

"Of course!" he muttered audibly. "I should have recognized the crest on the carriage! It is Prince . . ."

"Hush!" commanded the veiled figure. "No names!" She rose and walked to the door. "Time, Mr. Homes, is of the essence!"

"I swear I shall not rest until I resolve this," Homes promised fervently. "If your Ladyship could call at this hour to-morrow, I hope to have a definite answer for you."

"Oh, pray heaven that you shall!" came the muffled reply, and with no further word she passed through the door, to be followed immediately by the silent, liveried servant.

As soon as the sound of the carriage had died away in Bagel Street, Homes fell into a chair and began studying the note with fierce concentration. I stood behind him and also reread it, but it provoked no startling ideas.

"Do you suspect it of being in code, Homes?" I asked, watching his frowning features carefully.

"No, no, Watney!" he replied impatiently. "It is precisely what it purports to be – a note demanding ransom. Still, a fairly clear picture of the writer begins to emerge from his note."

I studied the wrinkled paper in his hand once again. "But I see nothing in it to give any clue whatsoever as to its author," I objected.

Homes laughed shortly. "Do you not? Really, Watney, there are times when I despair of you! Certainly it should be evident to all that the writer of this note comes from a tropical climate, is visiting London for the first time, and is a great admirer of George Bernard Shaw!"

"Now really, Homes!" I cried. "This is a serious case! You gain nothing by levity at a time like this."

"Oh, I am quite serious! In time you shall know all, Watney, but at the moment, there is little time to lose." He sprang from his chair, beginning to undo the cravat. "It is essential that I get out for a few hours. If you would be so kind as to arrange a hansom for me, I shall hurry and change into more suitable vestments."

"But, Homes," I said, studying his neat clothing with surprise, "there is nothing wrong with your present costume."

He smiled enigmatically and disappeared into his room. I sent our page to flag down a passing cab, and he managed to have one waiting at our portal when Homes emerged once again. I gaped in astonishment; for had it not been for the familiar grin of my old friend, I should have sworn that I was facing the actress, Diana Dors.

"Homes!" I cried in astonishment.

"Later, Watney," he chuckled, and with the supreme artistry that marked every detail of his incredible impersonations, he rearanged his features and minced from the room.

It was dusk before Homes returned. His high heels tapped quickly up the steps, and once in the room he removed his spiked shoes, slipped off his blonde wig, and flung himself into a chair.

"It is as I suspected," he said. "An inside job! However, I have the miscreants located, and to-night we shall see the end of this foul plan! I suggest, Watney, that we have a bite of supper, for we must go out again to-night. And you had best arrange a bull's-eye lantern and also take along your pistol, for I know not what deviltry we may encounter."

"You mean –" I began.

"Yes," he said. "Our case is nearly finished. To-night, I hope to effect the rescue. But now, if you will call for Mrs. Essex, I suggest we satisfy the inner man, for I have gone without lunch, and we have a long night ahead of us."

He refused to speak further until our supper had been placed upon the table, and then the only words he offered was a curt request for the salt. It was not until our supper was represented by soiled dishes that Homes leaned back and sought solace from his hookah. Another person might have appeared ridiculous sitting there in a low-cut dress sucking on the curved pipe, but Homes appeared quite natural.

"Well, Homes," I said, leaning back in surfeit, "if we have time I would certainly appreciate an explanation of this very odd affair."

"Certainly, Watney," he replied, his eyes twinkling. "Actually, we have several hours until we must leave." He laid aside his hookah, and reached for the note which he had left upon the desk.

"There are several things which are evident from this note, Watney. First, you may note that they request eleven million pounds to be placed in a shoe-box. It should have been apparent to you at first glance that this amount of money, even in the maximum of denomination, is far too great for the capacity of even the largest shoe-box; hence the deduction that the writer was unfamiliar with shoe-boxes, and therefore with shoes. The only conclusion one could logically draw was that he came from a tropical climate where shoes were not a necessity.

"Then, too, you will note his instruction to pass the money to one of Cook's boys. It is evident that the writer of the note did not realize that Thomas Cook have eleven branches in London, or he would have been more specific. From the fact that this was unknown to him, it must be deduced that this was his first visit to London."

"But his admiration for George Bernard Shaw?" I cried.

"That was the most simple of all," Homes replied. "You must have noted that the ransom note was written in reformed spelling!"

I sat in silent admiration of this masterful analysis. "But even knowing all this, Homes," I finally said, "I fail to see how you were able to locate the miscreants."

Homes reached over and took the *Daily Times* from the pile in the corner. "You have a short memory, Watney," he said, smiling briefly. "Do you not recall that just this morning I mentioned an article regarding the visit of an African potentate and his retinue? In that retinue there are bound to be some who are visiting London for the first time; moreover, they come from a climate where shoes are unnecessary; and among other things, they came to enjoy the theatre season. I would wager that Shaw was their first choice!"

"And from this you deduced an inside job?"

Homes nodded. "They are guests at the Palace," he said. "I know it is difficult to pass the Palace guards at any time. Surely any attempt to take a small boy past – a boy who would certainly be recognized, or who might attract attention by screaming – that is quite impossible. No, Watney, there is no doubt. He is being held in the Palace itself."

"In their quarters?"

Homes shook his head. "I do not believe so. With the constant presence of upstairs maids and housekeepers, it would be extremely dangerous. I should imagine they have him locked in one of the unused basement rooms – possibly one of the coal-cellars, since in this weather they would be unused."

He arose and, stepping into his high-heeled shoes, adjusted his wig. "But it is getting onto the hour for our departure. I suggest you arrange your accoutrements, for we must be on our way."

Moments later we were seated in a cab heading for the Palace. I had slipped the bull's-eye lantern under my cape, and my pistol was concealed in my waistcoat pocket. "But are you familiar with the room arrangements at the Palace?" I asked, as our cab clattered over the cobbled pavement along Piccadilly.

"I spent the afternoon there," replied my friend simply. "The guard allowed me, as a returning celebrity, to visit my humble old aunt, who is housekeeper in charge of the royal linens. And I explained, as I left, that

I would be coming back tonight with an aged uncle to have one last chat before sailing for the colonies." He turned to me seriously. "In the course of searching for the powder-room, I was able to make a complete search of the premises. When we arrive, I suggest you allow me to do the talking, as I made, I believe, quite an impression upon the guard!"

Our hansom drew up to a back entrance of the great, ornate building, and moments later we found ourselves inside, in a long empty corridor. "This way, Watney!" Homes whispered in great excitement.

He drew me by the hand to a staircase in one corner, leading downward. The lower level was dark, and I handed him the lantern. Removing the cover, he sent the light flickering over a series of cellar doors. We made our way silently along the narrow passageway, as Homes paused at each door, listening intently. Suddenly he raised his hand for complete quiet and turned to me with triumphant satisfaction engraved in every line of his face.

"In here, Watney!" he whispered. "Come, we must break it down!"

Making as little noise as possible, we placed our shoulders to the door and heaved with all our might. The door sprang open with a clatter we feared might bring our adversaries down upon us, but apparently the heavy floors and thick walls of the Palace contained the sound, for there was no outcry.

Homes immediately swung the lantern about the small room, and there in one corner, as he had so accurately predicted, was the figure of a small boy hunched back in terror on a pile of coal. At his feet was a dog who came bounding up, licking our hands.

"There, there!" said Homes soothingly, drawing the terrified boy to his breast. "It is all right – we are friends."

He stroked the boy's silky hair as I inspected the young lad. It was true that his ears were slightly pointed, but the smear of coal dust across his face prevented me from noticing any speckles on his nose. The small figure clung to Homes, weeping copiously.

"There is nothing to fear, your Highness," Homes said in a kindly voice. "Come, let us take you to your suite. I am sure that no further attempt will be made against your person."

He led us from the cellar, up the stairway to the upper corridor, with the dog following behind, trying to lick our heels. Once in the upper reaches, however, the boy suddenly broke away and dashed down the corridor and out of sight. I began to follow, but Homes laid a restraining hand upon my arm.

"Let him go his way alone," he said, a happy smile creasing his face. "It will be a nice surprise for their Majesties!"

He turned to the door, with the little dog following us.

"But what shall we do with the dog, Homes?" I queried.

He paused in thought. "Why, Watney," he finally said, "we have long needed a mascot. Let us take him home with us, in memory of a case where we have been able to serve our country!"

I lifted the little creature, placing him under my cape for warmth, and we made our way back to our cab.

Although our activities the previous evening had consumed many hours normally devoted to sleep, the following morning found us both dressed and at breakfast at eight o'clock, prepared to welcome the veiled emissary form the Palace. Our little mascot lay quietly at our feet, while Homes fed him scraps from the table.

At the sound of the carriage below, the great detective quickly arose and opened the door to our quarters, and before anyone could stop him, our little mascot had sprung outside and was racing down the steps. "After him, Homes!" I cried, jumping to my feet.

"Not now," Homes replied. "We cannot keep a messenger from her Majesty waiting."

There appeared to be a commotion in the street, but we waited patiently at the door. Moments later, the sound of footsteps came hurrying up, and the lady from the carriage stood before us. Her veil was tossed back from her radiant face, and her eyes glowed.

"Mr. Homes!" she cried. "You have done it! You have found him!" She was clasping the dog tightly as she lifted her shining eyes to his in profound gratitude.

"It was really nothing," Homes said modestly, although the sparkle of satisfaction gleamed in his eyes.

She pressed a signet ring firmly into his hand. "This is in gratitude from an appreciative country," she said, and without another word, turned and left our quarters.

The impression of the signet ring is still there, and Homes often looks at it in contemplation on those long winter evenings when we sit about the fireplace and recall his most successful case.

FLORENCE V. MAYBERRY
Woman Trouble

I never did like living in Reno. I'm a desert woman, born and raised just outside Winnemucca, Nevada. Trees and buildings, and all those crowds milling around day and night on the streets get in my way. I like to see clear and far off. Horizons, mountains. Even people stand out better in the open desert. You can see them coming, all alone and separate instead of muffled up in all that town stuff.

Have you ever smelled, real good, the sage coming in off the desert after a rain? Clean, heady, sweet. Seems to scour out the lungs and makes your brain fresh. You can remember you've got a heart, even a soul. Well, that's what I wanted for Paddy.

Paddy belongs to the desert. Wyoming country, he was born there. Up where buttes are swept by winds and you have to struggle a little to fill your lungs with oxygen, it's so high in the sky, you know. Couple of years after we were married Paddy took me back to his old home ranch. Well, it wasn't his any longer – he'd lost it fooling around in Nevada's gambling clubs. But the people who bought it from the bank are nice folks, old friends of the family, and they pretended the ranch was still Paddy's.

Paddy and I rode alongside the buttes, sometimes stopping the horses and edging them together so we could kiss. "Paddy," I told him, "let's save up and buy back your ranch. Town's no good for us, we're open-country people." Especially town's no good for Paddy, I was thinking, and he knew it.

He grinned and said, "You're right, girl. No dice tables out here on the open range." He patted my arm and added, "First big killing I make, and I sure ought to be due for one soon, we'll buy us a spread. Build us a brand-new house on it with all the fixings, good as back in Reno."

Good as! My God. A two-room-with-kitchenette apartment. A stove with an oven that baked lopsided. A dwarf-sized refrigerator. And all the gambling tables in the world, it seemed, just down the street.

"Paddy, I don't need fine things, I'm not used to them. It would be fun to camp out in a cabin, cook on a wood-stove – nothing bakes good like a wood range. It would be like when I was a kid. Home-baked bread – my mother always did her own baking and

110

she taught me. And we could have a little garden, Paddy. You'd be outdoors a lot – indoors don't suit you, Paddy, staying in that warehouse all the time, lifting those heavy loads."

"Lifting loads, woman?" His face took on that remote expression he always got when he decided I had gone too far interfering in men's ways. "You mean pushing so hard on those little levers that do all the lifting? With a hundred-eighty-pounds, six-one of a man to do the pushing? Well, Angie, I sure got a hard life."

I wanted to say it was lifting the dice, shaking them, tossing them out that was too much for a hundred-eighty-pounds, six-one of a man. But when he got that look Paddy scared me. No, no, I don't mean he ever hit me or roughed me up. He never did. Why, Paddy would just spit on the ground when he heard about men who hit women. Said only feisty little men did that who were too scared to tackle a man. But once, after that look, Paddy had walked out of our apartment and didn't come back. It took me a week to find him. Down in Vegas. And another week to beg him back.

That time I wished he had hit me instead. All the money we had in our joint savings account, $715, went that time. To the last

111

penny. It takes a lot of standing on your feet and waiting on customers in a department store to get that much put away above what it costs to live these days.

Paddy didn't believe in savings accounts, even though I had his name on the bank book. Said it was for men who didn't have the guts to take a chance, or for women. That's why it didn't bother him when he drew it out. Grinned, patted me on the back, and said he'd pay it back one of these days with interest.

Me, I didn't care if he ever paid it back. All I wanted back was Paddy.

Like that evening later on when I was snuggling my face against his, whispering I wouldn't trade him for the whole world tied in ribbons.

He kissed me and whispered back, "You're a good kid." Then he scooted me off his lap, stood up, gave me a little smack on the bottom, and said, "Think I'll hit the clubs a while. Think I'll begin my first million tonight. So I can get you that little ranch you're always talking about. Only it'll be a big one. Maybe I'll try for two million, so's I can fence it in with those ribbons you're always talking about."

"Oh, Paddy, please! Don't go, Paddy. I don't want to be rich. I don't even need the ranch. Paddy, you know it's just you I need. And you've been away so much lately. Every night, Paddy, the last few weeks."

"Maybe there'll be a few more nights, too," he said easily. "Stick with it, one of these nights I'll strike it rich."

"I'll go with you, Paddy."

His face set. "No. You bug me at the tables."

No use arguing with Paddy. Unless I wanted to set out on another search all over Nevada.

I remember it rained that night in Reno. A good steady rain. Once I thought, I'll just go along Virginia Street, down the alley by the clubs, find out which one Paddy's in, say it was raining hard and that I'd brought him an umbrella. But it scared me to think of the way his face would look – *I'm a man, Angie, don't wet-nurse me. You bug me at the tables, Angie.* Or maybe he wouldn't say anything. Just never come home.

I'd rather he hit me every day, honest I would.

I woke up in the morning and felt for him next to me. The sheet was cool, untouched. All around me, all through the apartment, was the sweet sage smell that rises off the desert after a rain. But it wouldn't make the ache in my head go away. I perked some coffee, waited a while to eat, and hoped he'd show up before he had to go to work. And I said to myself, *Damn the gambling and the gamblers, damn Reno to hell.*

Reno would have been a nice place, you know. A sweet hometown with the Truckee River running through, willows all along it. Over to the west, Mount Rose with snow still on it in summer. Old brown fat Peavine Mountain squatting toward the north. And the clean lovely desert spread to the east. My God, it could have been nice to live in with the man you love. Only it wasn't.

I left a place set at the table in case he showed up. Then I went down on Virginia Street, making like I was window shopping. At 6:30 in the morning, yet! Hoping I'd see him, but that he wouldn't see me: *Angie, you trying to make a woman out of me? I thought you married me because I was a man.* At 6:30 he could be grabbing a bite to eat at one of the club lunch counters, because he had to be at work by seven.

Then I saw him. Coming out of a club with a tall red-blonde holding onto his arm, almost head-high with him. Laughing, throwing her head back, tossing her long shiny hair. She had on a long black dress and it fit her like she was the model on which all women ought to be patterned. I noticed that especially because I'm short and stocky-built. Not fat or anything, just short and stocky-built, the strong kind. I used to help my Dad chop wood – Mother and Dad never had any boys.

I wanted to walk over and sock the girl in the nose. But I always have a sense to be fair about things. It was Paddy who needed the sock in the nose. How would the girl know Paddy belonged to me if he didn't tell her?"

I speeded up and came even with them just as she leaned toward him and kissed his cheek. Paddy had his arm up hailing a taxi. I said, "Hi, Paddy, won't you be late for work?"

Paddy was a gambler. His face stayed cool and easy, and it was like hoods dropped over his eyes so I couldn't see into them. "Hi, Angie," he said with his mouth. But I could feel the inside of him saying, *Get the hell out of here.* That wasn't fair. He was the one on the spot, not me. Besides, this was woman trouble. I'd never had woman trouble with Paddy before. Far as I knew. A wife can't buckle under when it's woman trouble.

"I laid out your breakfast on the table – you shouldn't go to work on an empty stomach. Paddy, I don't think I've met your friend."

I was talking to Paddy, but I was looking square at this woman. Woman she was, somewhere between twenty-five and thirty, not much younger than me. She had the skin and the looks of an eighteen-year-old, only young kids don't get that confident look on them. This woman looked strong and sure of herself, like maybe she'd fought her way up.

She was beautiful, I'll say that. Her eyes were so blue their color almost hurt you to look at. Big, too. Only thing, they stared at me bold as brass, shrewd too. Had me figured first look, and it was striking her funny. She took on a little half smile like she was holding back a laugh.

She knew how to put on makeup, just enough to turn her skin to honey and rose. Or maybe the Lord shot the works on her, maybe she was born that way. Makeup on her eyes, though, and lashes that almost brushed her cheeks. And like a halo, all that red-blonde hair.

"Is this your wife?" she asked Paddy.

He nodded and said, easy, "Sure is. Angie, meet Molly."

She looked him level in the eye, laughed, and said, "You're a cool one, I'll say that for you." She turned to me. "Chin up, lady, so he can take a poke at it for good measure."

She laughed again, climbed in the taxi, and drove off.

What she said shook Paddy. He whipped his face away from the taxi like he'd been slapped, and he didn't give me that goodbye look like he had just before he'd hopped off for Vegas. He said, "I'm sorry, Angie. But you shouldn't have come looking for me. And I'm not going to lie to you, tell you I was just coming out to put her in the taxi. I was going with her."

Well, I couldn't hardly jump on him after that. I mean, he'd come square with me. So I said, "I'm sorry, too, Paddy. See you tonight. I've fixed up a good roast for dinner." *Last night while you made up to this Molly with her bold, laughing, beautiful face, I was home cooking for you. I'm not ugly, Paddy. I got big brown eyes, nice features – you told me it's brown eyes you like, not blue like yours. You said brown eyes always got you.*

He let a deep breath sigh out and said, "Okay. See you tonight."

"You've never hit me, Paddy. Not once. She shouldn't have said that."

Kind of like it hurt as the words came out he said, "She's seen 'em hit." Then he turned and walked off.

What do you do when you love a man and

117

as far as you know he's never two-timed you before, and then you find out he did – or was going to? And you begin thinking maybe all those gambling nights and the money gone, that $715 out of the savings account – maybe it wasn't all for gambling?

You brood on it, if you're like me.

All day long while I was selling girdles, pantyhose, and things, I couldn't stop thinking about that tall bold Molly. The way she laughed and told off Paddy, and him standing there looking like he could eat her. And the contempt she'd had for his little dumb wife.

Paddy was there when I got home. He didn't say anything, just pulled me down on his lap and kissed my forehead and my eyes. "You got nice eyes, Angie," he said. "They never did see nothing bad about me. You got nice lovin' eyes."

That's all. What I wanted to say was such a big lump in me that I was afraid to let it out. So I just kissed him.

But after dinner I said, "Paddy, let's pull out and go on up to Wyoming. We could save for our own place up there as well – maybe better – as here in Reno. I could find a job and maybe you could get us a little house on a ranch where you'd work. There's an old cabin on your home place, maybe

118

they'd rent it to us and we could fix it up. Get your roots in."

"One of these days," he said. "Maybe."

He helped me with the dishes that night – usually he didn't do that, said he felt silly lifting teacups with a rag in his hand. But that night he helped me. And he kissed me sweet. Tender, it was. Never once mentioned going to the clubs. It was wonderful.

But sometime in the night – well, it was two o'clock when I turned on the light – I found myself alone in the bed. Paddy was nowhere in the apartment.

Molly, her name was. *Angie, meet Molly.* That's all, no last name. How do you find a Molly in a place as big as Reno?

You get up and dress and go down to the gambling clubs and start looking for Paddy. Or Molly.

But I didn't go. Paddy needed some kind of honor, even if it was the kind I made up myself.

Around four o'clcok I laid out some potatoes, ready to fry the way Paddy likes them. Set the table pretty. Listened for the creak of the elevator which meant somebody was coming up. Went to the bathroom to do what I could about my face. Bluish circles under my eyes smudged the upper part of my face. Face puffy from worry and lack of sleep – or like a puff adder getting mad, ready to strike. I was only in my early thirties, but this morning I looked forty or more. Little dumpy woman. Why wouldn't Paddy, eyes blue as heaven, six-one of muscle, a sidewise grin, why wouldn't –

"Stop it!" I told myself in the mirror. "Stop it!"

Paddy loved me. He told me so lots of times. And Paddy never lied, no matter what else he did.

I put the potatoes away in the refrigerator, drank a cup of coffee, and walked to work. It wasn't far, and besides we didn't have a car any more. Used to, but Paddy hit a winning streak a year or so back and wanted to raise his bets. So I signed the car over – it was in my name – and Paddy sold it. Oh, well, it costs money for gas.

It's tough to stand on your feet all day, straightening up counters that customers are always messing up the minute you've folded things. It's tough smiling, when you ache all over from wondering where Paddy's gone to. I thought once I'd call him at work. But if he was there he'd be mad. And if he wasn't there his boss would be mad knowing Paddy's wife was hunting for him again.

I tried to eat a sandwich at lunch, but it

just wouldn't go down. So I asked my boss could I go home, I didn't feel good. He was real nice, told me not to come back till I felt completely okay. They like me at work. Steady, always on time. Just a dumb, steady, day-after-day salesclerk that red-headed Molly wouldn't be caught dead being.

I went home and took a couple of aspirins. Tried to lie down and relax. Got up and mopped the kitchen and bathroom. Took a shower. Put on my new coral pants suit. Took it off. Broad as a barn door from the rear. Put on a long straight jersey dress. Looked like a Japanese wrestler in a nightgown. Finally put back on the dark dress I had worn to work. And it was past five o'clock and no Paddy.

Well, Reno's free and open – anybody can go in the clubs and play a few nickels and dimes in the slot machines. That's what I'd tell Paddy if I saw him. But maybe he wouldn't see me. I could hide behind the machines, leave once I knew where – no. Not if he was with Molly.

I walked my legs off that night. Tried to eat a hamburger. Couldn't make it. Got to bed around three in the morning. Alone.

Next morning I called at work and said I was still sick. It was no lie. I was sick. The boss was nice, said to take care of myself. So

121

I was ashamed to walk the streets, running in and out of clubs. I stayed in the apartment. Which was good, because Paddy's boss telephoned and asked what happened to him the last two days. "We're sick," I said. What kind of sick? "We must have eaten something funny. Sick to our stomachs."

"Yeah," his boss said. "Not down in Vegas again, is he, Angie, and you packing to go find him?"

"Listen, Pete, you got no right to say that – my God, can't a man have a stomach ache without –"

"Okay, okay, Angie, cool it. Take care of yourselves. Tell Paddy to forget about tomorrow, it's Saturday, he might as well get a good start on Monday."

"Thanks Pete, I'll tell him."

If Paddy was in the clubs he was like a ghost slipping in and out, because I hit them all. And that wasn't Paddy's style. Even losing, he'd stick at one table, waiting for the odds to break his way. And Paddy hadn't left for Vegas, he was still in Reno. My insides told me so.

They kept telling me something else. Paddy was with Molly.

So I concentrated on how I could find Molly.

You ever looked over the list of attorneys in the phonebook yellow pages? In Reno? You wonder how they all eat, except Reno's built on divorce as well as gambling – some fine recommendation for your hometown, huh? I started calling attorneys' offices and ran smack into, "Molly? The last name, please? You say you saw this lady drop her purse in one of the clubs and there's no identification in it, so how do you know the name is Molly? Oh. One of the dealers. Well, my suggestion would be to ask that dealer about her, or turn over the purse to the cashier or the police." A long pause. "May I ask why you didn't just give it to the lady?" Or, "I'm sorry, but we never give out clients' names. Why don't you try the police?"

Well, it was a dumb try anyway.

I thought, why not go down to that club where I first saw Paddy with her and ask around?

Down to the club. Jangling, brassy sound of slot machines, busy, busy. Everybody pulling handles like it was a job doing some good, like cleaning up the world or something every time a coin dropped in. Most of the time nothing was coming out, no loaf of bread or can of beans, nothing.

Once in a while a little money to be stuffed back into the machine.

"Say, do you know a pretty redhead named Molly? Tall girl, dressed good. She was here the other night. I – I've got something I think may belong to her. I got to find her."

The dealer at the blackjack table grinned sidewise and said, "Honey, I hope it's something nice you got for her. If it is, you might try the office. Something different, you better take it home. No, I don't know any tall redhead named Molly."

I tried a couple of other dealers. Then the lunch counter. A waitress there said, "Say, aren't you Paddy Finley's wife?"

I nodded and she said, "I thought so. I used to live in your same apartment house, couple of floors below – I used to see you come in together."

"I've got something may be this Molly's," I said again. "The other day down here I saw her with – something like it. But I don't know where to find her. I just thought someone here might know her."

She gave me a quirky smile. "I don't know her, honey, but I do know Paddy – he's here a lot. Hard to miss Paddy, looks like kids used to think cowboy heroes ought to look. Eastern divorcees still think that. You know what I'd do, Mrs. Finley – I'd go home, take two-three aspirins, and have yourself a nice rest. Then when Paddy came home you'd be in shape to flatten him. Want a cup of coffee? I'll throw in the aspirin."

It's peculiar how when your mind's upset it's the middle of your stomach that hurts. Like a knot tied in it. But all the time the real hurt is in your mind where you can't touch it.

Out on the street, up a way, I got this queer feeling. Like I wanted to shake all over but was too frozen to do it. I felt something either pulling on me or breathing on me. I mean, it was screwy, like I was a Geiger counter and had run into what I was looking for. I turned.

Across Second Street, headed towards the alley that leads into the clubs, was Molly. Wearing a long bright-green skirt and a white turtleneck sweater. With all that pretty reddish hair in a big top-knot, like she was deliberately making herself taller than she already was. Conspicuous, you know?

Paddy wasn't with her.

I was so relieved I felt like I ought to walk over and apologize to her. Instead I went close to the store windows, turned, and watched her swing along the street. Like she'd owned Reno so long she'd even forgotten it belonged to her.

Then I saw him, Paddy. Walking fast behind her, his long legs giving at the knee in that little bend that cowpunchers never quite lose. He came up to her, grabbed her arm, flung her face to face with him. She wasn't surprised. Just took on a strong bold look. Said something. Laughed. He grabbed her throat and shook her back and forth. Her long legs kicked at him, her fingers raked his cheeks. Her knee came up hard. Paddy staggered back, bent over. Even from across the street I could see he was pale, sick.

Molly turned away, cool as you please, not even touching her throat, though it was bound to be hurting. Bold as brass. Still owning the town.

I cut across the traffic to Paddy. He was leaning against a building, while people clustered around staring, eyes thrilled like they were watching a movie being shot.

"Paddy, let's go home."

Somebody snickered.

Flames shot through me. Like a chimney long unused and then too much paper is put in the firepot and the soot blazes and sets the house on fire. I plunged into the ring of gawkers, punching, slapping, screaming for them to mind their own business, to leave my Paddy alone.

I felt hands on my shoulders, Paddy's hands. "Angie, that's enough. Let's get out of here."

The crowd parted and we walked through it, turned towards the river. Paddy hailed a taxi and we got in it. Paddy wasn't walking too good.

"That Molly – that Molly, why did you –" I began after we shut the door of our apartment.

"I don't want to talk about it," Paddy said, his face white and drawn. He went in the bathroom and closed the door.

I made some coffee, then stood by the stove wondering whether he'd rather have steak or soup. Or if either of us ever wanted to eat again.

It's hard for a wife of twelve years not to ask her man why he chokes a girl he's just met. If he just met her. Especially with Paddy always spitting on the ground at the mention of men who hit women. Said they ought to take out their mad on wrangling horses or find a man their size or bigger. Now he was choking Molly. Like she had set him crazy.

And then she bested him, right in the

middle of Reno with his wife and a crowd watching. *Damn you, Paddy, how'd that look in the papers if a cop had been around and taken you both to the station and me, too? The papers saying your girl friend beat you up and your wife beat up the crowd for snickering. Like you were some ragdoll for women to toss around. Damn you, Paddy, how'd you like that?*

Paddy was a long time in the bathroom. I heard the bath water running. When he came out he was shaved and had on clean underthings I kept in a bureau for him in the bathroom. "I got soup hot and steak ready to broil," I said as he went through the living room to the bedroom, that's the screwy way our apartment was.

"I don't want anything."

I heard him moving around the bedroom. Pretty soon he came out, dressed up, and his suitcase in his hand. "So long, Angie," he said.

"You can't go like this, Paddy. It's not right, it's not fair to me. We got to talk. Listen, Paddy, I can overlook what happened. Just tell me why, then we won't talk about it any more."

"This time don't come looking for me," he said, staring straight ahead at the outside door.

"Paddy, you don't want her after what she done – she don't want you, you don't want a woman don't want you. But I want you."

"So long, Angie."

"Paddy, let's pack up and head for Wyoming, get out of this damn state with its no-good life, gambling, and loose women like –"

He wheeled on me, his eyes blue fire. "Don't say her name!"

He opened the door and went out. I just followed him, like a puppy dog that's been kicked but won't stay home. Down the hall after him. He took the stairs instead of the elevator, his long legs going fast. I kept up. Outside on the sidewalk, down to the corner, me with no purse or anything.

He turned and said, "Angie, I don't want you no more." He started walking again, with me right behind.

He began running. I'm stubby-built, but I've got lasting power. I ran behind him, down almost to Virginia Street. Paddy stopped and I stood beside him.

"You want to go along and hear me tell her I love her before I kill her?"

"You're not going to kill anybody."

"Okay, just keep hanging onto my tail." He started walking, and I did too. We crossed the Truckee Bridge, over by the old

129

Post Office, past the Holiday Hotel. Turned back again, the opposite direction, with him trying to lose me, up the hill above the river, then we turned again.

"You got no pride, Angie," he said over his shoulder.

What's pride? It don't fill emptiness. I kept walking.

Finally he stopped in front of a fine old house above the river, not far from downtown, that was split into apartments. "She lives here," Paddy said. "I'm going in. And if she's not there I'll wait for her. Because she's mine, she's not going to change her mind just because she's got her divorce and is tired of playing around. Angie, you got get you a divorce. I'm taking Molly. One way or another."

He went up the porch steps, through the entrance, up the stairs. Me back of him. At the top of the stairs he turned and said, "You're asking for it, Angie," and hauled back his arm. I stood, waiting for it. If he hit me, maybe he'd think of me the way he did Molly. But his hand dropped.

He knocked on a door, with a number 3 on it. Inside were footsteps and a woman asked, "Who is it?" Molly.

"You know who," Paddy said.

She laughed. "You want to get messed up

again?" She slid a bolt fast on the other side and walked away.

Paddy stepped back and kicked the door. Ordinarily a kick that hard would have gone on through. But this was an old-fashioned house with heavy oak doors. Nothing happened except a big deep scar on the finish.

Paddy kicked again. Then he went crazy. Kept kicking that door like a bronco with a cactus under its saddle, his face a sick-gray and his eyes blazing. I pulled at him. He shook me off and kept kicking. Nobody came out of the apartment across the hall – the folks must have been gone. Downstairs a woman was yelling. The landlady, it turned out, who went back inside and called the police.

Suddenly the cops were there, no sirens or anything, and they were manhandling Paddy. It took the two of them to handcuff him and drag him downstairs. I stood there, frozen. One cop came back, knocked on Molly's door, asked her to open up and tell him what the trouble was. "No trouble of mine," she said through the door. "I didn't call you. Nobody came in my apartment. Just some stupid idiot kicking my door. Go talk to the one who called you."

"It's the police. We need information."

131

She didn't answer. He turned to me. "You in on this, lady? You trying to get inside, too?"

I shook my head. "I'm his wife. I never touched the door. He just wanted to talk to her. She wouldn't talk to him and he got mad. There wasn't any more to it than that, he just lost his temper."

"Some temper, the way the door's beat up. You better come down to the station and tell the chief about it."

"I'm his wife. I've got no complaint. And if I did, you can't make me say anything against Paddy. I'm his wife. I've got no complaint."

"Well, I have!" the landlady yelled behind us. "Breaking up my door, disturbing my tenants, you bet I'll complain, I'll follow you down to the station in my car!"

"I'll pay for all the damage," I said. "You tell the chief that."

The policeman and the landlady left and I sat down on the top stairstep, shaking like a Washoe Zephyr had struck me. After a bit the bolt slid on Molly's door and the door slowly opened.

She saw me. "Oh," she said.

"I didn't say anything.

"You're his wife, aren't you?"

I nodded.

132

"Listen, I'll be straight with you. When I first hit this town I bumped into Paddy. In one of the clubs. I was just getting my bearings, had noplace to go or anyone to see. And Paddy – well, he has a way with him. Anyway, I didn't know he was married, so we played around. Then you showed up, talking about breakfast. So I split. But he looked me up after that and said he'd left you. Kept hanging around. But frankly, lady, I run on a different track than Paddy. With bosses, not hired help. So I said bye-bye and he wouldn't listen. So he tried muscling me around." She laughed, high and hard. "Shows how stupid a good-looking guy can be. I was trained by pros, and he's an amateur."

"Paddy never once raised his hand to me."

She looked at me wise, and a little sad. "Maybe it would have worked out better if he had. Honest to God. Women!" She went back inside and closed the door.

I'd been trying to hate her. But I couldn't. I felt nothing but sick, sitting there in a strange place like a cast-off ragdoll with its stuffing out.

I got up and went outdoors.

Like I said, it was an old-fashioned house turned into apartments. Whoever had changed it had made kind of a thing out of

133

it being old-fashioned. They'd kept the old veranda, shaped like an L, and put up an old-time hanging porch swing around the corner from the house front. I felt so done in that I went and rested in the swing.

After a while a car drove up. It was the landlady looking like she'd bit into a chunk of iron. She stomped inside, never saw me. It got dark, but I just kept sitting there.

Maybe I had a hunch what would happen.

Molly came out of the house. She went down the steps to the sidewalk, her hair shimmering under the porch light, and her long black dress swirled with embroidery that matched the color of her hair. When she reached the sidewalk, she turned towards town.

I heard footsteps, running from a clump of trees across the street. I stood up, my heart feeling like it filled my whole chest. Molly stopped, tall and defiant, turning towards the man who rushed at her. Paddy. I knew it would be Paddy. She laughed, never a flinch out of her. "Did that poor fool woman bail you out?"

"They didn't hold me. I paid for the door."

"Well, scram! You can't pay for me. The price is too high."

He called her a name. Then, pleading like,

134

his hands reaching out almost as if he was trying to climb up some slick and muddy riverbank, "Please, Molly! Please! I'm begging, Molly. I never felt this way before about anybody. I've got to have you, Molly!"

"Go to hell," she said. "I'm no horse you can break. So lay off the big he-man Wild West stuff with me."

Paddy swung. She dodged but the blow glanced her head. She staggered back. He came at her again, both his hands grabbing.

She must have reached in her purse. I couldn't see. I only heard a sharp crack, the sound reverberating in my ears until it made me dizzy. Paddy was on the ground, crawling around like he was trying to find something.

I floated down the steps, no feet, out to the sidewalk. Then Molly was on the pavement and I was pounding her head onto the concrete.

See Paddy out there? Gentlest man in the world. Sweet and quiet, just rocking on the porch. Hums to himself and rocks. Oh, now and again he walks out to the little corral I built and pets the mare I bought after I moved us up here to Wyoming. But Paddy just stays gentle and quiet, that's his real nature. That Molly had no right to stir him up, make fun of him. Then try to kill him.

She turned him crazy, her face and her bigtime ways.

Right after the trial I brought Paddy back to Wyoming.

Yes, the trial scared me. Not so much for myself as for Paddy. Because if I got sent to the penitentiary, who'd look after him? That shot of Molly's addled him. Struck his head. Made him like a child. Sometimes he cries at night, gets on the floor and crawls around. Just like he did that night. Like he's looking for something he'll never find.

Molly didn't die right away. Not for almost two weeks after that night. But that didn't get me off. Manslaughter it was. In the heat of passion. And my lawyer brought out that I was protecting my husband. So they gave me a suspended sentence. On probation for three years. I have to check in every month.

So I rent this little house on Paddy's old home place from the folks who own it now. Family friends. They keep an eye on Paddy while I'm at work. Except for some nights Paddy's happy. Thinks the mare is a whole string of horses, calls her a lot of different names.

Me?

Well, I'm kind of happy, too. Kind of. No

more worry about Paddy running off to the clubs. And by now I'm used to it.

Used to what?

Oh, like the mare, Paddy calls me by a different name. Just one. Molly. So it hurts a little, but I just figure it's me who answers. Me, Angie.

RICHARD M. GORDON

Death of a Harvard Man

For reasons which he considered sufficient
and which we need not consider here at all,
young Dyer, Harvard '56, had decided to
take arms against a sea of troubles and, by
opposing, end them.

To do this as decently as he might, he had
left his native Boston where any such act of
self-expression is looked on askance and had
journeyed to New York where the
nonconformists and the dramatic fail to raise
even an eyebrow. They were better able to
handle this sort of thing in New York, he felt,
and in any case, he would rather his shattered
remains were collected by the callous hands
of insensitive strangers than by the shocked
and disapproving hands of his fastidious
Boston friends.

He had had a busy day, but now his affairs
were in order: his last will and testament lay
on the dresser of his room at the Harvard
Club among three touching letters of farewell
and apology to his parents, his fiancée, and
the Alumni Secretary of the Class of '56. He

was prepared to meet the sole confidants of his fellow Bostonians, the Cabots.

He had chosen the 42nd Street station of the Sixth Avenue Subway at his point of departure from this vale of tears. It was dark, dank, depressing, and, at 4:30 on a Sunday morning, nearly deserted. There was only a ragged bum sprawled on a bench at the rear of the platform, an empty pint bottle which had contained a cheap California Muscatel beside him. The derelict was staring vacantly into his own world of sordid misery – a world which could not possibly touch on young Dyer's world of high tragedy.

Young Dyer paced impatiently as he waited for his train. And then, far away uptown in the darkness, there came a rumbling. The approaching train was only a local, but young Dyer was not going far. He watched fascinated as the lights materialized out of the gloom of the tunnel. Destiny and a Sixth Avenue local rushed down upon him as he poised tensely at the edge of the platform.

But young Dyer was the sort of man (boy, rather) who could not, even in his extremity, resist an ironic gesture to demonstrate his superiority to the common, non-Harvard humanity which was content to persist in a world he was rejecting.

With an exaggerated bow to the bum on the bench, he uttered the despairing cry of the gladiators of Rome: *"Morituri te salutamus!* – we who are about to die salute you!"

Rather surprisingly, before he could turn to the business at hand, there was a reply. The derelict, reclining languidly like a spectator in a loge at the Colosseum, turned up his thumb and said, *"Vive!"* – the "Live" of the Caesars.

Young Dyer was stopped in his tracks but not on them. By the time he had collected himself, the first car of the local had passed him, and the train was grinding to a halt.

"I thought I had better stop you," said the tramp, rising. His voice was well modulated, and his accent strangely familiar. "It's none of my business, of course," he continued, "but it does seem rather wasteful that a man who has his youth, his health, a Brooks Brothers suit, and a knowledge of Latin should squander all these assets under the wheels of a train. There are those who have a great deal less and still manage to carry on."

Young Dyer was ashamed; he looked down at his hand-lasted, hand-stitched, three-eyelet oxfords, and realized they contrasted sharply with the cracked, lop-heeled, shapeless lumps of dirty leather on the feet of the older man. He had been a bit lacking in courage, he thought. After all, he was a Harvard Man. There was always a comfortable, dignified place in the world for one such as he, if not in Boston, in the wilderness elsewhere. His pioneer blood came to the fore; in spite of all the slings and arrows of outrageous fortune, he would continue living.

"Thank you," he said simply and sincerely. "You saved my life, and I'd like to help you get back on your feet again. A pair of shoes – a new suit. I've got some extra things in my room at the Harvard Club. Come with me – it's not far, just over at 44th and –"

"I know where it is," interrupted the derelict, taking young Dyer by the arm. "I spent some time there myself years ago." And then, through the swelling roar of a southbound express, young Dyer heard the bum say, "I'm Hugh Haven, Class of '34 –"

With a cry of horror, Dyer tore himself from the other's grasp and hurled himself under the wheels of the oncoming D train.

Of course, we could end it here – it ended here for young Dyer. But there are at least three other possible endings. See the next page.

141

Ending One

Hugh Haven, Harvard '34, shook his head sadly as he sauntered unhurriedly toward the exit. For some reason, which it is just as well not to examine, an old college song came as if of its own accord to his lips. "With Crimson in triumph flashing..." he hummed absently to himself as he started up the stairs to the street.

There would now be a delay on the downtown express, and he thought he might as well again try to get a taxi. It is difficult to get a driver to pick you up when you are returning from a masquerade after winning first prize for authenticity as a bum. However, Mr. Haven was, on the whole, well satisfied with his prize-winning costume and the impression it made even on passing strangers.

Ending Two

Hugh Haven Glass, of 34 West 3rd Street, shrugged disconsolately and ambled away from the gathering crowd.

"Now why did he do that?" he said to himself, wondering if the young man had been hard of hearing. "I only wanted to give him my name and address in case he wanted to send me a check."

In his days as a busboy at the Harvard Club bar, before he was fired for reaching above himself into the members' rooms upstairs, he had learned all about Harvard men – what they drank, how they dressed, how they spoke. He had even learned a bit of Latin while he was there.

Ending Three

Hugh Haven, Yale '34, smiled a satisfied smile and relapsed on his bench. He hummed *Boola Boola* softly under his breath.

Once again Yale had triumphed over her ancient adversary.

EDNA FERBER

The Man Who Came Back

There are two ways of doing battle against
Disgrace. You may live it down; or you may
run away from it and hide. The first method
is heartbreaking, but sure. The second
cannot be relied upon because of the
uncomfortable way Disgrace has of turning
up at your heels just when you think you've
eluded her in the last town but one.

Ted Terrill did not choose the first
method. He had it thrust upon him. After
Ted had served his term he came back home
to visit his mother's grave, intending to take
the next train out. He wore none of the
prison pallor that you read about in books,
because he had been shortstop on the
penitentiary all-star baseball team, and
famed for the dexterity with which he could
grab up red-hot grounders. The storied
lockstep and the clipped-hair effect also were
missing. The superintendent of Ted's prison
had been one of the reform kind.

You never would have picked Ted for a
criminal. He had none of those interesting

phrenological bumps and depressions that usually are shown to such frank advantage in the Bertillon photographs. Ted had been assistant cashier in the Citizens' National Bank. In a mad moment he had attempted a little sleight-of-hand act in which certain Citizens' National funds were to be transformed into certain glittering shares and back again so quickly that the examiners couldn't follow it with their eyes. But Ted was unaccustomed to these now-you-see-it-and-now-you-don't feats and his hand slipped. The trick dropped to the floor with an awful clatter.

Ted had been a loveable young kid, six feet high, and blond, with a great reputation as a dresser. He had the first yellow plush hat in our town. It sat on his golden head like a halo.

The women all liked Ted. Mrs. Dankworth, the dashing widow (why will widows persist in being dashing?), said he was the only man in our town who knew how to wear a dress suit. The men were forever slapping him on the back and asking him to have a little something. Ted's good looks and his clever tongue and a certain charming Irish way he had with him caused him to be taken up by the smart set. Now, if you've never lived in a small town you will be much amused at the idea of its boasting a smart set. Which proves your ignorance. The small-town smart set is deadly serious about its smartness. It likes to take three-hour runs down to the city to fit a pair of shoes and attend the opera. Its clothes are as well made, and its scandals as crisp, and its pace as hasty, and its golf club as dull as the clothes, and scandals, and pace, and golf club of its city cousins.

The hasty pace killed Ted. He tried to keep step in a set of young folks whose fathers had made our town. And all the time his pocketbook was yelling, "Whoa!" The young people ran largely to leather-upholstered convertibles and country-club doings and house parties, as small-town younger generations are apt to. When Ted went to high school half the boys in his little clique spent their after-school hours dashing up and down Main Street in their big glittering cars, sitting slumped down on the middle of their spines in front of the steering wheel, their sleeves rolled up, their hair combed in a militant crewcut. One or the other of them always took Ted along. It is fearfully easy to develop a taste for that kind of thing. As he grew older, the taste took root and became a habit.

Ted came out after serving his term, still

handsome in spite of all that story-writers may have taught to the contrary. But we'll make this concession to the old tradition. There was a difference. His radiant blondeur was dimmed in some intangible, elusive way. Birdie Callahan, who had worked in Ted's mother's kitchen for years, and who had gone back to her old job at the Haley House after her mistress's death, put it sadly, thus:

"He was always th' han'some divil. I used to look forward to ironin' day just for the pleasure of pressin' his fancy shirts for him. I'm that partial to them swell blonds. But I dinnaw, he's changed. Doin' time has taken the edge off his hair an' complexion. Not changed his color, do yuh mind, but dulled it, like a gold ring, or the like, that has tarnished."

Ted was seated in the smoker, with a chip on his shoulder, and a sick horror of encountering someone he knew in his heart, when Joe Haley of the Haley House got on at Westport, homeward bound. Joe Haley is the most eligible bachelor in our town, and the slipperiest. He has made the Haley House a gem, so that traveling men will cut half a dozen towns to Sunday there. If he should say, "Jump through this!" to any girl in our town she'd jump and be very glad to do it.

Joe Haley strolled leisurely up the car aisle toward Ted. Ted saw him coming and sat very still, waiting.

"Hello, Ted! How's Ted?" said Joe Haley, casually. And dropped into the adjoining seat without any more fuss.

Ted wet his lips slightly and tried to say something. He had been a breezy talker. But the words wouldn't come. Joe Haley made no effort to cover the situation with a rush of conversation. He didn't seem to realize that there was any situation to cover. He champed the end of his cigar and handed one to Ted.

"Well, you've taken your lickin', kid. What you going to do now?"

The rawness of it made Ted wince. "Oh, I don't know," he stammered. "I've got a job half promised in Chicago."

"What doing?"

Ted laughed a short and ugly laugh. "Driving a brewery truck."

Joe Haley tossed his cigar dexterously to the opposite corner of his mouth and squinted thoughtfully along its bulging sides.

"Remember that Wenzel girl that's kept books for me for the last six years? She's leaving in a couple of months to marry a New

148

York guy that travels for ladies' cloaks and suits. After she goes, it's nix with the lady bookkeepers for me. Not that Minnie isn't a good, straight girl, and honest, but no girl can keep books with one eye on a column of figures and the other on a traveling man in a brown suit and a red necktie, unless she's cross-eyed, and you bet Minnie ain't. The job's yours if you want it. Eighty a month to start on, and board."

"I – can't, Joe. Thanks just the same. I'm going to try to begin all over again, somewhere else, where nobody knows me.

"Oh, yes," said Joe. "I knew a fellow that did that. After he came out he grew a beard, and wore eyeglasses, and changed his name. Had a quick, crisp way of talkin', so he cultivated a drawl and went west and started in business. Real estate, I think. Anyway, the second month he was there, in walks a fool he used to know and bellows: 'Why, if it ain't Bill! Hello, Bill! I thought you was doing time yet.' That was enough. Ted, you can black your face, and dye your hair, and squint, and some fine day, sooner or later, somebody'll come along and blab the whole thing. And say, the older it gets the worse it sounds when it does come out. Stick around here where you grew up, Ted."

Ted clasped and unclasped his hands

uncomfortably. "I can't figure out why you should care how I finish."

"No reason," answered Joe. "Not a darned one. I wasn't ever in love with your ma, like the guy on the stage; and I never owed your pa a cent. So it ain't a guilty conscience. I guess it's just pure cussedness, and a hankerin' for a new investment. I'm curious to know how'll you turn out. You've got the makin's of what the newspapers call a Leading Citizen, even if you did fall down once. If I'd ever had time to get married, which I never will have, a first-class hotel bein' more worry and expense than a Pittsburgh steel magnate's whole harem, I'd have wanted somebody to do the same for my kid. That sounds slushy, but it's straight."

"I don't seem to know how to thank you," began Ted, a little husky as to voice.

"Call around tomorrow morning," interrupted Joe Haley briskly, "and Minnie Wenzel will show you the ropes. You and her can work together for a couple of months. After then she's leaving to make her underwear, and that. I should think she'd have a bale of it by this time. Been embroidering them shimmy things and lunch cloths back of the desk when she thought I wasn't lookin' for the last six months."

Ted came down next morning at 8:00 with his nerve between his teeth and the chip still balanced lightly on his shoulder. Five minutes later, Minnie Wenzel knocked it off. When Joe Haley introduced the two jocularly, knowing that they had originally met in the First Reader room, Miss Wenzel acknowledged the introduction icily by lifting her left eyebrow slightly and drawing down the corners of her mouth. Her air of hauteur was a triumph, considering that she was handicapped by black sateen sleevelets.

I wonder how one could best describe Miss Wenzel? There is one of her in every small town. Let me think (business of hand on brow). Well, she always paid $8.00 for her girdles when most girls in a similar position got theirs for $1.59 in the basement. Nature had been kind to her. The hair that had been a muddy brown in Minnie's schoolgirl days it had touched with a magic red-gold wand. Birdie Callahan always said that Minnie was working only to wear out her old clothes.

After the introduction, Miss Wenzel followed Joe Haley into the lobby. She took no pains to lower her voice.

"Well, I must say, Mr. Haley, you've got a fine nerve! If my gentleman friend was to hear of my working with an ex-con I wouldn't be surprised if he'd break off the engagement. I should think you'd have some respect for the feelings of a lady with a name to keep up, and engaged to a swell fellow like Mr. Stone."

"Say, listen, m'girl," replied Joe Haley. "The law don't cover all the tricks. But if stuffing an order was a criminal offense I'll bet your swell traveling man would be doing a life term."

Ted worked that day with his teeth set so that his jaws ached next morning. Minnie Wenzel spoke to him only when necessary and then in terms of dollars and cents. When dinnertime came she divested herself of the black sateen sleevelets and disappeared in the direction of the washroom. Ted waited until the dining room was almost deserted. Then he went in to dinner alone. Someone in white wearing an absurd little pocket handkerchief of an apron led him to a seat in a far corner of the big room. Ted didn't lift his eyes higher than the snowy square of the apron. The Apron drew out a chair, shoved it under Ted's knees in the way Aprons have, and thrust a printed menu at him.

"Roast beef, medium," said Ted, without looking up.

"Bless your heart, yuh ain't changed a bit.

I remember how yuh used to jaw when it was too well done," said the Apron fondly.

Ted's head came up with a jerk.

"So yuh will cut yer old friends, is it?" grinned Birdie Callahan. "If this wasn't a public dining room maybe yuh'd shake hands with a poor but proud workin' girrul. Yer as good-lookin' a divil as ever, Mister Ted."

Ted's hand shot out and grasped hers. "Birdie! I could weep on your apron! I never was so glad to see anyone in my life. Just to look at you makes me homesick. What in Sam Hill are you doing here?"

"Waitin'. After yer ma died, seemed like I didn't care t'work fer no other privit fam'ly, so I came back here on my old job. I'll bet I'm the homeliest headwaitress in captivity."

Ted's nervous fingers were pleating the tablecloth. His voice sank to a whisper. "Birdie, tell me the God's truth. Did those three years cause her death?"

"Niver!" lied Birdie. "I was with her to the end. It started with a cold on th' chest. Have some French-fried with yer beef, Mr. Teddy. They're illigant today."

Birdie glided off to the kitchen. Authors are fond of the word "glide." But you can take it literally this time. Birdie had a face that looked like a huge mistake, but she

walked like a panther, and they're said to be
the last cry as gliders. She walked with her
chin up and her hips firm. That comes from
juggling trays. You have to walk like that to
keep your nose out of the soup. After a while
the walk becomes a habit. Any seasoned
dining-room girl could give lessons in
walking to the Delsarte teacher of an Eastern
finishing school.

From the day that Birdie Callahan served
Ted with the roast-beef medium and the
elegant French fries, she appointed herself
monitor over his food and clothes and
morals. I wish I could find words to describe
his bitter loneliness. He did not seek
companionship. The men, although not
directly avoiding him, seemed somehow to
have pressing business whenever they
happened in his vicinity. The women ignored
him. Mrs. Dankworth, still dashing and still
widowed, passed Ted one day and looked
fixedly at a point one inch above his head.

In a town like ours the Haley House is like
a big, hospitable clubhouse. The men drop
in the first thing in the morning, and the last
thing at night, to hear the gossip and buy a
cigar and jolly the girl at the cigar counter.
Ted spoke to them when they spoke to him.
He began to develop a certain grim line about

the mouth. Joe Haley watched him from afar, and the longer he watched the kinder and more speculative grew the look in his eyes. And slowly and surely there grew in the hearts of our townspeople a certain new respect and admiration for this boy who was fighting his fight.

Ted got into the habit of taking his meals late, so that Birdie Callahan could take the time to talk to him.

"Birdie," he said one day when she brought his soup, "do you know that you're the only decent woman who'll talk to me? Do you know what I mean when I say that I'd give the rest of my life if I could just put my head in my mother's lap and have her muss up my hair and call me foolish names?"

Birdie Callahan cleared her throat and said abruptly: "I was noticin' yesterday your gray pants needs pressin' bad. Bring 'em down tomorrow mornin' and I'll give 'em th' elegant crease in the laundry."

So the first weeks went by, and the two months of Miss Wenzel's stay came to an end. Ted thanked his God and tried hard not to wish that she was a man so that he could punch her head.

The day before the time appointed for her departure she was closeted with Joe Haley for a long, long time. When finally she emerged, a bellboy lounged up to Ted with a message.

"Wenzel says th' Old man wants t' see you. 'S in his office. Say, Mr. Terrill, do yuh think they can play today? It's pretty wet."

Joe Haley was sunk in the depths of his big leather chair. He didn't look up as Ted entered. "Sit down," he said. Ted sat down and waited, puzzled.

"As a wizard at figures," mused Joe Haley at last, softly as though to himself, "I'm a frost. A column of figures on paper makes my head swim. But I can carry a whole regiment of 'em in my head. I know every time the barkeeper draws one in the dark. I've been watchin' this thing for the last two weeks, hopin' you'd quit and come and tell me." He turned suddenly and faced Ted. "Ted, old kid," he said sadly, "what'n'ell made you do it again?"

"What's the joke?" asked Ted.

"Now, Ted," remonstrated Joe Haley, "that way of talkin' won't help matters none. As I said, I'm rotten at figures. But you're the first investment that ever turned out bad, and let me tell you I've handled some mighty bad-smelling ones. Why, kid, if you had just come to me on the quiet and asked for the loan of a hundred or so, why –"

156

"What's the joke, Joe?" said Ted again, slowly.

"This ain't my notion of a joke," came the terse answer. "We're three hundred short."

The last vestige of Ted Terrill's old-time radiance seemed to flicker and die, leaving him ashen and old.

"Short?" he repeated. Then, "My God!" in a strangely colorless voice – "My God!" He looked down at his fingers impersonally, as though they belonged to someone else. Then his hand clutched Joe Haley's arm with the grip of fear.

"Joe! Joe! That's the thing that's haunted me day and night till my nerves are raw. The fear of doing it again. Don't laugh at me, will you? I used to lie awake nights going over that cursed business of the bank – over and over – till the cold sweat would break out all over me. I used to figure it all out again, step by step, until – Joe, could a man steal and not know it? Could thinking of a thing like that drive a man crazy? Because if it could – if it could – then –"

"I don't know," said Joe Haley, "but it sounds darned fishy." He had a hand on Ted's shaking shoulder and was looking into the white, drawn face. "I had great plans for you, Ted. But Minnie Wenzel's got it all down on slips of paper. I might as well call her in again, and we'll have the whole blamed thing out."

Minnie Wenzel came. In her hand were slips of paper, and books with figures in them, and Ted looked and saw things written in his own hand that should not have been there. And he covered his shamed face with his two hands and gave thanks that his mother was dead.

There came three sharp raps at the office door. The tense figures within jumped nervously.

"Keep out!" called Joe Haley, "whoever you are!" Whereupon the door opened and Birdie Callahan breezed in.

"Get out, Birdie Callahan," roared Joe, "you're in the wrong pew!"

Birdie closed the door behind her composedly and came farther into the room. "Pete th' pasthry cook just tells me that Minnie Wenzel told th' day clerk, who told the barkeep, who told th' janitor, who told th' chef, who told Pete, that Minnie had caught Ted stealin' some three-hundred dollars."

Ted took a quick step forward. "Birdie, for heaven's sake, keep out of this. You can't make things any better. You may believe in me, but –"

"Where's the money?" asked Birdie.

Ted stared at her a moment, his mouth open ludicrously.

"Why, I don't – know," he articulated painfully.

Birdie snorted defiantly. "I thought so. D'ye know," sociably, "I was visitin' with my aunt, Mis' Mulcahy, last evenin'."

There was a quick rustle of silks from Minnie Wenzel's direction.

"Say, look here –" began Joe Haley impatiently.

"Shut up, Joe Haley!" snapped Birdie. "As I was sayin', I was visitin' with my aunt, Mis' Mulcahy. She does fancy washin' an' ironin' for the swells. An' Minnie Wenzel, there bein' none sweller, hires her to do up her weddin' linens. Such smears av hand embroidery an' Irish crochet she never see th' likes. Mis' Mulcahy says, and she's seen a lot. And as a special treat to the poor owld soul, why Minnie Wenzel lets her see some av her weddin' clothes. There never yet was a woman who cud resist showin' her weddin' things to every other woman she cud lay hands on.

"Well, Mis' Mulcahy, she see that grand trewsow and she said she never saw th' beat. Dresses! Well, her going-away suit alone comes to eighty dollars, for it's bein' made by Molkowsky, the little Polish tailor. An'

159

her weddin' dress is satin, do yuh mind! Oh, it was a real treat for my aunt, Mis' Mulcahy."

Birdie walked over to where Minnie Wenzel sat, very white and still, and pointed a stubby red finger in her face. "'Tis the grand manager ye are, Miss Wenzel, gettin' satins an' tailor-mades on yer salary. It takes a woman, Minnie Wenzel, to see through a woman's thricks."

"Well I'll be dinged!" exploded Joe Haley.

"Yuh'd better be!" retorted Birdie Callahan.

Minnie Wenzel stood up, her lip caught between her teeth.

"Am I to understand, Joe Haley, that you dare to accuse me of taking your filthy money, instead of that miserable ex-con there who has done time?"

"That'll do, Minnie," said Joe Haley gently. "That's a-plenty."

"Prove it," went on Minnie, and then looked as though she wished she hadn't.

"A business college edjication is a grand foine thing," observed Birdie. "Miss Wenzel is a graduate av wan. They teach you everything from drawin' birds with tail feathers to plain and fancy penmanship. In fact, they teach everything in the writin' line

160

except forgery, an' I ain't so sure they haven't got a coorse in that."

"I don't care," whimpered Minnie Wenzel suddenly, sinking in a limp heap on the floor. "I had to do it. I'm marrying a swell fellow and a girl's got to have some clothes that don't look like a Bird Center dressmaker's work. He's got three sisters. I saw their pictures and they're coming to the wedding. They're the kind that wear low-necked dresses in the evening and have their hair and nails done downtown. I haven't got a thing but my looks. Could I go to New York dressed like a rube? On the square, Joe, I worked here six years and never took a sou. But things got away from me. The tailor wouldn't finish my suit unless I paid him fifty dollars down. I only took fifty at first, intending to pay it back. Honest to goodness, Joe, I did."

"Cut it out," said Joe Haley, "and get up. I was going to give you a check for your wedding, though I hadn't counted on no three hundred. We'll call it square. And I hope you'll be happy, but I don't gamble on it. You'll be goin' through your man's pants pockets before you're married a year. You can take your hat and fade. I'd like to know how I'm ever going to square this thing with Ted and Birdie."

161

"An' me standin' gassin' while them fool girls in the dinin' room can't set a table decent, and dinner in less than ten minutes," cried Birdie, rushing off. Ted mumbled something unintelligible and at once was after her.

"Birdie! I want to talk to you," he said earnestly.

"Say it quick then," said Birdie, over her shoulder. "The doors open in three minnits."

"I can't tell you how grateful I am. This is no place to talk to you. Will you let me walk home with you tonight after your work's done?"

"Will I?" said Birdie, turning to face him. "I will not. Th' swell mob has shook you, an' a good thing it is. You was travelin' with a bunch of racers when you was only built for medium speed. Now you've got your chance to a fresh start and don't you ever think I'm going to be the one to let you spoil it by beginnin' to walk out with a dinin'-room Lizzie like me."

"Don't say that, Birdie," Ted put in.

"It's the truth," affirmed Birdie. "Not that I ain't a perfec'ly respectable girrul, and ye know it. I'm a good slob, but folks would be tickled for the chance to say that you had nobody to go with but the likes av me. If I was to let you walk home with me tonight, yuh might be askin' to call next week. Inside half a year, if yuh was lonesome enough, yuh'd ask me to marry yuh. And b'gorra," she said softly, looking down at her unlovely red hands, "I'm dead scared I'd do it. Get back to work, Ted Terrill, and hold yer head up high, and when yuh say your prayers tonight, thank your lucky stars I ain't a hussy."

MICHAEL GILBERT
The Wrong Fox

Sergeant Torrero, who was in charge of the in-lying picquet at the San Stefano Military Academy, made his final rounds at five o'clock in the morning.

The two previous rounds – at midnight and at three o'clock – had encompassed the buildings and courtyards. On this occasion, at 5:00, he and his four-man escort made a detour around the inside of the walls that surrounded the sports ground.

A single light showed from one of the small sheds behind the pavilion. It was instinct which sent the Sergeant's hand to the butt of his revolver before he kicked open the door. He stood staring into the room for a long moment. He was a veteran of the War of Liberation. When he turned around at last, his face, seamed and scarred like a stump of old oak, betrayed no hint of his feelings.

Indicating each member of the patrol in turn he said, "You will stay here, outside the door, and allow no one to enter. You will

164

fetch the Commandante. You two will come back with me to the guardroom. At the double."

The telephone buzzed softly in the office of Colonel Cristobal Ocampos, in the Seguridad Building on the Avenue Diaz. Ocampos, who appeared to be expecting the call, put down the file he was studying, picked up the receiver, and said, "Ocampos here. Cardozo? Yes. Where are you speaking from?"

"The guardroom. The telephone is an outside line. It is not connected with the Academy exchange."

"Excellent. Proceed."

"The boy has been identified. He was Basilio de Casal. A first-year cadet at the Academy."

"And it was suicide?"

"Our first conclusion was that it could have been suicide. He would appear to have hanged himself by climbing onto a pile of benches, then jumping from the top. The rope he used came from a longer piece, in a corner of the shed."

"Your *first* conclusion?"

"Then I noticed blood on the boy's shirt, at the back –"

Lieutenant Cardozo continued to speak

for nearly two minutes. At the end of it Ocampos said, "So then the Commandante arrived. What is his name? General Ramirez. Yes, I know him. And he warned you off, eh?"

"He took charge of the matter."

"We can be frank with each other, Lieutenant. Did the General order you to stop your investigation?"

"In effect, yes."

"Did he give any reason?"

"He said that it was clearly a suicide. The matter would be fully looked into by the Police of the Military District."

"Who could be trusted to act discreetly?"

"That was the impression I obtained. You know there have been other – incidents – at the Academy."

"Yes," said the Colonel. "You say that you are in the guardroom. Who is the Sergeant in charge?"

"His name is Torrero. He seems to be a good man."

"Where is General Ramirez?"

"Still down at the pavilion, I imagine. There are quite a few men there now. The doctor has come, and there is a Colonel Villagra, of the Military District, who seems to be in charge –"

Ocampos was not really listening. He said,

"Never mind that. Ask Torrero to take you to Cadet de Casal's room."

"To his room?"

"He will know where it is. Get there quickly and examine it. If you find anything of interest, bring it back here with you."

"I don't think General Ramirez will like it."

"The quicker you move," said Ocampos smoothly, "the less likely General Ramirez will know anything about it."

He hung up and resumed his study of the file. It was a fat file, labeled *Siriola*. It had three red stars pasted on its cover.

He was still reading an hour later when Lieutenant Cardozo was shown in. He was a good-looking young man, with thick black hair and a nose which had an attractive bend in it, the result of a difference of opinion with a drunken mestizo during his recruit service.

"How I wish," said Ocampos, closing the file, "that we had a Smersh here."

"A Smersh?"

"You have not heard of Smersh? It is a famous Russian organization. It removes traitors who have taken refuge in other countries. Think how useful such an organization would be to us, if only a poor country like this could afford it. What luxury! How easily it would dispose of some

167

of our problems! I would simply summon the Chief of Smersh to my office and say to him, 'Proceed to such-and-such a neighboring country and dispose of General Siriola.' And poof!" Ocampos blew a cloud of cigar smoke toward the ceiling. "No more Siriola. Please be seated, Lieutenant. You were up early. You have had a tiring morning."

"I managed to get into his room –"

"What is our major problem? It is that we are a small country. We are surrounded on all sides by larger countries, all hostile to us. So, when he is unmasked, what does a traitor like General Siriola do? He simply drives to one or another of our frontiers. How can poor ignorant soldiers be blamed for not stopping him – a General, in full uniform, flying an official flag on the front of his car? He crosses the bridge. He is among our enemies who are, automatically, his friends. But I am interrupting you, Lieutenant."

"I have here with me –" Cardozo indicated the bulging briefcase.

"Your worm."

Cardozo looked baffled.

"It is a saying. The early bird catches the worm. You were at the vital point ahead of General Ramirez. You have been rewarded."

As he spoke, Ocampos was plucking out

the contents of the briefcase, one by one, and laying them out on his desk – a fat blackbird picking a worm from the lawn.

A white linen robe. A red-covered exercise book with the words *Field Fortification* written in purple ink on the cover. Then half a dozen books, none of them new. Finally, a framed photograph.

"There are other things, of course," said Cardozo. "Many other things. Textbooks of military science, uniforms, underclothes, personal belongings of the sort one would expect to find in the room of a cadet."

"Yes," said Ocampos. He was examining the books. "Then why did you select these books in particular?"

"They were not on the shelves with the other books. They were in a closet, at the back. Almost, one might say, hidden."

Ocampos was examining the most battered of the books. It had no front cover or flyleaf, but the title could still be read in faded gold lettering along the spine: *Galizische Geschichten.*

"Do you speak German?"

"No, Colonel. What does it mean?"

"It means *Tales from Galicia.* It has the date of publication here – see? MDCCCLXXVI."

"That I *can* translate," said Cardozo with a smile. "1876, is it not?"

"Correct. Since it has only the one date it could be a first edition. If it were not in such a deplorable condition it might be valuable." He was opening the other books as he spoke. Four of them were medical textbooks, also in German. The sixth, and last, was in Spanish, and was titled *The Lives of the Martyrs.*

"A curious soldier, young Basilio," said Ocampos. He opened the red-covered notebook.

"I happened to glance inside it," said Cardozo. "It did not appear to be concerned with Field Fortification or, indeed, with any other branch of military service. It had more the appearance of a private diary, or memorandum book. Did I do rightly to take it?"

"Who can tell?" said the Colonel. He walked across to the big safe, spun the dial, opened the door, and placed the book inside. "Who can tell? Scraps of paper, they can be the most important things in the world. A scrap of paper sent Captain Dreyfus to Devil's Island. Another scrap of paper brought him out again."

He closed the safe and returned to the table.

"And this photograph?" It was a framed enlargement, inscribed and signed, of an informal snapshot. It showed a big handsome young man with an arrogant beak of a nose and rather full lips. He was dressed in riding togs, with polished boots and spurs, and had a riding switch tucked under one arm. "Why, particularly, did you bring this to me?"

Lieutenant Cardozo said, the embarrassment evident in his voice, "I recognized it. I thought –"

"You thought – yes?"

"It is the Leader's son, Juvenal Valdez, is it not?"

"Correct. Juvenal is a cadet at the College. In his third year. No doubt he is a friend of Basilio's. Did you find the idea surprising?"

Ocampos was grinning at his Lieutenant's discomfort.

"Basilio de Casal, they told me, came from a poor family. Moreover, it is a Febrerista family. His father was arrested during the Troubles when our Leader came to power. He was kept for some months under house arrest, I believe."

"Your information is accurate. But youth pays little attention to wealth or politics. The boys could have been friends. However –"

The Colonel reopened the safe and put the

photograph in beside the red-covered notebook . . .

It was two hours later and Colonel Ocampos was drinking a cup of coffee, his third of the day, when Colonel Villagra of the Military District Police was shown in. Since the two men were of equal rank, neither wasted effort on ceremony. Ocampos waved Villagra toward a chair. Villagra ignored the gesture, put his broad bottom on the edge of the table, and said, "I am told that one of your men, Lieutenant Cardozo, visited the room of Cadet de Casal this morning and removed certain items of his property."

"Indeed?"

"No doubt he was under the impression that he was doing his duty, but I must point out that General Ramirez has entrusted me with the conduct of this case."

"What case?"

"The case of Cadet de Casal. You are surely aware that he hanged himself last night."

"I was aware that his body was found suspended from a hook, in a shed behind the sports pavilion. Does that constitute a case? And if so, against whom? Or is it intended that there should be some procedure taken against this cadet for the crime of committing suicide?"

"You know very well that a matter like this must be investigated. Particularly since there have been other incidents."

"Two other incidents. Three years ago Cadet Ruffio was shot in the armory. A Court of Inquiry decided that it was an accident. Twelve months ago Cadet Under-Officer Perez, a very promising young man, jumped from the roof of the drill hall, fell sixty feet, and broke his neck.

"There was a suggestion, I believe, that he might have been engaged in some skylarking escapade. Incidentally, *how* long ago did General Ramirez assume control of the Academy? Three years ago, was it? Or four? Times goes so fast."

"Your remarks," said Colonel Villagra, his face distorted with anger, "shall be transmitted to General Ramirez. He may see fit to overlook your innuendos – or he may not."

"Innuendos? You are imagining things. I was pointing out that General Ramirez must naturally investigate every – episode – which occurs under his jurisdiction. Particularly if there have been such a number of them."

"Very well, then. And since I have been charged with this investigation –"

"I am sure you will carry it out very

thoroughly. For instance, you will no doubt come to some decision on the question of whether Cadet de Casal was flogged before or after he was hanged."

Colonel Villagra said, in a choked voice, "Who told you – this story?"

"One of my subordinates, Lieutenant Cardozo. He happens to live near the Academy. When the Sergeant of the Guard telephoned me I alerted him. Thus he was the first one on the scene. He noticed some blood on the back of the boy's shirt and was interested enough to remove his shirt. The weals were very plain. He had been savagely flogged. Incidentally" – Ocampos deposited an inch of ash from his cigar onto the onyx ashtray on his desk – "the Sergeant and the members of the guard *all* saw the marks."

Colonel Villagra said, "Why did he report this to you and not to me?"

"Two reasons, I imagine. First, because he is my subordinate and would naturally report to me. Second, because I am in charge of the investigation."

"Possibly you did not hear me. I told you that General Ramirez had specifically placed me in charge."

"Do I gather that General Ramirez is questioning the direct order of our Leader?"

"The direct –?"

"Given to me, personally, an hour ago. If you would like to confirm it my telephone is at your disposal. The red one has a direct line to the Chancellery."

"I will inform General Ramirez," said Colonel Villagra in a stifled voice.

"I'm afraid he was angry with me," said Ocampos to Lieutenant Cardozo ten minutes later. "General Ramirez will be angry, too. It is a mistake to get angry, particularly at this hot and humid season. It engorges the arteries and thus places a strain on the heart." He considered whether he should light another cigar, and rejected the idea.

"What shall we do now?"

"We have been charged with this investigation. We shall proceed with it. *You* will proceed with it. You will go down to the Academy and question all concerned. By now General Ramirez will have received confirmation of our Leader's edict, and you will find that you will receive full cooperation. I am afraid it will be a considerable task. You may take as much assistance as you wish. Two Sergeants, half a dozen men. Shorthand writers. I leave the details to you with every confidence, Lieutenant."

"I will do my best."

"I'm sure you will. And, by the way, a suggestion. You should certainly have a word with the boy's term officer. A Captain Hernandez. I believe he has a reputation as a disciplinarian – a very strict disciplinarian."

It was the custom of Dr. Chavez, the benign and bespectacled editor of the *Corriera Nacionale,* personally to sign his more provocative editorials. Some were so provocative that simple-minded readers wondered why the Doctor was not arrested. The more cynical suggested that there was a private telephone line between his office and the Chancellery. Certainly some of his guesses had proved inspired. The *Corriera,* for instance, had been the first and only newspaper to attack General Siriola for misappropriating foreign relief funds, and that was three weeks before the General's hurried departure to a neighboring country.

Three days after the discovery of Basilio's body a signed editorial appeared under banner headlines:

"*Academia De Tragedias*

"The discovery, three days ago, of the body of Cadet Basilio de Casal, a young first-year student at the San Stefano Military Academy, hanging in a shed behind the sports pavilion, has raised in many people's minds serious questions of the administration and discipline at this important national institution. People will surely not have forgotten –"

And in case they had forgotten, Dr. Chavez reminded them in a succession of pungent paragraphs of the deaths of Cadet Ruffio and Cadet Under-Officer Perez.

"Where a hundred high-spirited young men are congregated, no one need be surprised at an occasional mishap. But *three* unexplained deaths in less than three years seem to us to be too many. There are two possible explanations. Either the discipline and supervision is too lax, permitting horseplay, bullying and excesses of this sort. Or, as seems more probable, the discipline is too strict.

"Young officers must be taught the value of military discipline, but to enforce it in a barbaric manner, upon their own bodies, does not seem to us to be a course likely to benefit either the recipients of the punishment or its enforcers. Cadets are slow to talk about such matters. Loyalty often blocks criticism. Nevertheless, certain stories are in circulation which are too often repeated to be completely dismissed. Is it, for instance, a coincidence that all three cadets were in the Squadra commanded by

177

Captain Hernandez? Or that Captain Hernandez should be known to his squadristas – jokingly, no doubt – as the 'Slave Driver?'"

Dr. Chavez did not think it a coincidence, and did not scruple to say so, on that day and in the days that followed. Interviews were obtained with members of the Academy staff. Letters were printed from anxious parents of cadets. The name of Captain Hernandez was featured in most of them. His background was investigated by Dr. Chavez's reporters and the results of their researches were set out in many columns of print.

Captain Hernandez came of an aristocratic family, linked by direct descent from the Conquistadores, slave owners and autocrats. His father had fought in the War of Liberation and had been a notorious disciplinarian. Photographs of Captain Hernandez appeared in the papers, grim and unsmiling, a slash of black mustache across a tight-lipped mouth.

It was at the end of the first week that the barrage lifted to a higher target. Dr. Chavez treated his readers to a further signed editorial and a large headline in Latin.

"Quis custodiet ipsos custodes?"

On the assumption that most of his readers

would have neglected their classical studies, this was followed by a translation: *Who controls the controllers?*

"If, as has been widely suggested," the editorial began, "there exists in the Military Academy a system of private discipline which differs little from sadistic bullying, must one not cast a critical eye on the head of that institution?"

Ocampos, who got advance copies of all newspapers, read this with his first cup of coffee and smiled. He said to Lieutenant Cardozo, "I don't think General Ramirez will like this, do you?"

"I'm afraid he won't."

"How is your investigation proceeding?"

"It would be simpler if it were the only investigation."

"Explain."

"I am not being obstructed, you understand. I have been allowed free access to witnesses. As far as I know they have answered my questions frankly. But the fact that I – that we – are investigating the matter has not stopped General Ramirez from continuing a private investigation of his own. We are using the resources of the Military Police. It might be described not only as a double inquiry, but an investigation in parallel."

179

Ocampos considered the matter in silence for some minutes, drawing evenly on his cigar and watching the blue smoke climb into a curtain over his head.

He said, "Parallel lines never meet. I was taught that at school. Or rather, they meet only at infinity, which is an inconclusive destination. The problem then is, which of you will arrive at the truth first? Tell me frankly, what progress have you made so far?"

"You ask me to speak frankly and I will do so. Progress? Very little."

"I see."

"A number of cadets visited Basilio in his room that night at different times, up to nine o'clock. I have spoken to all of them, and all agree on one point: they say that Basilio was undoubtedly worried."

"Worried about what?"

"It was assumed that he was in some trouble with Captain Hernandez."

"Tell me, Lieutenant. In talking to these cadets did you get an impression of what sort of person Basilio was?"

"Reserved to the point almost of unapproachability. Extremely law-abiding – no one could recollect that he had ever been guilty of the least breach of discipline.

Religious in an austere way, which is uncommon in these laxer times."

"And did that not strike you as a curious contradiction?"

"A contradiction?"

"The estimate you have just given me of Basilio's character. And the fact that, on that one evening, a number of different cadets should have dropped in to his room to talk to him. A perfectly normal proceeding, I agree, if he had been a popular, easy-going, social-minded youth. But not so easy to explain if he was the latter-day saint you depict."

Lieutenant Cardozo considered the matter, and then said, with a smile, "One must remember that he was very good-looking."

"True," said Ocampos. "Much is forgiven to those whom providence has endowed with good looks. Proceed."

"One of the servants who visited Basilio's room on some errand at about ten o'clock found it empty. When he went back at half past ten it was still empty."

"And was Captain Hernandez in the building at this time?"

"Yes. He was working late that night."

"Was this usual?"

"Quite usual. In term time, when he was

181

busy, he slept more often in the Academy than in his apartment outside."

"One assumption is that Basilio visited Captain Hernandez that evening? That something – untoward – occurred? And that the hanging was an effort to cover it up?"

"Those are certainly possible assumptions."

"But you have no evidence? No actual proof?"

"No."

"And we cannot move without proof?"

"It would be difficult."

"Difficult," agreed Ocampos. "But, so far as our opponents are concerned, not impossible, apparently. Or have they, perhaps, discovered some vital facts which have escaped our notice?"

Cardozo stared at him.

"Just before you arrived," said Ocampos, "I learned that General Ramirez had ordered the arrest of Captain Hernandez."

"On what charge?"

"The charge is causing the death of Cadet Basilio in the course of unauthorized disciplinary proceedings."

"But –"

"Let us restrain our impatience. I have no doubt we shall read all about it in the *Corriera* tomorrow."

And not only the *Corriera* on the next day but all the newspapers of the capital for many days spread themselves on these exciting topics: the background of the accused and of his supposed victim; the membership of the military tribunal which had been summoned with exemplary speed; the zeal of General Ramirez in seeking out the truth, and the earnest desire of their Leader that justice should not only be done but be seen to be done.

During the whole of this time Colonel Cristobal Ocampos hardly left his office. Insofar as he interested himself in the case at all he seemed to be concentrating his attention on the red-covered exercise book which was locked in his safe and labeled in purple ink, *Field Fortification*. Each of the scribbled names, addresses, and telephone numbers in the book had been typed out by the Colonel's own podgy fingers onto a file card, and each card accumulated, as the days went by, a series of further annotations in the Colonel's sprawling handwriting.

On the evening of the seventh day he sent once more for Lieutenant Cardozo.

The Lieutenant received his orders with evident surprise. He said, "Certainly I will do it. But I was under the impression –" He paused.

"Under what impression, Lieutenant?"

"I had imagined that, in effect, the conduct of this case had passed out of our hands. That it was being conducted by General Ramirez."

"Now I wonder why you should think that," said Ocampos sleepily. "True, I have made no positive move in the matter over the past week. But that was because I could not see that any actual move was called for. You appeared to me to have made all the necessary preliminary investigations in a thorough and painstaking manner –"

The Colonel tapped the bulky folder on his desk. "However, on rereading your reports I did note one omission. You do not appear to have interrogated Cadet Juvenal Valdez. Why was that?"

The Lieutenant shifted uncomfortably.

"Particularly, Lieutenant, when we have evidence that he was a friend of Basilio's. Had he not a photograph of Juvenal on his mantelshelf?"

"Juvenal Valdez, being our Leader's son, is a popular figure in the Academy. Many cadets have such a photograph."

"And were all these photographs

personally inscribed to their recipients and signed Juvenal?"

"Well – no."

"I think, Lieutenant, that you had better have a word with this young man, and the sooner the better. In fact, immediately."

It was the veteran Sergeant Torrero who accompanied Lieutenant Cardozo across the graveled acres of the parade ground, past the old-fashioned cannon with its perimeter of neatly piled shot, up an echoing flight of stone stairs, along a bare corridor. The Military Academy by night was a place of silence, deep shadows, and sharp lights.

"It's not very homey," said the Lieutenant.

"Soldiers must learn to live without luxury," said the Sergeant. He knocked at a door at the end of the corridor, opened it, and stood aside for the Lieutenant to go in.

Juvenal Valdez was seated in a wicker chair in front of the fire, his slippered feet stretched out to the blaze. He waved a friendly hand and said, "Come along in, Lieutenant. Sit down. If I'm to be grilled I insist on being grilled in comfort."

He was a thickly built, well muscled young man with the shoulders of a boxer, black hair, and a handsome face which he must

185

have derived, the Lieutenant concluded, from his mother, Juanita. It had little in common with the thin, bloodless look of his father, except possibly for the eyes, which had a certain shrewdness behind the curtain of their candor.

"I have no intention of grilling you," said the Lieutenant, trying to keep the respect out of his voice. "But I thought – we thought – that you might be able to help us on a few points –"

"Does one gather that Colonel Ocampos is hunting a different line from our respected Commandante?"

The directness of the question took the Lieutenant by surprise. He said, "Well –"

"No need to answer if it embarrasses you. Speaking personally, I think General Ramirez is after the wrong fox."

"You do? Who then should he be chasing?"

"It's a difficult question. To answer it you would have to know something of Academy politics and personalities. Ramirez is an old-style aristocrat. He does not approve of my father's policy of allowing young men to come to this college on a basis of ability alone, without regard to family background. In the General's view, our Army should be officered only by gentlemen and the sons of gentlemen."

"And you do not agree?"

"I wasn't giving you *my* ideas. They are my father's."

"And as such, entitled to all respect."

"Within these four walls, Lieutenant, and in the confidence that it will not be repeated, I will tell you something. My father is not God. He is not infallible. Nevertheless, on this point I think he is right. There are not enough gentlemen of appropriate military talent to officer the Army. But you can appreciate that a boy like Basilio, son of an impoverished family – and a Febrerista family into the bargain – would hardly appeal to our Commandante."

"I understand that. Yes."

"And that was why poor Basilio" – there was a glint in Juvenal's eyes as he said it – "had to walk so circumspectly. Indeed, it was a narrow and thorny path he trod with bare feet. A path which led through torment to destruction."

"At the hands of whom?"

The walls of the Academy were so thick, the silence was so complete, that they might have been isolated in a capsule in space.

"It is not difficult to guess," said Juvenal at last. The words seemed to be forced out of him by an inner pressure that he was unable to resist. "If not by General Ramirez himself, then by his creatures. The Military Police. It would need only the slightest pretext –"

"Such as?"

"A hint from above that Basilio was engaged in treasonable activities. Rigorous questioning. Then a faked suicide to conceal the truth."

"And you do not think that Captain Hernandez had anything to do with it?"

Juvenal laughed. It was a sudden, harsh bray of laughter. "Hernandez? Of course not. He is a martinet, a disciplinarian certainly. But not a sadist. Besides, though he might conceivably have beaten him, how could he, single-handed, have arranged the so-called suicide?"

"No doubt the prosecution will have a theory, and witnesses to support it."

"Certainly they will have witnesses. All of them will be Villagra's policemen. They will tell a most convincing story. One of them will have seen Basilio going to Captain Hernandez's room. Another will have heard screams. A third will have noticed Captain Hernandez driving his car in the direction of the pavilion. After all, they have two successful precedents. Why should they not follow them? You have read the accounts of the Ruffio and Perez cases."

"Yes," said the Lieutenant. "I have read the accounts."

He left Juvenal Valdez's room a badly disturbed man. He was pondering deeply on what he had learned. He was still pondering when he realized that he was being followed.

It was the tink of a steel-capped boot against stone. He swung round, but could see nothing. Or was there a darker shadow in the shadows behind the floodlights?

Cardozo hesitated for a moment, then he swung round and started to walk fast across the large open parade ground. He heard nothing. The sound of his own footsteps, crunching on the gravel, effectively blocked out other sounds. It was instinct which made him turn his head. Three men were coming after him and coming fast.

He had a gun, but it was in a shoulder holster, inside his belted topcoat. Before he could reach it his pursuers would be on top of him.

He took to his heels.

The difficulty was that he had no clear idea where the main gate lay. The parade ground stretched out unhelpfully in the darkness.

A building loomed ahead. At the last moment, Cardozo realized that it was the sports pavilion, the very one behind which Basilio's body had been found. He had come too far to the right. But it gave him his bearings. He had only to swing left on the path behind the pavilion and it would bring him to the main gate and the guardhouse.

As his feet touched the path he realized something else. The men behind him, appreciating his blunder, had spread out on both sides and one of them had already reached the path to the Lieutenant's left.

Cardozo changed his plan, stopped in his tracks, and then quickly swung round.

The man behind him was so close, and coming so fast, that he could not conform to the move. As he went past, Cardozo thrust out a foot and saw his pursuer go sprawling. Then the Lieutenant was racing for the pavilion.

The third man, who had moved out to the right, was waiting for him in the shadow of the building, crouched low, his head forward, his arms hanging. A professional fighter.

Cardozo ran straight at him. Then, at the very last moment, he swerved to one side and sprinted up the pavilion steps.

At the top of the steps there was a broad railing. He put one hand on it, vaulted it, and
190

landed, in the comfortable darkness, among a pile of benches.

But he had gained the time he needed.

As the dark shape of his pursuer loomed at the foot of the steps Cardozo fired once, aiming carefully above the pursuer's head. The crack of the shot split open the quietness of the night.

The Lieutenant smiled happily. He had his back to a solid building. He had seven more shots in his police automatic, and a spare magazine in his pocket. He was quite prepared, if necessary, to wait for daylight.

It did not prove necessary. Five minutes later Sergeant Torrero, who had come with the picquet to investigate the sound of the shot, accompanied him back to the main gate.

At the Seguridad Building he found Colonel Ocampos, still engrossed in his study of the red-covered exercise book. He had just deciphered another name in it. It was in pencil scribble on the inside of the cover, so faint that it looked as though someone had written it and then changed his mind and tried to erase it. At first sight it had looked like *Gonzalez*. But careful work with a magnifying glass, under oblique light, had clarified the first few letters. It was *Benitez*. And the letter in front of it was a capital *A*.

"Andrea Benitez," said Ocampos. He said it aloud as Lieutenant Cardozo came into the room. The discovery had excited him. It excited him more than the Lieutenant's story, which seemed only to amuse him.

"They chased you out, did they?" he said. "It was to be expected. They're very sensitive about poaching on their preserves."

"It wasn't at all funny," said Cardozo. "Or it wouldn't have been if they'd caught me."

"You should wear your gun where you can always get at it," said Ocampos unsympathetically. "Now, to something important. Andrea Benitez. We have a file on him. A silly little man who tried to stir up trouble in the University. He cooled his heels in prison for a few months last year. He's free now. He lives in an apartment house near the airport. The address is in the file. Bring him in."

"Tonight?"

Ocampos looked at his watch. It was five minutes to midnight.

"Well, first thing tomorrow," he said grudgingly.

After breakfast on the following day, Cadet Under-Officer Juvenal Valdez obtained permission to leave the Academy and drove his neat and inconspicuous American car to the private parking lot at the back of the Chancellery Building. He left it in charge of the one-armed parking attendant, then walked through the private entrance, where the door was held open for him by a doorman who had lost most of his face. He then took the elevator, which went only to the sixth floor and was operated by a man who perched all day on a stool because he had only half a leg. All three men were veterans of the War of Liberation and owed their jobs to this fact.

Juvenal entered an unmarked door at the end of the corridor.

General Rafael Valdez, Chancellor, Minister of Defense, and Leader of his country, was not, at first sight, an impressive figure. He was six inches shorter than his son, a lack of height emphasized by a stoop which brought his shoulders forward and revealed the top of his head with its yellowish skin and thinning hair. For some years now he had abandoned the habit of wearing a uniform, and although the suit which he wore had been cut in London, and fitted him accordingly, it was hardly the expected garb of a South American dictator.

Yet he was formidable. In spite of the grayness and neutrality of his appearance he seemed to sound a warning. Partly it was in his eyes, partly in the way he held himself. Some of it was in his voice when he spoke.

He greeted his son formally. They shook hands. They settled themselves at a table, in the big bay window, the son holding the chair for his father to be seated before sitting himself.

"Well?" said Valdez.

"I wish that all *were* well, but it is not," said Juvenal.

He continued for some minutes. Then his father said, speaking slowly and dispassionately, as a judge might have done if he were summing up a case which interested but did not really concern him, "So. Your thesis is that my old friend and comrade in arms, General Ramirez, is plotting against me. That he is in touch with that other old comrade of mine, General Siriola, now a resident out of the country. The plotters, you suggest, come chiefly from the establishment of the Military District Police, under Colonel Villagra – I cannot, for the moment, recall him."

"You would not know him. Until recently he was only a Captain. He has been promoted rapidly by General Ramirez."

"Villagra. But yes. I do remember a man of that name. Large, red-faced, and with

194

somewhat prominent side teeth – tusks, almost."

Juvenal smiled. "Your memory for faces is infallible."

"And you tell me that these plotters have tried to involve you?"

"More than simply involve me," said Juvenal indifferently. "They wished me to lead the coup. I was to take your place as head of the State. I should, of course, have been a puppet only."

"And that was why you refused?"

"I admit an ambition to succeed you," said Juvenal with a smile. "But not to replace you."

"I wonder if you are wise," said Valdez. "It is a position with few attractions and many headaches. Was the approach made to you direct?"

"No. They used this boy, Basilio, as a go-between. They knew that he was a friend of mine. Possibly, since his father is of the Febrerista party, they considered that he might be on their side. If so, they misjudged him."

"And having taken him too far into their confidence, and found him loyal to me, they first flogged him, and then hanged him."

"Yes."

"One might conclude, perhaps, that they

made similar approaches – and similar mistakes – with the other two cadets, Ruffio and Perez."

"I think that is a fair assumption."

"But you have no proof of it?"

"I have no proof at all."

"Then what do you suggest that we can do?"

Juvenal looked at his father. There were times when he understood him and liked him, other times when he did not understand him and feared him.

He said, "If you do nothing, you realize that this conspiracy may grow?"

"A fish should not be caught until it has attained a certain size."

"You realize too that injustice will be done? That an innocent man will be condemned and shot?"

"Captain Hernandez?"

"Yes."

"Thin, dark, with a rather large dark mustache?"

"That's the man."

"And you are certain that he had no hand in this boy's death?"

"Oh, quite certain."

Juvenal said this with such emphasis that his father looked up for a fleeting second, seeing in the big proud young man a startling reflection of the passionate girl he had married twenty-five years before.

Juvenal became conscious of his father's gaze. He shifted uncomfortably and repeated, "Quite certain. It would be entirely out of character."

"Are you telling me all this for my own protection? Or because you respect Captain Hernandez and wish to prevent an injustice? Or because you were fond of Basilio and desire to avenge his death?"

"Something of all three."

"Yes. I see."

His father got up, stepped to the window, and stood staring down at the traffic crawling round the Piazza. He stood so for a long time in silence. Then he said, "When no truly effective course of action suggests itself, it is better to do nothing. Sometimes a small injustice will result. Sometimes something will happen to prevent it."

Juvenal realized that the interview was over, and departed the way he had come.

After he had driven off, the legless elevator operator said to the faceless doorman, "He has his father's temper."

That was on Friday.

The military tribunal to try Captain Hernandez was convoked for the following

Wednesday. On the intervening Sunday, Father Domenico Santos, Superior of the Jesuit Order of Our Lady at Quyguyho, preached in the Cathedral Church of the Asuncion.

What he said was reported under banner headlines in every newspaper in the capital for Father Santos was a nationally respected figure, a man of iron integrity and proved courage.

"If the trial of Captain Hernandez proceeds," he was reported as saying, "for a crime of which his accusers well know that he is innocent, I shall deem it my duty to offer evidence at the hearing. To do so will involve breaking the sacred seal of the confessional. But in order to prevent injustice and save an innocent life I should not hesitate to do even that."

The newspapers then pointed out that Basilio's family came from the neighborhood of Quyguyho, and that it was reasonable to assume that Father Santos had been the dead boy's confessor.

So great was the excitement over this unexpected development that a number of lesser occurrences escaped notice. A retired Major living alone took his dog for a walk that Sunday night. The dog returned, but the Major did not. On Monday morning a junior official in the Ministry of the Interior failed to arrive at his office; and an employee at the airport, a man named Andrea Benitez, did not report for duty.

To Lieutenant Cardozo and the other members of his staff who had carried out these three arrests it appeared that Colonel Ocampos had taken root in the Seguridad Building. He had a bed in his office, and his meals were brought in to him. His only excursions into the open air were a walk to the tobacconist's shop on the corner, where he purchased every day a fresh box of cigars.

On Tuesday morning he left his office and paid a visit to the lower part of the building. Here were the cells in which prisoners were kept in temporary confinement for interrogation, before they were passed on to permanent establishments. Here also were certain interview rooms, soundproofed, with concrete floors and tiled walls. The interrogation of Andrea Benitez was starting as he arrived.

At the end of it he said to the Sergeant in charge, "Show him the photographs of the last man who was obstinate. I should like him to see particularly the photographs of his back. Give him plenty of time to study them. I will be down again in an hour."

When he got back to his office there was

a message that Father Santos had arrived. He said, "Show him in at once," and lit a cigar.

The Jesuit was six-foot tall and his robes hung down over a body that was as thin as a sword. His lips were indrawn and bloodless, his face carved out of yellowing stone. He refused the offer of a chair and remained standing. The light from the window threw his menacing shadow across the room.

"I come here under compulsion," he said.

"Then those who brought you shall be reprimanded, Father. My instructions were that you be invited to attend."

"When an armed policeman invites you it is an order. Now that you have me here, what do you intend to do to me? Subject me to your special interrogation techniques?"

"That would hardly be profitable, I imagine."

The thin lips cracked into a bitter smile. "Under the old regime, when I was tortured, it is true that I was not broken. But I am an older man now. Old men are less tolerant of pain. If you were to whip me hard enough, you might whip a few words out of me."

"The question does not arise," said Ocampos. "I repeat, Father, that you are here by invitation. I desire your help. If you do not choose to give it you are free to depart."

"What do you wish of me?"

"I want you to tell me, now, what you would tell the military tribunal were you to give evidence before it."

"With what object?"

"My object, curiously enough, is the same as yours. To prevent injustice. Indeed, if the truth is what I suspect it to be, there can be no injustice. Because there will be no trial."

The flint-colored eyes held the Colonel's deep brown ones for a full ten seconds. Then Father Santos said, "If you promise me that, Colonel, then this would seem to be one occasion on which the Church and the State can act together."

At half past two on that same Tuesday afternoon Cristobal Ocampos rose from his chair. He had already donned the service uniform of a Colonel in the Presidential Guard. Now, opening the closet, he took the dress overcoat from its hanger and put it on, draping it carefully to conceal the bulge made by the big revolver in its holster on his left hip.

He examined himself critically in the glass. There was no doubt about it. The coat had become too tight around the waist. It would

201

have to be let out. To Lieutenant Cardozo, also in uniform, he said, "I think everything will be ready for us now."

The two men left by the entrance at the rear of the building. The courtyard was crammed with soldiers. There were four troop carriers, each with a full complement of steel-helmeted infantry men; a section of armored cars with machine guns mounted fore and aft; a dozen motorcyclists; and an open olive-green command car with a soldier at the wheel and another beside him.

Ocampos and Cardozo got into the command car, which moved slowly out of the courtyard and into the street. Behind them they could hear the roar of the other vehicles starting up.

Colonel Villagra was in his office in the headquarters of the Military District Police when the head of the cavalcade arrived. He looked out of the window and saw the soldiers jumping from the carriers and running to surround the building, saw the machine guns being set up and the armored cars moving to strategic points. He was still standing, staring out, when Colonel Ocampos came into the room.

Villagra said, "Might I ask what this – this charade – means?"

Files of soldiers were already moving

through the building, bringing out policemen and disarming them. There was no resistance. The demonstration of overwhelming force had been sufficient.

Ocampos said, "Your gun, please."

Villagra unbuckled his belt without a word. His red face was a mottled gray, and his plump cheeks seemed to have caved in.

Ocampos said, "You are under arrest."

"Is it permitted to know the charge?"

"The charge is conspiring against our Leader, the object of the conspiracy being to bring back the traitor, Siriola, from his well merited exile."

"I take it that you have some evidence to support this charge?"

"Two of your agents have made full confessions."

(Of the three, only the retired and solitary Major had refused to speak. His body had been buried early that morning behind the Seguridad Building.)

"I have no doubt," said Colonel Villagra, attempting a sneer which lifted his lip and exposed his tusklike side teeth, "that you can produce perjured testimony against me."

"You speak as an expert," said Ocampos. He turned to Lieutenant Cardozo and said, "It would be more fitting, I think, if we continued this conversation alone." As he spoke he was unbuckling the holster strap on Colonel Villagra's belt, and now he held Villagra's automatic pistol loosely in his gloved right hand.

Lieutenant Cardozo turned on his heel and went quickly out, shutting the door behind him. He had got halfway down the passage when he heard the shot. He did not even turn his head.

That evening Colonel Ocampos called on his Leader – not at the Chancellery but at his villa in the foothills above the city. The nights were cold at that time of year, and the two men sat in deep leather armchairs in front of a snapping fire.

It was the Leader who broke a long silence.

"After Colonel Villagra, by shooting himself, had admitted his treachery," he said, "what did you do?"

"I placed his principal officers under arrest and then I spoke to the men. I felt no doubt that they were innocent dupes. I considered that it was sufficient to disarm them and send each man home, with orders to stay there. We will, of course, examine their records. If any of them appears unreliable he will be dismissed."

"And the officers?"

"The decision must be yours," said Ocampos. "We could treat them in the same way as the men, or we could stage a mass trial."

"I dislike propaganda trials. They usually backfire."

"They harm our public image," agreed Ocampos, "and achieve little."

"Was it while you were making these arrangements, Colonel, that General Ramirez escaped?"

"That is so."

"The Academy is some little way from the Military Police Headquarters. Your preparations were made in strict secrecy. How did he get the news in time, I wonder?"

Ocampos considered his reply. He had worked with the Leader for a decade, and had been his friend before the Leader came to power. But there was a saying that blood was thicker than water. He realized that he would be taking a considerable risk if he spoke now. And for what?

The silence must have lasted a long time, because it was broken by the Leader who said, "I asked you a question, Colonel."

"Yes," said Ocampos, "and I will answer it. General Ramirez escaped because I sent him word. I sent it by Sergeant Torrero. He is one of my men. I placed him at the

Academy some time ago, to watch other events."

"Let us forget Sergeant Torrero, who is no doubt an honest policeman, and find out why you, the head of my Security Police, should have taken such a step."

"If General Ramirez had not fled, it would have been necessary to bring him to trial and to execute him. He would have been more dangerous to us as a martyr than he will be as a pensioner of one of our neighboring countries. As a student of English history, I have often thought that the Jacobite cause would have been greatly strengthened had the Young Pretender been executed on Tower Hill. It withered away as its hero grew fat, debauched, and ludicrous in the French Court."

"Even supposing you are right, was not this a matter of policy, which I should have been asked to decide for myself? Do such matters come within the province of the Security Police?"

"In the ordinary way," said Ocampos, "they would certainly not do so. But there was a further aspect of this matter. At his trial, if there was a trial, one of the matters General Ramirez would have been accused of would have been the death of three cadets under his charge as the Commandante. As

206

to that, certain facts are now much clearer. All three, Perez, Ruffio, and Basilio de Casal, had become involved, to a greater or lesser extent, in the treacherous schemes of the General and his immediate circle. In the case of the first two, the cadets had been indiscreet, or perhaps had shown an inclination to defect. So they were eliminated. The case of Basilio de Casal was somewhat different."

"Different? How?"

"Father Santos, who was the boy's confessor, has told me some odd facts about him – facts which seemed to me, in the context of other evidence which I had, to be significant. Basilio had read deeply in the lives of the Saints, particularly the ones who practised extreme forms of self-mortification. He had a white robe, and whenever he convicted himself, before the tribunal of his own conscience, of some sin or peccadillo, he would dress himself in this garment, and kneel, silent and motionless, in the attitude of a penitent."

"Father Santos told you this?"

"This, and more. Basilio was, it appears, a student of the works of Count von Sacher-Masoch. This book was found in his room – it is the Count's best-known work."

He took from his pocket the tattered

volume of the *Galiziche Geschichten* and handed it to the Leader, who placed it on the arm of his chair without opening it. "This Count. He was the man who originated the cult of masochism, was he not? The idea that you could obtain sexual satisfaction from the infliction of pain on yourself."

"Spiritual satisfaction also, in certain cases. He makes that plain in his writings."

"And are you suggesting that when Basilio found himself helplessly enmeshed in treachery, he sentenced himself to death by hanging? And carried out the sentence himself?"

"Not only to death. For a nature like this, a quick and simple death would have been entirely inadequate to the crimes he felt he had committed. It was necessary that he suffer first."

"He could not have flogged himself, surely?"

"No."

"Then who did it? General Ramirez? Colonel Villagra and his policemen? Captain Hernandez?"

"None of those appear to me to be at all likely," said Ocampos. He was picking his words with great care. "As I understand the cult of masochism, it is an essential element that the pain be inflicted by a friend. One for whom the sufferer has a warm and reciprocated affection. Almost, one might say, one with whom he was in love."

He was thinking, as he spoke, of the photograph of a big handsome young man with an arrogant beak of a nose and rather full lips, dressed in riding clothes, with a riding switch tucked under one arm.

What the Leader was thinking was not apparent.

When he broke the long silence he said, in a toneless voice, "One gets these relationships between young men who are thrown together. They are inevitable, I imagine."

"Inevitable," said Ocampos. "And usually, they are quite transient."

A log fell from the fire, blazing brightly. The Leader leaned forward, picked it up with his bare fingers, and threw it back into the flames. He said, "If there is no trial, then there will be no occasion for Father Santos to give evidence?"

"None at all."

"And you would advise that course?"

"I would advise it."

"I accept your advice," said the Leader. And as Ocampos rose to go, the Leader added, "Thank you, Colonel."

JON L. BREEN

The Number 12 Jinx

Before I tell you about the impossible disappearance at Surfer Stadium, a little anecdote might be appropriate.

In a game at one of the midwestern ball parks last season, I'm umpiring behind home plate – my name is Ed Gorgon, and I've been a major-league umpire for close to three decades. Anyway, in this particular park you can't see all of the bullpen from home plate. You can tell when a relief pitcher is warming up, but you can't see who he is because he's hidden by a fence.

On this occasion I see the bullpen catcher hunker down and start to receive warmup pitches from a reliefer, and I casually say to the batter coming up to hit, "I see ol' Spook Durkin is heatin' up out there." The batter, a rookie and not the smartest guy in the league, looks at me like I'm Sherlock Holmes in a chest protector and says, "Ed, how can you tell that? How do you know who's warming up?"

It's so simple, I'm ashamed to explain it.

"The bullpen catcher has his mask on. These masks aren't so comfortable you wear 'em without a reason, and you don't warm a guy up with a mask on unless he's a knuckleballer who has no idea where the ball he's throwing is going. And the only knuckler out there is Spook Durkin. Strike!"

The kid shakes his head in wonder before getting back in the box. "It's simple when you explain it, Ed."

"Yeah," I say. "Strike two!" The kid better get his mind on the game or he'll be back in the Coast League before he knows what hit him.

Anyway, that little story just shows how a man's acumen can get overrated, and it leads into the story I really want to tell you – about "Honey" Reed and his short career with the Los Angeles Surfers.

John "Honey" Reed, who could play six positions well and two others adequately, who could hit with power and run like your basic deer, came to the Surfers from Chicago with a reputation as a troublemaker. He seemed to need an excuse to live up to it, and he found it over the simple matter of choosing a number for his uniform.

The number Honey Reed wanted was the one he'd worn throughout his career – in high school, college, the minors, the majors

– the number 6. And there was the problem. Although no L.A. Surfer was wearing number 6 when Reed came to the club, he was told he couldn't wear it.

Six had been retired by the Surfers, having been worn by the great ballplayer of years ago, Fritz Krieg, who had played for the Surfers back when they were the Bronx Lions, long before they moved west. Though nobody in L.A. had ever seen Krieg play, he was one of the greats who, if he hadn't had the misfortune of being the only Major Leaguer killed in World War II, might have been greater still.

The controversy raged throughout spring training. Reed reported and agreed reluctantly to train wearing number 7, but he swore that if he couldn't wear 6 on opening day he wouldn't play ball with the Surfers. The papers and TV had a field day with it, making Fritz Krieg into a local hero on the order of Sandy Koufax, and reviving the old rumor that Krieg had actually met his death in a bombed brothel.

The long rhubarb came to a climax when the Surfers returned to town from Arizona for two exhibitions in their home park prior to the opening of the season. A meeting was called in the office of Frances Gabrielson, owner of the Surfers, and present besides

Honey Reed were Surfer player-representative Mort Fredericks; Florence Krieg, the widow of Fritz; team publicist Terry Takamoto; general manager Roy Giddings; and field manager Barney Dunlap.

The way the meeting was described to me later, everybody there except Fredericks is trying to get Reed to knuckle under and wear another number. Mrs. Gabrielson, a cool and elegant elderly lady, tries sweet reason and an appeal to team tradition, a tough case to make since the name Lions had been dropped for Surfers when the team came to L.A. Barney Dunlap's method of argument is loud and red-faced incredulity and an apparently genuine inability to comprehend anyone else's arguments.

The widow underlines the necessity she feels for keeping Fritz's memory alive, and Roy Giddings makes reference to Krieg's war record. At this point Takamoto, whose Nisei parents were interred during World War II, blows his top, swearing that Reed said under his breath, "On which side?" Reed denies the charge but apologizes to Mrs. Krieg and tells her he never believed the rumors about Fritz's death. Mrs. Krieg, white-faced, claims she doesn't know what rumors he's referring to.

One point of discussion is whether the

Bronx Lions that Krieg played for and the Los Angeles Surfers are really the same organization for number-retiring purposes. Giddings claims they are, regardless of the move of several thousand miles, and Reed surprisingly backs him up. He says, "I've done a lot of research into the history of this club, and it is for sure the same organization." Is there some implied threat in Reed's voice, a slight chilling of the atmosphere for a moment? My informants disagree on that point.

Anyway, after much more discussion and replowing of the same ground, with Mort Fredericks halfheartedly defending Reed's right to the number he wants, the slugger suddenly decides to give in, to give up number 6.

There are smiles all around and mutual congratulations until general manager Giddings asks, "So what number do you want, John?"

"Well, if I can't wear 6, I'll make it twice 6. I'll be number 12."

Barney Dunlap groans, and there is an awkward silence.

Reed breaks it by asking his teammate, "Mort, there's nobody on the club wearing 12, is there?"

"No," Fredericks admits, "there isn't."

"We don't wear 12 on the Surfers," says Barney Dunlap flatly. "We just don't."

In a low voice Honey Reed inquires, "Is it retired, too, in memory of some Bronx Lion who died in World War I in a –"

Mrs. Gabrielson breaks in quietly on Reed's offensive crack, and it's possible not everyone in the room even hears it. "Mr. Reed," she says, keeping her cool, "you must believe me that there are good and sound reasons for our unwillingness to have you wear number 12 and that they spring from nothing so much as a concern for your own well-being."

Reed will not be brought down, however. He blows up. "Look, I've gone out of my way to cooperate with you people on this. I wanted 6 and you said I couldn't have 6 and I said okay. Now I want 12 and for some reason you say I can't have 12, either. Well, I'm gonna have 12. If I play baseball for this club, that is. I don't need to play this game another day, you know – I have a restaurant. I have a bowling alley, and I have three offers to broadcast ball games. I can announce my retirement right here and now, it won't hurt me one bit."

"Cool off, Honey," says Barney Dunlap. "Let us explain it." Barney, though, seems disinclined to start.

215

Finally, rather embarrassed, Terry Takamoto says, "Number 12 is jinxed."

"Jinxed? Look, I know most ballplayers are superstitious, but I'm not."

"Why were you so attached to number 6, then? Isn't that superstition?"

"No. It's a sentimental thing with me, but I don't really think 6 is particularly lucky –"

"John, I'm not superstitious, either," says Mrs. Gabrielson, "but the history of number 12 on this club is really quite remarkable – horrible, actually – and I wouldn't want to take any chances with it. Tell him about it, Roy."

"Right," says Giddings. "You remember Alvin Hudspith?"

"Sure I do. Second baseman. Didn't he die . . . ?"

"Of a beanball thrown by a Chicago pitcher named Abramowicz. One of only two men in baseball history to die as the result of a thrown ball."

"I was on that club with Abramowicz," says Barney Dunlap. "It ruined his career, too. He lost all heart for the game."

"Anyway, Alvin Hudspith was number 12 for the Bronx Lions. The next guy to wear number 12 was Ingemar Lundquist, a rookie first baseman for the Lions who could have been another Lou Gehrig. But one night he was out after curfew, had too much to drink, and wandered in front of a subway train. Nobody wore number 12 again until after the team moved west. Mort can tell you about the next guy to wear number 12. You were a rookie catcher with the club the year Willie Washington came up, weren't you, Mort?"

"Yeah, we came up together through the minor-league system. I caught nearly all his games, minors and majors. He won eight in a row wearing number 13 – ol' Willie's not a superstitious dude, you see. But one day on the road his uniforms got lost in transit, so he wore number 12 instead. That day something popped in his arm, and he was never the same again. Two years later he was making a living tending bar."

Reed laughs and that doesn't endear him to Mort Fredericks. "An old story. Pitchers are just freaks anyway, and I don't think Willie Washington was cut out for great things. Damned if you need a curse to explain a sore-armed pitcher."

Fredericks looks fighting-mad for an instant, but Reed laughs again, disarmingly. "Do you really believe in it, Mort?"

They look at each other for a few seconds, challengingly some think, then Mort laughs, too, with an effort. "No, not really. I think it's pretty silly."

"I don't," Barney Dunlap mumbles.

Reed adds, "Anyhow, at least Washington lived. Maybe the curse is wearing off." He laughs again, and those who were there swear it has a hollow sound, echoing off the walls of the office. "I'm wearing 12. Take it or leave it."

After a few moments of pensive silence Mrs. Gabrielson decrees that they take it. Maybe because, after that meeting, nobody in the room cares too much if the number 12 jinx keeps working or not.

Of course the papers pick it up, and they like the curse angle even better than they did the Fritz Krieg controversy. By the next night, when Reed is scheduled to make his debut in Los Angeles in the last exhibition game of the season, all L.A. and all baseball are waiting to see what terrible fate is going to befall John "Honey" Reed in his indifference to the number 12 curse.

All the parties to the meeting I described are there, too. Fredericks, of course, on the field; Barney Dunlap in the dugout; Roy Giddings and Terry Takamoto in the press box; and even Florence Krieg as a guest in owner Frances Gabrielson's private box.

The game goes along in orderly fashion until the top half of the fifth inning. I'm umpiring at first base, and Joe Bidwell, a rookie ump, is behind the plate. Mort Fredericks is catching for the Surfers, who lead in the game 8 to 1, and Honey Reed, wearing number 12, and with a homer and single in defiance of the curse already, is playing first.

On a one-ball and two-strike count, the Surfer pitcher misses the outside corner of the plate with his pitch and Joe Bidwell calls it a ball. Fredericks, thinking the guy has struck out, is all ready to throw the ball around the infield and reacts violently to Joe's call. He tears off his mask, throws it into the dirt, gets red in the face, and starts jumping up and down. No call for it, as far as I can see. The pitch was close, but not that close, and Fredericks' team is leading by seven runs. The Surfer pitcher just stands there watching, as much puzzled by the theatrics as I am.

"That rookie ump's got a lot to learn, Ed," Honey Reed says to me at first base.

"You just play your position," I tell him, and I start toward home plate to make sure things don't get out of hand. As senior ump, I have to watch out for Bidwell.

When he sees me coming, Fredericks turns to me. Bidwell should have chased him

219

already, and I'm determined not to take any guff from him.

"You saw it, Ed. We had him struck out."

"You can't appeal to me on a called strike, Mort, and you know it. Now this is just an exhibition game, and I don't want to toss anybody, but one more word from you and you are gone."

"Well, if the league's gonna recruit blind umpires –"

"That's it. Take a hike." I speak softly but give him the thumb so everybody in the ball park gets the message.

With an angry snort Mort picks his mask up from the dirt and goes storming toward the Surfer dugout. Barney Dunlap is till there, looking more puzzled at his catcher's behavior than mad at me. Of course, he knows if he comes out to argue a called strike, he'll be gone, too.

I return to my position behind first. Honey Reed says, "That's a cheap shot, Ed."

"You do your job and I'll do mine," I say, baffled by all this fuss and rancor in an 8-to-1 exhibition game.

The batter hits the next pitch deep to shortstop. The Surfer infielder makes a great stop on the ball, but he's too far back and can't get enough on the throw, and on a close play I call the runner safe. All of a sudden Honey Reed is all over me.

"Ed, I had him and you know it!"

"Shut up and play ball," I say, beginning to run short of patience.

"It wasn't even close, damn it!"

"Reed, if you want to join Fredericks for an early shower just keep on talking."

This time Barney Dunlap comes out and starts jawing at me, too, mainly to save his first baseman from ejection. I have the feeling Dunlap's heart isn't in his protest and he's as baffled by his players' antics as I am.

Barney's intervention does Reed no good. He can't stay away from me and before long I have no choice. He, too, gets a decisive thumb. Like Fredericks, he doesn't stick around once he's been bounced – why make the fine bigger? He just turns around and walks toward the Surfer dugout.

Barney gives me a last managerial glare, but his eyebrows do a sort of nothing-personal shrug, and he waddles back to the dugout. I suspect now we can play ball, and for a couple of innings I'm right.

But around the end of the seventh, Barney Dunlap calls me over to the dugout.

"Ed," he says, "the damnedest thing has happened. Honey Reed has disappeared."

"Probably just went home early.

Something was eating him, and I don't think it was just my calls."

"You don't understand, Ed. I mean he's vanished. Between the dugout and the clubhouse. He started down the tunnel, but he never got to the other end. It's impossible, Ed. It couldn't happen."

"Better get on the phone and tell Roy Giddings," I say.

"Ed, you're the big detective. Won't you sort of look into it?"

"I can't till after the game. I'm sure nothing happened to Reed and there's a simple explanation for whatever seems to have happened."

"There's an explanation, all right. He was wearing number 12 – that's the explanation." Barney's fat face looks comically but sincerely terrified.

Of course, it's none of my business what happens to a player after he leaves the field, and I have no choice but to keep the game going. But all the way to the ninth inning the little puzzle of how Honey Reed could have disappeared on his way from the dugout to the locker room niggles at me.

After the game is over, I walk back to the locker room through the Surfers' tunnel, though the umps have our own route to our cramped dressing-room facilities. The one important point about the tunnel is that it makes two turns along the way, so that you can't see the whole tunnel from the dugout to the locker room. I'm pretty sure the walls of the tunnel are innocent of secret panels – there's no excuse for gothic trappings in a new baseball park. (Or in an old one, come to think of it.)

When I get to the end of the tunnel, Roy Giddings approaches me.

"Found him?" I ask the worried-looking general manager.

"No, we haven't. Ed, it's unreal. I can't figure it."

Naturally, it has occurred to me the whole thing may be a publicity stunt dreamed up by the Surfer management, but Giddings' look of worry appears genuine to me. Gradually, with unwelcome help from Barney Dunlap and other players, Giddings gives me the details of the mystery.

Gus Brend, the clubhouse attendant, was sitting in the doorway to the Surfer locker room when the ejected Mort Fredericks came storming through. Fifteen minutes later the team trainer came back for a forgotten piece of equipment, and at this time the tunnel was empty. Gus swears that between the time Mort came through and the time the trainer did, *no one came through*

223

the tunnel. the ballplayers in the dugout are just as sure Honey Reed walked down the tunnel and never came back. Thus, number 12 has vanished with not so much as a puff of smoke.

A nice little problem, but surely still a joke of some sort, not a police matter just yet. I yield to the flattery of Giddings about my detective prowess and agree to do a little investigation of my own.

First I interview Mort Fredericks.

"What did you do when you came back to the clubhouse?"

"What I normally do – took a shower. I felt like breaking up the place, you guys had me so steamed, but I like old Gus and didn't want to make extra work for him."

"Gus didn't follow you into the clubhouse?"

"No, I motioned him to stay put in his chair. I didn't need anything and he looked kind of worn out."

"What was he doing? Did he have the game on the radio?"

"Naw, old Gus is stone-deaf. He just sat there – oh, I think he had the morning paper."

"Could he have missed anybody coming through the tunnel?"

"Not old Gus. He's sharp-eyed. If he says

nobody came through the tunnel after me, I have to believe nobody did."

"And you never saw Honey Reed?"

"Hell, no. I was still in the shower when the excitement started. First time I heard Honey was missing I had a towel wrapped around me and was wringing wet."

Next I have a word with Gus Brend. Gus looks right at my lips when I talk and doesn't miss a word.

"You're sure nobody came down the tunnel after Mort Fredericks?"

"Sure I'm sure."

"You were reading the paper, though?"

"Off and on. Mostly just sittin', smoking my pipe."

"Weren't you curious about what happened when Fredericks came back?"

"Yeah, but his way of walkin' looked angry to me, and he motioned to me to just stay in my chair, so I did. I let 'em alone when they're that mad."

"You say he walked angry. How did his face look?"

"Didn't see it. He had his catcher's mask on."

"Does Fredericks usually smash up the place when he's mad?"

"Been known to. Not this time, though."

"Were you sitting in your chair all the time

between the beginning of the game and the time Fredericks came storming through the tunnel?"

"Nope, I had my work to do, keeping the locker room and the clubhouse tidy."

"Nobody back there but you?"

"Nope."

When I'm through with Gus, I'm summoned again by Roy Giddings and Barney Dunlap, demanding amazing deductions. I'm a little short with them – of course, I have it figured out now, as you will too, and I decide my time's been wasted with something purely silly. Sick of playing games, I retreat to the umps' room, where my three colleagues haven't even started getting dressed, so fervently are they discussing the foibles of major-league ballplayers.

I strip off my uniform and step into the shower room, and at that moment the shoddy, publicity-smelling vanishing of Honey Reed becomes police business. He's lying dead on the floor of the umpires' shower, blood drying on a vicious wound on his skull.

A few hours later I'm sitting in Mrs. Gabrielson's private box, more an apartment really, overlooking a darkened ballfield. I'm nursing a drink and feeling a little uneasy – a man of my position as neutral arbiter fraternizing with the officials of a major-league club. Still, we've all been of interest to the police the last few hours and thrown together that way. So I sit sharing a drink with the publicist, the general manager, the field manager, and the owner of the L.A. Surfers. I'm telling them a little story. The police have left, taking the killer of Honey Reed with them.

"So when I went back to the dugout, leaving my fellow umps to watch over the body, I got Roy here to call the police and I immediately told Mort what had happened. What Mort told me then convinced me I knew who had killed Honey Reed and how the killing tied in with his disappearance."

"But Mort didn't tell you anything," Roy Giddings says.

"That's right – he didn't tell me anything," I reply, sipping my drink and enjoying myself. My Sherlock Holmes qualities may be overrated, but that doesn't mean I don't play them to the hilt when I'm in the mood.

"The meeting in my office," muses Mrs. Gabrielson. "That should have warned us something like this could happen. Reed seemed to have a threat in every word he said, as if he knew all sorts of terrible things about the Surfers organization and about all of us. Did he really?"

"I don't know how many terrible things there are to know," I say. "But basically I don't think so. He'd just heard a lot of rumors, and he was in a really nasty mood from the way you described it to me. It was easy for one of you to infer he knew something he really didn't."

"The disappearance," says Mrs. Gabrielson. "How did that work?"

"Simple. Did it ever occur to you that the catcher and the plate umpire are the only two people who appear on the ballfield in *disguise?* When Mort gets to that point halfway through the tunnel, where he can't be seen from either end, he stops and strips off his jersey, his chest protector, his shin guards, everything that identifies him as a catcher. His mask is already off. He leaves them there in a little pile and goes on down the tunnel. Old Gus isn't in his chair yet. If he was, Mort would have to do something to distract him and sneak by. At any rate, he goes into the clubhouse unseen. He doesn't have to worry about deaf Gus hearing him, of course.

"Then, when Honey Reed gets himself tossed out – like Mort, quite intentionally –

he goes halfway through the tunnel, picks up the jersey and puts it on over his own, plus the chest protector, shin guards, and mask. Of course, he has to make sure Gus is in the chair before he comes storming past him, motioning him to stay there and going into the clubhouse. The key to it is that he has the mask on – no catcher goes around with his mask on except in the game, unless of course he aims to *disguise* himself – which is just what Reed was doing, pretending to be Fredericks.

"There's another tipoff about the mask. Why would a guy as mad as Fredericks is supposed to be when I kick him out even bother to pick up his mask out of the dirt, unless he has some particular use for it?

"If old Gus could hear and was listening to the game on the radio, the whole illusion could never work, because he'd know the different times of the ejections, and the time of 'Fredericks' passing him would be too late."

"Then," says Terry Takamoto, "the whole vanishing was just a practical joke worked out between Fredericks and Reed?"

"Right. Mainly by Reed, I think. It couldn't have been anything more important than a joke, because too many things could go wrong for anything really important to be riding on it. Gus could have seen Fredericks sneak into the clubhouse. Or he could have left his chair later and left the tunnel unviewed, blowing the whole illusion. The players all know Gus is in the habit of sitting there during the game, after an hour or so of working in the clubhouse, but it's not something you can absolutely count on. For a while I thought you were behind this, Mr. Takamoto – more space in the papers couldn't hurt the Surfers."

"I hope we have a classier operation than that, Mr. Gorgon," says Takamoto.

"And that we take the number 12 jinx more seriously, as well," says Mrs. Gabrielson. "Reed mocked it, and it punished him."

"In a way I suppose it did," I reply. "Anyway, I knew that as soon as Mort heard what happened to Reed, he'd own up right away to his part in the prank unless –"

"– he was the murderer," Takamoto finishes.

"Right, though I don't know if murderer is the precise term. Maybe manslaughterer, or anyway, for now, suspect. Fredericks apparently hoped, stupidly, that the vanishing trick wouldn't be seen through and we'd think the curse had reached out and struck Honey Reed down. He confessed readily enough with a little questioning from the police. Not any kind of premeditated murder; I'm sure of that.

"Reed goes to hide in the umps' dressing room, and after Fredericks gets out of the shower, before the game is over, Fredericks goes down there probably to help Reed escape to some safer hiding place. They know we'll be back there when the game is over. The two of them get into a quarrel. Maybe Reed makes a crack about Mort's friend Willie Washington that hits too close to home. It seems for all these years Mort has felt guilty about the end of Washington's career. Washington really hurt his arm rough-housing in a hotel room with Fredericks, and the two of them kept it a secret from the club. Mort was afraid that Reed, with his act of knowing everything, had found out all about it and would tell the club officials, though what Mort thought you folks would do to him for it I can't imagine. Anyway, the fear of Reed's giving him away is what persuaded him to go along with the joke in the first place.

"Anyhow, in the umps' room, Fredericks for whatever reason takes a poke at Reed who, says Mort, hits his head hard on a sharp corner in the shower room and dies. Mort decides to brazen it out. But if the vanishing

231

trick is figured out, he's the obvious suspect – only he would know that Reed hid out in the umps' room."

There is a short silence. Then Mrs. Gabrielson speaks up grimly. "No Surfer," she says, "will ever again wear number 12."

KATHERINE BRUSH

Silk Hat

With a pass-key the superintendent unlocked the door, and they filed solemnly in: the detective, the man from the corporation that owned the apartment house, and the superintendent. Through the foyer they went without pausing, their footsteps mute on the rug, and into the big, bright living room beyond.

The superintendent began silently switching off lights.

"Left 'em on, didn't he?" the detective said. And added in a jocular way, "Sure! What'd *he* care!"

"Do you think," the man from the corporation began, but stopped abruptly, startled into silence by the ring of the telephone.

The detective answered. "Hello?" he said, and cleared' his throat. "Hello? . . . Why, no, he – who is this? . . . What? . . . Oh, I see. Well – Kemble's dead. . . . Yeah, *dead*. That's right. Suicide. . . . Yeah. Fished him out of the river early this morning. This is Mahoney

233

of Headquarters talking. Listen, what do you know about him? Don't, eh? ... I see ... No. No, I don't know, can't say as to that ..."

He hung up presently. "His tailor," he explained to the two who had listened. "Kemble's owed him for three suits since last April. *Sa-ay!* Who's the dame?"

He referred to a photograph in a giant Italian leather frame which stood on the desk in the corner. A photograph of a woman not quite young, with strange, sacrilegious eyes. A blonde woman. She was rather beautiful in a way – the New York way, sleek, lacquered. A costly woman. You thought of shops. Avenue salons. "I will have this, and this." In the photograph her mouth was black, but you knew how red it would be. Her eyebrows were big commas. Snobbish. She wore an evening gown and a rope of pearls, and in the pearls the fingers of one hand were twined, the slim first finger pointed up and curved a little, as if she indicated herself.

"I've seen her," said the superintendent. "She's been here many's the time."

"How old a fellow was Kemble?" asked the man from the corporation.

"Twenty-two, twenty-three, somewhere along there."

234

The man from the corporation stared harder at the picture.

"Know her name?" the detective queried of the superintendent. "She might give us the dope we need."

"No. I never heard her name."

"Well," said the detective, "let's get busy. I got other things to do today."

Suddenly brisk, he seated himself before the desk and pulled out the nearest drawer. It was choked with papers.

He removed them by handfuls, piled them on the desk, and began to go through them. They were chiefly bills – huge bills, that made the superintendent's pale eyes bulge and drew from the detective soft, low whistles. Bills for food, for wine, for flowers, for garage rent, for a silk hat, for a jazz band. Bills marked "Please Remit" and "Overdue." Letters: "Your attention is respectfully called –" And other letters not so respectful.

"This guy," said the detective, "was cert'ny a bird. Bought things like money grew on trees – and ain't paid a cent in six months."

"I remember when he come," put in the superintendent quickly, importantly. "I remember the day well. I showed him three apartments – this one and two cheaper. He took this, and the next day he brought a decorator, and pretty soon the stuff began arrivin'. All this stuff. All new, it was. Every bit."

"Don't know where he came from, eh?" the detective asked.

"No."

"All we need to find out is who to notify. It don't take a Sherlock Holmes to guess why he did it." The detective's fat hand slapped the bills. "If there's anybody cares," he added.

He gathered up the bills and stuffed them back into their drawer and yanked out the drawer below.

There was a checkbook; a bank book; a stack of theater programs; a souvenir hammer from a nightclub in the Forties; a box of stationery, engraved; a book on good manners. Below all these, thrust into the back of the drawer, were newspaper clippings, together with a telegram, held by a rubber band:

GEORGE KEMBLE
CARE OF WARREN'S GARAGE
GREEN FALLS, INDIANA
TAKE GREAT PLEASURE IN IN-FORMING YOU THAT CONTEST PRIZE TWENTY THOUSAND DOLLARS FOR

BEST NAME FOR OUR NEW GOLF BALL HAS BEEN AWARDED YOU FOR YOUR SUGGESTION "LINDY" STOP OUR REPRESENTATIVE EN ROUTE TO YOU BEARING OUR CHECK AND OUR CONGRATULATIONS STOP RUSH PHOTOGRAPH AND DATA FOR PUBLICITY USE

UNION SPORTS PRODUCTS CO.
T.M. SOMERS, PRESIDENT

The date was not quite a year old.

"My gosh!" said the detective. "What do you know about that!"

They turned to the clippings. There were pictures of George Kemble, a smiling, dark-haired boy, and small-town large-type headlines like KEMBLE WINS! and LOCAL LAD MAKES FORTUNE OVERNIGHT! There were paragraphs and paragraphs of facts. George Kemble was twenty-two years old. His parents were dead. He had been born and raised in Green Falls. At the age of seventeen he had left high school and associated himself in business with William H. Warren, proprietor of Warren's Garage, South Walnut Street. He had a natural aptitude for things mechanical and he had rapidly become known as one of the best garage repair men in Lane County.

237

The detective returned to the telegram. He read and reread it again. "Twenty grand!" he kept saying. "*Twenty* grand! And *any* damn fool could've thought of that!"

The man from the corporation had the clippings in his hands. "Listen," he commanded, and his voice was low and grave and compassionate. "Listen to this: 'Lucky' Kemble, as he is now called, today told reporters that he expected to leave for New York City as soon as possible. 'That's the town for people with money,' he said."

There was a short silence.

"And he went through it," murmured the man from the corporation, "in half a year."

"And *how!*" the detective said. And he snorted: "*Silk hat!*"

They opened the bank book, which before they had passed by. There it was. The single entry: $20,000 no cents. They opened the checkbook and glanced over it, marveling. Incredible that such a sum could shrink so swiftly.

"Well," said the detective finally, slamming the checkbook shut, "anyway, we got what we need. A wire to Green Falls, now –"

"Look here," interrupted the man from the corporation.

He had picked up a magazine lying on the

desk, and parted its leaves at the place where a pencil and several sheets of rough paper were thrust in. Here was an announcement, an offer, screaming in red from a page: *$50,000 Cash for Ten Best Letters on "Why I Prefer Lait's Shaving Cream."* The sheets of loose paper were covered with scrawled, half hearted, short attempts to write such a letter. "I prefer Lait's because –" Scratched out. "It seems to me that of all the shaving creams on the market today –" Scratched out.

The detective stood up, folding the telegram into his wallet. "Poor dumb fool, I'd call him," he said. "He might've known he couldn't repeat. Stands to reason."

"It looks," said the man from the corporation, "as though he did know."

The detective tucked his wallet into an inner pocket and buttoned his coat with stubby fingers. He turned to go.

"What I can't see is," he said, "why, if he was such a mechanic, he didn't get busy again, and *be* a mechanic. Eh?"

The question was an observation merely. The detective did not expect anyone to answer him. And no one did – unless you count the woman in the frame, whose slim first finger pointed up, through pearls, and curved a little, as if she indicated herself.

ROBERT EDWARD ECKELS
Only One Way To Go

A uniformed maid with a face as sharp and shiny as a new ax led me back through the cool entrance corridor and up a short flight of stairs to a second-floor sitting room. "Mr. Howard will be with you in a moment," she said. Then she was gone. There were a number of chairs scattered about, but not wanting Howard to find me sitting I walked over to the wall that was mostly windows and looked out. A vast expanse of well trimmed lawn sloped down to the screen of trees that marked the end of the property.

Unless you liked grass it wasn't much of a view. Off to my left, though, a blonde girl in a white tennis dress was practising serves on a clay court. She worked with single-minded intensity, smashing her supply of balls into the far corner, then walking around to retrieve them and smash them back. I was still watching her when Howard came in.

"Mr. Thomas," he said without preamble. "Good of you to come on such short notice." He was a short, slightly built man in his mid to late sixties, with glasses that looked too big for his narrow triangular face. He was bald except for a close-clipped fringe around the ears and a few scattered wisps across the crown.

I wasn't put off by the unprepossessing appearance, because I'd taken the trouble to look him up in *Who's Who* before coming out. It was a short entry with the usual biographical trivia: Wendell Howard, born 1920, married Elizabeth Bolton Wainwright (deceased). The important thing was occupation: Chairman of the Board and Chief Operating Officer, Wainwright Pharmaceuticals.

I'd also looked up Wainwright Pharmaceuticals. It had started out as a patent-medicine company in the Thirties, expanding into true pharmaceuticals with the War, but like so many essentially one-man operations it barely managed to survive the almost simultaneous deaths of its founder and his only child, a son. It had been almost bankrupt when Howard had come along to marry the son's widow, take charge, and build it up to where it once again controlled a respectable share of the legitimate drug market. And since the older Wainwright had held most of the stock and it was still largely family-owned, most of the money had stayed home, too.

A taller, younger man had come in behind him. Now he closed the door and came over to take a position just to his employer's left as Howard sat down and leaned back to eye me speculatively.

"You come very highly recommended," he said.

"Thank you."

A faint smile tugged at the corner of Howard's mouth. "That was a statement, Mr. Thomas," he said, "not a compliment. However, there's no point wasting your time or mine on nonessentials." He glanced up at the man beside him. "I believe you've already met Mr. Lawson, my attorney."

Lawson looked at me impassively. He was about my age, with a round pug-nosed face and pitted cheeks.

"I understand your boy is missing," I said matter-of-factly.

Howard smiled again. "You don't waste time on nonessentials, either, do you, Mr. Thomas? That's good. I like that in a man. In any case, you're right. The boy left the house six weeks ago, ostensibly to join some friends backpacking in the Rockies. The problem is, the others returned two days ago. Billy wasn't with them. He had, in fact, never been with them. He'd lied from the start about where he was going and what he intended to do."

"How old is he?"

"Twenty. He'll be twenty-one in March."

"Was he unhappy at home?"

"He had no reason to be," Howard said sharply. "But whether he was or not, he's a minor and I want him found and brought home. When he's of age he can do as he pleases, but now he's my responsibility and I intend to exercise that responsibility."

"Have you notified the police?"

"No, I have not. I saw no reason to expose myself and the rest of the family to that kind of scandal and publicity when he has so obviously run off to 'find' himself in some long-haired hippie commune or something equally foolish. If I had reason to be concerned about his health or safety it would be a different matter, but under the circumstances I much prefer one man, working alone and sensitive to my concerns for privacy. That's why I had Lawson contact you. And, as I say, you were highly recommended."

"You can only go so far on recommendations," I said. "After six weeks he could be very hard to find."

"Possibly," Howard said. "But we won't

know until you've tried. And I'm not a poor man. You'll be well paid for your efforts."

He looked at me unblinkingly. I shrugged. "It's your money," I said.

"So it is," Howard said. He put his hands on the arms of his chair and pushed himself up. "Well, now that that's settled I'll leave you and Lawson to work out the details." He went to the door, then paused with his hand on the knob. "By the way," he said, "I understand you've been having some difficulty with the state licensing board. Over a shooting, I believe."

I looked away, but not before I caught a glimpse of Lawson's eyes glinting with silent amusement. "It'll work itself out," I said.

Howard nodded soberly. "Yes, Mr. Thomas," he said, "it will." He smiled. "I'm not in any sense a 'public' man but I'm not without influence – or above the will to use it when I choose. Good day, Mr. Thomas," he said. "And good luck in your search."

He went out. Lawson closed the door after him, then turned back to me. His eyes were impersonal again. "You'll need some money for a retainer," he said, "and to cover your expenses. Mr. Howard asked me to give you this. If and when you need more you can let me know."

I took the check he held out. It was for

$1,000. I put it in my pocket. "You'll want an accounting, of course," I said.

Lawson shrugged. "As far as Mr. Howard is concerned, success is the best accounting. However, yes, you should keep a record – in case one is needed. Now, what else do you need?"

"A picture would be helpful."

Lawson nodded. "There's one in his room. I'll get it."

"I'd also like to talk to whoever saw him last."

Lawson smiled faintly. "Oddly enough," he said, "that was me. I'd come by quite late that evening with some papers for Mr. Howard to sign and as I came in Billy was going up to his room. He said he'd just seen his father and he'd tell me goodbye now as well because he planned to leave early the next morning. I have no idea what time he actually did leave, but he was gone when the first servants arrived at six."

"How did he seem?"

"As you might expect. Excited. Almost exuberant. At the time I put it down to the prospect of the trip. But now, of course –" He shrugged.

"Where do you think he might have gone?"

Lawson shook his head. "I'd have to agree

with Mr. Howard, but beyond that it's impossible to say. He was a very withdrawn, almost secretive boy." He smiled wryly. "That's why Mr. Howard was so pleased when he brought up the backpacking trip. One of the leaders of the group – Brian Mercer – is the son of one of Mr. Howard's closest business associates and Mr. Howard thought it might mean Billy was opening up, becoming part of the team."

"I see," I said.

"I hope so," Lawson said. He rubbed his hands together briskly. "Now let's get you that photograph."

After I'd gotten the photo – a standard studio portrait of a good-looking boy with dreamer's eyes and a still unformed face – the same hatchet-faced maid who'd brought me in escorted me out. My car was parked at the head of the looping drive, but on impulse I left it there and walked around the house to the tennis court I'd seen from the window. The blonde girl was still there, still smashing away at the opposite corner.

She kept at it for several minutes after she became aware of my presence, then carefully put her racquet down, and, tossing her head to free her hair, came over to where I stood. She was a tall girl, in her mid to late twenties at the most, and only the strong jaw and concentration lines above her eyes kept her from being beautiful.

"They said you'd be coming this morning," she said. She gave her head a final toss. "You're the detective they hired to find my brother, aren't you?"

"That's right, Miss Howard."

"Wainwright." Her voice was sharp. "And I prefer Pat to Miss."

"Billy's your half brother, then?"

She shook her head. "No, we're full brother and sister. When Mother married Wendell Howard, she wanted us to stay one family. So she asked us to use his name. Billy still does. I don't. Not that it matters. The important question is whether you have any realistic hope of finding him."

"That depends on whether he wants to be found or not," I said. "Fortunately, most runaways do. It's the whole point of their running away."

"I see," Pat said. She looked off, beyond me. "If you do find him – or rather, when you find him – what happens then?"

"I'm not a social agency," I said. "I just make my report, and that's it."

"How nice for you. Unfortunately, it's not so easy for the rest of us who have to live with the problem." She looked away again. "I might have prevented all this if I'd been here. But I was in Europe and Billy had already gone when I got back. Even so, I'm not going to let everything we've planned for be ruined by an impulsive act – or my stepfather's preconceptions." Her eyes swung back to hold mine. "When you find him," she said, "I want to know it first. Before you tell anybody else."

"Even before your stepfather?"

"Especially before my stepfather," she said. She smiled cynically. "He wouldn't have to know," she said. "And I'd make it worth your while, of course."

"Of course," I said. "Mind telling me why?"

She looked up sharply. "Does it matter?"

"It might," I said. When she still hesitated, I shrugged. "You've gone this far," I said, "you might as well go the rest of the way. If I can't be trusted, the mistake's already been made."

"Yes," she said, "I suppose it has." She was silent another moment, then looked up at me again. "Do you know what a spendthrift trust is?"

"Basically," I said, "it's a provision put in a will when there's a large amount of money involved and some question about the ability of the heir to handle it. The principal is put in trust and the heir is given an allowance from the income either forever or until his competence is proved or disproved."

"Exactly," Pat said. "So you can understand the situation here. When Grandfather died, he left the bulk of his estate to Billy in trust until he was twenty-one – unless since Billy was only a baby at the time he turned out to be incapable of handling money; in which case the trust would continue indefinitely." Her eyes held mine steadily now. "Howard's been Billy's guardian under the trust ever since Mother died and I know he's going to claim Billy's disappearance proves he's incapable of handling the money and stock. But if I can reach Billy first, together we can work out a defense to counter that so that Billy won't be denied his inheritance."

"Unless," I said, "the facts prove he is incapable."

"Let me worry about that," she said. "You just tell me where he is."

I shook my head. "I don't think so," I said.

Pat's eyes blazed. "I knew you couldn't be trusted!"

"As far as it goes, I can," I said. "I'm not going to tell your stepfather what you've asked me to do. On the other hand, I'm not going to step into the middle of a family squabble, either."

She looked at me for a long moment, then nodded soberly, the anger gone from her eyes and manner. "Very wise," she said. "Except that like it or not you're already in the middle. Think about it." And with that she turned on her heel and marched back to pick up her racquet. It flashed suddenly and the ball slammed down with more than usual force on the chalk lines across the net. I watched for several minutes, then walked back to my car.

There was a pile of mail waiting for me when I got back to my office. Six months earlier there would have been a fair amount of incoming cash mixed with the bills, some of them now second notices. But then Continental Bank had hired me to stop a series of break-ins at a warehouse they were holding in trust. It started out nice and clean-cut. I staked the place out and caught the punk climbing in an unlocked window the first night. Unfortunately, when I challenged him he made the bad mistake of reaching under his jacket. A mistake for him because I shot him twice before he could bring his hand out again. A mistake for me because there was no gun under the jacket, only a handkerchief, and no witnesses to back up my side of it.

The State's Attorney waffled for most of a month, then declined prosecution. The state licensing board was a lot less charitable and, on the basis that what happened was less important than what might happen, raised questions about my judgment and fitness to continue to operate. They didn't pull my license but they were well on their way to it. Which, of course, was one more reason, family squabble or not, I couldn't afford to turn down Howard's $1,000. I marked his check for deposit and dropped it in an envelope to my bank.

First thing the next morning I looked up Brian Mercer.

"I don't know what it's got to do with me," he said. He was a stocky boy, Billy's age or a little older, dressed in the uniform of the day: faded jeans and jacket. "What I mean is, I knew Billy from school and, you know, around, but we weren't really what you'd call close."

"Close enough, though, for him supposed to be going along with you on a camping trip," I said.

Mercer shook his head. "That's what he told his old man," he said. "He never said anything to the rest of us going. To tell you the truth, I would have been surprised if he had. Physical activity wasn't particularly his thing."

"What was?"

Mercer hesitated, then shook his head again. "Look," he said, "I really don't want to get involved with this. I figure if somebody wants to take off and live his own life, that's his business. Why not let him?"

"If that's what he wanted," I said, "he could have saved himself and everybody else a whole lot of trouble by waiting until he was twenty-one."

"Or maybe he figured it was better to take off while the going was good," Mercer said. "Look, man, I don't know what you know about the family, but they had Billy's life planned out for him from the day he was born. He was the male heir and that meant someday he was going to step in and take over where Grampa left off. That's why the old man left him all the stock. If he'd been smart, he'd have given it to Billy's sister. She's the real take-over kind."

"And Billy isn't."

Mercer shrugged. "Guess not, or he wouldn't have taken off."

"You know," I said, "for somebody who wasn't close, you seem to know a lot."

Mercer shrugged again. "You know how it is," he said. "You hear things."

"Maybe you heard something else."

He shook his head. "I told you, man," he said. "I don't want to get involved."

"Sure," I said. "But if you know something and you don't tell, you're just as involved as if you did. More even, because you've made a judgment and taken sides, which means if things don't work out the way you think they ought to, then maybe you have to share some of the guilt, too."

Mercer looked at me for a long time. "You really dig in, don't you?"

I shrugged and rose. "I think the phrase is 'telling it like it is,'" I said. He didn't rise to show me out, and I didn't make any move to leave on my own. Finally he said, "Look, maybe this is a mistake, but I can tell you this. Billy used to have a pad over on Auburn. I was there once for a party with some other guys. It wasn't all that much, but he acted like he thought it was some kind of big deal."

"You remember the address?"

"Sure," Mercer said. "3650 West. If he really wants to lose himself, though, he won't be there. It was supposed to be a big secret, but everybody knew."

253

"It's something to check out anyway," I said. "Thanks."

Mercer smiled wryly. "For nothing," he said, "I hope."

The address wasn't hard to find. It was half of a duplex on a street that had just started to turn shabby. Nobody was home the first time I called, but when I went back that evening, lights were on inside and two cars were parked in the short side drive. A tall dark-haired girl opened the door to my ring.

"Billy home?" I said.

The girl looked at me curiously, then shook her head.

"That's funny," I said. "He said he'd meet me here."

The girl continued to shake her head. "The hell he did," she said.

I shrugged and handed her one of my cards. "It was worth a try," I said.

"Sure," she said and stepped back to let me enter. The room was small and overfurnished. Along the far wall a cabinet-sized TV flickered its bluish images. Just beyond it was a door, closed now, leading back into the rest of the house. The girl moved past me to turn off the TV.

"What do you want Billy for?" she said.

"Not that it'll make any difference. I'm the last person who'd know where he is."

"You're living in his house, though."

"Sure," she said, "why not? I'm his wife."

The girl's name was Myra Dawn, and according to the leatherette-bound certificate she dug out she and Billy Howard had been married four days after he had ostensibly left for the camping trip.

"I guess it was kind of dumb," she said. We sat facing each other across the width of the room. "I knew he was only marrying me because I was pregnant, but I thought, you know, maybe it would work out anyway. And at first it looked like maybe it would. We drove over to Indiana and spent the three days' waiting period in a Holiday Inn – almost like a honeymoon, you know? Then I don't know whether it got through to him at last that he was stuck with me or what, but after the ceremony Billy got real uptight and I couldn't do anything to please him. I mean, not anything.

"Finally I told him that since the kid was going to have a name it didn't matter to me whether we stayed together or not. As far as I cared, he could do what he pleased. He gave me a real funny look then and said,

'That shows what you know.' The next morning, he was gone."

"And you haven't seen him or made any effort to get in touch with him since?"

Myra shrugged. "What would be the point? If he wants me, he knows where I am. I figure, though, he's gone back home for good."

"Not quite," I said.

"What's that mean?"

I told her.

Both cars were still in the drive when I left. There could be any number of different explanations, but I wasn't paid to make assumptions. So as soon as I was far enough down the block to be out of sight, I cut my lights and motor and pulled over to the curb.

Forty-five minutes later Myra's door opened again and a man came out and trotted across the lawn to the rear car. It was too dark and I was too far away to make out his features, but I'd already gotten a good long look at his license plate.

Howard sat quietly for a long moment after I finished my report. We were back in that same second-floor sitting room, he, Lawson, and I. It might have been the day before repeating itself, except that now Pat

Wainwright sat, grim-faced and silent, with her back to the windows. Finally Howard stirred, the corners of his mouth curving down even more markedly.

"A fine mess," he said.

"But not irremediable," Lawson said. He looked down his nose at me as if somehow that made it my fault. "Billy's a minor. The marriage can be set aside."

"And the child?" Howard said. "Can you set that aside too?"

Lawson didn't reply. Howard continued to look up at him for another long moment, then turned back to me and sighed. "Well, Mr. Thomas, I can't say I particularly care for the news you bring. But you have done your job and done it well. Send me your bill. I'll pay whatever you ask."

"If that's what you want," I said.

"Why wouldn't it be?"

I shrugged. "You did hire me to find him," I said.

Howard smiled grimly. "I don't think we need worry too much about Billy now," he said. "This isn't the first time he's run off and left someone else to clean up after him. Once the heat is off, he'll be back soon enough" – he glanced over at Pat – "just like before."

257

"He was only thirteen then," Pat flashed, "and still upset because –"

"And he's twenty now," Howard snapped back, "and upset because he got some tramp pregnant and was damn fool enough to marry her. When he's thirty it'll be something else. He hasn't changed, and despite what you say it's obvious he never will."

"And neither will you, will you?" Pat turned to me. "If you were going to continue to look for Billy," she said, "what would be your next step?"

"The obvious one," I said. "Track down Myra's visitor last night and see where he led."

"Do it then. Or is there still some reason you wouldn't want to work for me?"

Howard's face crimsoned, but before he could explode Lawson put a restraining hand on the back of his chair. "I shouldn't think it need come to that," Lawson said. "How long do you think it would take to find this person?"

He was asking me. I shrugged. "A couple of days," I said. "A week at the most."

"I think we can go with that," he said to Howard. "Having gone as far as we have already, it would be foolish not to take another step." He smiled faintly. "And even if Thomas finds nothing, we're no worse off."

"All right," Howard said. The corners of his mouth turned down again and he looked straight at me. "You have until the end of the week," he said. "Then we'll decide what we do next." He glanced at his stepdaughter. "Fair enough?"

She nodded.

Nobody said anything more about paying me, but there was more than enough of Howard's $1,000 left to cover my time. So as soon as I got back to my office I put in a call to the Department of Motor Vehicles. I had to talk to four clerks in three different offices but in the end I got what I wanted. The car in Myra's drive was registered to a Charles Michaels, 1832 S. Beeler.

It was a big old house long since gone down in the world and cut up into single-occupancy rooms. According to the row of mail slots just inside the doorway, Charles's was number 2C. It was empty, but on my third knock a birdlike old woman stuck her head out of the door across the hall.

"You just missed him," she said. "He left early this morning."

"You know when he'll be back?"

"He won't," she said. "Not any more. He moved out." She twisted her neck to cast a long conspiratorial look up and down the hallway. "It was none of my business," she said, "but there was a big row about it on the stairs. You're supposed to give notice and the manager wouldn't let him take his suitcase because he owed two weeks' rent."

"I see," I said. I went back downstairs to the apartment marked *Manager* and told the woman who answered that Charles Michaels had asked me to pay his rent and pick up his things.

It was even later than usual when I got back to my office and the building was dark. I let myself in with my key and took Charles's suitcase inside, where I could go through it undisturbed.

There wasn't much – just a jumble of clothes and shaving gear, all of it as essentially characterless as a YMCA towel, and I was just about to write it off as $76 wasted when I found the photograph, apparently overlooked and left in an inside jacket pocket. It was an unframed Polaroid print of a man and woman standing on an old-fashioned front porch. The man I assumed to be Charles. The woman, glowering into the camera and holding a small bunch of nondescript flowers, was Myra Dawn. I put the picture in my pocket, then shoved the rest of Charles's things back into the suitcase even more carelessly than he had, and, leaving the bag behind, left the building.

I was halfway across the lot to my car when I heard somebody coming up fast behind me. Instinct said turn, but before I could even start I was caught from behind and pulled back. Something hard smashed down against the side of my head and I fell into complete darkness.

When I came to, I was still on my back on the pavement and a woman was bending over me. It took a full minute for my eyes to focus and recognize Myra.

"Thank God," she said. "I thought you were dead."

It took several tries but finally I managed to sit up. Myra looked at me anxiously. "Are you all right?" she said.

"As much as I will be," I said. I had a good-sized lump where I'd been hit but no blurring or double vision. No nausea, either, and with Myra's help I got the rest of the way up and went back inside.

My office was a shambles – furniture overturned and smashed and what had been the contents of file drawers scattered everywhere. Charles's suitcase was gone, of course. Even worse, the one locked drawer had been forced and the gun inside taken, too.

Myra stood just inside the door, looking dismayed. "My God," she said, "what *happened?*"

"I thought maybe you could tell me."

"No," she said. "No, honest. All I know is that Billy told me to come here tonight to see if I couldn't find you. He wants to talk to you."

"Why didn't he come himself?"

"Because he's afraid," she said. She shrugged helplessly. "What I told you last night," she said, "wasn't all the truth. After we were married, Billy and I didn't really split. He had some business he said he had to take care of down in Florida. I wanted to go along with him and make it, you know, kind of a real honeymoon. But he said it wasn't that kind of business and that I'd be better off waiting at home. The next time I heard from him was last week.

"I don't know what happened and maybe I don't want to. But he's in trouble and he's scared. Right after that, too, Charles Michaels showed up, looking for him. The only good thing Charles ever did in his life was introduce me to Billy. So I made up that story to get rid of him. I don't think he bought it, though, because he keeps hanging around. He was the one you saw leaving my house the other night."

"I know," I said. "Where's Billy now?"

"At the St. Clair Hotel," Myra said, "registered under the name of Brown. I don't know for how long, though. He's really scared."

What I should have done, by all the rules, was call the police and report the mugging and the theft of my pistol. What I did was take Myra home, then drive back across town to the St. Clair.

It was a second-rate commercial hotel at the wrong end of Michigan Avenue and at this time of night the lobby was deserted except for an elderly clerk in shirt sleeves nodding behind the desk. He woke up long enough to give me Billy's room number, then he was dozing off again even before I had punched the button to call the elevator down.

The number he gave me was on the third floor at the end of a corridor. There was no answer to my knock, but the latch hadn't quite caught and the door moved slightly under my hand. After a moment's hesitation I pushed it all the way open. Charles

Michaels – or at least the man in Charles's photograph – sprawled in a chair facing me. Blood still oozed from his chest.

I fought down the impulse to run, took a deep breath, stepped into the room, and pressed the back of my hand down along the side of his neck. He was still warm but there wasn't a trace of the carotid pulse. He had been shot twice close enough to where the physiology books say the heart is to make no difference. The gun that apparently had done it lay on the floor beside his outflung left foot where the killer might have dropped it in his haste. Beautiful. Because even despite the unfamiliar silencer I had no difficulty recognizing it as the one stolen from my desk.

There was nothing else in the room – not even clothes – and I backed out carefully, resisting the second idiot urge of the evening – to take the gun with me – and closed the door behind me just as I had found it. The only thing I did was wipe my fingerprints from the knob. Then I went back down to the lobby. The clerk was still asleep behind the desk. I went out without disturbing him.

There was a phonebooth on the corner that somehow hadn't been vandalized, and I used it to call Myra at her home. She answered on the second ring, but I put the receiver back without speaking. A black-and-white patrol car had swung around the other end of the street, blinker lights flashing, and now it pulled to a halt in front of the St. Clair. Two blue caps piled out and dashed inside. In a very short time there were going to be a whole lot more people around, and I wanted to get the hell away from there before they had a chance to arrive.

Without traffic, it was less than ten minutes to Lawson's apartment but it was very definitely at the right end of Michigan Avenue, not quite on the lake but high enough to overlook its neighbors for a view almost as good as if it had been.

Lawson himself answered the door. He was wearing a plum-colored dressing gown and his hair was rumpled. "Couldn't this have waited?" he said.

"Not this time," I said. "I think I've found Myra's visitor."

"You *think?*"

"He was dead," I said. "So I couldn't ask him to be sure."

Lawson looked at me for a long moment, then opened the door wider.

"Come in," he said.

The room was furnished simply but expensively. Lawson sat down in the one chair with arms and faced me. "Now," he said, "what's this all about?"

"It's a pretty straightforward story," I said, "on the surface. Myra gave me what may or may not be a cock-and-bull story about Billy being on the run from the consequences of some shady deal he was involved in and sent me off to meet him. When I got where he was supposed to be I found a corpse waiting for me with my own gun on the floor beside him. If I'm right, he was a punk named Charles Michaels, who may or may not have been involved with Billy in that so-called shady deal but who definitely was Myra's visitor the other night."

"You think she killed him and set you up to take the blame?"

"Not by herself," I said. "Charles had been dead only a matter of minutes when I found him and I called Myra right afterward. She couldn't possibly have killed him and gotten back across town in time to answer her phone. But there she was."

"I see," Lawson said. He was silent for another long moment. "Have you decided what you're going to tell the police yet?"

"What's wrong with the truth?"

Lawson smiled cynically. "You know the answer to that," he said, "or you wouldn't be here." He sighed. "You can't help being involved, of course. If nothing else, the desk clerk will identify you as having been where you were, and I think you can rest assured that once the police identify the gun as yours they'll make sure the clerk gets a chance to see you again. Coupled with the attack on you earlier, it adds up to a very damning case. On the other hand, you shouldn't have too much difficulty copping a plea. Self-defense might be a little much this time, but I think the State's Attorney would buy manslaughter." He nodded as if pleased with himself. "Yes, that should work out very well."

"For whom?"

"For everybody, Mr. Thomas. For you as well as for Mr. Howard and Billy. After all, what would you serve? A few years at the most. With Mr. Howard's influence behind you, you might even draw a suspended sentence. But whatever the penalty, there would be a place for you when you came out. Mr. Howard takes good care of his employees – particularly those who put his interests first."

I let my eyes drift around the room. "I can see that," I said.

"I'm sure you can," Lawson said, unruffled. He rose and went to the door.

"Let me know your decision," he said. "Soon."

I was pretty sure the police couldn't have managed to trace the gun back to me yet, but I spent the night in a motel rather than risk finding them waiting when I got home. Then first thing the next morning I drove down to Headquarters and asked for Dave Minor. Minor was Robbery-Burglary and not likely to be up on a homicide investigation. But on the other hand he was the closest friend I had left on the force and, considering what I had to say, a little sympathy up front wouldn't hurt.

"Well," Minor said, "this is a surprise." He was a burly man with pale-reddish hair and a fleshy strong-chinned face suffused with the subcutaneous flush that seems to go with fair skin and overweight. "Somebody did tell me you were back in business."

"Maybe more than I'd like to be," I said. "Suppose I told you I killed a man last night."

Minor's face lost its friendliness. "You damn fool," he said.

I spent the rest of the day going over my story to successive sets of police onlookers both in uniform and out. Finally, Minor told me I could use the phone on his desk to make my call. Two hours later, after Lawson had

had time to make *his* calls, Minor told me I could go.

Myra didn't seem particularly happy to see me, leaving the door on the chain and peering out through the narrow gap. I held up my hands to show they were empty. "No hard feelings, Myra," I said. "You only did what you were told. I know that."

She continued to regard me suspiciously. "Is that what you came to say?"

"Partly, but mostly that it's past time you met your in-laws."

"Why?"

"There's a lot of money there, Myra," I said. "More than enough for both of us if we play it right."

"How much?"

"A half million," I said. "Maybe more."

Myra released the chain. "What would I have to do?" she said.

"Like I said. Come out and meet your in-laws."

Howard sat back and looked around at the four of us: Lawson, Pat Wainwright, Myra and myself. It was later that same evening. The servants had been dismissed for the night and we were assembled in what I took to be Howard's study – at least, it was furnished with a massive desk. On closer inspection, though, what I had taken for a bookcase on the opposite wall turned out to be a dry sink and bar.

"I'm not sure I understand why you felt it necessary to have this meeting," he said. He might have been addressing a recalcitrant board of directors. "I thought you and Lawson had agreed on how this matter was to be handled."

"We discussed it," I said. "We didn't agree."

"I see." He looked at me unblinkingly. "It's your decision," he said. "Obviously, I can't force you to do anything you don't want to do. However, if you act against what I consider my interest you do it at your own risk. You get no support here." He broke off to glance over at Pat and was apparently satisfied with what he saw. "No support at all," he added.

"Even if I could prove Billy wasn't involved?"

Howard shook his head. "Unfortunately," he said, "you can't. The facts are against you."

"Not the facts," I said. "Only what Myra *says* are the facts, and Myra's a liar."

"Why, you –" Myra burst out. She turned to Howard. "You know what he's after?

Money. He told me we could rip you off for a half million between us."

Howard looked at me. I shrugged. "I had to tell her something to get her out here," I said.

"Of course," Howard said drily. "But go on. Let's hear what you have to tell the rest of us."

"All right," I said. "Let's work on the theory that Myra is lying. She needed a partner, and you can almost sense his – or her – presence the way astronomers do with planets by the way the visible objects behave. In this case the visible objects are Myra and Charles. It's a little much that Charles should have gone on the run just as I started looking for him. Then later, when she was selling me the bill of goods about Billy, Myra identified Charles as the one I had seen leaving her house. The trouble is I was careful not to be seen staking out the house. So how did she know I'd seen anybody?"

I looked around. No one offered an answer. "Of course," I said, "it's not the sort of proof that would stand up in court. But this just might." I tossed the photograph I'd found in Charles's suitcase onto Howard's desk. "It could have been taken any time, of course, and Myra never denied she knew Charles before she met Billy. But the

271

bouquet in the picture suggests some kind of occasion. A wedding maybe? It just might be interesting to backtrack Myra to see if she wasn't married before. Or better still, show the picture to the J.P. she says married her and Billy to see how many of the participants he recognizes."

Lawson brought the gun out from under his jacket. "You had to keep pushing, didn't you?" he said. "You couldn't just leave well enough alone."

"Neither could you," I said, "although when you come right down to it, you really gave yourself away last night when you pointed out that the desk clerk could identify me. I hadn't said anything about a desk clerk – or a hotel, for that matter."

"Then the more fool you."

"Or you," I said. "You ought to take your own advice and quit while you're ahead."

Lawson shook his head.

"I can't," he said. "None of us can. Once these things start there's only one way to go."

He was facing me but he wasn't really addressing me, and after a long moment Howard pushed himself up out of his chair. "Do what you have to," he said. He sounded old and tired, and he left the room, moving as if a hundred years had hit him all at once.

Pat jerked around nervously in her chair.

"I don't understand this," she said. "What's going on here?"

"It's very simple," I said. "Your brother never married Myra. It was Charles impersonating Billy – and your stepfather and his attorney set it up."

"But where's Billy then?"

"The only place he could be," I said. "He's dead. He's been dead all along. The whole idea was to set up Myra and her baby as Billy's heirs so his share of your grandfather's estate wouldn't pass to you and leave Howard and Lawson out in the cold. I'll bet Howard doesn't have much stock in his own name and it's quite a comedown to find yourself suddenly dependent on the good will of somebody who's hated your guts all along. Right, Lawson?"

"What does it matter?" he said. "It's not going to help you." He gestured with the gun. "Get up."

"No," Myra said. "There's a better way." She crossed over to the bar and came back with a bottle and glass. "Nobody's going to get too worked up about a couple of drunks killed in a smash-up. Just one of those things." She set the bottle and glass down where I could reach them. "Go ahead," she said. "Pour yourself a drink unless you'd prefer a bullet right now."

273

I shrugged and picked up the bottle. "It's not going to work, Lawson," I said. "There's a squad car waiting outside now. I just convinced them to let me go it alone until we were sure if it was only you and Myra or whether Howard was in it too."

Lawson smiled bleakly. "You keep trying, don't you?" he said. "But nobody believes you any more." He gestured again with the gun.

I poured a hefty drink into the glass, drank it down, and on order followed it with a second and a third. Lawson moved over to stand behind Pat.

"All right," he said. "Now the girl."

I got up, a little unsteadily, and carried the bottle and glass across to Pat. At the moment, the whiskey I'd drunk was still concentrated in my stomach but it wouldn't be long before it sped through my bloodstream to the motor centers of my brain. And all the police in the world wouldn't help me then.

Pat took the glass I poured for her and held it stubbornly clenched in her hand. Lawson nudged her shoulder with the gun. "Drink," he said.

With a swift unhesitating motion she threw the whiskey back into his face.

He recoiled instinctively and before he

could recover I swung the bottle as hard as I could, catching him square across the bridge of the nose. He went down like a stone, the gun skittering off somewhere behind him.

Myra started for the gun, then, when she saw that Pat was going to beat her to it, turned and dashed for the door. I let her go. I was in no condition to catch her and the police really were outside anyway.

With one final effort, I heaved the bottle out through the window. It wasn't the agreed-upon signal, but it would bring them charging in just the same.

Minor was waiting for me when I came down the stairs. I was still feeling the effects of the whiskey.

"You don't look so good," he said.

"I don't feel so good," I said. "If you were a gentleman instead of a cop, you'd let me sleep it off."

"If I was a gentleman instead of a cop, I wouldn't have to worry about whether I was going to need a statement from you or not." He shrugged. "The way it turned out, though, Myra's already maneuvering for a deal to turn State's evidence – although it's a good question how she's going to feel once the high-powered lawyers start getting to her."

"That's your problem," I said. "All I wanted was to come out of this with my neck and my license intact."

Minor nodded. "You've done that," he said.

Pat Wainwright came out of one of the side rooms and crossed the hallway, looking grim and efficient. She reminded me of somebody. It took me a minute to realize it was her stepfather. "Yeah," I said. "The good guys always win."

MICHAEL INNES
A Test of Identity

"Yes," Inspector Appleby said as we strolled to the far end of his study, "I do keep a bit of a museum in this room. A sign of old age and the reminiscent mood, no doubt."

He pointed to a range of well ordered shelves. "You may find them depressing. For these things connect up, one way or another, with every sort of wickedness under the sun."

"All of them?"

"Well, no. One or two recall affairs that would have to be termed bizarre, I suppose, rather than nefarious. For example, that photograph. What do you make of it?"

I found myself studying a formal, three-quarter length portrait of a young man, taken full face and looking straight at the camera. A professional job, I thought, but of rather an old-fashioned sort.

"Attract you?" No comment had occurred to me, and Appleby appeared to feel I needed prompting. " Or do you prefer a man to be handsome in a more regular way?"

"The features are certainly irregular enough," I said. "But they have vitality. For what it is worth, then, your specimen *does* attract me. Was he a great criminal?"

Appleby smiled. "That was the question which confronted us. Did you ever hear of Leonard Morton?"

"Never. Is this his photograph?"

Appleby smiled. "Sit down, my dear chap, and I'll tell you the tale."

"It is sometimes said that if the whole population was finger-printed the police and the law courts would be saved some pretty large headaches. And Morton is a case in point.

"His parents had been wealthy folk who lost their lives in some accident when he was a baby. There were no near relatives, and young Leonard was brought up in a careful enough, but rather impersonal way. Nobody had much occasion to be interested in him, and he seems to have had no talent for impressing himself upon the world.

"You spoke of vitality. I suspect he shoved most of that into a rugger scrum. And by his companions there, I suppose, he was remembered only as so much heave and shove. He made no *print*, so to speak, as a

278

personality. Which was awkward, in view of what happened.

"He took off into the skies one day – it was for the purpose of bombing Berlin – and ceased to be a recognizable physical object some hours later."

I was horrified. "Do you mean," I asked Appleby, "that he was charred to a cinder?"

"Nothing so drastic. But he was abominably burned. Or that was the story the world was asked to believe later. At the time, Morton was posted as missing, believed killed. No word of him came through, you see, as a P.O.W. or anything else. Then the war ended, and suddenly there was this mutilated man with his story – his story of being Leonard Morton.

"There was nothing out of the way in it. He had baled out; every rag had been blasted or burned off him; and for a long time he had suffered a complete loss of memory. And now here he was back in England, proposing to claim quite a substantial fortune. But was he Morton?

"If he wasn't, he had certainly *known* Morton – and known him as quite a young man, before the war started. There could, it seemed, be no doubt about that. If he was an impostor, he wasn't impersonating a dead man whom he had met for the first time in a hospital or prison camp. But here certainty ended."

Appleby paused at this to stare thoughtfully at the photograph, and a question occurred to me. "At which point did you come into the affair?"

"In the first few days. There was, you see, an important time element in the matter. For a reason I'll presently explain, it was essential that the truth be got at quickly.

"Sooner or later, of course, it was *bound* to be got at – although a bold impostor might well persuade himself it wasn't so. The claimant – as I suppose he should be called – hadn't materialized miraculously on a frontier of postwar Germany. He had come out in a train, and the train had had a starting point, and so on. There existed, as you can guess, a highly efficient organizsation for tackling just such problems, and there was little doubt that in the end the facts would be run to earth."

"But meanwhile there was this important time element?"

"Precisely. Nearly everybody's relations with Morton had been impersonal, as I've said. Or, if not impersonal, say professional. Schoolmasters, holiday tutors, trustees, executors, bankers – and so on. They could none of them be confident, one way or the other. Quite early they got together and held a sort of committee of inquiry on the young man, with a fellow called Firth, who was senior trustee, in the chair.

"Well, the claimant did pretty well. When he realized that they conceived it their duty to question his identity, he behaved very much as the genuine man might have been expected to do – if the genuine man was a pretty decent and forbearing sort of fellow. The committee was impressed, but by no means convinced.

"And then the claimant sprang a bombshell. There was after all, it appeared, one highly personal relationship in his life. Shortly before that bombing trip he had met and become engaged to a young lady. He demanded to be confronted with her. And the young lady, when named, proved to be the only daughter of the occasion's Grand Inquisitor."

I stared. "Firth?"

Appleby bobbed his head.

"Exactly ... and that was where I came in. Miss Firth – at least, according to her father's idea of her – was a young person of an extremely delicate nervous constitution; and to be presented with a lover from the grave, and later see him unmasked as an impostor, would be quite, quite fatal to her. So Firth

281

came and besought me. Could I resolve the puzzle straightaway, or at least arrive at some reliable opinion? I said I thought I could."

"And you did?"

"Yes. Not in a fashion that would have had much value as evidence in a court. But at least it gave Firth confidence in choosing a line.

"I did a quick rake around photographers who might have had dealings with young Morton just before the war – and then some equally quick work in our own laboratories and files. When I met the young man – whose face was certainly badly disfigured – I had a batch of portraits, including the one that you see hanging here. I asked him to select his own portrait, and he promptly chose this one. I wonder if you can see what that meant to me?"

"I don't know that I can."

"I was able to tell Firth that the claimant was certainly genuine, and that his daughter might be brought along."

This floored me completely.

"My dear Appleby, I don't see –"

"I realize you don't. Imagine you're a tailor, and try again."

Inspiration came to me. "The buttons and buttonholes!"

282

Appleby was delighted. "Splendid! What about them?"

"They're on the wrong side. *The printing has been reversed!*"

"Exactly. I found a photograph of Morton, and had this reverse print prepared. The two looked substantially different, because human features are never symmetrical, and his were more irregular than most. *Both* prints were included in the batch he was to sort through to find himself. You see what was involved?"

"I'm blessed if I do still."

"If he chose the original print, he was choosing a Leonard Morton he recognized from life. If he chose the reverse print, he was choosing a Leonard Morton he had never seen – *except in a mirror.*

"That, you see, was how I knew he was the genuine Morton."

STANLEY ELLIN
The Blessington Method

Mr. Treadwell was a small, likeable man who worked for a prosperous company in New York City, and whose position with the company entitled him to an office of his own. Late one afternoon of a fine day in June a visitor entered this office. The visitor was stout, well dressed, and imposing. His complexion was smooth and pink, his small, near-sighted eyes shone cheerfully behind heavy, horn-rimmed eyeglasses.

"My name," he said, after laying aside a bulky portfolio and shaking Mr. Treadwell's hand with a crushing grip, "is Bunce, and I am a representative of the Society for Gerontology. I am here to help you with your problem, Mr. Treadwell."

Mr. Treadwell sighed. "Since you are a total stranger to me, my friend," he said, "and since I have never heard of the outfit you claim to represent, and, above all, since I have no problem which could possibly concern you, I am sorry to say that I am not in the market for whatever you are peddling. Now, if you don't mind –"

"Mind?" said Bunce. "Of course, I mind. The Society for Gerontology does not try to sell anything to anybody, Mr. Treadwell. Its interests are purely philanthropic. It examines case histories, draws up reports, works toward the solution of one of the most tragic situations we face in modern society."

"Which is?"

"That should have been made obvious by the title of the organization, Mr. Treadwell. Gerontology is the study of old age and the problems concerning it. Do not confuse it with geriatrics, please. Geriatrics is concerned with the diseases of old age. Gerontology deals with old age as the problem itself."

"I'll try to keep that in mind," Mr. Treadwell said impatiently. "Meanwhile, I suppose, a small donation is in order? Five dollars, say?"

"No, no, Mr. Treadwell, not a penny, not a red cent. I quite understand that this is the traditional way of dealing with various philanthropic organizations, but the Society for Gerontology works in a different way entirely. Our objective is to help you with your problem first. Only then would we feel we have the right to make any claim on you."

"Fine," said Mr. Treadwell more amiably. "That leaves us all even. I have no problem, so you get no donation. Unless you'd rather reconsider?"

"Reconsider?" said Bunce in a pained voice. "It is you, Mr. Treadwell, and not I who must reconsider. Some of the most pitiful cases the Society deals with are those of people who have long refused to recognize or admit their problem. I have worked months on your case, Mr. Treadwell. I never dreamed you would fall into that category."

Mr. Treadwell took a deep breath. "Would you mind telling me just what you mean by that nonsense about working on my case? I was never a case for any damned society or organization in the book!"

It was the work of a moment for Bunce to whip open his portfolio and extract several sheets of paper from it.

"If you will bear with me," he said, "I should like to sum up the gist of these reports. You are forty-seven years old and in excellent health. You own a home in East Sconsett, Long Island, on which there are nine years of mortgage payments still due, and you also own a late-model car on which eighteen monthly payments are yet to be made. However, due to an excellent salary you are in prosperous circumstances. Am I correct?"

"As correct as the credit agency which gave you that report," said Mr. Treadwell.

Bunce chose to overlook this. "We will now come to the point. You have been happily married for twenty-three years, and have one daughter who was married last year and now lives with her husband in Chicago. Upon her departure from your home your father-in-law, a widower and somewhat crotchety gentleman, moved into the house and now resides with you and your wife."

Bunce's voice dropped to a low, impressive note. "He is seventy-two years old, and, outside of a touch of bursitis in his right shoulder, admits to exceptional health for his age. He has stated on several occasions that he hopes to live another twenty years, and according to actuarial statistics which my Society has on file *he has every chance of achieving this*. Now do you understand, Mr. Treadwell?"

It took a long time for the answer to come. "Yes," said Mr. Treadwell at last, almost in a whisper. "Now I understand."

"Good," said Bunce sympathetically. "Very good. The first step is always a hard one – the admission that there *is* a problem hovering over you, clouding every day that passes. Nor is there any need to ask why you make efforts to conceal it even from yourself. You wish to spare Mrs. Treadwell your unhappiness, don't you?"

Mr. Treadwell nodded.

"Would it make you feel better," asked Bunce, "if I told you that Mrs. Treadwell shared your own feelings? That she, too, feels her father's presence in her home as a burden which grows heavier each day?"

"But she can't!" said Mr. Treadwell in dismay. "She was the one who wanted him to live with us in the first place, after Sylvia got married, and we had a spare room. She pointed out how much he had done for us when we first got started, and how easy he was to get along with, and how little expense it would be – it was she who sold me on the idea. I can't believe she didn't mean it!"

"Of course she meant it. She knew all the traditional emotions at the thought of her old father living alone somewhere, and offered all the traditional arguments on his behalf, and was sincere every moment. The trap she led you both into was the pitfall that awaits anyone who indulges in murky, sentimental thinking. Yes, indeed, I'm sometimes inclined to believe that Eve ate the apple just to make the serpent happy," said Bunce, and shook his head grimly at the thought.

"Poor Carol," groaned Mr. Treadwell. "If I had only known that she felt as miserable about this as I did –"

"Yes?" said Bunce. "What would you have done?"

Mr. Treadwell frowned. "I don't know. But there must have been something we could have figured out if we put our heads together."

"What?" Bunce asked. "Drive the man out of the house?"

"Oh, I don't mean exactly like that."

"What then?" persisted Bunce. "Send him to an institution? There are some extremely luxurious institutions for the purpose. You'd have to consider one of them, since he couldn't possibly be regarded as a charity case; nor, for that matter, could I imagine him taking kindly to the idea of going to a public institution."

"Who would?" said Mr. Treadwell. "And as for the expensive kind, well, I did look into the idea once, but when I found out what they'd cost I knew it was out. It would take a fortune."

"Perhaps," suggested Bunce, "he could be given an apartment of his own – a small, inexpensive place with someone to take care of him."

"As it happens, that's what he moved out

of to come live with us. And on that business of someone taking care of him – you'd never believe what it costs. That is, even allowing we could find someone to suit him."

"Right!" Bunce said, and struck the desk sharply with his fist. "Right in every respect, Mr. Treadwell."

Mr. Treadwell looked at him angrily. "What do you mean – right? I had the idea you wanted to help me with this business, but you haven't come up with a thing yet. On top of that you make it sound as if we're making great progress."

"We are, Mr. Treadwell, we are. Although you weren't aware of it, we have just completed the second step to your solution. The first step was the admission that there was a problem; the second step was the realization that no matter which way you turn there seems to be no logical or practical solution to the problem. In this way you are not only witnessing, you are actually participating in the marvelous operation of The Blessington Method, which, in the end, places the one possible solution squarely in your hands."

"The Blessington Method?"

"Forgive me," said Bunce. "In my enthusiasm I used a term not yet in scientific vogue. I must explain, therefore, that The

Blessington Method is the term my co-workers at the Society for Gerontology have given to its course of procedure. It is so titled in honor of J. G. Blessington, the Society's founder, and one of the great men of our era. He has not achieved his proper acclaim yet, but he will. Mark my words, Mr. Treadwell, someday his name will resound louder than that of Malthus."

"Funny I never heard of him," reflected Mr. Treadwell. "Usually I keep up with the newspapers. And another thing," he added, eyeing Bunce narrowly, "we never did get around to clearing up just how you happened to list me as one of your cases, and how you managed to turn up so much about me."

Bunce laughed delightedly. "It does sound mysterious when you put it like that, doesn't it? Well, there's really no mystery to it at all. You see, Mr. Treadwell, the Society has hundreds of investigators scouting this great land of ours from coast to coast, although the public at large is not aware of this. It is against the rules of the Society for any employee to reveal that he is a professional investigator – he would immediately lose effectiveness.

"Nor do these investigators start off with some specific person as their subject. Their interest lies in *any* aged person who is willing to talk about himself, and you would be astonished at how garrulous most aged people are about their most intimate affairs. That is, of course, as long as they are among strangers.

"These subjects are met at random on park benches, in saloons, in libraries – in any place conducive to comfort and conversation. The investigator befriends the subjects, draws them out – seeks, especially, to learn all he can about the younger people on whom they are dependent."

"You mean," said Mr. Treadwell with growing interest, "the people who support them."

"No, no," said Bunce. "You are making the common error of equating *dependence* and *finances*. In many cases, of course, there is a financial dependence, but that is a minor part of the picture. The important factor is that there is always an *emotional* dependence. Even where a physical distance may separate the older person from the younger, that emotional dependence is always present. It is like a current passing between them. The younger person by the mere realization that the aged exist is burdened by guilt and anger. It was his personal experience with this tragic dilemma of our times that led J. G. Blessington to his great work."

"In other words," said Mr. Treadwell, "you mean that even if the old man were not living with us, things would be just as bad for Carol and me?"

"You seem to doubt that, Mr. Treadwell. But tell me, what makes things bad for you now, to use your own phrase?"

Mr. Treadwell thought this over. "Well," he said, "I suppose it's just a case of having a third person around all the time. It gets on your nerves after a while."

"But your daughter lived as a third person in your home for over twenty years," pointed out Bunce. "Yet I am sure you didn't have the same reaction to her."

"But that's different," Mr. Treadwell protested. "You can have fun with a kid, play with her, watch her growing up –"

"Stop right there!" said Bunce. "Now you are hitting the mark. All the years your daughter lived with you you could take pleasure in watching her grow, flower like an exciting plant, take form as an adult being. But the old man in your house can only wither and decline now, and watching that process casts a shadow on your life. Isn't that the case?"

"I suppose it is."

"In that case, do you suppose it would make any difference if he lived elsewhere?

Would you be any the less aware that he was withering and declining and looking wistfully in your direction from a distance?"

"Of course not. Carol probably wouldn't sleep half the night worrying about him, and I'd have him on my mind all the time because of her. That's perfectly natural, isn't it?"

"It is indeed, and, I am pleased to say, your recognition of that completes the third step of The Blessington Method. You now realize that it is not the *presence* of the aged subject which creates the problem, but his *existence*."

Mr. Treadwell pursed his lips thoughtfully. "I don't like the sound of that."

"Why not? It merely states the fact, doesn't it?"

"Maybe it does. But there's something about it that leaves a bad taste in the mouth. It's like saying that the only way Carol and I can have our troubles settled is by the old man's dying."

"Yes," Bunce said gravely, "it is like saying that."

"Well, I don't like it – not one bit. Thinking you'd like to see somebody dead can make you feel pretty mean, and as far as I know it's never killed anybody yet."

Bunce smiled. "Hasn't it?" he said gently.

He and Mr. Treadwell studied each other in silence. Then Mr. Treadwell pulled a handkerchief from his pocket with nerveless fingers and patted his forehead with it.

"You," he said with deliberation, "are either a lunatic or a practical joker. Either way, I'd like you to clear out of here. That's fair warning."

Bunce's face was all sympathetic concern. "Mr. Treadwell," he cried, "don't you realize you were on the verge of the fourth step? Don't you see how close you were to your solution?"

Mr. Treadwell pointed to the door. "Out – before I call the police."

The expression on Bunce's face changed from concern to disgust. "Oh, come, Mr. Treadwell, you don't believe anybody would pay attention to whatever garbled and incredible story you'd concoct out of this. Please think it over carefully before you do anything rash, now or later. If the exact nature of our talk were even mentioned you would be the only one to suffer, believe me. Meanwhile, I'll leave you my card. Anytime you wish to call on me I will be ready to serve you."

"And why should I ever want to call on

you?" demanded the white-faced Mr. Treadwell.

"There are various reasons," said Bunce, "but one above all." He gathered his belongings and moved to the door. "Consider, Mr. Treadwell: anyone who has mounted the first three steps of The Blessington Method inevitably mounts the fourth. You have made remarkable progress in a short time, Mr. Treadwell – you should be calling soon."

"I'll see you in hell first," said Mr. Treadwell.

Despite this parting shot, the time that followed was a bad one for Mr. Treadwell. The trouble was that having been introduced to The Blessington Method he couldn't seem to get it out of his mind. It incited thoughts that he had to keep thrusting away with an effort, and it certainly colored his relationship with his father-in-law in an unpleasant way.

Never before had the old man seemed so obtrusive, so much in the way, and so capable of always doing or saying the thing most calculated to stir annoyance. It especially outraged Mr. Treadwell to think of this intruder in his home babbling his private affairs to perfect strangers, eagerly spilling out details of his family life to paid investigators who were only out to make trouble. And, to Mr. Treadwell in his heated state of mind, the fact that the investigators could not be identified as such didn't serve as any excuse.

Within very few days Mr. Treadwell, who prided himself on being a sane and level-headed businessman, had to admit he was in a bad way. He began to see evidences of a fantastic conspiracy on every hand. He could visualize hundreds – no, thousands – of Bunces swarming into offices just like his all over the country. He could feel cold sweat starting on his forehead at the thought.

But, he told himself, the whole thing was *too* fantastic. He could prove this to himself by merely reviewing his discussion with Bunce, and so he did, dozens of times. After all, it was no more than an objective look at a social problem. Had anything been said that a *really* intelligent man should shy away from? Not at all. If he had drawn some shocking inferences, it was because the ideas were already in his mind looking for an outlet. Perfectly human ideas, and who could fault him for being as human as the next one? On the other hand –

It was with a vast relief that Mr. Treadwell

finally decided to pay a visit to the Society for Gerontology. He knew what he would find there: a dingy room or two, a couple of underpaid clerical workers, the musty odor of a piddling charity operation – all of which would restore matters to their proper perspective again. He went so strongly imbued with this picture that he almost walked past the gigantic glass-and-aluminum tower which was the address of the Society, rode its softly humming elevator in confusion, and emerged in the anteroom of the main office in a daze.

And it was still in a daze that he was ushered through a vast and seemingly endless labyrinth of rooms by a sleek, long-legged young woman, and saw, as he passed, hosts of other young woman no less sleek and long-legged, multitudes of brisk, square-shouldered young men, rows of streamlined machinery clicking and chuckling in electronic glee, mountains of stainless-steel card indexes, and, over all, the bland reflection of modern indirect lighting on plastic and metal – until finally he was led into the presence of Bunce himself, and the door closed behind him.

"Impressive, isn't it?" said Bunce, obviously relishing the sight of Mr. Treadwell's stupefaction.

"Impressive?" croaked Mr. Treadwell hoarsely. "Why, I've never seen anything like it. It's a ten-million-dollar outfit!"

"And why not? Science is working day and night like some Frankenstein, Mr. Treadwell, to increase longevity past all sane limits. There are fourteen million people over sixty-five in this country right now. In twenty years their number will be increased to twenty-one million. Beyond that no one can even estimate what the figures will rise to!

"But the one bright note is that each of these aged people is surrounded by many young donors or potential donors to our Society. As the tide rises higher, we too flourish and grow stronger to withstand it."

Mr. Treadwell felt a chill of horror penetrate him. "Then it's true, isn't it?"

"I beg your pardon?"

"This Blessington Method you're always talking about," said Mr. Treadwell wildly. "The whole idea is just to settle things by getting rid of old people!"

"Right!" said Bunce. "That is the exact idea. And not even J. G. Blessington himself ever phrased it better. You have a way with words, Mr. Treadwell. I always admire a man who can come to the point without sentimental twaddle."

"But you can't get away with it!" said Mr. Treadwell incredulously. "You don't really believe you can get away with it, do you?"

Bunce gestured toward the expanses beyond the closed door. "Isn't that sufficient evidence of the Society's success?"

"But all those people out there! Do they realize what's going on?"

"Like all well trained personnel, Mr. Treadwell," said Bunce reproachfully, "they know only their own duties. What you and I are discussing here happens to be upper echelon."

Mr. Treadwell's shoulders drooped. "It's impossible," he said weakly. "It can't work."

"Come, come," Bunce said not unkindly, "you mustn't let yourself be overwhelmed. I imagine that what disturbs you most is what J. G. Blessington sometimes referred to as the Safety Factor. But look at it this way, Mr. Treadwell: isn't it perfectly natural for old people to die? Well, our Society guarantees that the deaths will appear natural. Investigations are rare – not one has ever caused us any trouble.

"More than that, you would be impressed by many of the names on our list of donors.

People powerful in the political world as well as the financial world have been flocking to us. One and all, they could give glowing testimonials as to our efficiency. And remember that such important people make the Society for Gerontology invulnerble, no matter at what point it may be attacked, Mr. Treadwell. And such invulnerability extends to every single one of our sponsors, including you, should you choose to place your problem in our hands."

"But I don't have the right," Mr. Treadwell protested despairingly. "Even if I wanted to, who am I to settle things this way for anybody?"

"Aha." Bunce leaned forward intently. "But you do want to settle things?"

"Not this way."

"Can you suggest any other way?"

Mr. Treadwell was silent.

"You see," Bunce said with satisfaction. "The Society for Gerontology offers the one practical answer to the problem. Do you still reject it, Mr. Treadwell?"

"I can't see it," Mr. Treadwell said stubbornly. "It's just not right."

"Are you sure of that?"

"Of course I am!" snapped Mr. Treadwell. "Are you going to tell me that it's right and proper to go around killing people just because they're old?"

"I am telling you that very thing, Mr. Treadwell, and I ask you to look at it this way. We are living today in a world of progress, a world of producers and consumers, all doing their best to improve our common lot. The old are neither producers nor consumers, so they are only barriers to our continued progress.

"If we want to take a brief, sentimental look into the pastoral haze of yesterday we may find that once they did serve a function. While the young were out tilling the fields, the old could tend to the household. But even that function is gone today. We have a hundred better devices for tending the household, and they come far cheaper. Can you dispute that?"

"I don't know," Mr. Treadwell said doggedly. "You're arguing that people are machines, and I don't go along with that at all."

"Good heavens," said Bunce, "don't tell me that you see them as anything else! Of course, we are machines, Mr. Treadwell, all of us. Unique and wonderful machines, I grant, but machines nevertheless. Why, look at the world around you. It is a vast organism made up of replaceable parts, all striving to produce and consume, produce and consume until worn out. Should one permit the worn out part to remain where it is? Of course not! It must be cast aside so that the organism will not be made inefficient. It is the whole organism that counts, Mr. Treadwell, not any of its individual parts. Can't you understand that?"

"I don't know," said Mr. Treadwell uncertainly. "I've never thought of it that way. It's hard to take in all at once."

"I realize that, Mr. Treadwell, but it is part of The Blessington Method that the sponsor fully appreciate the great value of his contribution in all ways – not only as it benefits him, but also in the way it benefits the entire social organism. In signing a pledge to our Society a man is truly performing the most noble act of his life."

"Pledge?" said Mr. Treadwell. "What kind of pledge?"

Bunce removed a printed form from a drawer of his desk and laid it out carefully for Mr. Treadwell's inspection. Mr. Treadwell read it and sat up sharply.

"Why, this says I'm promising to pay you two thousand dollars in a month from now. You never said anything about that kind of money!"

"There has never been any occasion to

raise the subject before this," Bunce replied. "But for some time now a committee of the Society has been examining your financial standing, and it reports that you can pay this sum without stress or strain."

"What do you mean, stress or strain?" Mr. Treadwell retorted. "Two thousand dollars is a lot of money, no matter how you look at it."

Bunce shrugged. "Every pledge is arranged in terms of the sponsor's ability to pay, Mr. Treadwell. Remember, what may seem expensive to you would certainly seem cheap to many other sponsors I have dealt with."

"And what do I get for this?"

"Within one month after you sign the pledge, the affair of your father-in-law will be disposed of. Immediately after that you will be expected to pay the pledge in full. Your name is then enrolled on our list of sponsors, and that is all there is to it."

"I don't like the idea of my name being enrolled on anything."

"I can appreciate that," said Bunce. "But may I remind you that a donation to a charitable organization such as the Society of Gerontology is tax-deductible?"

Mr. Treadwell's fingers rested lightly on the pledge. "Now just for the sake of argument," he said, "suppose someone signs one of these things and then doesn't pay up. I guess you know that a pledge like this isn't collectible under the law, don't you?"

"Yes," Bunce smiled, "and I know that a great many organizations cannot redeem pledges made to them in apparently good faith. But the Society for Gerontology has never met that difficulty. We avoid it by reminding all sponsors that the young, if they are careless, may die as unexpectedly as the old . . . No, no," he said, steadying the paper, "just your signature at the bottom will do."

When Mr. Treadwell's father-in-law was found drowned off the foot of East Sconsett pier three weeks later (the old man fished from the pier regularly although he had often been told by various local authorities that the fishing was poor there), the event was duly entered into the East Sconsett records as Death by Accidental Submersion, and Mr. Treadwell himself made the arrangements for an exceptionally elaborate funeral.

And it was at the funeral that Mr. Treadwell first had the Thought. It was a fleeting and unpleasant thought, just disturbing enough to make him miss a step as he entered the church. In all the confusion

305

of the moment, however, it was not too difficult to put aside.

A few days later, when he was back at his familiar desk, the Thought suddenly returned. This time it was not to be put aside so easily. It grew steadily larger and larger in his mind, until his waking hours were terrifyingly full of it, and his sleep a series of shuddering nightmares.

There was only one man who could clear up the matter for him, he knew; so he appeared at the offices of the Society for Gerontology burning with anxiety to have Bunce do so. He was hardly aware of handing over his check to Bunce and pocketing the receipt.

"There's something that's been worrying me," said Mr. Treadwell, coming straight to the point.

"Yes?"

"Well, do you remember telling me how many old people there would be around in twenty years?"

"Of course."

Mr. Treadwell loosened his collar to ease the constriction around his throat. "But don't you see? I'm going to be one of them!"

Bunce nodded. "If you take reasonably good care of yourself there's no reason why you shouldn't be," he pointed out.

306

"You don't get the idea," Mr. Treadwell said urgently. "I'll be in a spot then where I'll have to worry all the time about someone from this Society coming in and giving my daughter or my son-in-law ideas! That's a terrible thing to have to worry about all the rest of your life."

Bunce shook his head slowly. "You can't mean that, Mr. Treadwell."

"And why can't I?"

"Why? Well, think of your daughter, Mr. Treadwell. Are you thinking of her?"

"Yes."

"Do you see her as the lovely child who poured out her love to you in exchange for yours? The fine young woman who has just stepped over the threshold of marriage, but is always eager to visit you, eager to let you know the affection she feels for you?"

"I know that."

"And can you see in your mind's eye that manly young fellow who is her husband? Can you feel the warmth of his handclasp as he greets you? Do you know his gratitude for the financial help you give him regularly?"

"I suppose so."

"Now, honestly, Mr. Treadwell, can you imagine either of these affectionate and devoted youngsters doing a single thing – the slightest thing – to harm you?"

307

The constriction around Mr. Treadwell's throat miraculously eased; the chill around his heart departed.

"No," he said with conviction, "I can't."

"Splendid," said Bunce. He leaned far back in his chair and smiled with a kindly wisdom. "Hold onto that thought, Mr. Treadwell. Cherish it and keep it close at all times. It will be a solace and comfort to the very end."

EDWARD D. HOCH

Thirteen

Renger looked up from the crude map on the table before him and studied the newcomer with critical eyes. "You're Hallman?"

"That's right."

"They tell me you're a good man with a gun."

"I get by."

"Then I guess you're the man we need for this job. Ever used an automatic carbine?"

"Plenty of times."

"Like this one?" Renger asked, bringing out a new Plainfield carbine very much like the standard military weapon. "It uses thirty-shot clips. All right?"

"Fine." Hallman glanced around at the five other men in the room. The only one he knew was Asmith, a part-time heroin pusher who'd been in and out of prison. He nodded to him and waited for Renger to introduce the others.

"That's Crowthy and Evans and Asmith and Galliger and Yates. A damn good team

309

for this job. But we needed a good man with a gun – somebody who's not afraid to use it."

"That's me," Hallman said. He had earned the reputation.

"Good! We'll have smoke bombs and stuff, but I'm not kidding myself that we're going to get in there without killing a few people."

"What about guards?" Hallman asked. "And patrol cars?"

Renger pushed back his graying hair and stabbed at the map with a pencil. "The only guard you need to worry about is right here. Take him out and it's smooth sailing. Now, a patrol car comes down this street about once every hour. We're timed to miss it, but we can't be sure. All I can tell you is that Crowthy here will be covering you from across the street. If the patrol car surprises us, you'll have to deal with it."

"I understand," Hallman said.

"Your job is to take out this guard, get into the place, and fire a few shots. Create confusion. Make them think we've got a whole army out here. Then I'll toss a few smoke bombs and the rest of us will move in."

Asmith spoke up from his corner. "What about the getaway?"

"We'll leave the truck at this point and go the

310

rest of the way on foot. Afterwards each of you will have to get back to the truck on your own. Evans will stay with the truck as a lookout. But at ten o'clock we pull out. Anyone not back to the truck by ten, we figure they're caught. Any questions?"

As they went over the plan step by step, Hallman found his attention wandering. He was twenty-four years old, and already he had the reputation of being good with a gun. Anyone who bothered to check his record would know he was equally good with a knife. The first man he'd ever killed had been with a knife, and he still remembered the expression of shock in the man's eyes as Hallman's blade slid deep between his ribs.

That was the way it had been the other times, too, though he remembered that first one best of all. Sometimes he had not even seen the men he'd killed. They'd merely been figures to be gunned down at a distance, or sometimes men to be blown up in their beds by a well tossed bomb. And people knew that Hallman was an expert. They came to Hallman when the killing had to be neat and swift and efficient.

"All right," Renger said. "It's set, then. We go at dawn."

The men nodded silently and left the room. There was very little conversation, and

311

Hallman was glad of that. He was not much of a talker.

The early morning was usually best for a job of this sort, Hallman had discovered. It was especially good if you could hit a place just a few minutes before eight, when people were arriving for the day's work. The patrol cars were generally off the road then, too, changing crews for the day tour.

This morning was especially good, because a light mist from the river hung over the streets of the town. Evans had parked the truck an hour earlier, and they'd come the rest of the way on foot, moving singly to avoid attracting attention. The town was quiet, with only a few people moving about, when Hallman poked his head around a tree across the street from their target.

The first thing he saw was the uniformed guard by the gate. He seemed to know everyone who entered, though occasionally he glanced at a pass when it was held out to him. The holstered revolver at his side presented no difficulty to Hallman, who could have, if necessary, killed the man from across the street.

Hallman broke from cover and walked directly toward the guard, carrying the carbine casually in his left hand, pointed at the ground. The man didn't notice him until he was almost up to him, and then the guard's hand dropped uncertainly to the holstered revolver. "You need a pass here," he said. "A pass."

Hallman smiled and kept walking toward the man, as if he didn't understand the language. When he was close enough he brought his right arm up quickly to the guard's throat, plunging his knife deep into the flesh. The man went down with the gurgling sound they always made. Already, before the guard hit the ground, Hallman swung his automatic carbine up to cover the doorway ahead of him, and that was almost a fatal mistake.

From behind him he heard Crowthy shout a warning, and he whirled to see the patrol car traveling fast down the street. They'd already spotted him and screeched to a stop. Crowthy fired a quick wild shot and retreated toward the woods. Two officers jumped out of the car and one of them fired three rapid shots at Crowthy's retreating back. Hallman saw him topple in the dirt as Hallman brought his own weapon up. He fired a quick burst, dropping one officer in his tracks and the other dived behind the patrol car. A third man, the driver, started out his side and then fell back, bleeding from the shattered wind-shield.

Hallman moved backward into the building, firing as he went, and saw the second officer fall over. Then he was inside, running down a dingy hallway, ramming another 30-shot clip into the weapon. He hoped the others would be coming soon.

A man appeared ahead of him at the end of the passage, like a pop-up target in a shooting gallery, and Hallman sprayed him with bullets. Then he ran on, into the first room, firing quick shots to clear the way. He'd got the rhythm of it now, the half forgotten feel for killing that left him at times but always returned.

In the second office a screaming woman was hunched in one corner, covering her face. Hallman paused only an instant, and then fired a short burst into her body. She slid down the wall, torn and bleeding and already without life. She was the first woman he'd ever killed, and he was surprised at how little it bothered him.

He smashed out the window in a front room, seeking the others, and saw two more uniformed guards running around the front of the building. He fired fast, cutting them both down with a line of bullets across their backs. Then he saw the others break from the cover of the trees. Renger was in the lead, running with his gun ready, and he hurled a smoke bomb as he crossed the road. Then someone on the floor above cut loose with three quick shots and Hallman saw Yates stagger and go down in the street, just before the smoke obscured him.

Hallman found the stairs and started up. A figure appeared at the top and Hallman let go with the rest of the clip. Before he could reload, a second man fell on him with a roar, toppling him backward halfway down the steps. He felt the carbine slide away from him, but he rolled over and managed to get his knife out. He plunged it into the fleshy man's side, heard his grunt of pain, and plunged it again. The man went suddenly limp, and Hallman rolled his body down the stairs.

There was shooting below him now, and he knew Renger and the others were past the gate. He made it the rest of the way to the top of the stairs, finding his weapon and then reloading it as he climbed. He burst through the door at the top landing and killed the man at the window with a sudden spray of bullets. Two others – short frightened men – raised their hands and backed against the wall. Hallman shot them both.

He could feel the warmth of blood on his

lower lip now, and he realized the man on the stairs had landed some damaging punches. But there was no pain. The exhilaration of the moment had blotted it out. He glanced out the window, but the smoke was too thick to see anything.

Leaning against the wall, he tried to remember how many he'd killed. The guard, and at least two of the three in the patrol car, and the man in the passage. And the woman. The two guards out the window. And the two on the stairs. And three in this room. That made twelve, in just under five minutes. Fast work. Good work.

He took out his knife again and made sure they were dead. He was on his last clip of bullets, so he couldn't waste any more. Then he heard someone coming up the stairs, calling his name. It was Renger, carrying two suitcases. Hallman licked the blood from his lip, savoring it, and went to meet him.

"You did a damn good job," Renger told him. "You're a regular one-man army!"

"I said I was good with a gun. How many men did we lose?"

"Crowthy and Yates. The others are all right. Let's plant these explosives and get the hell out of here!"

They did their job, working fast, and then left the building with the others.

"Damn!" Renger said as they started across the muddy road toward the shelter of the woods. "I'm going to see that you get a medal for this, Hallman!"

"Thank you, Major."

"When they hear back home how you led an attack on the enemy's forward command post and helped destroy it, almost singlehanded, they'll make you a hero. How many did you kill?"

"Twelve."

"Damn good shooting!"

They passed the enemy patrol car, parked at a crazy angle on the road, and Hallman saw that the driver was still alive, gasping for breath behind the shattered windshield. He raised his carbine with one hand and killed the man with a single shot.

"That makes thirteen," he said, and walked on.

JOHN DICKSON CARR
The One Real Horror

Hargreaves did not speak until he had turned on two lamps. Even then he did not remove his overcoat. The room, though cold, was stuffy, and held a faintly sweet odor. Outside the Venetian blinds, which were not quite closed, you saw the restless, shifting presence of snow past street lights. For the first time Hargreaves hesitated.

"The – the object," he explained, indicating the bed, "was there. *He* came in by this door, here. Perhaps you understand a little better now?"

Hargreaves' companion nodded.

"No," said Hargreaves, and smiled. "I'm not trying to invoke illusions. On the contrary, I'm trying to dispel them. Shall we go downstairs?"

It was a tall, heavy house where no clocks ticked. But the treads of the stairs creaked and cracked sharply, even under their padding of carpet. At the back, in a kind of small study, a gas fire had been lighted. Its hissing could be heard from a distance; it

318

roared up blue like solid blue flames into the white fretwork of the heater, but it did little to dispel the chill of the room.

Hargreaves motioned his companion to a chair at the other side of the fire.

"I want to tell you about it," he went on. "Don't think I'm trying to be –" his wrist hesitated over a word, as though over a chess piece "– highbrow. Don't think I'm trying to be highbrow if I tell it to you" – again his wrist hesitated – "objectively. As though you knew nothing about it. As though you weren't concerned in it. It's the only way you will understand the problem he had to face."

Hargreaves was very intent when he said this. He was bending forward, looking up from under his eyebrows; his heavy overcoat flopped over the sides of his knees, and his gloved hands, seldom still, either made a slight gesture or pressed flat on his knees.

"Take Tony Marvell, to begin with," he argued. "A good fellow whom everybody liked. Not a good businessman, perhaps – too generous to be a good businessman; but as conscientious as the very devil, and with so fine a mathematical brain that he got over the practical difficulties.

"Tony was Senior Wrangler at Cambridge, and intended to go on with his mathematics. But then his uncle died, so he had to take over the business. You know what the business was then: three luxury hotels, built, equipped, and run by Old Jim, the uncle, in Old Jim's most flamboyant style; and all going to rack and ruin.

"Everybody said it was madness for Tony to push his shoulder up against the business world. His brother – that's Stephen Marvell, the former surgeon – said Tony would only bring Old Jim's card houses down on everybody and swamp them all with more debts.

"But you know what happened. At twenty-five, Tony took over the business. At twenty-seven, he had the hotels on a paying basis. At thirty, they were hotels to which everybody went as a matter of course – blazing their sky signs, humming with efficiency, piling up profits which startled even Tony.

"And all because he sneered at the idea that there could be any such thing as overwork. He never let up. You can imagine that dogged expression of his: 'Well, I don't like this work, but let's clean it up satisfactorily so that we can get on to more important things' – like his studies. He did it partly because he had promised Old Jim he would, and partly *because* – you see? – he

320

thought the business so unimportant that he wanted to show how easy it was.

"But it wasn't easy. No man could stand that pace. London, Brighton, Eastbourne; he knew everything there was to know about the Marvell Hotels, down to the price of a pillow case and the cost of grease for the lifts. At the end of the fifth year he collapsed one morning in his office. His brother Stephen told him what he had to do.

" 'You're getting out of this,' Stephen said. 'You're going clear away. Round the world – anywhere – but for six or eight months at least. During that time you're not even so much as to think of your work. Is that clear?'

"Tony told me the story himself last night. He says that the whole thing might never have happened if he had not been forbidden to write to anybody while he was away.

" 'Not even so much as a postcard,' snapped Stephen, 'to anybody. If you do, it'll be more business; and then God help you.'

" 'But Judith –' Tony protested.

" 'Particularly to Judith,' said Stephen. 'If you insist on marrying your secretary, that's your affair. But you don't ruin your rest cure by exchanging long letters about the hotels.'

"You can imagine Stephen's over-aristocratic, thin-nosed face towering over him, dull with anger. You can imagine

Stephen in his black coat and striped trousers, standing up beside the polished desk of his office in Harley Street. Stephen Marvell – and, to a certain extent, Tony, too – had that overbred air which Old Jim Marvell had always wanted and never achieved.

"Tony didn't argue. He was willing enough, because he was tired. Even if he were forbidden to write to Judith, he could always think about her. In the middle of April, more than eight months ago, he sailed by the *Queen Anne* from Southampton. And on that night the terrors began."

Hargreaves paused. The gas fire still hissed in the little dim study. You would have known that this was a house in which death had occurred, and occurred recently, by the look on the face of Hargreaves' companion.

Hargreaves went on: "The *Queen Anne* sailed at midnight. Tony saw her soaring up above the docks, as high as the sky. He saw the long decks, white and shiny like shoeboxes, gleaming under skeins of lights; he saw the black dots of passengers moving along them; he heard the click rattle-rush of winches as great cranes swung over the crowd on the docks; and he felt the queer, pleasurable, restless feeling which stirs the nerves at the beginning of an ocean voyage.

"At first he was as excited as a schoolboy. Stephen Marvell and Judith Gates, Tony's fiancée, went down to Southampton with him. Afterwards he recalled talking to Judith, holding her arm, piloting her through the rubbery-smelling passages of the ship to show her how fine it was. They went to Tony's cabin, where his luggage had been piled together with a basket of fruit. Everybody agreed that it was a fine cabin.

"It was not until a few minutes before the 'all ashore' gong that the first pang of loneliness struck him. Stephen and Judith had already gone ashore, for all of them disliked these awkward, last-minute leavetakings. They were standing on the dock, far below. By leaning over the rail of the ship he could just see them.

"Judith's face was tiny, remote, and smiling; infinitely loved. She was waving to him. Round him surged the crowd – faces, hats, noise under naked lights, accentuating the break with home and the water that would widen between. Next he heard the gong begin to bang – hollow, quivering, pulsing to loudness over the cry 'All ashore that's going ashore!'' and dying away into the ship.

"He did not want to go. There was still plenty of time. He could still gather up his luggage and get off.

"For a time he stood by the rail with the breeze from Southampton Water in his face. Such a notion was foolish. He would stay. With a last wave to Judith and Stephen, he drew himself determinedly away. He would be sensible. He would go below and unpack his things.

"Feeling the unreality of that hollow night he went down to his cabin on C Deck. And his luggage was not there! He stared round the stuffy cabin with its neat curtains at the portholes. There had been a trunk and two suitcases, gaudily labeled, to say nothing of the basket of fruit. Now the cabin was empty.

"Tony ran upstairs again to the Purser's office. The Purser, a harassed man behind a kind of ticket-window desk, was just getting rid of a clamoring crowd. In the intervals of striking a hand bell and calling orders, he caught Tony's eye.

" 'My luggage –' Tony said.

" 'That's all right, Mr. Marvell,' said the harassed official. 'It's been taken ashore. But you'd better hurry yourself.'

"Tony had here only a feeling of extreme stupidity. 'Taken ashore?' he said. 'But why? Who told you to send it ashore?'

" 'Why, *you* did,' said the Purser, looking up suddenly from a sheet of names and figures.

"Tony only stared at him.

" 'You came here,' the Purser went on, with sharply narrowing eyes, 'not ten minutes ago. You said you had decided not to take the trip, and asked for your luggage to be taken off. I told you that at this late date we could not, of course, refund the –'

" 'Get it back!' said Tony. His own voice sounded wrong. 'I couldn't have told you that. Get it back!'

" 'Just as you like, sir,' said the Purser, smiting on the bell, *if* there's time.'

"Overhead the hoarse blast of the whistle, that mournfullest of all sounds at sea, beat out against Southampton Water. B Deck, between open doors, was cold and gusty.

"Now Tony Marvell had not the slightest recollection of having spoken to the Purser before. That was what struck him between the eyes like a blow, and what, for the moment, almost drove him to run away from the *Queen Anne* before they should lift the gang-plank.

"It was the nightmare again. One of the worst features of his nervous breakdown had been the conviction, coming in flashes at night, that he was not real any longer; that

· 325

his body and his inner self had moved apart, the first walking or talking in everyday life like an articulate dummy, while the brain remained in another place. It was as though he were dead, and seeing his body move. Dead.

"To steady his wits, he tried to concentrate on familiar human things. Judith, for instance. He recalled Judith's hazel eyes, the soft line of her cheek as she turned her head, the paper cuffs she wore at the office. Judith, his fiancée, his secretary, who would take care of things while he was away; whom he loved, and who was so maddeningly close even now. But he must not think of Judith.

"Instead, he pictured his brother Stephen, and Johnny Cleaver, and any other friends who occurred to him. He even thought of Old Jim Marvell, who was dead. And – so strong is the power of imaginative visualization – at that moment, in the breezy lounge room facing the Purser's office, he thought he saw Old Jim looking at him round the corner of a potted palm.

"All this, you understand, went through Tony's mind in the brief second while he heard the ship's whistle hoot out over his head.

"He made some excuse to the Purser, and went below. He was grateful for the chatter of noise, for the people passing up and down below decks. None of them paid any attention to him but at least they were there. But, when he opened the door of his cabin, he stopped and stood very still in the doorway.

"The propellers had begun to churn. A throb, a heavy vibration, shook upwards through the ship; it made the tooth-glass tinkle in the rack and sent a series of creaks through the bulkheads. The *Queen Anne* was moving.

"Tony Marvell took hold of the door as though that movement had been a lurch, and he stared at the bed across the cabin. On the white bedspread, where it had not been before, lay an automatic pistol."

The gas fire had heated its asbestos pillars to glowing red. Again there was a brief silence in the little study of the house in St. John's Wood. Hargreaves – Sir Charles Hargreaves, Commissioner of Police for the Criminal Investigation Department – leaned down and lowered the flame of the heater. Even the tone of his voice seemed to change when the gas ceased its loud hissing.

"Wait!" he said, lifting his hand. "I don't want you to get the wrong impression. Don't think that the fear, the slow approach of what was going to happen, pursued Tony all through his trip round the world. It didn't. That's the most curious part of the whole affair.

"Tony has told me that it was a brief, bad bout, lasting perhaps fifteen minutes in all, just before and just after the *Queen Anne* sailed. It was not alone the uncanny feeling that things had ceased to be real. It was a sensation of active malignancy – of hatred, of danger – surrounding him and pressing on him. He could feel it like a weak current from a battery.

"But five minutes after the ship had headed out to open sea, every such notion fell away from him. It was as though he had emerged out of an evil fog. That hardly seems reasonable. Even supposing that there are evil emanations, or evil spirits, it is difficult to think that they are confined to one country; that their tentacles are broken by half a mile's distance; that they cannot cross water.

"Yet there it was. One moment he was standing there with the automatic pistol in his hand, the noise of the engines beating in his ears, and a horrible impulse joggling his elbow to put the muzzle of the pistol into his mouth and –

"Then – snap! Something broke: that is

the only way he can describe it. He stood upright. He felt like a man coming out of a fever, shaken and sweating, but back from behind the curtain into the real world again. He gulped deep breaths. He went to the porthole and opened it. From that time on, he says, he began to get well.

"How that automatic had got into his cabin he did not know. He knew he must have brought it himself, in one of those blind flashes. But he could not remember. He stared at it with new eyes, and new feeling of the beauty and sweetness of life. He felt as though he had been reprieved from execution.

"You might have thought that he would have flung the pistol overboard in sheer fear of touching it. But he didn't. To him it was the part of a puzzle. He stared much at it: a Browning .38, of Belgian manufacture, fully loaded. After the first few days, when he did keep it locked away out of sight in his trunk, he pondered over it. It represented the one piece of evidence he could bring back home with him, the one tangible reality in a nightmare.

"At the New York Customs shed it seemed to excite no surprise. He carried it overland with him – Cleveland, Chicago, Salt Lake City – to San Francisco, in a fog, and then down the kindled sea to Honolulu. At Yokohama they were going to take it away from him; only a huge bribe retrieved it. Afterwards he carried it on his person, and was never searched.

"As the broken bones of his nerves knitted, as in the wash of the propellers there was peace, it became a kind of mascot. It went with him through the blistering heat of the Indian Ocean, into the murky Red Sea, to the Mediterranean. To Port Said, to Cairo in early winter. To Naples and Marseilles and Gibraltar. It was tucked away in his hip pocket on the bitter cold night, a little more than eight months after his departure, when Tony Marvell – a healed man again – landed back at Southampton in the *Chippenham Castle*.

"It was snowing that night, you remember? The boat train roared through thickening snow. It was crowded, and the heat would not work.

"Tony knew that there could be nobody at Southampton to meet him. His itinerary had been laid out in advance, and he had stuck to the bitter letter of his instructions about not writing even so much as a postcard. But he had altered the itinerary so as to take a ship that would get him home in time for Christmas; he would burst in on them a week early. For eight months he had lived. in a void. In an hour or two he would be home. He would see Judith again.

"In the dimly lighted compartment of the train his fellow passengers were not talkative. The long voyage had squeezed their conversation dry; they almost hated each other. Even the snow roused only a flicker of enthusiasm.

" 'Real old-fashioned Christmas!' said one.

" 'Hah!' said another appreciatively, scratching with his fingernails at the frosted window.

" 'Damn cold, *I* call it,' snarled a third. 'Can't they ever make the heat work in these trains? I'm damn well going to make a complaint!'

"After that, with a sympathetic grunt or mutter, each retired behind his newspaper – a white, blank wall which rustled occasionally, and behind which they drank up news of home.

"In other words – Tony remembers that he thought it then – he was in England again. He was home. For himself, he only pretended to read. He leaned back in his seat, listening vaguely to the clackety-clack of the wheels and the long blast of the whistle that was torn behind as the train gathered speed.

"He knew exactly what he would do. It

331

would be barely ten o'clock when they reached Waterloo. He would jump into a cab and hurry home – to this house – for a wash and brush-up. Then he would pelt up to Judith's flat at Hampstead as hard as he could go.

"Yet this thought, which should have made him glow, left him curiously chilly round the heart. He fought the chill. He laughed at himself. Determinedly he opened the newspaper, distracting himself, turning from page to page, running his eye down each column. Then he stopped. Something familiar caught his eye, a familiar name. It was an obscure item on a middle page.

"He was reading in this paper the news of his own death. Just that.

"'Mr. Anthony Dean Marvell, of Upper Avenue Road, St. John's Wood, and owner of Marvell Hotels, Ltd., was found shot dead last night in his bedroom at home. A bullet had penetrated up through the roof of the mouth into the brain, and a small-calibre automatic was in his hand. The body was found by Mrs. Beach, Mr. Marvell's housekeeper, who . . .'

"A suicide!

"And once again, as suddenly as it had left him aboard ship, the grasp fell on him, shutting him off from the real world into the unreal. The compartment, as I told you, was very dimly lighted. So it was perhaps natural that he could only dimly see a blank wall of upheld newspapers facing him; as though there were no fellow passengers there, as though they had deserted him in a body, leaving only the screen of papers that joggled a little with the rush of the train.

"Yes, he was alone.

"He got up blindly, dragging open the door of the compartment to get out into the corridor. The confined space seemed to be choking him. Holding his own newspaper up high so as to catch the light from the compartment, he read the item again.

"There could be no possibility of a mistake. The account was too detailed. It told all about him, his past and present.

" '... His brother, Mr. Stephen Marvell, the eminent Harley Street surgeon, was hurriedly summoned.... His fiancée, Miss Judith Gates... It is understood that in April, Mr. Anthony Marvell suffered a nervous breakdown, from which even a long rest had not effected a cure...'

"Tony looked at the date of the newspaper, afraid of what he might see. But it was the date of that day – the twenty-third of December. From this account it appeared that he had shot himself forty-eight hours before.

"And the gun was in his hip pocket now.

"Tony folded up the newspaper. The train moved under his feet with a dancing sway, jerking above the click of the wheels, and another thin blast of the whistle went by. It reminded him of the whistle aboard the *Queen Anne*.

"He glanced along the dusky corridor. It was empty except for someone, whom he supposed to be another passenger, leaning elbows on the rail past the windows and staring out at the flying snow.

"He remembers nothing else until the train reached Waterloo. But something – an impression, a subconscious memory – registered in his mind about that passenger he had seen in the corridor. First, it had to do with the shape of the person's shoulders. Then Tony realized that this was because the person was wearing a greatcoat with an old-fashioned brown fur collar.

"Tony was jumping blindly out of the train at Waterloo when he remembered that Old Jim Marvell always used to wear such a collar.

"After that he seemed to see it everywhere.

"When he hurried up to the guard's van to claim his trunk and suitcases, the luggage ticket in his hand, he was in such a crowd that he could not move his arms. But he thought he felt brown fur press the back of his shoulders.

"A porter got him a taxi. It was a relief to see a London cab again, in a coughing London terminus, and hear the bump of the trunk as it went up under the strap, and friendly voices again. He gave the address to the driver, tipped the porter, and jumped inside. Even so, the porter seemed to be holding open the door of the taxi longer than was necessary.

" 'Close it, man!' Tony found himself shouting. 'Close it, quick!'

" 'Yes, sir,' said the porter, jumping back. The door slammed. Afterwards, the porter stood and stared after the taxi. Tony, glancing out through the little back window, saw him still standing there.

"It was dark in the cab, and as close as though a photographer's black hood had been drawn over him. Tony could see little. But he carefully felt with his hands all over the seat, all over the open space; and he found nothing."

At this point in the story Commissioner Hargreaves broke off for a moment or two. He had been speaking with difficulty – not as though he expected to be doubted, but as though the right words were hard to find. His gloved fingers opened and closed on his knee.

For the first time, his companion – Miss Judith Gates – interrupted him. Judith spoke from the shadow on the other side of the gas fire.

"Wait!" she said. "Please!"

"Yes?" said Hargreaves.

"This person who was following Tony." She spoke also with difficulty. "You aren't telling me that it was – well, was –?"

"Was what?"

"Dead," said Judith.

"I don't know who it was," answered Hargreaves, looking at her steadily. "Except that it seemed to be somebody with a fur collar on his coat. I'm telling you Tony's story, which I believe."

Judith's hand shaded her eyes. "All the same," she insisted, and her pleasant voice went high, "even supposing it was! I mean, even supposing it was the person you think. *He* of all people, living or dead, wouldn't have tried to put any evil influence round Tony. Old Jim loved Tony. He left Tony every penny he owned, and not a farthing to Stephen. He always told Tony he'd look after him."

"And so he did," said Hargreaves.

"But –"

"You see," Hargreaves told her slowly. "You still don't understand the source of the evil influence. Tony didn't, himself. All he knew was that he was bowling along in a dark taxi, through slippery, snowy streets; and whatever might be following him, good or bad, he couldn't endure it.

"Even so, everything might have ended well if the taxi driver had been careful. But he wasn't. That was the first snowfall of the year, and the driver miscalculated. When they were only two hundred yards from Upper Avenue Road, he tried to make a turn too fast.

"Tony felt the helpless swing of the skid; he saw the glass partition tilt and a black tree trunk rush up at them until it exploded against the outer windscreen. They landed upright against the tree, with a buckled wheel.

" 'I 'ad to swerve,' the driver was crying. 'I 'ad to! An old gent with a fur collar walked smack out in front of –"

"And so, you see, Tony had to walk home alone."

"He knew something was following him before he had taken half a dozen steps. Two hundred yards don't sound like a great distance. First right, then left, and you're home. But here it seemed to stretch out interminably, as such things do in dreams.

"He did not want to leave the taxi driver. The driver thought this was because Tony doubted his honesty about bringing the luggage on when the wheel was repaired. But it was not that.

"For the first part of the way Tony walked rapidly. The other thing walked at an equal pace behind him. By the light of a street lamp Tony could see the wet fur collar on the coat, but nothing else. Afterwards he increased his pace to what was almost a run; and, though no difference could be seen in the gait of what was behind him, it was still there.

"Unlike you, Tony didn't wonder whether it might be good or evil. These nice differences don't occur to you when you're dealing with something that may be dead. All he knew was that he mustn't let it *identify* itself with him or he was done for.

"Then it began to gain on him, and he ran.

"The pavement was black, the snow dirty gray. He saw the familiar turning, where front gardens were built up above the low stone walls; he saw the street sign fastened to one of those corners, white lettering on black; and in sudden blind panic he plunged for the steps that led up to his home.

"The house was dark. He got the cold keys out of his pocket, but the key ring slipped round in his fingers like soap in bathweater and fell on the tiled floor of the vestibule. He groped after it in the dark – just as the thing turned in at the gate. In fact, Tony heard the gate creak. He found the keys, found the lock by a miracle, and opened the door.

"But he was too late, because the other thing was already coming up the front steps. Tony says that at close range, against a street lamp, the fur collar looked more wet and motheaten; that is all he can describe. He was in a dark hall with the door open. Even familiar things had fled his wits and he could not remember the position of the light switch.

"The other person walked in.

"In his hip pocket, Tony remembered, he still had the weapon he had carried round the world. He fumbled under his overcoat to get the gun out of his pocket; but even that weak gesture was no good to him, for he dropped the gun on the carpet. Since the visitor was now within six feet of him, Tony did not stop. He bolted up the stairs.

"At the top of the stairs he risked a short glance down. The other thing had stopped. In the faint bluish patches of light which came through the open front door, Tony could see that it was stooping down to pick up the automatic pistol from the carpet.

"Tony thinks – now – that he began to switch on lights in the upper hall. Also, he shouted something. He was standing before the door of his bedroom. He threw open this door, blundered in, and began to turn on more lamps. He had got two lamps lighted before he turned to look at the bed, which was occupied.

"The man on the bed did not, however, sit up at the coming of noise or lights. A sheet covered him from head to feet, and even under the outline of the sheet you could trace the line of the wasted, sunken features.

"Tony Marvell then did what was perhaps the most courageous act of his life. He had to know. He walked across and turned down the upper edge of the sheet, and looked down at a dead face, turned sightlessly up from the bed. His own face.

"Shock? Yes. But more terror? No. For this dead man was real, he was flesh and blood – as Tony was flesh and blood. He looked exactly like Tony. But it was now no question of a real world and an unreal world; it was no question of going mad. This man was real; and that meant fraud and imposture.

"A voice from across the room said: '*So*

you're alive!' And Tony turned round – to find his brother Stephen looking at him from the doorway.

"Stephen wore a red dressing gown, hastily pulled round him, and his hair was tousled. His face was one of collapse.

"'I didn't mean to do it!' Stephen was crying out at him. Even though Tony did not understand, he felt that the words were a confession of guilt; they were babbling words – words which made you pity the man who said them.

"'I never really meant to have you killed aboard that ship,' said Stephen. 'It was all a joke. You know I wouldn't have hurt you; you know that, don't you? Listen –'

"Now Stephen was standing in the doorway, clutching his dressing gown round him. What made him look round towards the hall behind, Tony did not know. Perhaps he heard a sound behind him. Perhaps he saw something out of the corner of his eye. But Stephen did look round, and he began to scream.

"Tony saw no more, for the light in the hall went out. The fear was back on him again, and he could not move. He saw a hand. It was only, so to speak, the flicker of a hand.

"This hand darted in from the darkness
341

out in the hall; it caught hold of the knob on the bedroom door, and closed the door. It turned a key on the outside, locking Tony into the room. It kept Stephen outside in the dark hall – and Stephen was still screaming.

"A good thing, too, that Tony had been locked in the room. That saved trouble with the police afterwards.

"The rest of the testimony comes from Mrs. Beach, the housekeeper. Her room was next door to Stephen's bedroom at the end of the upstairs hall. She was awakened by screams, by what seemed to be thrashing sounds, and the noise of hard breathing. These sounds passed her door towards Stephen's room.

"Just as she was getting out of her bed and putting on a dressing gown, she heard Stephen's door close. Just as she went out into the hall, she heard, for the second time in forty-eight hours, the noise of a pistol shot.

"Now, Mrs. Beach will testify in a coroner's court that nobody left or could have left Stephen's room after the shot. She was looking at the door, though it was several minutes before she could screw up enough courage to open the door. When she did open it, all sounds had ceased.

"He had been shot through the right temple at close range – presumably by himself, since the weapon was discovered in a tangle of stained bed-clothing. There was nobody else in the room, and all the windows were locked on the inside. The only other thing Mrs. Beach noticed was an unpleasant – an intensely unpleasant – smell of mildewed cloth and wet fur."

Again Commissioner Hargreaves paused. It seemed that he had come to the end of the story. An outsider might have thought, too, that he had emphasized these horrors too much, for the girl across from him kept her hands pressed against her eyes. But Hargreaves knew his business.

"Well?" he said gently. "You see the explanation, don't you?"

Judith took her hands away from her eyes. "Explanation?"

"The natural explanation," repeated Hargreaves, spacing his words. "Tony Marvell is not going mad. He never had any brain-storms or 'blind flashes.' He only thought he had. The whole thing was a cruel and murderous fake, engineered by Stephen, and it went wrong. But if it had succeeded, Stephen Marvell would have committed a perfect murder."

The relief he saw flash across Judith's face, the sudden dazed catching at hope, went to Hargreaves' heart. But he did not show this.

"Let's go back eight months," he went on, "and take it from the beginning. Now, Tony is a very wealthy young man. The distinguished Stephen, on the other hand, was swamped with debts and always on the thin edge of bankruptcy. If Tony were to die, Stephen, the next of kin, would inherit the whole estate. So Stephen decided that Tony had to die.

"But Stephen, a medical man, knew the risks of murder. No matter how cleverly you plan it, there is always *some* suspicion; and Stephen was bound to be suspected. He was unwilling to risk those prying detectives, those awkward questions, those damning post-mortem reports – until, more than eight months ago, he suddenly saw how he could destroy Tony without the smallest suspicion attaching to himself.

"In St. Jude's Hospital, where he did some charity work, Stephen had found a broken-down ex-schoolmaster named Rupert Hayes. Every man in this world, they say, has his exact double. Hayes was Tony's double to the slightest feature. He was, in fact, so uncannily like Tony that the very sight of him made Stephen flinch.

"Now, Hayes was dying of tuberculosis. He had, at most, not more than a year to live. He would be eager to listen to any scheme

344

which would allow him to spend the rest of his life in luxury and die of natural causes in a soft bed. To him, Stephen explained the trick.

"Tony should be ordered off – apparently – on a trip round the world. On the night he was to sail, Tony should be allowed to go aboard.

"Hayes should be waiting aboard that same ship, with a gun in his pocket. After Stephen or any other friends had left the ship conveniently early, Hayes should entice Tony up to the dark boat-deck. Then he was to shoot Tony through the head and drop the body overboard.

"Haven't you ever realized that a giant ocean liner, just before it leaves port, is the ideal place to commit a murder? Not a soul will remember you afterwards. The passengers notice nothing; they are too excited. The crew notice nothing; they are kept too busy. The confusion of the crowd is intense.

"And what happens to your victim after he goes overboard? He will be sucked under and presently caught by the terrible propellers, to make him unrecognizable. When a body is found – if it is found at all – it will be presumed to be some dock roisterer. Certainly it will never be connected with the ocean liner, because there will be nobody missing from the liner's passenger list.

"Missing from the passenger list? Of course not! Hayes, you see was to go to the Purser and order Tony's luggage to be sent ashore. He was to say he was cancelling the trip, and not going after all. After killing Tony he was then to walk ashore as –"

"The girl uttered an exclamation.

Hargreaves nodded. "You see it now. He was to walk ashore *as Tony*. He was to say to his friends that he couldn't face the journey after all; and everybody would be happy. Why not? The real Tony was within an ace of doing just that.

"Then, Hayes, well coached, would simply settle down to play the part of Tony for the rest of his natural life. Mark that: his natural life – a year at most. He would be too ill to attend to the business, of course. He wouldn't even see you, his fiancée, too often. If ever he made any bad slips, that, of course, would be his bad nerves. He would be allowed to 'develop' lung trouble. At the end of a year, amid sorrowing friends ...

"Stephen had planned brilliantly. 'Murder'? What do you mean, murder? Let the doctors examine as much as they like! Let the police ask what questions they like!

346

Whatever steps are taken, Stephen Marvell is absolutely safe. For the poor devil in bed really has died a natural death.

"Only – well, it went wrong. Hayes wasn't cut out to be a murderer. I hadn't the favor of his acquaintance, but he must have been a decent sort. He promised to do this. But when it came to the actual fact, he couldn't force himself to kill Tony – literally, physically couldn't.

"He threw away his pistol and ran. On the other hand, once off the ship, he couldn't confess to Stephen that Tony was still alive. He couldn't give up that year of sweet luxury, with all Tony's money at his disposal to soothe his aching lungs. So he pretended to Stephen that he had done the job, and Stephen danced for joy.

"But Hayes, as the months went on, did not dance. He knew Tony wasn't dead. He knew there would be a reckoning soon. And he couldn't let it end like that. A week before he thought Tony was coming home, after writing a letter to the police to explain everything, Hayes shot himself rather than face exposure."

There was a silence. "That, I think," Hargreaves said quietly, "explains everything about Tony."

Judith Gates bit her lips. Her pretty face

347

was working, and she could not control the twitching of her capable hands. For a moment she seemed to be praying.

"Thank God!" she murmured. "I was afraid –"

"Yes," said Hargreaves; "I know."

"But it still doesn't explain *everything*. It –"

Hargreaves stopped her.

"I said," he pointed out, "that it explains everything about Tony. That's all you need worry about. Tony is free. You are free. As for Stephen Marvell's death, it was suicide. That is the official record."

"But that's absurd!" cried Judith. "I didn't like Stephen; I always knew he hated Tony; but he wasn't one to kill himself, even if he was exposed. Don't you see, you haven't explained the one real horror? I must know. I mean, I must know if you think what I think about it.

"Who was the man with the brown fur collar? Who followed Tony home that night? Who stuck close by him, to keep the evil influences off him? Who was his guardian? Who shot Stephen in revenge?"

Sir Charles Hargreaves looked down at the sputtering gas fire. His face, inscrutable, was wrinkled in sharp lines from mouth to nostril. His brain held many secrets. He was ready to lock away this one, once he knew that they understood each other.

"You tell me," he said.

CLAYTON RAWSON

Off the Face of the Earth

The lettering in neat gilt script on the door read: *Miracles For Sale,* and beneath it was the familiar rabbit-from-a-hat trademark. Inside, behind the glass showcase counter, in which was displayed an unlikely an assortment of objects as could be got together in one spot, stood The Great Merlini.

He was wrapping up half a dozen billiard balls, several bouquets of feather flowers, a dove pan, a Talking Skull, and a dozen decks of cards for a customer who snapped his fingers and nonchalantly produced the needed number of five-dollar bills from thin air. Merlini rang up the sale, took half a carrot from the cash drawer, and gave it to the large white rabbit who watched proceedings with a pink skeptical eye from the top of a nearby escape trunk. Then he turned to me.

"Clairvoyance, mind-reading, extra-sensory perception," he said. "We stock only the best grade. And it tells me that you came to pick up the two Annie Oakleys I

350

promised to get you for that new hit musical. I have them right here."

But his occult powers slipped a bit. He looked in all his coat pockets one after another, found an egg, a three-foot length of rope, several brightly colored silk handkerchiefs, and a crumpled telegram reading: NEED INVISIBLE MAN AT ONCE. SHIP UNIONTOWN BY MONDAY. – NEMO THE ENIGMA. Then he gave a surprised blink and scowled darkly at a sealed envelope that he had fished out of his inside breast pocket.

"That," I commented a bit sarcastically, "doesn't look like a pair of theater tickets."

He shook his head sadly. "No. It's a letter my wife asked me to mail a week ago."

I took it from him. "There's a mail chute by the elevators about fifteen feet outside your door. I'm no magician, but I can remember to put this in it on my way out." I indicated the telegram that lay on the counter. "Since when have you stocked a supply of invisible men? That I would like to see."

Merlini frowned at the framed slogan: *Nothing Is Impossible* which hung above the cash register. "You want real miracles, don't you? We guarantee that our invisible man can't be seen. But if you'd like to see how impossible it is to see him, step right this way."

In the back, beyond his office, there is a larger room that serves as workshop, shipping department and, on occasion, as a theater. I stood there a moment later and watched Merlini step into an upright coffin-shaped box in the center of the small stage. He faced me, smiled, and snapped his fingers. Two copper electrodes in the side walls of the cabinet spat flame, and a fat green electric spark jumped the gap just above his head, hissing and writhing. He lifted his arms; the angry stream of energy bent, split in two, fastened on his fingertips, and then disappeared as he grasped the gleaming spherical electrodes, one with each hand.

For a moment nothing happened; then, slowly, his body began to fade into transparency as the cabinet's back wall became increasingly visible through it. Clothes and flesh melted until only the bony skeletal structure remained. Suddenly, the jawbone moved and its grinning white teeth clicked as Merlini's voice said:

"You must try this, Ross. On a hot day like today, it's most comfortable."

As it spoke, the skeleton also wavered and grew dim. A moment later it was gone and
352

the cabinet was, or seemed to be, empty. If Merlini still stood there, he was certainly invisible.

"Okay, Gypsy Rose Lee," I said. "I have now seen the last word in strip-tease performances." Behind me I heard the office door open and I looked over my shoulder to see Inspector Gavigan giving me a fishy stare. "You'd better get dressed again," I added. "We have company."

The Inspector looked around the room and at the empty stage, then at me again, cautiously this time. "If you said what I think you did –"

He stopped abruptly as Merlini's voice, issuing from nowhere, chuckled and said, "Don't jump to conclusions, Inspector. Appearances are deceptive. It's not an indecent performance, nor has Ross gone off his rocker and started talking to himself. I'm right here. On the stage."

Gavigan looked and saw the skeleton shape taking form within the cabinet. He closed his eyes, shook his head, then looked again. That didn't help. The grisly spectre was still there and twice as substantial. Then, wraithlike, Merlini's body began to form around it and, finally, grew opaque and solid. The magician grinned broadly, took his hands from the electrodes, and bowed as the spitting green discharge of energy crackled once more above him. Then the stage curtains closed.

"You should be glad that's only an illusion," I told Gavigan. "If it were the McCoy and the underworld ever found out how it was done, you'd face an unparalleled crime wave and you'd never solve a single case."

"It's the Pepper's Ghost illusion brought up to date," Merlini said as he stepped out between the curtains and came toward us. "I've got more orders than I can fill. It's a sure-fire carnival draw." He frowned at Gavigan. "But *you* don't look very entertained."

"I'm not," the Inspector answered gloomily. "Vanishing into thin air may amuse some people. Not me. Especially when it really happens. Off stage in broad daylight. In Central Park."

"Oh," Merlini said. "I see. So that's what's eating you. Helen Hope, the chorus girl who went for a walk last week and never came back. She's still missing then, and there are still no clues?"

Gavigan nodded. "It's the Dorothy Arnold case all over again. Except for one thing we haven't let the newspapers know about – Bela Zyyzk."

"Bela what?" I asked.

354

Gavigan spelled it.

"Impossible," I said. "He must be a typographical error. A close relative of Etoain Shrdlu."

The Inspector wasn't amused. "Relatives," he growled. "I wish I could find some. He not only claims he doesn't have any – he swears he never has had any! And so far we haven't been able to prove different."

"Where does he come from?" Merlini asked. "Or won't he say?"

"Oh, he talks all right," Gavigan said disgustedly. "Too much. And none of it makes any sense. He says he's a momentary visitor to this planet – from the dark cloud of Antares. I've seen some high, wide, and fancy screwballs in my time, but this one takes the cake – candles and all."

"Helen Hope," Merlini said, "vanishes off the face of the earth. And Zyyzk does just the opposite. This gets interesting. What else does he have to do with her disappearance?"

"Plenty," Gavigan replied. "A week ago Tuesday night she went to a Park Avenue party at Mrs. James Dewitt-Smith's. She's another candidate for Bellevue. Collects Tibetan statuary, medieval relics, and crackpots like Zyyzk. He was there that night – reading minds."

"A visitor from outer space," Merlini said, "and a mindreader to boot. I won't be happy until I've had a talk with that gentleman."

"I have talked with him," the Inspector growled. "And I've had indigestion ever since. He does something worse than read minds. He makes predictions." Gavigan scowled at Merlini. "I thought fortune tellers always kept their customers happy by predicting good luck?"

Merlini nodded. "That's usually standard operating procedure. Zyyzk does something else?"

"He certainly does. He's full of doom and disaster. A dozen witnesses testify that he told Helen Hope she'd vanish off the face of the earth. And three days later that's exactly what she does do."

"I can see," Merlini said, "why you view him with suspicion. So you pulled him in for questioning and got a lot of answers that weren't very helpful?"

"Helpful!" Gavigan jerked several typewritten pages from his pocket and shook them angrily. "Listen to this. He's asked: 'What's your age?' and we get: 'According to which time – solar, sidereal, galactic, or universal?' Murphy of Missing Persons, who was questioning him, says: 'Any kind. Just tell us how old you are.' And Zyyzk replies:

356

'I can't answer that. The question, in that form, has no meaning.'" The Inspector threw the papers down disgustedly.

Merlini picked them up, riffled through them, then read some of the transcript aloud. "Question: How did you know that Miss Hope would disappear? Answer: Do you understand the basic theory of the fifth law of interdimensional reaction? Murphy: Huh? Zyyzk: Explanations are useless. You obviously have no conception of what I am talking about."

"He was right about that," Gavigan muttered. "Nobody does."

Merlini continued. "Question: Where is Miss Hope now? Answer: Beyond recall. She was summoned by the Lords of the Outer Darkness." Merlini looked up from the papers. "After that, I suppose, you sent him over to Bellevue?"

The Inspector nodded. "They had him under observation a week. And they turned in a report full of eight-syllable jawbreakers all meaning he's crazy as a bedbug – but harmless. I don't believe it. Anybody who predicts in a loud voice that somebody will disappear into thin air at twenty minutes after four on a Tuesday afternoon just before it actually happens, knows plenty about it!"

Merlini is a hard man to surprise, but even

he blinked at that. "Do you mean to say that he foretold the exact time, too?"

"Right on the nose," Gavigan answered. "The doorman of her apartment house saw her walk across the street and into Central Park at four-eighteen. We haven't been able to find anyone who has seen her since. And don't tell me his prediction was a long shot that paid off."

"I won't," Merlini agreed. "Whatever it is, it's not coincidence. Where's Zyyzk now? Could you hold him after that psychiatric report?"

"The D.A.," Gavigan replied, "took him into General Sessions before Judge Keeler and asked that he be held as a material witness." The Inspector looked unhappier than ever. "It would have to be Keeler."

"What did he do?" I asked. "Deny the request?"

"No. He granted it. That's when Zyyzk made his second prediction. Just as they start to take him out and throw him back in the can, he makes some funny motions with his hands and announces, in that confident manner he's got, that the Outer Darkness is going to swallow Judge Keeler up, too!"

"And what," Merlini wanted to know, "is wrong with that? Knowing how you've

358

always felt about Francis X. Keeler, I should think that prospect would please you."

Gavigan exploded. "Look, blast it! I have wished dozens of times that Judge Keeler would vanish into thin air, but that's exactly what I don't want to happen right now. We've known at headquarters that he's been taking fix money from the Castelli mob ever since the day he was appointed to the bench. But we couldn't do a thing. Politically he was dynamite. One move in his direction and there'd be a new Commissioner the next morning, with demotions all down the line. But three weeks ago the Big Guy and Keeler had a scrap, and we get a tip straight from the feed box that Keeler is fair game. So we start working overtime collecting the evidence that will send him up the river for what I hope is a ninety-nine-year stretch. We've been afraid he might tumble and try to pull another 'Judge Crater.' And now, just when we're almost, but not quite, ready to nail him and make it stick, this has to happen."

"Your friend, Zyyzk," Merlini said, "becomes more interesting by the minute. Keeler is being tailed, of course?"

"Twenty-four hours a day, ever since we got the word that there'd be no kick-back." The phone on Merlini's desk rang as

Gavigan was speaking. "I get hourly reports on his movements. Chances are that's for me now."

It was. In the office, we both watched him as he took the call. He listened a moment, then said, "Okay. Double the number of men on him immediately. And report back every fifteen minutes. If he shows any sign of going anywhere near a railroad station or airport, notify me at once."

Gavigan hung up and turned to us. "Keeler made a stop at the First National and spent fifteen minutes in the safety-deposit vaults. He's carrying a suitcase, and you can have one guess as to what's in it now. This looks like the payoff."

"I take it," Merlini said, "that this time the Zyyzk forecast did not include the exact hour and minute when the Outer Darkness would swallow up the Judge?"

"Yeah. He sidestepped that. All he'll say is that it'll happen before the week is out."

"And today," Merlini said, "is Friday. Tell me this. The Judge seems to have good reasons for wanting to disappear which Zyyzk may or may not know about. Did Miss Hope also have reasons?"

"She had one," Gavigan replied. "But I don't see how Zyyzk could have known it. We can't find a thing that shows he ever set eyes on her before the night of that party. And her reason is one that few people knew about." The phone rang again and Gavigan reached for it. "Helen Hope is the girl friend Judge Keeler visits the nights he doesn't go home to his wife!"

Merlini and I both tried to assimilate that and take in what Gavigan was telling the telephone at the same time. "Okay, I'm coming. And grab him the minute he tries to go through a gate." He slammed the receiver down and started for the door.

"Keeler," he said over his shoulder, "is in Grand Central. There's room in my car if you want to come."

He didn't need to issue that invitation twice. On the way down in the elevator Merlini made one not very helpful comment.

"You know," he said thoughtfully, "if the Judge does have a reservation on the extra-terrestrial express – destination: the Outer Darkness – we don't know what gate that train leaves from."

We found out soon enough. The Judge stepped through it just two minutes before we hurried into the station and found Lieutenant Malloy exhibiting all the symptoms of having been hit over the head with a sledge hammer. He was bewildered and dazed, and had difficulty talking coherently.

Sergeant Hicks, a beefy, unimaginative, elderly detective who had also seen the thing happen, looked equally groggy.

Usually Malloy's reports were as dispassionate, precise, and factual as a logarithmic table. But not today. His first paragraph bore a much closer resemblance to a first-person account of a dope addict's dream.

"Malloy," Gavigan broke in icily. "Are you tight?"

The Lieutenant shook his head sadly. "No, but the minute I go off duty, I'm going to get so plas –"

Gavigan cut in again. "Are all the exits to this place covered?"

Hicks replied, "If they aren't, somebody is sure going to catch it."

Gavigan turned to the detective who had accompanied us in the Inspector's car. "Make the rounds and double-check that, Brady. And tell headquarters to get more men over here fast."

"They're on the way now," Hicks said. "I phoned right after it happened. First thing I did."

Gavigan turned to Malloy. "All right.

Take it easy. One thing at a time – and in order."

"It don't make sense that way either," Malloy said hopelessly. "Keeler took a cab from the bank and came straight here. Hicks and I were right on his tail. He comes down to the lower level and goes into the Oyster Bar and orders a double brandy. While he's working on that, Hicks phones in for reinforcements with orders to cover every exit. They had time to get here, too; Keeler had a second brandy. Then, when he starts to come out, I move out to the center of the station floor by the information booth so I'm ahead of him and all set to make the pinch no matter which gate he heads for. Hicks stands pat, ready to tail him if he heads upstairs again.

"At first, that's where I think he's going because he starts up the ramp. But he stops here by this line of phone booths, looks in a directory, and then goes into a booth halfway down the line. And as soon as he closes the door, Hicks moves up and goes into the next booth to the left of Keeler's." Malloy pointed. "The one with the Out-of-Order sign on it."

Gavigan turned to the Sergeant. "All right. You take it."

Hicks scowled at the phone booth as he

spoke. "The door was closed and somebody had written 'Out of Order' on a card and stuck it in the edge of the glass. I lifted the card so nobody'd wonder why I was trying to use a dead phone, went in, closed the door, and tried to get a load of what the Judge was saying. But it was no good. He was talking, but so low I couldn't get it. I came out again, stuck the card back in the door, and walked back toward the Oyster Bar so I'd be set to follow him either way when he came out. And I took a gander into the Judge's booth as I went past. He was talking with his mouth up close to the phone."

"And then," Malloy continued, "we wait. And we wait. He went into that booth at five-ten. At five-twenty I get itchy feet. I begin to think maybe he's passed out or died of suffocation or something. Nobody in his right mind stays in a phone booth for ten minutes when the temperature is ninety like today. So I start to move in just as Hicks get the same idea. He's closer than I am, so I stay put.

"Hicks stops just in front of the booth and lights a cigarette, which gives him a chance to take another look inside. Then I figure I must be right about the Judge having passed out. I see the match Hicks is holding drop, still lighted, and he turns quick and plasters

364

his face against the glass. I don't wait. I'm ready on my way when he turns and motions for me."

Malloy hesitated briefly. Then, slowly and very precisely, he let us have it. "I don't care if the Commissioner himself has me up on the carpet, one thing I'm sure of – *I hadn't taken my eyes off that phone booth for one single split second since the Judge walked into it.*"

"And neither," Hicks said with equal emphasis, "did I. Not for one single second."

"I did some fancy open-field running through the commuters," Malloy went on, "skidded to a stop behind Hicks, and looked over his shoulder."

Gavigan stepped forward to the closed door of the booth and looked in.

"And what you see," Malloy finished, "is just what I saw. You can ship me down to Bellevue for observation, too. It's impossible. It doesn't make sense. I don't believe it. But that's exactly what happened."

For a moment Gavigan didn't move. Then, slowly, he pulled the door open.

The booth was empty.

The phone receiver dangled off the hook, and on the floor there was a pair of horn-rimmed spectacles, one lens smashed.

"Keeler's glasses," Hicks said. "He went

into that booth and I had my eyes on it every second. He never came out. And he's not in it."

"And that," Malloy added in a tone of utter dejection, "isn't the half of it. I stepped inside, picked up the phone receiver Keeler had been using, and said, 'Hello' into the mouthpiece. There was a chance the party he'd been talking to might still be on the other end." Malloy came to a full stop.

"Well?" Gavigan prodded him. "Let's have it. Somebody answered?"

"Yes. Somebody said: *'This is the end of the trail, Lieutenant.'* Then – hung up."

"You didn't recognize the voice?"

"Yeah, I recognized it. That's the trouble. It was *Judge Keeler!*"

Silence.

Then, quietly, Merlini asked, "You are quite certain it was his voice, Malloy?"

The Lieutenant exploded. "I'm not sure of anything any more! But if you've ever heard Keeler – he sounds like a bullfrog with a cold – you'd know it couldn't be anyone else."

Gavigan's voice, or rather a hollow imitation of it, cut in. "Merlini. Either Malloy and Hicks have both gone completely off their chumps or this is the one phone booth in the world that has two exits. The

366

back wall is sheet metal backed by solid marble, but if there's a loose panel in one of the side walls, Keeler could have moved over into the empty booth that is supposed to be out of order."

"Is supposed to be," Malloy repeated. "so that's it! The sign's a phony. That phone isn't on the blink, and his voice –" Malloy took two swift steps into the booth. He lifted the receiver, dropped a nickel, and waited for the dial tone. He scowled. He jiggled the receiver. He repeated the whole operation.

This specimen of Mr. Bell's invention was definitely not working.

A moment or two later Merlini reported another flaw in the Inspector's theory. "There are," he stated after a quick but thorough inspection of both booths, "no sliding panels, hinged panels, removable sections, trap doors, or any other form of secret exit. The side walls are single sheets of metal, thin but intact. The back wall is even more solid. There is one exit and one only – the door through which our vanishing man entered."

"He didn't come out," Sergeant Hicks insisted again, sounding like a cracked phonograph record endlessly repeating itself. "I was watching that door every single second. Even if he turned himself into an invisible man like in a movie I saw once, he'd still have had to open the door. And the door didn't budge. I was watching it every single –"

"And that," Merlini said thoughtfully, "leaves us with an invisible man who can also walk through closed doors. In short – a ghost. Which brings up another point. Have any of you noticed that there are a few spots of something on those smashed glasses that look very much like – blood?"

Malloy growled. "Yeah, but don't make any cracks about there being another guy in that booth who sapped Keeler – that'd mean *two* invisible men."

"If there can be one invisible man," Merlini pointed out, "then there can be two."

Gavigan said, "Merlini, that vanishing gadget you were demonstrating when I arrived – it's just about the size and shape of this phone booth. I want to know –"

The magician shook his head. "Sorry, Inspector. That method wouldn't work here under these conditions. It's not the same trick. Keeler's miracle, in some respects, is even better. He should have been a magician; he's been wasting his time on the bench. Or has he? I wonder how much cash he carried into limbo with him in that suitcase?" He paused, then added, "More than enough, probably, to serve as a motive for murder."

And there, on that ominous note, the investigation stuck. It was as dead an end as I ever saw. And it got deader by the minute. Brady, returning a few minutes later, reported that all station exits had been covered by the time Keeler left the Oyster Bar and that none of the detectives had seen hide nor hair of him since.

"Those men stay there until further notice," Gavigan ordered. "Get more men – as many as you need – and start searching this place. I want every last inch of it covered. And every phone booth, too. If it was Keeler's voice Malloy heard, then he was in one of them, and –"

"You know, Inspector," Merlini interrupted, "this case not only takes the cake but the marbles, all the blue ribbons, and a truckload of loving cups, too. That is another impossibility."

"What is?"

"The voice on the telephone. Look at it. If Keeler left the receiver in this booth off as Malloy and Hicks found it, vanished, then reappeared in another booth and tried to call this number, he'd get a busy signal. He couldn't have made a connection. And if he left the receiver on the hook, he could have called this number, but someone would have had to be here to lift the receiver and leave it off as it was found. It keeps adding up to two invisible men no matter how you look at it."

"I wish," Malloy said acidly, "that you'd disappear, too."

Merlini protested. "Don't. You sound like Zyyzk."

"That guy," Gavigan predicted darkly, "is going to wish he never heard of Judge Keeler."

Gavigan's batting average as a prophet was zero. When Zyyzk, whom the Inspector ordered brought to the scene and who was delivered by squad car twenty minutes later, discovered that Judge Keeler had vanished, he was as pleased as punch.

An interstellar visitor from outer space should have three eyes, or at least green hair. Zyyzk, in that respect, was a disappointment. He was a pudgy little man in a wrinkled gray suit. His eyes, two only, were a pale washed-out blue behind gold-rimmed bifocals, and his hair, the color of weak tea, failed miserably in its attempt to cover the top of his head.

His manner, however, was charged with an abundant and vital confidence, and there was a haughty, imperious quality in his high thin voice which hinted that there was much more to Mr. Zyyzk than met the eye.

"I issued distinct orders," he told Gavigan in an icy tone, "that I was never, under any circumstances, to be disturbed between the sidereal hours of five and seven post-meridian. You know that quite well, Inspector. Explain why these idiots have disobeyed. At once!"

If there is any quicker way of bringing an inspector of police to a boil, I don't know what it is. The look Gavigan gave the little man would have wrecked a Geiger counter. He opened his mouth. But the searing blast of flame which I expected didn't issue forth. He closed his mouth and swallowed. The Inspector was speechless.

Zyyzk calmly threw more fuel on the fire. "Well," he said impatiently, tapping his foot, "I'm waiting."

A subterranean rumble began in Gavigan's interior and then, a split second before he blew his top, Merlini said quietly, "I understand, Mr. Zyyzk, that you read minds?"

Zyyzk, still the Imperial Roman Emperor, gave Merlini a scathing look. "I do," he said. "And what of it?"

"For a mind-reader," Merlini told him,

371

"you ask a lot of questions. I should think you'd know why you've been brought here."

That didn't bother the visitor from Outer Space. He stared intently at Merlini for a second, glanced once at Gavigan, then closed his eyes. The fingertips of one white hand pressed against his brow. Then he smiled.

"I see. Judge Keeler."

"Keeler?" Gavigan pretended surprise. "What about him?"

Zyyzk wasn't fooled. He shook his head. "Don't try to deceive me, Inspector. It's childish. The Judge has vanished. Into the Outer Darkness – as I foretold." He grinned broadly. "You will, of course, release me now."

"I'll – I'll *what?*"

Zyyzk spread his hands. "You have no choice. Not unless you want to admit that I could sit in a police cell surrounded on all sides by steel bars and cause Judge Keeler to vanish off the face of the earth by will power alone. Since that, to your limited, earthly intelligence, is impossible. I have an impregnable alibi. Good day, Inspector."

The little man actually started to walk off. The detectives who stood on either side were so dazed by his treatment of the Inspector that Zyyzk had gone six feet before they came to life again and grabbed him.

Whether the strange powers he claimed were real or not, his ability to render Gavigan speechless was certtainly uncanny. The Inspector's mouth opened, but again nothing came out.

Merlini said, "You admit then that you are responsible for the Judge's dis-appearance?"

Zyyzk, still grinning, shook his head. "I predicted it. Beyond that I admit nothing."

"But you know how he vanished?"

The little man shrugged. "In the usual way, naturally. Only an adept of the seventh order would understand."

Merlini suddenly snapped his fingers and plucked a shiny silver dollar from thin air. He dropped it into his left hand, closed his fingers over it, and held his fist out toward Zyyzk. "Perhaps Judge Keeler vanished – like this." Slowly he opened his fingers. The coin was gone.

For the first time a faint crack appeared in the polished surface of Zyyzk's composure. He blinked. "Who," he asked slowly, "are you?"

"An adept," Merlini said solemnly, "of the eighth order. One who is not yet satisfied that you are what you claim to be." He snapped his fingers again, almost under Zyyzk's nose, and the silver dollar reappeared. He offered it to Zyyzk. "A test," he said. "Let me see you send that back into the Outer Darkness from which I summoned it."

Zyyzk no longer grinned. He scowled and his eyes were hard. "It will go," he said, lifting his hand and rapidly tracing a cabalistic figure in the air. "And you with it!"

"Soon?" Merlini asked.

"Very soon. Before the hour of nine strikes again you will appear before the Lords of the Outer Darkness in far Antares. And there –"

Gavigan had had enough. He passed a miracle of his own. He pointed a cabalistic but slightly shaking finger at the little man and roared an incantation that had instant effect.

"Get him out of here!"

In the small space of time that it took them to hurry down the corridor and around a corner, Zyyzk and the two detectives who held him both vanished.

Gavigan turned on Merlini. "Isn't one lunatic enough without you acting like one, too?"

The magician grinned. "Keep your eyes on me, Inspector. If I vanish, as predicted, you may see how Keeler did it. If I don't,

374

Zyyzk is on the spot and he may begin to make more sense."

"That," Gavigan growled, "is impossible."

Zyyzk, as far as I was concerned, wasn't the only thing that made no sense. The Inspector's men turned Grand Central Station inside out and the only trace of Judge Keeler to be found were the smashed spectacles on the floor of that phone booth. Gavigan was so completely at a loss that he could think of nothing else to do but order the search made again.

Merlini, as far as I could tell, didn't seem to have any better ideas. He leaned against the wall opposite the phone booth and scowled darkly at its empty interior. Malloy and Hicks looked so tired and dispirited that Gavigan told them both to go home and sleep it off. An hour later, when the second search had proved as fruitless as the first, Gavigan suddenly told Lieutenant Doran to take over, turned, and started to march off.

Then Merlini woke up. "Inspector," he asked, "where are you going?"

Gavigan turned, scowling. "Anywhere," he said, "where I don't have to look at telephone booths. Do you have any suggestions?"

Merlini moved forward. "One, yes. Let's eat."

Gavigan didn't look as if he could keep anything in his stomach stronger than weak chicken broth, but he nodded absently. We got into Gavigan's car and Brady drove us crosstown, stopping, at Merlini's direction, in front of the Williston Building.

The Inspector objected, "There aren't any decent restaurants in this neighborhood. Why –"

"Don't argue," Merlini said as he got out. "If Zyyzk's latest prediction comes off, this will be my last meal on earth. I want to eat here. Come on." He crossed the pavement toward a flashing green-and-purple neon sign that blinked: *Johnson's Cafeteria. Open All Night*.

Merlini was suddenly acting almost as strangely as Zyyzk. I knew very well that this wasn't the sort of place he'd pick for his last meal and, although he claimed to be hungry, I noticed that all he put on his tray was crackers and a bowl of soup. Pea soup at that – something he heartily disliked.

Then, instead of going to a table off in a corner where we could talk, he chose one right in the center of the room. He even selected our places for us. "You sit there, Inspector. You there, Ross. And excuse me a moment. I'll be right back." With that he turned, crossed to the street door through which we had come, and vanished through it.

"I think," I told Gavigan, "that he's got a bee in his bonnet."

The Inspector grunted. "You mean bats. In his belfry." He gave the veal cutlet on his plate a glum look.

Merlini was gone perhaps five minutes. When he returned, he made no move to sit down. He leaned over the table and asked, "Either of you got a nickel?"

I found one and handed it to him. Suspiciously, Gavigan said, "I thought you wanted to eat?"

"I must make a phone call first," the magician answered. "And with Zyyzk's prediction hanging over me, I'd just as soon you both watched me do it. Look out the window behind me, watch that empty booth – the second from the right. And keep your eyes on it every second." He glanced at his wristwatch. "If I'm not back here in exactly three minutes, you'd better investigate."

I didn't like the sound of that. Neither did Gavigan. He started to object. "Now, wait a minute. You're not going –"

But Merlini had already gone. He moved

with long strides toward the street door, and the Inspector half rose from his chair as if to go after him. Then, when Gavigan saw what lay beyond the window, he stopped. The window we both faced was in a side wall at right angles to the street, and it opened not to the outside but into the arcade that runs through the Williston Building.

Through the glass we could see a twenty-foot stretch of the arcade's opposite wall and, against it, running from side to side, was a row of half a dozen phone booths.

I took a quick look at the clock on the wall above the window just as Merlini vanished through the street door. He reappeared at once in the arcade beyond the window, went directly to the second booth from the right, and went inside. The door closed.

"I don't like this," I said. "In three minutes the time will be exactly –"

"Quiet!" Gavigan commanded.

"– exactly nine o'clock," I finished. "Zyyzk's deadline!"

"He's not going to pull this off," Gavigan said. "You keep your eyes on that booth. I'm going outside and watch it from the street entrance. When the time's up, join me."

I heard his chair scrape across the floor as he got up, but I kept my eyes glued to the scene beyond the window – more precisely, to one section of it – the booth into which Merlini had gone. I could see the whole face of the door from top to bottom and the dim luminescence of the light inside.

Nothing happened.

The second hand on the wall clock moved steadily, but much too slowly. At five seconds to the hour I found myself on my feet. And when the hand hit twelve I moved fast. I went through the door, turned left, and found Gavigan just inside the arcade entrance, his eyes fixed on the booth.

"Okay," he said without turning his head. "Come on."

We hurried forward together. The Inspector jerked the door of the second booth open. The light inside blinked out.

Inside, the telephone receiver dangled, still swaying, by its cord.

The booth was empty.

Except for one thing. I bent down and picked it up off the floor – Merlini's shiny silver dollar.

Gavigan swore. Then he pushed me aside, stepped into the booth, and lifted the receiver. His voice was none too steady. He said one word into the phone.

"Hello?"

Leaning in behind him, I heard the voice that replied – Merlini's voice making a statement that was twice as impossible as anything that had happened yet.

"Listen carefully," it said. "And don't ask questions now. I'm at 1462-12 Astoria Avenue, The Bronx. Got that? 1462-12 Astoria. Keeler's here – and a murderer! *Hurry!*"

The tense urgency of that last command sent a cold shiver down my spine. Then I heard the click as the connection was broken.

Gavigan stood motionless for a second, holding the dead phone. Then the surging flood of his emotions spilled over. He jiggled the receiver frantically and swore again.

"Blast it! This phone is dead!"

I pulled myself out of a mental tailspin, found a nickel, and dropped it in the slot. Gavigan's verbal fireworks died to a mutter as he heard the dial tone and he jabbed savagely at the dial.

A moment later the Telegraph Bureau was broadcasting a bowdlerized version of Gavigan's orders to the prowl cars in the Astoria Avenue neighborhood. And Gavigan and I were running for the street and his own car. Brady saw us coming, gunned his motor, and the instant we were aboard took off as though jet-powered. He made a banked turn into Fifth Avenue against a red light and we raced uptown, siren screaming.

If Zyyzk had been there beside us, handing out dire predictions that we were headed straight for the Pearly Gates, I wouldn't have doubted him for a moment. We came within inches of that destination half a dozen times as we roared swerving through the cross-town traffic.

The Astoria address wasn't hard to find. There were three prowl cars parked in front of it and two uniformed cops on the front porch. One sat on the floor, his back to the wall, holding a limp arm whose sleeve was stained with blood. There were two round bullet holes in the glass of the door above him. As we ran up the walk, the sound of gunfire came from the rear of the house and the second cop lifted his foot, kicked in a front window, and crawled in through the opening, gun in hand.

The wounded man made a brief report as we passed him. "Nobody answered the door," he said. "But when we tried to crash the joint, somebody started shooting."

Somebody was still shooting. Gavigan, Brady, and I went through the window and toward the sound. The officer who had preceded us was in the kitchen, firing around the jamb of the back door. An answering gun blazed in the dark outside and the cop fired at the flash.

"Got him, I think," the cop said. Then he slipped out through the door, moved quickly across the porch, and down the steps. Brady followed him.

Gavigan's pocket-flash suddenly sent out a thin beam of light. It started a circuit of the kitchen, stopped for a moment as it picked up movement just outside the door, and we saw a third uniformed man pull himself to a sitting position on the porch floor, look at the bloodstain on his trouser leg, and swear.

Then the Inspector's flash found the open cellar door.

And down there, beside the beginning of a grave, we found Judge Keeler.

His head had been battered in.

But we couldn't find Merlini anywhere in the house. It wasn't until five minutes later, when we were opening Keeler's suitcase, that Merlini walked in.

He looked at the cash and negotiable securities that tumbled out. "You got here," he said, "before that vanished, too, I see."

Gavigan looked up at him. "But you just arrived this minute. I heard a cab out front."

Merlini nodded. "My driver refused to ignore the stop lights the way yours did. Did you find the Judge?"

"Yes, we found him. And I want to know how of all the addresses in Greater New York you managed to pick this one out of your hat?"

Merlini's dark eyes twinkled. "That was the easy part. Keeler's disappearance, as I said once before, added up to *two* invisible men. As soon as I knew who the second one must be, I simply looked the name up in the phone book."

"And when you vanished," I asked, "was that done with two invisible men?"

Merlini grinned. "No. I improved on the Judge's miracle a bit. I made it a one-man operation."

Gavigan had had all the riddles he could digest. "We found Keeler's body," he growled ominously, "beside an open grave. And if *you* don't stop–"

"Sorry," Merlini said, as a lighted cigarette appeared mysteriously between his fingers. "As a magician I hate to have to blow the gaff on such a neatly contrived bit of hocus-pocus as The Great Phone Booth Trick. But if I must – well, it began when Keeler realized he was going to have to take a runout powder. He knew he was being watched. It was obvious that if he and Helen Hope tried to leave town by any of the usual methods, they'd both be picked up at once.

383

Their only chance was to vanish as abruptly and completely as Judge Crater and Dorothy Arnold once did. I suspect it was Zyyzk's first prediction that Miss Hope would disappear that gave Keeler the idea. At any rate, that was what set the wheels in motion."

"I thought so," Gavigan said. "Zyyzk was in on it."

Merlini shook his head. "I'm afraid you can't charge him with a thing. He was in on it – but he didn't know it. One of the subtlest deceptive devices a magician uses is known as 'the principle of the impromptu stooge.' He so manages things that an unrehearsed spectator acts as a confederate, often without ever realizing it. That's how Keeler used Zyyzk. He built his vanishing trick on Zyyzk's predictions and used them as misdirection. But Zyyzk never knew that he was playing the part of a red herring."

"He's a fraud though," Gavigan insisted. "And he does know it."

Merlini contradicted that, too. "No. Oddly enough, he's the one thing in this whole case that is on the level. As you yourself pointed out, no fake prophet would give such precisely detailed predictions. He actually does believe that Helen Hope and Judge Keeler vanished into the Outer Darkness."

"A loony," Gavigan muttered.

"And," Merlini added, "a real problem, at this point, for any psychiatrist. He's seen two of his prophecies come true with such complete and startling accuracy that he'll never believe what really happened. I egged him into predicting my disappearance in order to show him that he wasn't infallible. If he never discovers that I did vanish right on time, it may shake his belief in his occult powers. But if he does, the therapy will backfire; he'll be convinced when he sees me that I'm a doppelganger or an astral double the police have conjured up to discredit him."

"If you don't stop trying to psychoanalyze Zyyzk," Gavigan growled impatiently, "the police are going to conjure up a charge of withholding information in a murder case. Get on with it. Helen Hope wasn't being tailed, so her disappearance was a cinch. She simply walked out, without even taking her toothbrush – to make Zyyzk's prediction look good – and grabbed a plane for Montana or Mexico or some such place where Keeler was to meet her later. But how did Keeler evaporate? And don't you give me any nonsense about two invisible men."

Merlini grinned. "Then we'd better take my disappearance first. That used only one

385

invisible man – and, of course, too many phone booths."

Then, quickly, as Gavigan started to explode, Merlini stopped being cryptic. "In that restaurant you and Ross sat at a table and in the seats that I selected. You saw me, through the window, enter what I had been careful to refer to as the second booth from the right. Seen through the window, that is what it was. But the line of phone booths extended on either side beyond the window and your field of vision. Viewed from outside, there were nine – not six – booths, and the one I entered was actually the third in line."

"Do you mean," Gavigan said menacingly, "that when I was outside watching the second booth, Ross, inside, was watching the third – and we both thought we were watching the same one?"

"Yes. It isn't necessary to deceive the senses if the mind can be misdirected. You saw what you saw, but it wasn't what you thought you saw. And that –"

Then Gavigan did explode, in a muffled sort of way. "Are you saying that we searched the *wrong* phone booth? And that you were right there all the time, sitting in the next one?"

Merlini didn't need to answer. That was obviously just what he did mean.

"Then your silver dollar," I began, "and the phone receiver –"

"Were," Merlini grinned, "what confidence men call 'the convincer' – concocted evidence which seemed to prove that you had the right booth prevented any skeptical second thoughts and kept you from examining the other booths just to make sure you had the right one."

I got it then. "That first time you left the restaurant, before you came back with that phony request for the loan of a nickel – that's when you left the dollar in the second booth."

Merlini nodded. "I made a call, too. I dialed the number of the second booth. And when the phone rang, I stepped into the second booth, took the receiver off the hook, dropped the silver dollar on the floor, then hurried back to your table. Both receivers were off and the line was open."

"And when we looked into the second booth, you were sitting right next door, three feet away, telling Gavigan via the phone that you were in The Bronx?"

Merlini nodded. "And I came out after you had gone. It's a standard conjuring principle. The audience doesn't see the coin, the rabbit, or the girl vanish because they actually disappear either before or after the magician pretends to conjure them into thin air. The audience is watching most carefully at the wrong time."

"Now wait a minute," the Inspector objected. "That's just exactly the way you said Keeler couldn't have handled the phone business. What's more, he couldn't. Ross and I weren't watching you the first time you left the restaurant. But we'd been watching Keeler for a week."

"And," I added, "Malloy and Hicks couldn't have miscounted the booths at the station and searched the wrong one. They could see both ends of that line of booths the whole time."

"They didn't miscount," Merlini said. "They just didn't count. The booth we examined was the fifth from the right end of the line, but neither Malloy nor Hicks ever referred to it in that way."

Gavigan scowled. "They said Keeler went into the booth *to the right of the one that was out of order.*' And the phone in the next booth *was* out of order."

"I know, but Keeler didn't enter the booth next to the one we found out of order. He went into a booth next to one that was

388

marked: Out of Order. That's not quite the same."

Gavigan and I both said the same thing at the same time: "The sign had been moved!"

"Twice," Merlini said, nodding. "First, when Keeler was in the Oyster Bar. The second invisible man – invisible because no one was watching him – moved it one booth to the right. And when Keeler, a few minutes later, entered the booth to the right of the one bearing the sign, he was actually in the second booth from the one whose phone didn't work.

"And then our second invisible man went into action again. He walked into the booth marked out of order, smashed a duplicate pair of blood-smeared glasses on the floor, and dialed the Judge's phone. When Keeler answered, he walked out again, leaving the receiver off the hook. It was as neat a piece of misdirection as I've seen in a long time. Who would suspect him of putting through a call from a phone booth that was plainly labeled out of order?"

Cautiously, as if afraid the answer would blow up in his face, the Inspector asked, "He did all this with Malloy and Hicks both watching? And he wasn't seen – because he was invisible?"

"No, that's not quite right. He was invisible – because he wasn't suspected."

I still didn't see it. "But," I objected, "the only person who went anywhere near the booth next to the one Keeler was in –"

Heavy footsteps sounded on the back porch and then Brady's voice from the doorway said, "We found him, Inspector. Behind some bushes the other side of the wall. Dead. And do you know who –"

"I do now," Gavigan cut in. "Sergeant Hicks."

Brady nodded.

Gavigan turned to Merlini. "Okay, so Hicks was a crooked cop and a liar. But not Malloy. He says he was watching that phone booth every second. How did Hicks switch that Out-of-Order sign back to the original booth again without being seen?"

"He did it when Malloy wasn't watching quite so closely – *after* Malloy thought Keeler had vanished. Malloy saw Hicks look into the booth, act surprised, then beckon hurriedly. Those actions, together with Hicks's later statement that the booth was already empty, made Malloy think the judge had vanished sooner than he really did. Actually Keeler was still right there, sitting in the booth into which Hicks stared. It's the same deception as to time that I used."

"Will you," Gavigan growled, "stop lecturing on the theory of deception and just explain when Hicks moved that sign."

"All right. Remember what Malloy did next? He was near the information booth in the center of the floor and he ran across toward the phones. Malloy said, 'I did some fancy open-field running through the commuters.' Of course he did. At five-twenty the station is full of them and he was in a hell of a hurry. He couldn't run fast and keep his eyes glued to Hicks and that phone booth every step of the way; he'd have had half a dozen head-on collisions. But he didn't think the fact that he had had to use his eyes to steer a course rather than continue to watch the booth was important. He thought the dirty work – Keeler's disappearance – had taken place.

"As Malloy ran toward him through the crowd, Hicks simply took two steps sideways to the left and stared into the phone booth that was tagged with the Out-of-Order card. And, behind his body, his left hand shifted the sign one booth to the left – back to the booth that was genuinely out of order. Both actions took no more than a second or two. When Malloy arrived, 'the booth next to the one that was out of order' was empty. Keeler had vanished into Zyyzk's Outer Darkness *by simply sitting still and not moving at all!*"

"And he really vanished," Gavigan said, finally convinced, "by walking out of the next booth as soon as he had spoken his piece to Malloy on the phone."

"While Malloy," Merlini added, "was still staring goggle-eyed at the phone. Even if he had turned to look out of the door, all he'd have seen was the beefy Hicks standing smack in front of him, carefully blocking the view. And then Keeler walked right out of the station. Every exit was guarded – except one. An exit big enough to drive half a dozen trains through!"

"Okay," the Inspector growled. "You don't have to put it in words of one syllable. He went out through one of the train gates which Malloy himself had been covering, boarded a train a moment before it pulled out, and ten minutes later he was getting off again up at 125th Street."

"Which," Merlini added, "isn't far from Hicks's home, where we are now and where Keeler intended to hide out until the cops, baffled by the dead-end he'd left, relaxed their vigilance a bit. The Judge was full of cute angles. Who'd ever think of looking for

392

him in the home of one of the cops who was supposed to be hunting him?"

"After which," I added, "he'd change the cut of his whiskers or trim them off altogether, go to join Miss Hope, and they'd live happily ever after on his ill-gotten gains. Fadeout."

"That was the way the script read," Merlini said. "But Judge Keeler forgot one or two little things. He forgot what a man who has just vanished off the face of the earth, leaving a dead-end trail, is a perfect prospective murder victim. And he forgot that a suitcase full of folding money is a temptation one should never set before a crooked cop."

"Forgetfulness seems to be dangerous," I said. "I'm glad I've got a good memory."

"I have a hunch that somebody is going to have both our scalps," Merlini said ominously. "I've just remembered that when we left the shop –"

He was right. I hadn't mailed Mrs. Merlini's letter.

L. J. BEESTON
The Return of Backshaw

In the wet murk, in one corner of the seat, a woman was droning tipsily:

"If I had a thousand a year, Gaffer Gray,
"If I had a thousand a year –"

There passed by a stout gentleman with a light overcoat just showing his dress suit underneath. He went by slowly, staring hard.

" 'Evening, 'Orace," said the woman.

He came back. His kindly eyes, as they glimmered behind his gold spectacles, were fixed, not on the shattered derelict who accosted him, but at the hunched figure of a man in the other corner of the bench on the river embankment – the man whose frock coat was green with years, like lichen on an old wall, and whose boots were a grim joke.

"Backshaw, my dear fellow? Can it be you?" said the stroller in a shocked tone.

The other stirred restlessly, and shot an uneasy glance. He shook his head, and muttered something unintelligible.

The stout gentleman in the dress suit hesitated, then stooped and looked keenly into the white face with its red eyes, and the grossly disheveled hair.

"God bless me! It *is* Jimmy Backshaw!" he ejaculated.

The woman, careless of this drama, took up her drawl:

"What fun we would have, what sights we would see,

"If I had a thousand a year, Gaffer Gray,

"If I had a thousand a year –"

"Come, come, Jimmy," implored the stout gentleman affectionately, "you are not ashamed to recognize an old friend? I'm Conway – Sidney Conway. You haven't forgotten me? You must remember me!"

The other lifted again his bleared heavy eyes. He shook his head a second time, but with reluctance, and into his unshaved face crept an expression of cunning.

"Now you come along with me," urged the stout man gently, laying a gloved hand on the thin shoulder. "Thank heaven I ran up against you. I won't take a denial. My poor fellow, you have had a bad fall in this rough-and-tumble world. Forgive my alluding to it. Now you are coming home with me to a bite of supper, even if I have to carry you. You hear, Jimmy?"

The other rose stiffly, his muscles numbed with the rain and chill wind blowing off the river, and he trembled throughout his space body. Even his teeth rattled together. The cunning did not pass from his eyes as he tried to meet the gaze bent upon him.

"What did you say my name is?" he growled shiftily.

"Jimmy Backshaw, you old donkey. You are not afraid of me? Don't I look happy to meet you? Is this an occasion for a show of pride on your side? Are you going to insist that the name of Sidney Conway is unknown to you?"

"No!" blurted the other, with sudden, fierce vehemence. "I knew you directly you looked at me. And I'll go with you for that bite of supper and a glass of something hot. Heavens, do I look as if I could refuse?"

"That's better, Jimmy," answered Sidney Conway, his kindly eyes blinking behind his spectacles. "I'm still a bachelor. And who do you think I've got at my place tonight? Algy Wedgwood! You are not going to tell me that you've forgotten *him?*"

"Wedgwood?" echoed the other, with a sideways, very uneasy glance. "Of course I remember him. But suppose he doesn't remember me?"

"We'll see! Come along. My rooms are quite close."

He took his shivering companion by the

arm, turned his back on the river, and entered a labyrinth of streets which were deserted at that late hour.

At the end of ten minutes' walk he pulled up before a door in a narrow alley. On one side of this very grimy court was a high brick wall. On the other rose the side of a lofty block of buildings which were self-contained flats, having an iron stairway running zigzag from its topmost floor.

He pushed ajar the door in the alley, crossed a sodden piece of ground, which was dubiously adorned by sanitary dustbins, and fitted a key to the lock of another door close to the foot of the fire-escape stairway.

"I rent the bottom flat here," he explained, "and have the privilege of this side entrance."

They were in a small passage, where a single low-power electric bulb glowed. At the end of it Conway flung open a door.

"Nous sommes arrivés!" he cried cheerily. "Come right in, and welcome."

At that moment a man who was lounging in the padded depth of an armchair rose from his comfortable receptacle with a startled cry.

"What the devil have you got there, old man?"

"Easy, easy, Algy," laughed Conway,

almost dragging his reluctant visitor into the sociable warmth and light of the cosy room. "Try a more personal pronoun, as being more respectful to our guest."

"*Guest?*" echoed the other, with a look of open disgust. "What joke –"

"It is anything but a jest. I found him on a seat by the river, poor chap. Come, Algy, you don't want me to introduce an old pal, do you?"

With the words he pushed a second armchair toward the visitor, who sank into it, his eyes blinking painfully in the glare of the light.

"An old pal," Wedgwood echoed, his brows puckered in perplexity. He placed on the table a book he had been reading, then stepped up to the figure thawing its frozen fingers by the fireglow. A silence of a minute ensued. Conway, his face radiant, lighted a cigarette.

"Well?" said he, tossing aside the match.

"The – er – gentleman has the advantage of me," drawled Wedgwood.

"Not so," said Conway, crisply. "Look again. You know him perfectly well."

Wedgwood stared again.

"I'm hanged if I do," he dissented petulantly.

The figure in the chair raised himself

painfully. He growled, "I'm going. What did I tell you?"

"Stop!" interposed Conway. He wheeled sharply on Wedgwood, with the demand, "Perhaps the voice will assist your crass dullness?"

Wedgwood put his fingers to his chin, and his lips parted with an expression of astonishment and mental pain. He stammered, "It is not –not –"

"Out with it, man!" cried Conway.

"Not *Backshaw?*" he gasped, incredulously.

Conway shouted and clapped his hands.

"No other, I'll swear," he beamed.

"My soul!" said Wedgwood, unable to remove his fascinated gaze from the figure hunched in the cushioned chair.

"A find, you'll admit," went on Conway. "He denies his identity. I don't wonder; but we are going to knock that silly pride out of him, eh, Algy? Whines like an underdog; but we'll make him bark like the thoroughbred he is. D'ye blame me for bringing him along?"

"I should say not!" cried Wedgwood. He called the shivering guest on the shoulder.

"There's no other man in the wide-wide that I'd sooner see than you, Jimmy

Backshaw," he declared with quivering voice.

The man addressed lifted his eyes. A cunning light had again passed into them. He rubbed his palms, glanced shiftily round the well furnished room, and that artful glimmer deepened as he meditated.

"All right. I believe you," he answered thickly, and he shrugged imperceptibly.

In the meantime Conway was setting a cold supper on the table.

"My servant has leave for tonight," he explained. "At such times I generally eat at a restaurant. But we shall do very well in the circs, and we can chat at our ease in my rooms."

"Very true," Wedgwood assented. "And we won't make our friend open his lips for half an hour, save to put away good food."

He placed a seat for the guest, who accepted it. His red eyes followed with intense suspicion and uneasiness the movements of his hosts, and threw ravenous glances at the cold fowl and chunk of Stilton and bottle of wine. Conway was heating water over a spirit lamp, and he mixed a little brandy with it.

"Drink this first, Jimmy," he counseled. "It will stop that shivering."

The next minute they warmly engaged the

supper. After a few mouthfuls the guest showed signs of weariness. Soon his fork clattered to the floor, his head drooped, his limbs relaxed, and he fell into a profound slumber.

Conway rose cautiously, and peered into the white face.

"He's off," he grunted. "And serve him jolly well right for saying he was Jimmy Backshaw – that wholly imaginary person!"

"Pardon; *you* said he was," laughed Wedgwood.

"Same thing. He agreed with me – the liar!"

"He won't wake for a couple of hours at least," said Wedgwood. "You didn't put too much sleeping dope in the brandy?"

"I don't think I did. So far, good. Now to business."

He switched off the light and jerked the blind from the window. If the unconscious guest had opened his eyes he would doubtless have been astonished to perceive the river embankment facing the block of flats, and the bench he had occupied in view.

"Coast clear?" called Wedgwood in the darkness.

"Not a soul astir," answered Conway. He pulled up the lower window and peered to right and left. "Nobody near the house – as

401

yet. The place will be watched, but we have a start. Get busy."

He readjusted the blind and flicked on the light. In the palm of his hand. Wedgwood was holding a truly lustrous diamond of considerable size. It was a glorious sapphire-blue in color.

"You splendid creature, you," he mused, holding it to the light and peering into its velvet depths. "There are ten thousand pounds here, Conway, or I'm a minister of the Gospel."

Conway was doing a curious thing. With a small pair of sharp scissors he was ripping a hole in the bottom left-hand corner of the faded frock coat worn by their sleeping guest.

"I suggest this," he ventured. "As good as anywhere. There's plenty of padding in the corner which will make an admirable receptacle. Any objections?"

"None whatever. Here you are," answered Wedgwood.

Conway slipped in the stone, and with needle and thread repaired the slight damage neatly.

"Sharp's the word," he said briskly. "I don't fear he'll wake; but attention is bound to be focused on you, as I explained, and we have got to get the diamond safely away before the spotlight is turned on. Open the doors first. Luckily, the poor devil doesn't weigh much more than a hundred pounds."

Wedgwood hurried out and speedily returned. They placed their hands under the man's arms and lifted him to an upright posture. His head sagged over sideways with a rather sickening jerk. Only by main strength could they keep him upright. His teeth were clenched horribly tight; merely the whites of his eyes showed, and he breathed as one struck down by an apoplectic fit.

"He's dying!" whispered Wedgwood, appalled. "You didn't consider his weakness when you dosed him!"

"Rot! He'll pull out," replied Conway, with an anxious look into the sightless eyeballs. "Run him along, and don't lose your head if we're stopped."

They half dragged, half lifted their senseless burden through the short passage into the open, then through a doorway at the other end of the alley, which opened, in that direction, on the front of the building. They traversed a short gravel path, then the public pavement, then the silent and deserted road, while they held the man between them in a fairly natural posture.

But no eye saw them as they reached the bench on the riverfront. The bench had no occupant. They planted their burden in a corner and so left him. The rain had not ceased. A mist beat up from the stones; a ship's siren howled over the distorted surface of the water.

"I don't like it," admitted Wedgwood. "If the poor devil pegs out –"

"Bah! That sort never pegs out," scorned Conway.

In the sitting room ten minutes later Wedgwood, a newly lighted cigar between his lips, observed, "We have adopted a drastic policy. A desperate move, if you ask me."

"It had to be," smiled Conway, standing on the rug before the fire. "Yours the fault, if fault there was. Concerning your acquisition of Mrs. Goodsack's famous and wonderful blue diamond, I have nothing but praise, nothing but praise."

He waved his hand gently up and down. "But in coming to me with it three hours after, you acted – to be blunt – like a born fool. You, my dear Wedgwood, are not suspect; indeed, this is your first essay in the delicate art of jewel lifting, but I am just in the shadow.

"True, the only thing against me is that I was present at so many houses when losses were sustained; but I have felt in my bones of late that I am being talked about in an uncomfortable way. That being so, the presence in this flat of a famous stone of fabulous worth spells Danger – with a large and flame-painted capital D.

"Just now I am going easy – easy and ever so cautiously – waiting for the shadow to edge off me. And then, all at once, when I had resolved not to look at a diamond for six months, up turns my friend Wedgwood with a catch that would be the envy of the king of crooks. Very nice, and – very nasty."

"By Jove, Conway, it was opportunity that let me down, that made me a thief," said the other, fiercely troubled. "You know the state of my finances, that it is absolutely rotten. I was one of the earliest guests at Mrs. Goodsack's ball tonight – yesterday evening, I should say, for it's cursed late now. She was wearing the diamond pendant. I had no more idea of stealing it than of stealing you. An hour or two later a clumsy partner caused the thin gold chain to break, and the jewel fell to the floor.

"Mrs. Goodsack at once removed it – to her room. Well, I was feeling slack and seedy, and I left soon after. As I was leaving the house I noticed that one side of it was in repair, covered with builders' scaffolding.

And then it struck me that that meant a fairly easy access to Mrs. Goodsack's room.

"It was raining cats and dogs, and the night black as the pit. Temptation caught me by the throat. I leaped a wall and swarmed up the scaffolding, forced the window catch, and got through. I broke open two drawers in an escritoire, found the jewel box, and lifted the diamond.

"Everything worked easy as pie; but when I found myself at home I got the shivers. I was more scared then than at any other time. I began to want to see you, badly. Didn't I know it was a matter you could handle better than I? Wasn't I in the secret of your – er – profession? Hadn't you often tempted me to help you when you knew I was down at the heel? So I came to you, Conway."

"Wait. How long was that after your actual scoop?"

"Three hours, roughly."

"Too much if the loss was discovered at once."

"I hope not. I hope not, Conway. As I was the first guest to leave, they might have followed me –"

"Unlikely. What did you do with the gold setting of the pendant?"

"Flung it into the river. Look here, if you are so infernally nervy of having the stone

406

about you, why didn't you advise me to keep it?"

"*You?*" mocked Conway, throwing back his head in a silent laugh. "Your newly hurt conscious would have made you restore it in the morning. I cursed you for bringing it, but it was far too good a haul to let go. The police will search my rooms surreptitiously at least once. That will be because Algy Wedgwood, after leaving Mrs. Goodsack's ball early, paid me a late visit."

"But how can they find that out?"

"How? They will, sure as eggs. Trust Treadway of the Yard to get on that scent. I know him! Therefore, it was most important that I slip the diamond to a third person without delay. That I chose a dramatic method, you will allow."

"I should have thought it easy to find a dozen safe hiding places."

"Easy? Easy to hide a ten-thousand-pounds diamond? Good Lord, you don't know what you're talking about."

"But we shall have to keep a watchful eye on this vagrant."

"We? You will, you mean. So far as I'm concerned, the diamond does not exist – not for six months. I don't want even to think of it if I can help it, for fear of wiring a mental telegraphic message to New Scotland Yard.

But it is you who must keep our man under observation; and you must begin in a very few hours. If you ever lose sight of him I shall probably kill you."

"Suppose he pawns his coat?"

"Then you get the ticket."

"Easy said," grumbled Wedgwood. "Was it really necessary to pitch him that yarn about his being a wholly imaginary Jimmy Backshaw?"

"My dear fellow," beamed Conway. "In that matter it was your fortunate privilege to observe one of my most subtle touches. If I had gone out and fetched him here without that make-believe story, had drugged him and taken him back, what would have been his impression later on? That he had been victimized to some doubtful end, obviously. I do not want him to think any such thing; one could not tell where it would stop, just what he would do.

"As things are now, he will awake with a hazy idea in his poor fuddled brain of having been hailed as a dear old pal by a swell in evening dress, who took him home to supper in an expensive flat – only to find himself, when consciousness returned, in the same corner of the same bench he had occupied when the mysterious aforesaid swell took him to his bosom. Now, I put it to you – what will be his final conclusion?"

Wedgwood grinned. "He will think that he dreamed it," he replied.

"Exactly. You admit the subtlety of the move? Give me a good cigar. The room needs fumigating after our visitor. By George, he must have been saturated. See where the water has run from his clothes –"

"That is an error," said a quiet voice. "The moisture is a small quantity of brandy – drugged."

Wedgwood spun round, his face livid. Conway, the cigar an inch from his parted lips, had become paralyzed.

In the open doorway stood their late guest.

He rubbed his palms in a gentle motion, and his expression suggested a full-fed panther's contentment.

"Was I watching this flat when you first came along? Even so. And now? Now I have the entire story from its very beginning. That is highly gratifying to me, gentlemen," purred Inspector Treadway of New Scotland Yard.

BARRY PEROWNE

The Blind Spot

Annixter loved the little man like a brother. He put an arm around the little man's shoulders, partly from affection and partly to prevent himself from falling.

He had been drinking earnestly since seven o'clock the previous evening. It was now nudging midnight, and things were a bit hazy. The lobby was full of the thump of hot music; down two steps, there were a lot of tables, a lot of people, a lot of noise. Annixter had no idea what this place was called, or how he had got here, or when. He had been in so many places since seven o'clock the previous evening.

"In a nutshell," confided Annixter, leaning heavily on the little man, "a woman fetches you a kick in the face, or fate fetches you a kick in the face. Same thing, really – a woman and fate. So what? So you think it's the finish, an' you go out and get plastered. You get good an' plastered," said Annixter, "an' you brood.

"You sit there an' you drink an' you brood

– an' in the end you find you've brooded up just about the best idea you ever had in your life! 'At's the way it goes," said Annixter, "an' 'at's my philosophy – the harder you kick a playwright, the better he works!"

He gestured with such vehemence that he would have collapsed if the little man hadn't steadied him. The little man was pokerbacked, his grip was firm. His mouth was firm, too – a straight line, almost colorless. He wore hexagonal rimless spectacles, a black hardfelt hat, a neat pepper-and-salt suit. He looked pale and prim beside the flushed, rumpled Annixter.

From her counter, the hat-check girl watched them indifferently.

"Don't you think." the little man said to Annixter, "you ought to go home now? I've been honored you should tell me the scenario of your play, but –"

"I had to tell someone," said Annixter, "or blow my top! Oh, boy, what a play, what a play! What a murder, eh? That climax –"

The full, dazzling perfection of it struck him again. He stood frowning, considering, swaying a little – then nodded abruptly, groped for the little man's hand, warmly pumphandled it.

"Sorry I can't stick around," said Annixter. "I got work to do."

He crammed his hat on shapelessly, headed on a slightly elliptical course across the lobby, thrust the double doors open with both hands, lurched out into the night.

It was, to his inflamed imagination, full of lights, winking and tilting across the dark. *Sealed Room* by James Annixter. No. *Room Reserved* by James – No, no. *Blue Room. Room Blue. Room Blue* by James Annixter –

He stepped, oblivious, off the curb, and a taxi, swinging in toward the place he had just left, skidded with suddenly locked, squealing wheels on the wet road.

Something hit Annixter violently in the chest, and all the lights he had been seeing exploded in his face.

Then there weren't any lights.

Mr. James Annixter, the playwright, was knocked down by a taxi last last night when leaving the Casa Havana. After hospital treatment for shock and superficial injuries, he returned to his home.

The lobby of the Cassa Havana was full of the thump of music' down two steps there were a lot of tables, a lot of people, a lot of noise. The hat-check girl looked wonderingly at Annixter – at the plaster on his forehead, the black sling which supported his left arm.

"My," said the hat-check girl, "I certainly didn't expect to see *you* again so soon!"

"You remember me, then?" said Annixter, smiling.

"I ought to," said the hat-check girl. "You cost me a night's sleep! I heard those brakes squeal right after you went out the door that night – and there was a sort of a thud!" She shuddered. "I kept hearing it all night long. I can still hear it now – a week after! Horrible!"

"You're sensitive," said Annixter.

"I got too much imagination," the hat-check girl admitted. "F'rinstance, I just *knew* it was you even before I ran to the door and see you lying there. That man you was with was standing just outside. 'My heavens,' I says to him, 'it's your friend!'"

"What did he say?" Annixter asked.

"He says, 'He's not my friend. He's just someone I met.' Funny, eh?"

Annixter moistened his lips.

"How d'you mean," he said carefully, "funny? I *was* just someone he'd met."

"Yes, but – a man you been drinking with," said the hat-check girl, "killed before your eyes. Because he must have seen it; he went out right after you. You'd think he'd 'a' been interested, at least. But when the taxi

413

driver starts shouting for witnesses it wasn't his fault, I looks around for that man – an' he's gone!''

Annixter exchanged a glance with Ransome, his producer, who was with him. It was a slightly puzzled, slightly anxious glance. But he smiled, then, at the hat-check girl.

"Not quite 'killed before his eyes,'" said Annixter. "Just shaken up a bit, that's all."

There was no need to explain to her how curious, how eccentric, had been the effect of that "shaking up" upon his mind.

"If you could 'a' seen yourself lying there with the taxi's lights shining on you –"

"Ah, there's that imagination of yours!" said Annixter.

He hesitated for just an instant, then asked the question he had come to ask – the question which had assumed so profound an importance for him.

He asked, "That man I was with – who was he?"

The hat-check girl looked from one to the other. She shook her head.

"I never saw him before," she said, "and I haven't seen him since."

Annixter felt as though she had struck him in the face. He had hoped, hoped desperately, for a different answer; he had

414

counted on it. Ransome put a hand on his arm, restrainingly.

"Anyway," said Ransome, "as we're here, let's have a drink."

They went down the two steps into the room where the band thumped. A waiter led them to a table, and Ransome gave him an order.

"There was no point in pressing that girl," Ransome said to Annixter. "She doesn't know the man, and that's that. My advice to you, James, is: don't worry. Get your mind onto something else. Give yourself a chance. After all, it's barely a week since –"

"A week!" Annixter said. "Hell, look what I've done in that week! The whole of the first two acts, and the third act right up to that crucial point – the climax of the whole thing: the solution: the scene that the play stands or falls on! It would have been done, Bill – the whole play, the best thing I ever did in my life – it would have been finished two days ago if it hadn't been for this –" he knuckled his forehead "– this extraordinary blind spot, this damnable little trick of memory!"

"You had a very rough shaking-up –"

"That?" Annixter said contemptuously. He glanced down at the sling on his arm. "I never even felt it; it didn't bother me. I woke

415

up in the ambulance with my play as vivid in my mind as the moment the taxi hit me – more so, maybe, because I was stone cold sober then, and knew what I had. A winner – a thing that just couldn't miss!"

"If you'd rested," Ransome said, "as the doctor told you, instead of sitting up in bed there, scribbling night and day –"

"I had to get it on paper. Rest?" said Annixter, and laughed harshly. "You don't rest when you've got a thing like that. That's what you live for – if you're a playwright. That *is* living! I've lived eight whole lifetimes, in those eight characters, during the past five days. I've lived so utterly in them, Bill, that it wasn't till I actually came to write that last scene that I realized what I'd lost! Only my whole play, that's all! How was Cynthia stabbed in that windowless room into which she had locked and bolted herself? How did the killer get to her? *How was it done?*

"Hell," Annixter said, "scores of writers, better men than I am, have tried to put that sealed-room murder over – and never quite done it convincingly: never quite got away with it: been overelaborate, phony! I had it – heaven help me, *I* had it! Simple, perfect, glaringly obvious when you've once seen it! And it's my whole play – the curtain rises on

416

that sealed room and falls on it! That was my revelation – *how it was done!* That was what I got, by way of playwright's compensation, because a woman I thought I loved kicked me in the face – I brooded up the answer to the sealed room! And a taxi knocked it out of my head!"

He drew a long breath.

"I've spent two days and two nights, Bill, trying to get that idea back – *how it was done!* It won't come. I'm a competent playwright; I know my job; I could finish my play, but it'd be like all those others – not quite right, phony! It wouldn't be *my play!* But there's a little man walking around this city somewhere – a little man with hexagonal glasses – who's got my idea in his head! He's got it because I told it to him. I'm going to find that little man, and get back what belongs to me! I've got to! Don't you see that, Bill? I've *got* to!"

If the gentleman who, at the Casa Havana on the night of January 27th, so patiently listened to a playwright's outlining of an idea for a drama will communicate with the Box No. below he will hear something to his advantage.

A little man who had said, "He's not my friend. He's just someone I met –"

A little man who'd seen an accident but hadn't waited to give evidence –

The hat-check girl had been right. There *was* something a little queer about that.

A little queer?

During the next few days, when the advertisements he'd inserted failed to bring any reply, it began to seem to Annixter very queer indeed.

His arm was out of its sling now, but he couldn't work. Time and again, he sat down before his almost completed manuscript, read it through with close, grim attention, thinking. "It's *bound* to come back this time!" – only to find himself up against that blind spot again, that blank wall, that maddening hiatus in his memory.

He left his work and prowled the streets; he haunted bars and saloons; he rode for miles on buses and subway, especially at the rush hours. He saw a million faces, but the face of the little man with hexagonal glasses he did not see.

The thought of him obsessed Annixter. It was infuriating, it was unjust, it was torture to think that a little, ordinary, chance-met citizen was walking blandly around somewhere with the last link of his,

418

the celebrated James Annixter's play – the best thing he'd ever done – locked away in his head. And with no idea of what he had: without the imagination, probably, to appreciate what he had! And certainly with no idea of what it meant to Annixter!

Or *had* he some idea? Was he, perhaps, not quite so ordinary as he's seemed? Had he seen those advertisements, drawn from them tortuous inferences of his own? Was he holding back with some scheme for shaking. Annixter down for a packet?

The more Annixter thought about it, the more he felt that the hat-check girl had been right, that there was something very queer indeed about the way the little man had behaved after the accident.

Annixter's imagination played around the man he was seeking, tried to probe into his mind, conceived reasons for his fading away after the accident, for his failure to reply to the advertisements.

Annixter's was an active and dramatic imagination. The little man who had seemed so ordinary began to take on a sinister shape in Annixter's mind –

But the moment he actually saw the little man again, he realized how absurd that was. It was so absurd that it was laughable. The little man was so respectable; his shoulders

419

were so straight; his pepper-and-salt suit was so neat; his black hard-felt hat was set so squarely on his head –

The doors of the subway train were just closing when Annixter saw him, standing on the platform with a briefcase in one hand, a folded evening paper under his other arm. Light from the train shone on his prim, pale face; his hexagonal spectacles flashed. He turned toward the exit as Annixter lunged for the closing doors of the train and squeezed between them onto the platform.

Craning his head to see above the crowd, Annixter elbowed his way through, ran up the stairs two at a time, and put a hand on the little man's shoulder.

"Just a minute," Annixter said. "I've been looking for you."

The little man checked instantly at the touch of Annixter's hand. Then he turned his head an looked at Annixter. His eyes were pale behind the hexagonal, rimless glasses – a pale grey. His mouth was a straight line, almost colorless.

Annixter loved the little man like a brother. Merely finding the little man was a relief so great that it was like the lifting of a black cloud from his spirits. He patted the little man's shoulder affectionately.

"I've got to talk to you," said Annixter.

"It won't take a minute. Let's go somewhere."

The little man said, "I can't imagine what you want to talk to me about."

He moved slightly to one side, to let a woman pass. The crowd from the train had thinned, but there was still people going up and down the stairs. The little man looked, politely inquiring, at Annixter.

Annixter said, "Of course you can't, it's so damned silly! But it's about that play –"

"Play?"

Annixter felt a faint anxiety.

"Look," he said, "I was drunk that night – I was very, very drunk! But looking back, my impression is that you were dead sober. You were, weren't you?"

"I've never been drunk in my life."

"Thank heaven for that!" said Annixter. "Then you won't have any difficulty in remembering the little point I want you to remember." He grinned, shook his head. "You had me going there, for a minute. I thought –"

"I don't know what you thought," the little man said. "But I'm quite sure you're mistaking me for somebody else. I haven't any idea what you're talking about. I never saw you before in my life. I'm sorry. Good night."

He turned and started up the stairs. Annixter stared after him. He couldn't believe his ears. He stared blankly after the little man for an instant, then a rush of anger and suspicion swept away his bewilderment. He raced up the stairs, caught the little man by the arm.

"Just a minute," said Annixter. "I may have been drunk, but –"

"That," the little man said, "seems evident. Do you mind taking your hand off me?"

Annixter controlled himself. "I'm sorry," he said. "Let me get this right, though. You say you've never seen me before. Then you weren't at the Casa Havana on January twenty-seventh – somewhere between ten o'clock and midnight? You didn't have a drink or two with me, and listen to an idea for a play that had just come into my mind?"

The little man looked steadily at Annixter. "I've told," he said. "I've never set eyes on you before."

"You didn't see me get hit by a taxi?" Annixter pursued, tensely. "You didn't say to the hat-check girl, 'He's not my friend. He's just someone I met?'"

"I don't know what you're talking about," the little man said sharply.

He made to turn away, but Annixter gripped his arm again.

"I don't know," Annixter said between his teeth, "anything about your private affairs, and I don't want to. You may have had some good reason for wanting to duck giving evidence as a witness of that taxi accident. You may have some good reason for this act you're pulling on me now. I don't know and I don't care. But it is an act! You *are* the man I told my play to!

"I want you to tell that story back to me as I told it to you; I have my reasons – personal reasons, of concern to me and me only. I want you to tell the story back to me – that's all I want! I don't want to know who you are, or anything about you. *I just want you to tell me that story!*"

"You ask," the little man said, "an impossibility, since I never heard it."

Annixter kept an iron hold on himself.

He said, "Is it money? Is this some sort of a hold-up? Tell me what you want; I'll give it to you. Lord help me, I'd go so far as to give you a share in the play! That'll mean real money. I know, because I know my business. And maybe – maybe," said Annixter, struck by a sudden thought, "*you* know it, too! Eh?"

"You're insane or drunk!" the little man

said. With a sudden movement, he jerked his arm free, raced up the stairs. A train was rumbling in, below. People were hurrying down. He weaved and dodged among them with extraordinary celerity.

He was a small man, light, and Annixter was heavy. By the time he reached the street, there was no sign of the little man. He was gone.

Was the idea, Annixter wondered, to steal his play? By some wild chance did the little man nurture a fantastic ambition to be a dramatist? Had he, perhaps, peddled his precious manuscripts in vain, for years, around the managements? Had Annixter's play appeared to him as a blinding flash of hope in the gathering darkness of frustration and failure: something he had imagined he could safely steal because it had seemed to him the random inspiration of a drunkard who by morning would have forgotten he had ever given birth to anything but a hangover?

That, Annixter thought, would be a laugh! That would be irony –

He took another drink. It was his fifteenth since the little man with the hexagonal glasses had given him the slip, and Annixter was beginning to reach the stage where he lost count of how many places he had had drinks in tonight. It was also the stage, though, where he was beginning to feel better, where his mind was beginning to work.

He could imagine just how the little man must have felt as the quality of the play he was being told, with hiccups, gradually had dawned upon him.

"This is mine!" the little man would have thought. "I've got to have this. He's drunk, he's soused, he's bottled – he'll have forgotten every word of it by the morning! Go on! Go on, mister! Keep talking!"

That was a laugh, too – the idea that Annixter would have forgotten his play by the morning. Other things Annixter forgot, unimportant things; but never in his life had he forgotten the minutest detail that was to his purpose as a playwright. Never!

Except once, because a taxi had knocked him down.

Annixter took another drink. He needed it. He was on his own now. There wasn't any little man with hexagonal glasses to fill in that blind spot for him. The little man was gone. He was gone as though he'd never been. To hell with him! Annixter had to fill in that blind spot himself. He *had* to do it – somehow!

425

He had another drink. He had quite a lot more drinks. The bar was crowded and noisy, but he didn't notice the noise – till someone came up and slapped him on the shoulder. It was Ransome.

Annixter stood up, leaning with his knuckles on the table.

"Look, Bill," Annixter said, "how about this? Man forgets an idea, see? He wants to get it back – gotta get it back! Idea comes from inside, works outwards – right? So he starts on the outside, works back inward. How's that?" He swayed, peering at Ransome.

"Better have a little drink," said Ransome. "I'd need to think that out."

"I," said Annixter, "*have* thought it out!" He crammed his hat shapelessly onto his head. "Be seeing you, Bill. I got work to do!"

He started, on a slightly tacking course, for the door – and his apartment.

It was Joseph, his "man" who opened the door of his apartment to him some twenty minutes later. Joseph opened the door while Annixter's latchkey was still describing vexed circles around the lock.

"Good evening, sir," said Joseph.

Annixter stared at him. "I didn't tell you to stay in tonight."

"I hadn't any real reason for going out, sir," Joseph explained. He helped Annixter off with his coat. "I rather enjoy a quiet evening in, once in a while."

"You got to get out of here," said Annixter.

"Thank you, sir," said Joseph. "I'll go and throw a few things into a bag."

Annixter went into his big living room-study and poured himself a drink.

The manuscript of his play lay on the desk. Annixter, swaying a little, glass in hand, stood frowing down at the untidy stack of yellow paper, but he didn't begin to read. He waited until he heard the outer door click shut behind Joseph, then he gathered up his manuscript, the decanter and a glass, and the cigarette box. Thus laden, he went into the hall, walked across it to the door of Joseph's room.

There was a bolt on the inside of this door, and the room was the only one in the apartment which had no window – both facts which made the room the only one suitable to Annixter's purpose.

With his free hand, he switched on the light.

It was a plain little room, but Annixter noticed with a faint grin that the bedspread and the cushion in the worn basket-chair

427

were both blue. Appropriate, he thought – a good omen. *Room Blue* by James Annixter –

Joseph had evidently been lying on the bed reading the evening paper; the paper lay on the rumpled quilt, and the pillow was dented. Beside the head of the bed, opposite the door, was a small table littered with shoe-brushes and dusters.

Annixter swept this paraphernalia onto the floor. He put his stack of manuscript, the decanter and glass and cigarette box on the table, and went across and bolted the door. He pulled the basket-chair up to the table, sat down, lighted a cigarette.

He leaned back in the chair, smoking, letting his mind ease into the atmosphere he wanted – the mental atmosphere of Cynthia, the woman in his play, the woman who was afraid, so afraid that she had locked and bolted herself into a windowless room, a sealed room.

"This is how she sat," Annixter told himself, "just as I'm sitting now: in a room with no windows, the door locked and bolted. Yet he got at her. He got at her with a knife – in a room with no windows, the door remaining locked and bolted on the inside. *How was it done?*"

There was a way in which it could be done.

428

He, Annixter, had thought of that way; he had conceived it, invented it – and forgotten it. His idea had produced the circumstances. Now, deliberately, he had reproduced the circumstances, that he might think back to the idea. He had put his person in the position of the victim, that his mind might grapple with the problem of the murderer.

It was very quiet: not a sound in the room, the whole apartment.

For a long time, Annixter sat unmoving. He sat unmoving until the intensity of his concentration began to waver. Then he relaxed. He pressed the palms of his hands to his forehead for a moment, then reached for the decanter. He splashed himself a strong drink. He had almost recovered what he sought; he had felt it close, had been on the very verge of it.

"Easy," he warned himself, "take it easy. Relax. Try again in a minute."

He looked around for something to divert his mind, picked up the paper from Joseph's bed.

At the first words that caught his eye, his heart stopped.

The woman, in whose body were found three knife wounds, any of which might have been fatal, was in a windowless room, the only door to which was locked and bolted on the inside.

429

These elaborate precautions appear to have been habitual with her, and no doubt she went in continual fear of her life, as the police know her to have been a persistent and pitiless blackmailer.

Apart from the unique problem set by the circumstance of the sealed room is the problem of how the crime could have gone undiscovered for so long a period, the doctor's estimate from the condition of the body as some twelve to fourteen days.

Twelve to fourteen days –

Annixter read back over the remainder of the story, then let the paper fall to the floor. The pulse was heavy in his head. His face was grey. Twelve to fourteen days? He could put it closer than that. *It was exactly thirteen nights ago that he had sat in the Casa Havana and told a little man with hexagonal glasses how to kill a woman in a sealed room!*

Annixter sat very still for a minute. Then he poured himself another drink. It was a big one, and he needed it. He felt a strange sense of wonder, of awe.

They had been in the same boat, he and the little man – thirteen nights ago. They had both been kicked in the face by a woman. One, as a result, had conceived a murder play. The other had made the play reality!

And I actually, tonight, offered him a

430

share! Annixter thought. I talked about "real" money!

That was a laugh. All the money in the universe wouldn't have made that little man admit that he had seen Annixter before – that Annixter had told him the plot of a play how to kill a woman in a sealed room! Why, he, Annixter, was the one person in the world who could denounce that little man! Even if he couldn't tell them, because he had forgotten, just *how* he had told the little man the murder was to be committed, he could still put the police on the little man's track. He could describe him so that they would trace him. And once on his track, the police would ferret out links, almost inevitably, with the dead woman.

A queer thought – that he, Annixter, was probably the only menace, the only danger, to the little prim pale man with hexagonal spectacles. The only menace – as, of course, the little man must know very well.

He must have been very frightened when he had read that the playwright who had been knocked down outside the Casa Havana had only received "superficial injuries." He must have been still more frightened when Annixter's advertisements had begun to appear. *What must he have felt tonight when Annixter's hand had fallen on his shoulder?*

431

A curious idea occurred now to Annixter. It was from tonight, precisely from tonight, that he was a danger to that little man. He was, because of the inferences the little man must infallibly draw, a deadly danger as from the moment the discovery of the murder in the sealed room was published. That discovery had been published tonight and the little man had had a paper under his arm –

Annixter's was a lively and resourceful imagination.

It was, of course, just in the cards that, when he'd lost the little man's trail at the subway station, the little man might have turned back, picked up *his*, Annixter's, trail.

And Annixter had sent Joseph out. He was, it dawned slowly upon Annixter, alone in the apartment – alone in a windowless room, with the door locked and bolted on the inside, at his back.

Annixter felt a sudden, icy, and wild panic.

He half rose, but it was too late.

It was too late, because at that moment the knife slid, thin and keen and delicate, into his back, fatally, between the ribs.

Annixter's head bowed slowly forward until his cheek rested on the manuscript of his play. He made only one sound – a queer sound, indistinct, yet identifiable as a kind of laughter.

The fact was, Annixter had just remembered.

GRAHAM GREENE
The Third Man

When I saw Rollo Martins first I made this note on him for my security police files: "In normal circumstances a cheerful fool. Drinks too much and may cause a little trouble. Has never really grown up, and perhaps that accounts for the way he worshipped Lime."

I met him first as Harry Lime's funeral. It was February, and the gravediggers had been forced to use electric drills to open the frozen ground in Vienna's Central Cemetery. It was as if even nature were doing its best to reject Lime, but we got him in at last and laid the earth back on him like bricks. He was vaulted in, and Rollo Martins walked quickly away as though his long, gangly legs wanted to break into a run, and the tears of a boy ran down his thirty-five-year-old cheeks. Rollo Martins believed in friendship, and that was why what happened later was such a shock.

If you are to understand this strange, rather sad story you must have an impression, at least, of the background – the smashed, dreary city of Vienna divided up

434

in zones among the four powers: the Russian, the British, the American, the French zones, regions marked only by a notice board, and in the center of the city, surrounded by the Ring, with its heavy public buildings and its prancing statuary, the Inner Stadt under the control of all four powers.

In this once fashionable Inner Stadt, each power in turn, for a month at a time, takes, as we call it, "the chair," and becomes responsible for security. At night, if you were fool enough to waste your Austrian shillings on a nightclub, you would see the International Patrol at work – four military police, one from each power, communicating with one another, if they communicated at all, in the language of their enemy.

I never knew Vienna between the wars, and I am too young to remember the old Vienna, with its Strauss music and its bogus easy charm. To me, it is simply a city of undignified ruins which turned, that February, into great glaciers of snow and ice. The Danube was a gray, flat, muddy river a long way off across the Russian zone. The Prater lay smashed and desolate and full of weeds; only the Great Wheel moved, revolving slowly over the foundations of merry-go-rounds like abandoned milestones, the rusting iron of smashed tanks which nobody had cleared away, the frost-nipped weeds where the snow was thin.

At night, the kidnappings occur – such senseless kidnapings they sometimes seemed to us – a Ukrainian girl without a passport, an old man beyond the age of usefulness, sometimes, of course, the technician or the traitor. This was, roughly, the Vienna to which Rollo Martins had come on February 7 of last year.

A British subject can still travel if he is content to take with him only five English pounds, which he is forbidden to spend abroad, but if Rollo Martins had not received an invitation from Lime of the International Refugee Office he would not have been allowed to enter Austria, which counts still as occupied territory. Lime had suggested that Martins might "write up" the business of looking after the international refugees, and although it wasn't Martins's usual line, he had consented.

Rollo Martins's usual line was the writing of paper-covered westerns under the name of Buck Dexter. His public was large but unremunerative. He couldn't have afforded Vienna if Lime had not offered to pay his expenses when he got there out of some vaguely described propaganda fund. He could also, he said, keep him supplied with

436

paper *Bafs* – the only currency in use from a penny upward in British hotels and clubs. So it was with exactly five unusable pound notes that Martins arrived in Vienna.

An odd incident had occurred at Frankfurt, where the plane from London grounded for an hour. Martins was eating a hamburger in the American canteen (a kindly airline supplied the passengers with a voucher for 65 cents' worth of food) when a man he could recognize from twenty feet away as a journalist approached.

"You Mr. Dexter?" he asked.

"Yes," Martins said, taken off his guard.

"You look younger than your photographs," the man said. "Like to make a statement? I represent the local paper here. We'd like to know what you think of Frankfurt."

"I only touched down ten minutes ago."

"Fair enough," the man said. "What about views on the American novel?"

"I don't read them," Martins said.

"The well known acid humor," the journalist said. He pointed at a small, gray-haired man with two protruding teeth nibbling a bit of bread. "Happen to know if that's Carey?"

"No. What Carey?"

"J. G. Carey, of course."

"I've never heard of him."

"You novelists live out of the world. He's my real assignment." And Martins watched the journalist make across the room for the great Carey.

Dexter wasn't the man's assignment, but Martins couldn't help feeling a certain pride – nobody had ever before referred to him as a novelist; and that sense of pride and importance carried him over the disappointment when Lime was not there to meet him at the airport, nor at the Hotel Astoria, where the bus landed him, and no message – only a cryptic one for Mr. Dexter from someone he had never heard of called Crabbin: "We expected you on tomorrow's plane. Please stay where you are. On the way round. Hotel room booked." But Rollo Martins wasn't the kind of man who stayed around.

Martins had been given Lime's address, and he felt no curiosity about the man called Crabbin. It was too obvious that a mistake had been made, though he didn't yet connect it with the conversation at Frankfurt. Lime had written that he could put Martins up in his own flat, a large apartment on the edge of Vienna, so Martins drove straightaway to the building lying in the third (British) zone.

How quickly one becomes aware of silence even in so silent a city as Vienna, with the snow steadily settling. Martins hadn't reached the second floor before he was convinced that he would not find Lime there, and as he reached the fourth floor and saw the big black bow over the door handle, he knew he would not find Lime anywhere in the world. Of course, it might have been a cook who had died, a housekeeper, anybody but Harry Lime, but Martins knew that Lime, the Lime he had hero-worshipped now for twenty years, since the first meeting in a grim school corridor with a cracked bell ringing for prayers, was gone.

After he had rung the doorbell half a dozen times, a small man with a sullen expression put his head out from another flat and told him in a tone of vexation, "It's no use ringing like that. There's nobody there. He's dead."

Martins, as he told me later, asked him, "When did it happen? How?"

"He was run over by a car," the man said. "Last Thursday." He added sullenly, as if really this were none of his business, "They're burying him this afternoon. You've only just missed a couple of friends and the coffin."

"Wasn't he in a hospital?"

"There was no sense in taking him to a

hospital. He was killed here on his own doorstep – instantaneously."

"Where are they burying him?"

"In the Central Cemetery."

He had no idea how to pay for his taxi, or indeed where in Vienna he could find a room in which he could live for five English pounds, but that problem had to be postponed until he had seen the last of Harry Lime. He drove straight to Central Cemetery.

It was just chance that he found the funeral in time – one patch in the enormous park where the snow had been shoveled aside and a tiny group were gathered, apparently bent on some very private business. A priest had finished speaking and a coffin was on the point of being lowered into the ground. Two men in lounge suits were at the graveside. A girl stood a little way away with her hands over her face, and I stood twenty yards away by another grave watching with relief the last of Lime and noticing carefully who was there – just a man in a mackintosh I was to Martins. He came up to me and said, "Could you tell me who they're burying?"

"A fellow called Lime," I said, and was astonished to see the tears start to this stranger's eyes. He didn't look like a man

440

who wept, nor was Lime the kind of man who I thought was likely to have mourners.

Martins stood there till the end, close beside me. He said to me later that as an old friend he didn't want to intrude on these newer ones. As soon as the affair was over, Martins strode back to his taxi; he made no attempt to speak to anyone, and the tears now were really running. I followed him. I knew the other three; I wanted to know the stranger.

I caught him up by his taxi and said, "I haven't any transport. Would you give me a lift into town?"

"Of course," he said. I knew the driver of my jeep would spot me as we came out and follow us.

I said, "My name's Calloway."

"Martins," he said.

"You were a friend of Lime?"

"Yes." Most people in the last week would have hesitated before they admitted quite so much. "I came only this afternoon from England. Harry had asked me to stay with him. I hadn't heard."

"Bit of a shock?"

"Look here," he said; "I badly want a drink, but I haven't any cash – except five pounds sterling. I'd be awfully grateful if you'd stand me one."

It was my turn to say, "Of course." I thought for a moment, and told the driver the name of a small bar in the Kärtnerstrasse.

On the door was the usual notice saying the bar opened at six till ten, but one just pushed the door and walked through the front rooms. We had a whole small room to ourselves.

Martins said over his second quick drink, "I'm sorry, but he was the best friend I ever had."

I couldn't resist saying, knowing what I knew, and because I was anxious to vex him – one learns a lot that way – "That sounds like a cheap novelette."

He said quickly, "I write cheap novelettes."

I said, "Tell me about yourself – and Lime."

"Look here," he said, "I badly need another drink, but I can't keep scrounging on a stranger. Could you change me a pound or two into Austrian money?"

"Don't bother about that," I said, and called the waiter. "You can treat me when I come to London on leave. You were going to tell me about Lime and how you met him?"

The glass of liqueur might have been a

crystal the way he looked at it and turned it this way and that. He said, "It was a long time ago. I don't suppose anyone knows Harry the way I do." And I thought of the thick file of agents' reports in my office, each claiming the same thing.

"How long?"

"Twenty years – or a bit more. I met him my first term at school. I can see the place. I can see the notice-board and what was on it. I can hear the bell ringing. He was a year older and knew the ropes. He put me wise to a lot of things."

"Was he clever at school?"

"Not the way they wanted him to be. But what things he did think up! He was a wonderful planner. I was far better at subjects like history and English than Harry, but I was a hopeless mug when it came to carrying out his plans." He laughed; he was already beginning, with the help of drink and talk, to throw off the shock of the death. He said, "I was always the one who got caught."

"That was convenient for Lime."

"That was my fault, not his. He could have found someone cleverer if he'd chosen, but he liked me. He was endlessly patient with me."

"When did you see him last?"

"Oh, he was over in London six months

ago for a medical congress. You know, he qualified as a doctor, though he never practiced. That was typical of Harry. He just wanted to see if he could do a thing, and then he lost interest. But he used to say that it often came in handy."

And that, too, was true. It was odd how like the Lime he knew was to the Lime I knew; it was only that he looked at Lime's image from a different angle or in a different light.

He said, "One of the things I liked about Harry was his humor." He gave a grin which took five years off his age. "I'm a buffoon. I like playing the silly fool, but Harry had real wit. You know, he could have been a first-class light composer if he had worked at it."

He whistled a tune – it was oddly familiar to me. "I always remember that. I saw Harry write it. Just in a couple of minutes on the back of an envelope. That was what he always whistled when he had something on his mind. It was his signature tune."

He whistled the tune a second time, and I knew then who had written it – of course, it wasn't Harry. I nearly told him so, but what was the point?

The tune wavered and went out. He stared down into his glass, drained what was left, and said, "It's a damned shame to think of him dying the way he did."

"It was the best thing that ever happened to him," I said.

"You mean there wasn't any pain?"

"He was lucky in that way, too."

It was my tone of voice and not my words that caught Martins's attention. He asked gently and dangerously – I could see his right hand tighten – "Are you hinting at something?"

There is no point at all in showing physical courage in all situations; I eased my chair far enough back to be out of reach of his fist. I said, "I mean that I had his case completed at police headquarters. He would have served a long spell – a very long spell – if it hadn't been for the accident."

"What for?"

"He was about the worst racketeer who ever made a dirty living in this city."

I could see him measuring the distance between us and deciding that he couldn't reach me from where he sat.

"You're a policeman?" he asked.

"Yes."

"I've always hated policemen. They are always either crooked or stupid."

"Is that the kind of books you write?"

I could see him edging his chair round to

block my way out. I caught the waiter's eye and he knew what I meant – there's an advantage in always using the same bar for interviews.

Martins said gently, and brought out a surface smile: "I have to call them sheriffs."

"Been in America?"

"Is this an interrogation?"

"Just interest."

"Because if Harry was that kind of racketeer, I must be one, too. We always worked together."

"I daresay he meant to cut you in – somewhere in the organization. I wouldn't be surprised if he had meant to give you the baby to hold. That was his method at school – you told me, didn't you?"

"You are running true to form, aren't you? I suppose there was some petty racket going on with petrol and you couldn't pin it on anyone, so you've picked a dead man. That's just like a policeman. You're a real policeman, I suppose?"

"Yes, Scotland Yard, but they've put me into a colonel's uniform when I'm on duty."

He was between me and the door now. I couldn't get away from the table without coming into range. I'm no fighter, and he had six inches of advantage anyway. I said, "It wasn't petrol."

"Tires, saccharins – why don't you policemen catch a few murderers for a change?"

"Well, you could say that murder was part of his racket."

He pushed the table over with one hand and made a dive at me with the other. The drink confused his calculations. Before he could try again, my driver had his arms round him.

"Listen, Callaghan, or whatever your bloody name is –"

"Calloway. I'm English, not Irish."

"I'm going to make you look the biggest bloody fool in Vienna."

"I see. You're going to find me the real criminal?"

"You can let me go, Callaghan. I'd rather make you look the fool you are than black your eye. You'd only have to go to bed for a few days with a black eye. But when I've finished with you, you'll leave Vienna."

I took out a couple of pounds' worth of *Bafs* and stuck them in his breast pocket. "These will see you through tonight," I said, "and I'll make sure they keep a seat for you on tomorrow's London plane."

"You can't turn me out. My papers are in order."

"Yes, but this is not like other cities: You

need money here. If you change sterling on the black market I'll catch up on you inside twenty-four hours. – Let him go."

Rollo Martins dusted himself down. "I'll be seeing you again when I've got the dope," he said.

"I might come and see you off tomorrow," I said.

"I shouldn't waste your time. I won't be there."

"Paine here will show you the way to Sacher's. You can get a bed and dinner there. I'll see to that."

He stepped on one side as though to make way for the waiter, and slashed out at me. I just avoided him but stumbled against the table. Before he could try again, Paine had landed him on the mouth. He went bang over in the alleyway between the tables and came up bleeding from a cut lip.

I had had a long day and I was tired of Rollo Martins. I said to Paine, "See him safely into Sacher's. Don't hit him again if he behaves."

What happened next I didn't hear from Paine but from Martins a long time afterward. Paine simply saw him to the head porter's desk and explained there, "This gentleman came in on the plane from London. Colonel Calloway says he's to have a room." Having made that clear, he said, "Good evening, sir," and left.

"Had you already got a reservation, sir?" the porter asked.

"No. No, I don't think so," Martins said in a muffled voice, holding his handkerchief to his mouth.

"I thought perhaps you might be Mr. Dexter. We had a room reserved for a week for Mr. Dexter."

Martins said, "Oh, I am Mr. Dexter." He told me later that it occurred to him that Lime might have engaged him a room in that name because perhaps it was Buck Dexter and not Rollo Martins who was to be used propaganda purposes.

A voice said at his elbow, "I'm so sorry you were not met at the plane, Mr. Dexter. My name's Crabbin."

The speaker was a stout, middle-aged young man with one of the thickest pairs of horn-rimmed glasses that Martins had ever seen. He went apologetically on, "One of our chaps happened to ring up Frankfurt and heard you were on the plane. H.Q. made one of their usual foolish mistakes and wired you were not coming. Something about Sweden, but the cable was badly mutilated. Directly I heard from Frankfurt I tried to meet the plane, but I just missed you. You got my note?"

Martins held his handkerchief to his mouth and said obscurely, "Yes. Yes?"

"May I say at once, Mr. Dexter, how excited I am to meet you?"

"Good of you."

"Ever since I was a boy, I've thought you the greatest novelist of our century."

Martins winced; it was painful opening his mouth to protest. He took an angry look instead at Mr. Crabbin, but it was impossible to suspect that young man of a practical joke.

"You have a big Austrian public, Mr. Dexter, both for your originals and your translations. Especially for *The Curved Prow;* that's my own favorite."

Martins was thinking hard. "Did you say – room for a week?"

"Yes."

"Very kind of you."

"Mr. Schmidt here will give you tickets every day to cover all meals. But I expect you'll need a little pocket money. We'll fix that. Tomorrow we thought you'd like a quiet day – to look about."

"Yes."

"Of course, any of us are at your service if you need a guide. Then, the day after tomorrow in the evening there's a little quiet discussion at the Institute – on the contemporary novel. We thought perhaps you'd say a few words."

Martins at that moment was prepared to agree to anything, to get rid of Mr. Crabbin and also to secure a week's free board and lodging. He said, "Of course, of course," into his handkerchief.

"Excuse me, Mr. Dexter, have you got a toothache?"

"No. Somebody hit me, that's all."

"Good heavens! Were they trying to rob you?"

"No, it was a soldier. I was trying to punch his colonel in the eye."

He removed the handkerchief and gave Crabbin a view of his cut mouth. He told me that Crabbin was at a complete loss for words. Martins couldn't understand why, because he had never read the work of his great contemporary, Benjamin Dexter; he hadn't even heard of him. I am a great admirer of Dexter, so that I could understand Crabbin's bewilderment.

Dexter has been ranked as a stylist with Henry James, but he has a wider feminine streak than his master – indeed, his enemies have sometimes described his subtle, complex, wavering style as old-maidish. For a man still just on the right side of fifty, his

451

passionate interest in embroidery and his habit of calming a not very tumultuous mind with tatting – a trait beloved by his disciples – certainly to others seems a little affected.

"Have you ever read a book called *The Lone Rider from Santa Fe?*" Martins asked.

"No, I don't think so."

Martins said, "this lone rider had his best friend shot by the sheriff of a town called Lost Claim Gulch. The story is how he hunted that sheriff down – quite legally – until his revenge was completed."

"I never imagined you reading westerns, Mr. Dexter," Crabbin said.

"Well, I'm gunning just the same way for Colonel Callaghan."

"Never heard of him."

"Heard of Harry Lime?"

"Yes," Crabbin said cautiously, "but I didn't really know him. A friend of his – an actress, you know – is learning English at the Institute. He called once or twice to fetch her."

Martins remembered the girl by the grave with her hands over her face. He said, "I'd like to meet any friend of Harry's."

"She'll probably be at your lecture."

"Austrian?"

"She claims to be Austrian, but I suspect

she's Hungarian. She works at the Josefstadt."

"Why claims to be Austrian?"

"The Russians sometimes get interested in the Hungarians. I wouldn't be surprised if Lime hadn't helped her with her papers. She calls herself Schmidt. Anna Schmidt."

Martins felt he had got all he could from Crabbin, so he pleaded tiredness, a long day, promised to ring up in the morning, accepted ten pounds' worth of *Bafs* for immediate expenses, and went to his room.

He was tired. He realized that when he stretched himself out on his bed in his boots. Within a minute he was asleep. He woke suddenly, to hear the telephone ringing by his bed.

A voice with a trace of foreign accent – only a trace – said, "Is that Mr. Rollo Martins?"

"Yes."

"You wouldn't know me," the voice said unnecessarily, "but I was a friend of Harry Lime."

It was a change, too, to hear anyone claim to be a friend of Harry's; Martins's heart warmed toward the stranger. He said, "I'd be glad to meet you."

"I'm just around the corner at the Old Vienna."

"Wouldn't you make it tomorrow?"

"Harry asked me to see that you were all right. I was with him when he died."

"I thought –" Rollo Martins said, and stopped. He was going to say, "I thought he died instantaneously," but something suggested caution. He said instead, "You haven't told me your name."

"Kurtz," the voice said. "I'd offer to come round to you, only, you know, Austrians aren't allowed in Sacher's."

"Perhaps we could meet at the Old Vienna in the morning."

"Certainly," the voice said, "if you are quite sure that you are all right till then."

"How do you mean?"

"Harry had it on his mind that you'd be penniless."

Rollo Martins lay back on his bed with the receiver to his ear and thought, Come to Vienna to make money. This was the third stranger to stake him in less than five hours. He said cautiously, "Oh, I can carry on till I see you."

"Shall we say eleven, then, at Old Vienna in the Kärtnerstrasse? I'll be in a brown suit and I'll carry one of your books."

454

"That's fine. How did you get hold of one?"

"Harry gave it to me."

The voice had enormous charm and reasonableness, but when Martins had said good night and rung off, he couldn't help wondering how it was that if Harry had been so conscious before he died, he had not had a cable sent to stop him. Hadn't Callaghan, too, said that Lime had died instantaneously – or without pain, was it? Or had he, himself, put the words into Callaghan's mouth?

It was then that the idea first lodged firmly in Martins's mind that there was something wrong about Lime's death, something the police had been too stupid to discover. He tried to discover it himself with the help of two cigarettes, but he fell asleep without his dinner and with the mystery still unsolved.

"What I disliked about him at first sight," Martins told me, "was his toupee. It was one of those obvious toupees – flat and yellow, with the hair cut straight at the back and not fitting close. There *must* be something phony about a man who won't accept baldness gracefully."

This conversation took place some days later – he brought out his whole story when the trail was nearly cold. It appeared that Kurtz was sitting there at the Old Vienna making a great show of reading *The Lone Rider from Santa Fe*.

Martins introduced himself and sat down. "So you were a friend of Harry's," he said.

"I think his best," but Kurtz added, with the smallest pause in which his brain must have registered the error, "except you, of course."

"Tell me how he died."

"I was with him. We came out together from the door of his flat and Harry saw a friend he knew across the road – an American called Cooler. He waved to Cooler, and started across the road to him, when a jeep came tearing round the corner and bowled him over. It was Harry's fault really – not the driver's."

"Somebody told me he died instantaneously."

"I wish he had. He died before the ambulance could reach us, though."

"He could speak then?"

"Yes. Even in his pain he worried about you."

"What did he say?"

"I can't remember the exact words, Rollo – I may call you Rollo, mayn't I? He always

456

called you that to us. He was anxious that I should look after you when you arrived."

"But why didn't you cable to stop me?"

"We did, but the cable must have missed you."

"There was an inquest?"

"Of course."

"Did you know that the police have a crazy notion that Harry was mixed up in some racket?"

"They get rather absurd ideas sometimes," Kurtz said cautiously.

"I'm going to stay here till I prove them wrong."

"I don't see what you can do."

"I'm going to start working back from his death. You were there, and this man Cooler and the chauffeur. You can give me their addresses."

"I don't know the chauffeur's."

"I can get it from the coroner's records. And then there's Harry's girl –"

Kurtz said, "It will be painful for her."

"I'm not concerned about her. I'm concerned about Harry."

"Do you know what it is that the police suspect?"

"No. I lost my temper too soon."

"Has it occurred to you," Kurtz said

gently, "that you might dig up something – well, discreditable to Harry?"

"I'll risk that."

"It will take a bit of time – and money."

"I've got time and you were going to lend me some money, weren't you?"

"I'm not a rich man," Kurtz said. "I promised Harry to see you were all right and that you got your plane back."

"You needn't worry about the money – or the plane," Martins said. "But I'll make a bet with you – in pounds sterling – five pounds against two hundred schillings – that there's something queer about Harry's death."

It was a shot in the dark, but already he had this firm, instinctive sense that there was something wrong, though he hadn't yet attached the word "murder" to the instinct. Kurtz had a cup of coffee halfway to his lips and Martins watched him. The shot apparently went wide; an unaffected hand held the cup to the mouth and Kurtz drank, a little noisily, in long sips. Then he put down the cup and said, "How do you mean – queer?"

"It was convenient for the police to have a corpse, but wouldn't it have been equally convenient, perhaps, for the real racketeers?" When he had spoken he realized that, after

458

all, Kurtz had not been unaffected by his wild statement. The hands of the guilty don't necessarily tremble. Tension is more often shown in the studied action. Kurtz had finished his coffee as though nothing had been said.

"Well" – he took another sip – "of course, I wish you luck, though I don't believe there's anything to find. Just ask me for any help you want."

"I want Cooler's address."

"Certainly. I'll write it down for you. Here it is. In the American zone."

"And yours?"

"I've already put it – underneath. I'm unlucky enough to be in the Russian zone – so you shouldn't visit me very late. Things sometimes happen round our way." He rose, giving one of his studied Viennese smiles. "Keep in touch," he said, "and if you need help – but I still think you are very unwise."

Martins sat on a hard chair just inside the stage door of the Josefstadt Theater. He had sent up his card to Anna Schmidt after the matinee, marking it, "A friend of Harry's."

He had had time to think. He thought, "Kurtz is right. They're all right. I'm behaving like a romantic fool. I'll just have a word with Anna Schmidt, a word of commiseration, and then I'll pack and go."

A voice over his head called, "Mr. Martins," and he looked up at the face that watched him from between the curtains a few feet above his head. It wasn't a beautiful face, he firmly explained to me. Just an honest face with dark hair and eyes which looked brown; a wide forehead, a large mouth which didn't try to charm. She said, "Will you come up, please?" The second door on the right."

There are some people, he explained to me carefully, whom one recognizes instantly as friends. You can be at ease with them because you know that never, never will you be in danger. "That was Anna," he said.

He said to her, "I wanted very much to see you. About Harry."

It was the dreaded moment; he could see her mouth stiffen to meet it.

"Yes?"

"I was his friend. We were at school together, you know, and after that there weren't many months running when we didn't meet."

She said, "When I got your card I couldn't say no, but there's nothing, really, for us to talk about. Everything's over, finished."

"We both loved him."

460

"I don't know. You can't know a thing like that – afterward. I don't know anything any more except – that I want to be dead, too."

Martins told me, "Then I nearly went away. What was the good of tormenting her because of this wild idea of mine? But instead I asked her one question: 'Do you know a man called Cooler?' "

"An American?" she asked. "I think that was the man who brought me some money when Harry died. I didn't want to take it, but he said Harry had been anxious – at the last moment."

"So he didn't die instantaneously?"

"Oh, no."

Martins said to me later, "I began to wonder why I had got that idea into my head, and then I thought, it was only the man in the flat who told me so, no one else."

Martins said to Anna, "He must have been very clear in his head at the end, because he remembered about me, too. That seems to show that there wasn't really any pain."

"That's what I tell myself all the time," she said.

"Did you know the doctor?"

"Yes. Harry sent me to him once."

Martins suddenly saw in that odd chamber of the mind which constructs such pictures,

461

instantaneously, irrationally, a desert place, a body on the ground, a group of birds gathered. he thought, "How odd that they were all there, just at that moment, all Harry's friends – Kurtz, the doctor, this man Cooler; only the two people who loved him seemed to have been missing." He said, "And the driver? Did you hear his evidence?"

"He was upset, scared. But Cooler's evidence exonerated him. No, it wasn't his fault, poor man. I've often heard Harry say what a careful driver he was."

"*He* knew Harry, too?" Another bird flapped down and joined the others round the silent figure on the sand who lay face down.

Somebody called outside the window, "Fräulein Schmidt."

She said, "They don't like one to stay too long. It uses up their electricity."

He had given up the idea of sparing her anything. He told her, "The police say they were going to arrest Harry. They'd pinned some racket on him."

She took the news in much the same way as Kurtz. "Everybody's in a racket."

"I don't believe he was in anything serious. He may have been framed. Do you know a man called Kurtz?"

"I don't think so."

"He wears a toupee."

"Oh." He could tell that that struck home. He said, "Don't you think it was odd they were all there – at the death. Everybody knew Harry. Even the driver, the doctor –"

She said, with hopeless calm, "I've thought that, too, though I didn't know about Kurtz. I wondered whether they'd murdered him, but what's the use of wondering?"

"I'm going to find out," Rollo Martins said.

"Fräulein Schmidt," the voice called again.

"I must go."

"I'll walk with you a bit of the way."

It was almost dark. The snow had ceased. The great statues of the Ring, the prancing horses, the chariots, and the eagles, were gunshot-gray with the end of evening light. "It's better to give up and forget," Anna said.

"Will you give me the doctor's address?"

They stood in the shelter of a wall while she wrote it down for him.

"And yours, too?"

"Why do you want that?"

"I might have news for you."

"There isn't any news that would do any good now."

He watched her from a distance board her tram, bowing her head against the wind.

An amateur detective has this advantage over the professional, that he doesn't work set hours. Rollo Martins was not confined to the eight-hour day; his investigations didn't have to pause for meals. In his one day he covered as much ground as one of my men would have covered in two, and he had this initial advantage over us, that he was Harry's friend.

Dr. Winkler was at home. Perhaps he would not have been at home to a police officer. Again, Martins had marked his card with the sesame phrase: "A friend of Harry Lime's."

Dr. Winkler was the cleanest doctor Martins had ever seen. He was very small and neat, in a black tail coat and a high, stiff collar; his little black mustache was like an evening tie. He said, "Mr. Martins?"

"We were both friends of Harry Lime," Martins said.

"I was his medical adviser," Dr. Winkler corrected him, and waited obstinately.

"I arrived too late for the inquest. Harry had invited me out here to help him in

464

something. I don't quite know what. I didn't hear of his death till I arrived."

"Very sad," Dr. Winkler said.

"Naturally, under the circumstances, I want to hear all I can."

"There is nothing I can tell you that you don't know. He was knocked over by a car. He was dead when I arrived."

"Would he have been conscious at all?"

"I understand he was for a short time, while they carried him into the house."

"You're quite certain it was an accident?"

Dr. Winkler touched his mustache. "I was not there. My opinion is limited to the cause of death. Have you any reason to be dissatisfied?"

The amateur has another advantage over the professional: he can be reckless. He can tell unnecessary truths and propound wild theories.

Martins said, "The police had implicated Harry in a very serious racket. It seemed to me that he might have been murdered – or had even killed himself."

"I am not competent to pass an opinion," Dr. Winkler said.

"Do you know a man called Cooler?"

"I don't think so."

"He was there when Harry was killed."

"Then of course I have met him. He wears a toupee."

"That was Kurtz."

Dr. Winkler was not only the cleanest, he was also the most cautious doctor that Martins had ever met. His statements were so limited that you could not for a moment doubt their veracity. He said, "There was a second man there."

"Had you been Harry's doctor for long?"

"For about a year."

"Well, it's good of you to have seen me."

Dr. Winkler bowed. When he bowed there was a very slight creak, as though his shirt were made of celluloid.

When Rollo Martins left Dr. Winkler's he was in no danger. He could have gone home to bed at Sacher's and slept with a quiet mind. He could even have visited Cooler at this stage without trouble. No one was seriously disturbed. Unfortunately for him, he chose to go back to Harry's flat. He wanted to talk to the little vexed man who said he had seen the accident.

The little man – who bore the name of Koch – was friendly and quite ready to talk. He had just finished dinner and had crumbs on his mustache. "Ah, I remember you. You are Herr Lime's friend."

466

He welcomed Martins in with great cordiality and introduced him to a mountainous wife.

"Did you tell me that you had actually seen the accident?" Martins asked.

Herr Koch exchanged glances with his wife. "The inquest is over, Ilse. There is no harm. You can trust my judgment. The gentleman is a friend. – Yes, I saw the accident, but you are the only one who knows. When I say that I saw it, perhaps I should say that I heard it. I heard the brakes put on and the sound of the skid, and I got to the window in time to see them carry the body to the house."

"But didn't you give evidence?"

"It is better not to be mixed up in such things. My office cannot spare me. We are short of staff, and of course I did not actually *see* –"

"But you told me yesterday how it happened."

"That was how they described it in the papers."

"Was he in great pain?"

"He was dead. I looked right down from my window here and I saw his face. I know when a man is dead. You see, it is, in a way, my business. I am the head clerk at the mortuary."

"But the others say that he didn't die at once."

"Perhaps they don't know death as well as I do."

"I think, Herr Koch, that you should have given evidence."

"One must look after oneself, Herr Martins. I was not the only one who should have been there."

"How do you mean?"

"There were three people who helped to carry your friend to the house."

"I know – two men and the driver."

"The driver stayed where he was. He was very much shaken."

"Three men –" It was as though, suddenly fingering that bare wall, his fingers had encountered, not so much a crack perhaps but at least a roughness that had not been smoothed away by the careful builders.

"Can you describe the men?"

But Herr Koch was not trained to observe the living; only the man with the toupee had attracted his eyes; the other two were just men, neither tall nor short, thick nor thin. He had seen them from far above, foreshortened, bent over their burden. They had not looked up, and he had quickly looked away and closed the window, realizing at once the wisdom of not being seen himself.

"There was no evidence I could really give, Herr Martins."

No evidence, Martins thought, no evidence! He no longer doubted that murder had been done. Why else had they lied about the moment of death? And the third man? Who was he?

He said, "Did you see Herr Lime go out?"

"No."

"Did you hear a scream?"

"Only the brakes, Herr Martins."

It occurred to Martins that there was nothing – except the word of Kurtz and Cooler and the driver – to prove that in fact Harry had been killed at that precise moment. There was the medical evidence, but that could not prove more than that he had died, say, within a half hour, and in any case the medical evidence was only as strong as Dr. Winkler's word.

"Herr Martins, it just ocurs to me, if you need accommodation and spoke to the authorities quickly, you might secure Herr Lime's flat."

"Could I see the flat?"

"Ilse, the keys."

Herr Koch led the way into the flat that had been Harry's. In the little dark hall there was still the smell of cigarette smoke – the

469

Turkish cigarettes that Harry always smoked.

The living room was completely bare – it seemed to Martins too bare. The chairs had been pushed up against the walls; the desk at which Harry must have written was free from dust or any papers. Herr Koch opened a door and showed the bedroom – the bed neatly made with clean sheets.

"You see," Herr Koch said, "it is quite ready for a newcomer."

"Were there no papers, Herr Koch?"

"Herr Lime was always a very tidy man. His wastepaper basket was full and his briefcase, but his friend fetched that away."

"His friend?"

"The gentleman with the toupee."

It was possible, of course, that Lime had not taken the journey so unexpectedly, and it occurred to Martins that Lime had perhaps hoped he would arrive in time to help. He said to Herr Koch, "I believe my friend was murdered."

"Murdered?" Herr Koch's cordiality was snuffed out by the word. He said, "I would not have asked you in here if I had thought you would talk such nonsense."

"Why should it be nonsense?"

"We do not have murders in this zone."

470

"All the same, your evidence may be very valuable."

"I have no evidence. I saw nothing. I am not concerned. You must leave here at once, please. You have been very inconsiderate." He hustled Martins back through the hall; already the smell of the cigarette smoke was fading a little more. Herr Koch's last word before he slammed his own door was, "It's no concern of mine."

Poor Herr Koch! We do not choose our concerns. Later, when I was questioning Martins closely, I said to him, "Did you see anybody at all on the stairs, or in the street outside?"

"Nobody." He had everything to gain by remembering some chance passerby, and I believed him.

"Of course, it proves nothing. There is a basement where anybody who had followed you could hide."

"Yes."

"The whole story may be phony."

"Yes."

"The trouble is, I can see no motive for you to have done it. It's true you are already guilty of getting money on false pretenses: you came out here to join Lime, perhaps to help him –"

Martins said to me. "What was this racket you keep on hinting at?"

"I'd have told you all the facts when I first saw you if you hadn't lost your temper so damned quickly. Now, I don't think I shall be acting wisely to tell you. It would be disclosing official information, and your contacts, you know, don't inspire confidence. A girl with phony papers supplied by Lime, this man Kurtz –"

"Dr. Winkler –"

"I've got nothing against Dr. Winkler. No, if you are phony, you don't need the information, but it might help you to learn exactly what we know. You see, our facts are not complete."

"I bet they aren't. I could invent a better detective than you in my bath."

"Your literary style doesn't do your namesake justice." Whenever he was reminded of Mr. Crabbin, that poor, harassed representative of the British Council, Rollo Martins turned pink with annoyance, embarrassment, shame. That, too, inclined me to trust him.

He had certainly given Crabbin some uncomfortable hours. On returning to Sacher's Hotel after his interview with Herr Koch, he had found a desperate note waiting for him from the representative.

"I have been trying to locate you all day," Crabbin wrote. "It is essential that we should get together and work out a proper program for you. This morning by telephone I have arranged lectures at Innsbruck and Salzburg for next week, but I must have your consent to the subjects, so that proper programs can be printed.

"Apart from this, there are a great many people here who would like to meet you, and I want to arrange a cocktail party for early next week. But for all this I must have a few words with you." The letter ended on a note of acute anxiety: "You will be at the discussion tomorrow night, won't you? We all expect you at 8:30, and, needless to say, look forward to your coming. I will send transport to the hotel at 8:15 sharp."

Rollo Martins read the letter and, without bothering any further about Mr. Crabbin, went to bed.

Martins spent the greater part of the following day studying the reports of the inquest, thus again demonstrating the superiority of the amateur to the professional, and making him more vulnerable to Cooler's liquor (which the professional in duty-bound would have

473

refused). It was nearly five o'clock when he reached Cooler's flat.

Again the card marked "Harry's friend" was like an entrance ticket.

Cooler, a man with tousled gray hair, a worried, kindly face, and long-sighted eyes, was in officer's uniform, but wore no badges of rank. His maid referred to him as Colonel Cooler. His warm, frank handclasp was the most friendly act that Martins had encountered in Vienna.

"Any friend of Harry is all right with me," Cooler said.

"I wondered – you were there, weren't you? – if you'd tell me about Harry's death."

"It was a terrible thing," Cooler said. "I was just crossing the road to go to Harry. He and a Mr. Kurtz were on the sidewalk. Maybe if I hadn't started across the road he'd have stayed where he was. But he saw me and stepped straight off to meet me, and this jeep – it was terrible, terrible. The driver braked, but Harry didn't stand a chance –

"Have a drink, Mr. Martins. It's silly of me, but I get shaken up when I think of it."

"Was the other man in the car?"

Cooler took a long pull and then measured what was left with his tired, kindly eyes. "What man would you be referring to, Mr. Martins?"

"I was told there was another man there."

"I don't know how you got that idea. You'll find all about it in the inquest reports." He poured out two more generous drinks. "There were just the three of us – me and Mr. Kurtz and the driver. The doctor, of course. I expect you were thinking of the doctor."

"This man I was talking to happened to look out of a window – he has the next flat to Harry's – and he said he saw three men and the driver. That's before the doctor arrived."

"He didn't say that in court."

"He didn't want to get involved."

"You'll never teach these Europeans to be good citizens. It was his duty." Cooler brooded sadly over his glass. "It's an odd thing, Mr. Martins, with accidents. You'll never get two reports that coincide. Why, even I and Mr. Kurtz disagreed about the details. The thing happens so suddenly, you aren't concerned to notice things, until bang crash! And then you have to reconstruct, remember. I expect he got too tangled up trying to sort out what happened before and what after, to distinguish the four of us."

"The four?"

"I was counting Harry. What else did he see, Mr. Martins?"

"Nothing of interest – except he says Harry was dead when he was carried to the house."

"Well, he was dying – not much difference there. – Have another drink, Mr. Martins?"

"Perhaps one more – to keep you company," Martins said.

"Do you know Anna Schmidt?" he asked, while the whisky still tingled on his tongue.

"Harry's girl? I met her once, that's all. As a matter of fact, I helped Harry fix her papers. Not the sort of thing I should confess to a stranger, I suppose, but you have to break the rules sometimes. Humanity's a duty, too."

"What was wrong?"

"She was Hungarian and her father had been a Nazi, so they said. She was scared the Russians would pick her up."

"But she lives in the British zone."

"That wouldn't stop them. The streets aren't well lighted, and you haven't many police around."

"You took her some money from Harry, didn't you?"

"Yes, but I wouldn't have mentioned that. Did she tell you?"

The telephone rang, and Cooler drained his glass.

"Hullo," he said. – "Why, yes, this is

Colonel Cooler." Then he sat with the receiver at his ear and an expression of sad patience, while some voice a long way off drained into the room. "Yes," he said once. "Yes." His eyes dwelt on Martin's face, but they seemed to be looking a long way beyond him; flat and tired and kind, they might have gazing out over acres of sea. He said, "You did quite right," in a tone of commendation, and then, with a touch of asperity, "Of course they will be delivered. I gave my word. Goodbye."

He put the receiver down and passed a hand across his forehead wearily. It was as thought he were trying to remember something he had to do.

Martins said, "Had you heard anything of this racket the police talk about?"

"I'm sorry. What's that?"

"They say Harry was mixed up in some racket."

"Oh, no," Cooler said, "No. That's quite impossible. He had a great sense of duty."

"Kurtz seemed to think it was possible."

"Kurtz doesn't understand how an Anglo-Saxon feels," Cooler replied.

It was nearly dark when Martins made his way along the banks of the canal. Across the water lay the half destroyed Diana Baths and in the distance the great black circle of the Prater Wheel, stationary above the ruined houses. Coming up the Kärtnerstrasse, Martins passed the door of the Military Police station. The four men of the International Patrol were climbing into their jeep. The Russian M.P. sat beside the driver (for the Russians had that day taken over the chair for the next four weeks) and the Englishman, the Frenchman, and the American mounted behind. The third stiff whisky fumed in Martins's brain and he moved toward the only girl he knew in Vienna.

He hadn't, of course, known that she would be in, that her play was not on that night in the Josefstadt. She was sitting alone in an unheated room, with the bed disguised as a divan.

He saw awkwardly, "I thought I'd just look you up. You see, I was passing –"

"Passing? Where to?" It had been a good half hour's walk from the Inner City to the rim of the English zone, but he always had a reply: "I had too much whisky with Colonel Cooler. I needed a walk, and I just happened to find myself this way."

"I can't give you a drink here. Except tea."

"No. No, thank you." He said, "Can I stay a little?"

"I wish you would."

He slumped down on the divan, and he told me, a long time later, that there it was he took his second real look at her. She stood there as awkward as himself in a pair of old flannel trousers, with her legs firmly straddled as though she were opposing someone and was determined to hold her ground.

"One of those bad days?" he asked her.

"It's always bad about this time." She explained, "He used to look in, and when I heard your ring, just for a moment, I thought –" She sat down on a hard chair opposite him and said, "Please talk. You knew him. Just tell me anything."

And so he talked. He noticed after a while that their hands had met. He said to me, "I never meant to fall in love, not with Harry's girl."

"When did it happen?" I asked him.

"It was very cold and I got up to close the window curtains. I only noticed my hand was on hers when I took it away. As I stood up I looked down at her face, and she was looking up. It wasn't a beautiful face – that was the trouble. It was a face to live with, day in, day out. A face for wear. I felt as though I'd come into a new country where I couldn't speak the language. I had always thought it was beauty one loved in a woman.

"I stood there at the curtains, waiting to pull them, looking out. I couldn't see anything but my own face, looking back into the room, looking for her. She said, 'And what did Harry do that time?' and I wanted to say, 'Damn Harry. He's dead. We both loved him, but he's dead. The dead are made to be forgotten.' Instead, of course, all I said was, 'What do you think? He just whistled his old tune as if nothing was the matter,' and I whistled it to her as well as I could. I heard her catch her breath, and I looked round, and before I could think, is this the right way, the right card, the right gambit? I'd already said, 'He's dead. You can't go on remembering him forever.' "

She had answered, "I know, but perhaps something will happen first."

"What do you mean – something happen?" Martins had asked.

"Oh, I mean, perhaps there'll be another war, or I'll die, or the Russians will take me."

"You'll forget him in time. You'll fall in love again."

"I know, but I don't want to. Don't you see I don't want to?"

So Rollo Martins came back from the window and sat down on the divan again.

When he had risen, half a minute before, he had been the friend of Harry comforting Harry's girl; now he was a man in love with Anna Schmidt, who had been in love with a man they had both once known called Harry Lime. He didn't speak again that evening about the past. Instead, he began to tell her of the people he had seen.

"I can believe anything of Winkler," he told her, "but Cooler – I liked Cooler. He was the only one of his friends who stood up for Harry. The trouble is, if Cooler's right, then Koch is wrong, and I really thought I had something there."

"Who's Koch?"

He explained how he had returned to Harry's flat, and he described his interview with Koch, the story of the third man.

"It it's true," she said, "it's very important."

"It doesn't prove anything. After all, Koch backed out of the inquest; so might this stranger."

"That's not the point," she said. "It means that *they* lied, Kurtz and Cooler."

"They might have lied so as not to inconvenience this fellow – if he was a friend."

"Yet another friend – on the spot. And where's your Cooler's honesty then?"

481

"What do we do? Koch clamped down like an oyster and turned me out of his flat."

"He won't turn *me* out," she said, "or his Ilse won't."

They walked up the long road to the flat together. The snow clogged on their shoes and made them move slowly. Anna Schmidt said, "Is it far?"

"Not very far now. Do you see that knot of people up the road? It's somewhere about there." The group of people up the road was like a splash of ink on the whiteness that flowed, changed shape, spread out. When they came a little nearer Martins said, "I think that is his block. What do you suppose this is – a political demonstration?"

Anna Schmidt stopped. She said, "Who else have you told about Koch?"

"Only you and Colonel Cooler. Why?"

"I'm frightened. It reminds me –" She had her eyes fixed on the crowd and he never knew what memory out of her confused past had risen to warn her. "Let's go away," she implored him.

"You're crazy. We're onto something here, something big."

"I'll wait for you."

"But you're going to talk to him."

"Find out first what all those people –"

She said, strangely for one who worked behind the footlights, "I hate crowds."

He walked slowly on alone. He had the impression of heads turning to watch him come. When he reached the fringe of the little crowd he knew for certain that it was the house. A man looked hard at him and said, "Are you another of them?"

"Who do you mean?"

"The police."

"No. What are they doing?"

"They've been in and out all day."

"What's everybody waiting for?"

"They want to see him brought out."

"Who?"

"Herr Koch."

"What's he done?"

"Nobody knows that yet. They can't make their minds up in there – it might be suicide and it might be murder."

"Herr Koch?"

"Of course. There is talk of a foreigner who called on Herr Koch yesterday."

Martins walked back down the street toward Anna. He said, "Koch has been murdered. Come away from here." He walked as rapidly as the snow would let him, turning this corner and that. He paid no attention when Anna said to him, "Then

483

what Koch said was true. There *was* a third man."

The tram cars flashed like icicles at the end of the street; they were back at the Ring. Martins said, "You had better go home alone. I'll keep away from you a while till things have sorted out."

"But nobody can suspect you."

"They were asking about the foreigner who called on Koch yesterday. There may be some unpleasantness for a while."

"Why don't you go to the police?"

"They are so stupid. I don't trust them. See what they've pinned on Harry. And then I tried to hit this man Callaghan. They'll have it in for me. The least they'll do is send me away from Vienna. But if I stay quiet – There's only one person who can give me away: Cooler."

"And he won't want to."

"Not if he's guilty. But then I can't believe he's guilty."

Before she left him she said, "Be careful. Koch knew so very little and they murdered him. You know as much as Koch."

The warning stayed in his brain all the way to Sacher's. After nine o'clock the streets are very empty, and he would turn his head at every padding step coming up the street behind him, as though that third man whom

484

they had protected so ruthlessly was now following him like an executioner.

At Sacher's a desk man said, "Colonel Calloway has been in asking after you, sir. I think you'll find him in the bar."

"Back in a moment," Martins said, and walked straight out of the hotel again – he wanted time to think. But immediately he stepped outside a man came forward, touched his cap, and said firmly, "Please sir." He flung open the door of a khaki-painted truck with a Union Jack on the windscreen and firmly urged Martins within. He surrendered without protest. Sooner or later he had felt sure inquiries would be made; he had only pretended optimism to Anna Schmidt.

The driver drove too fast for safety on the frozen road, and Martins protested. All he got in reply was a sullen grunt and a muttered sentence containing the word "orders."

The car drew up before a building and the driver led the way up two flights of stairs. He rang the bell of a great double door, and Martins was aware beyond it of many voices. He turned sharply to the driver and said, "Where the –?" but the driver was halfway down the stairs and already the door was opening. His eyes were dazzled from the darkness by the lights inside; he heard but he could hardly see the advance of Mr. Crabbin: "Oh, Mr. Dexter, we have been so anxious, but better late than never. Let me introduce you to Miss Wilbraham and the Gräfin von Meyersdorf."

A buffet laden with coffee cups; an urn steaming; a woman's face shiny with exertion; two young men with the happy, intelligent faces of sixth formers; and huddled in the background, like faces in a family album, a multitude of the old-fashioned, the dingy, the earnest and cheery features of constant readers. Martins looked behind him, but the door had closed.

He said desperately to Mr. Crabbin, "I'm sorry, but –"

"Don't think any more about it," Mr. Crabbin said. "One cup of coffee and then let's go on to the discussion."

One of the young men placed a cup in his hand, the other shoveled in sugar before he could say he preferred his coffee unsweetened.

Martins was not able to tell me very much about the meeting; his mind was still dazed with the death. He could not say how he got through the discussion. Perhaps Crabbin took the brunt; perhaps he was helped by

486

some of the audience who got into an animated discussion about the film version of a popular American novel. He remembered very little more before Crabbin was making a final speech in his honor. Then one of the young men led him to a table stacked with books and asked him to sign them.

Martins took his pen and wrote: "From B. Dexter, author of *The Lone Rider from Santa Fe*," and the young man read the sentence and blotted it, with a puzzled expression.

Suddenly in a mirror Martins saw my driver, Sergeant Paine. He seemed to be having an argument with one of Crabbin's young henchmen. Martins thought he caught the sound of his own name. It was then he lost his nerve, and with it any relic of common sense. The young man, Crabbin, and Paine stood together at the entrance.

"And this gentleman?" Sergeant Paine asked.

"It's Mr. Benjamin Dexter," the young man said.

Paine said respectfully, "We were looking for you, sir. Colonel Calloway wants a word with you."

I had kept a very careful record of Martins's

movements from the moment I knew that he had not caught the plane home. Events had taken a disquieting turn, and it seemed to me that the time had come for another interview.

I put a good, wide desk between us and gave him a cigarette. I found him sullen but ready to talk, within strict limits. I asked him about Kurtz, and he seemed to me to answer satisfactorily. I then asked him about Anna Schmidt, and I gathered from his reply that he must have been with her after visiting Colonel Cooler. That filled in one of the missing points. I tried him with Dr. Winkler, and he answered readily enough.

"You've been getting around," I said, "quite a bit. And have you found out anything about your friend?"

"Oh, yes," he said. "It was under your nose but you didn't see it."

"What?"

"That he was murdered." That took me by surprise; I had at one time played with the idea of suicide, but I had ruled even that out.

"Go on," I said. He tried to eliminate from his story all mention of Koch, talking about an informant who had seen the accident. This made his story rather confusing, and I couldn't grasp at first why he attached so much importance to the third man.

"He didn't turn up at the inquest, and the others lied to keep him out."

"I don't see much importance in that. If it was a genuine accident, all the evidence needed was there. Why get the other chap into trouble?"

"There was more to it than that," he said. "The little chap who told me about the third man – they've murdered him. You see, they obviously didn't know what else he had seen."

"Now we have it," I said. "You mean Koch."

"Yes."

"As far as we know you were the last person to see him alive. The Austrian police are anxious to pin this on you. Frau Koch told them how disturbed her husband was by your visit. Who else knew about it?"

"I told Cooler." He said excitedly, "Suppose immediately I left he telephoned the story to someone – to the third man. They had to stop Koch's mouth."

"When you told Colonel Cooler about Koch, the man was already dead. That night he got out of bed, hearing someone, and went downstairs."

"Well, that rules me out. I was in Sacher's."

"But he went to bed very early. Your visit brought on a headache. It was soon after nine that he got up. You returned to Sacher's at nine-thirty. Where were you before that?"

He said gloomily, "Wandering round and trying to sort things out."

I wanted to frighten him, so there was no point in telling him that he had been followed all the time. I knew that he hadn't cut Koch's throat, but I wasn't sure that he was quite so innocent as he made out.

He said, "How did you know that I went to Koch's? That was why you pulled me here, wasn't it?"

"Immediately you left Colonel Cooler's, he telephoned to me."

"Then that lets him out. If he had been concerned, he wouldn't have wanted me to tell you my story – to tell Koch's story, I mean."

"He might assume that you were a sensible man and would come to me with your story as soon as you learned of Koch's death. By the way, how did you learn of it?"

He told me promptly, and I believed him. It was then I began to believe him altogether. He said, "I still can't believe Cooler's concerned. I'd stake anything on his honesty.

He's one of those Americans with a real sense of duty."

"Yes," I said, "he told me about that when he phoned. He apologized for it. He said it was the worst of having been brought up to believe in citizenship. He said it made him feel a prig. To tell you the truth, Cooler irritates me. Of course, he doesn't know that I know about his tire deals."

"Is he in a racket too, then?"

"Not a very serious one. I daresay he's salted away $25,000."

"I see." He said thoughtfully, "Is that the kind of thing Harry was up to?"

"No. It was not so harmless."

He said, "You know, this business – Koch's death – has shaken me. Perhaps Harry did get mixed up in something pretty bad. Perhaps he was trying to clear out again, and that's why they murdered him."

"Or perhaps," I said, "they wanted a bigger cut of the spoils. Thieves fall out."

He took it this time without any anger at all. He said, "We won't agree about motives, but I think you check your facts pretty well. I'm sorry about the other day."

"That's all right." There are times when one has to make a flash decision – this was one of them. I owed him something in return for the information he had given me. I said,

"I'll show you enough of the facts in Lime's case for you to understand. But don't fly off the handle. It's going to be a shock."

It couldn't help being a shock. The war and the peace let loose a great number of rackets, but none more vile than this one. The black marketeers in food did at least supply food, and the same applied to all the other racketeers who provided articles in short supply at extravagant prices. But the penicillin racket was a different affair altogether. Penicillin in Austria was supplied only to the military hospitals; no civilian doctor, not even a civilian hospital, could obtain it by legal means.

As the racket started, it was relatively harmless. Penicillin would be stolen by military orderlies and sold to Austrian doctors for very high sums – a phial would fetch anything up to $300.

This racket went on quite happily for a while. Occasionally an orderly was caught and punished, but the danger simply raised the price of penicillin. Then the racket began to get organized. The big men saw big money in it, and while the original thief got less for his spoils, he received, instead, a certain security.

This, I have sometimes called stage two.

492

Stage three was when the organizers decided that the profits were not large enough. Penicillin would not always be impossible to obtain legitimately; they wanted more money and quicker money while the going was good. They began to dilute the penicillin with colored water, and in the case of penicillin dust, with sand.

I keep a small museum in one drawer in my desk, and I showed Martins examples. He wasn't enjoying the talk, but he hadn't yet grasped the point. He said, "I suppose that makes the stuff useless."

I said, "We wouldn't worry so much if that was all, but just consider that you can be immunized from the effects of penicillin. At the best, you can say that the use of this stuff makes a penicillin treatment for the particular patient ineffective in the future. That isn't so funny, of course, if you are suffering from V.D. Then the use of sand on a wound that requires penicillin – well, it's not healthy. Men have lost their legs and arms that way – and their lives. But perhaps what horrified me most was visiting the children's hospital here. They had bought some of this penicillin for use against meningitis. A number of children simply died, and a number went off their heads. You can see them now in the mental ward."

He sat on the other side of the desk scowling into his hands.

I said, "It doesn't bear thinking about very closely, does it?"

"You haven't shown me any evidence yet that Harry –"

"We're coming to that now," I said. "Just sit still and listen." I opened Lime's file and began to read.

I am not going to bother the reader now, as I bothered Martins then, with all the stages – the long tussle to win the confidence of the go between, a man called Harbin. At last we had the screws on Harbin, and we twisted them until he squealed. "But he led us only as far as Kurtz," I said.

"Kurtz!" Martins exclaimed. "But why haven't you pulled him in?"

"Zero hour is almost here," I said.

Kurtz was a great step forward, for Kurtz was in direct communication with Lime – he had a small outside job in connection with international relief. With Kurtz, Lime sometimes put things on paper, if he was pressed. I showed Martins the photostat of a note. "Can you identify that?"

"It's Harry's hand." He read it through. "I don't see anything wrong."

"No, but now read this note from Harbin

494

to Kurtz, which we dictated. Look at the date. This is the result."

He read them both through twice.

"You see what I mean?"

If one watched a world come to an end, a planet dive from its course, I don't suppose one would chatter, and a world for Martins had certainly come to an end, a world of easy friendship, hero-worship, confidence, which had begun twenty years before.

While he sat there, looking at his hands and saying nothing, I fetched a precious bottle of whisky out of a cupboard and poured out two large doubles. "Go on," I said, "drink that," and he obeyed me as though I were his doctor. I poured him out another.

He said slowly, "Are you certain that he was the real boss?"

"It's as far back as we have got so far."

"Suppose," he said, "someone had got a line on him, forced him into this racket, as you forced Harbin to double-cross."

"It's possible."

"And they murdered him in case he talked when he was arrested."

"It's not impossible."

"I'm glad they did," he said. "I wouldn't have liked to hear Harry squeal." He made a curious little dusting movement of his hand

on his knee, as much as to say, "That's that."
He said, "I'll be getting back to England."

"I'd rather you didn't just yet. The
Austrian police would make an issue if you
tried to leave Vienna at the moment. You see,
Cooler's sense of duty made him call them
up, too."

"I see," he said hopelessly.

"When we've found the third man –" I
said.

"I'd like to hear *him* squeal," Martins said.

After he left me Martins went straight off to
drink himself silly. By the time the spots
were swimming in front of his eyes he was
oppressed by a sense of loneliness. The trams
had stopped, and he set out obstinately on
foot to find Harry's girl.

It must have been about three in the
morning when he climbed the stairs to
Anna's room. He was nearly sober by that
time and had only one idea in his head – that
she must know about Harry, too. He felt that
somehow this knowledge would pay the
mortmain that memory levies on human
beings, and he would stand a chance with
Harry's girl.

When Anna opened the door to him, with
astonishment at the sight of him, tousled, on

the threshold, he never imagined that she was opening the door to a stranger.

He said, "Anna, I've found out everything."

"Come in," she said. "You don't want to wake the house." She was in a dressing gown; the divan had become a bed.

"Now," she said, while he stood there, fumbling for words, "what is it? I thought you were going to keep away. Are the police after you?"

"No."

"You didn't really kill that man, did you?"

"Of course not."

"You're drunk, aren't you?"

"I am a bit," he said sulkily. The meeting seemed to be going on the wrong lines. "I've been with the British police. They are satisfied I didn't do it. But I've learned everything from them. Harry was in a racket – a bad racket." He said hopelessly, "He was no good at all. We were both wrong."

"You'd better tell me," Anna said.

She sat down on the bed and he told her.

"They really proved it?" Anna asked.

"Yes."

"I'm glad he's dead now," she said. "I wouldn't have wanted him to rot for years in prison."

"But can you understand how Harry – your Harry, my Harry – could have got mixed up –?" He said hopelessly, "I feel as though he had never really existed, that we'd dreamed him. Was he laughing at fools like us all the time?"

"He may have been. What does it matter?" she said. "Sit down. Don't worry." He had pictured himself comforting *her*, not this other way about. She said, "If he was alive now, he might be able to explain, but we've got to remember him as he was to us. There are always so many things one doesn't know about a person, even a person one loves – good things, bad things. We have to leave plenty of room for them."

"Those children –"

She said angrily, "For heaven's sake, stop making people in *your* image. Harry was real. He wasn't just your hero. He was Harry. He was in a racket. He did bad things. What about it? He was the man we knew."

He said, "Don't talk such bloody wisdom. Don't you see that I love you?"

She looked at him with astonishment. "You?"

"Yes, me. I don't kill people with fake drugs. I'm not a hypocrite who persuades people that I'm the greatest – I'm just a bad

498

writer who drinks too much and falls in love with girls –"

She said, "But I don't even know what color your eyes are. If you'd rung me up just now and asked me whether you were dark or fair or wore a mustache, I wouldn't have known."

"Can't you get him out of your head?"

"No."

He said, "As soon as they've cleared up this Koch murder I'm leaving Vienna. I can't feel interested any longer in whether Kurtz killed Harry – or the third man. Whoever killed him, it was a kind of justice. Maybe I'd kill him myself under those circumstances. But you still love him. You love a cheat, a murderer."

"I loved a man," she said. "I told you – a man doesn't alter because you find out more about him. He's still the same man."

"I hate the way you talk. I've got a splitting headache, and you talk and talk."

Suddenly she laughed. She said, "You are so comic. You come here at three in the morning – a stranger – and say you love me. Then you get angry and pick a quarrel. What do you expect me to do – or say?"

"I haven't seen you laugh before. Do it again. I like it."

"There isn't enough for two laughs," she said.

He took her by the shoulders and shook her gently. He said, "I'd make comic faces all day long. I'd learn a lot of jokes from the books on After-Dinner Speaking."

"Come away from the window. There are no curtains."

"There's nobody to see." But automatically checking his statement, he wasn't quite so sure; a long shadow that had moved, perhaps with the movement of clouds over the moon, was motionless again. He said, "You still love Harry, don't you?"

"Yes."

"Perhaps I do. I don't know." He dropped his hands and said, "I'll be pushing off."

He walked rapidly away. He didn't bother to see whether he was being followed, to check up on the shadow. But passing by the end of the street, he happened to turn, and there, just around the corner, pressed against a wall to escape notice, was a thick, stocky figure. Martins stopped and stared. There was something familiar about that figure. Perhaps, he thought, I've grown unconsciously used to him during these last twenty-four hours; perhaps he is one of those who have so assiduously checked my movements.

Martins stood there, twenty yards away, staring at the silent, motionless figure in the dark side street who stared back at him. A police spy, perhaps, or an agent of those other men, those men who had corrupted Harry first and then killed him. Even possibly the third man?'

It was not the face that was familiar, for he could not make out so much as the angle of the jaw; nor a movement, for the body was so still that he began to believe the whole thing was an illusion caused by shadow. He called sharply, "Do you want anything?" and there was no reply. He called again: "Answer, can't you?" And an answer came, for a window curtain was drawn petulantly back by some sleeper he had awakened and the light fell straight across the narrow street and lit up the features of Harry Lime.

"Do you believe in ghosts?" Martins asked of me.

"Do *you*?"

He hadn't come to me at once with his story – only the danger to Anna Schmidt tossed him back into my office, like something the sea has washed up, tousled, unshaven, haunted by an experience he couldn't understand.

He said, "If it had been just the face, I

wouldn't have worried. I'd been thinking about Harry, and I might easily have mistaken a stranger... The light was turned off again at once, you see; I only got one glimpse, and the man made off down the street – if he was a man. There was no turning for a long way, but I was so startled I gave him another thirty yards' start. He came to one of those newspaper kiosks, and for a moment moved out of sight. I ran after him. It only took me ten seconds to reach the kiosk, and he must have heard me running, but the strange thing was he never appeared again. I reached the kiosk. There wasn't anybody there. The street was empty. He couldn't have reached a doorway without my seeing him. He'd simply vanished."

"What did you do then?"

"I had to have another drink. My nerves were all to pieces."

"Didn't that bring him back?"

"No, but it sent me back to Anna's. But Anna was gone."

I think he would have been ashamed to come to me with his absurd story if it had not been for the attempt on Anna Schmidt. My theory when he did tell me his story was that there had been a watcher, though it was drink and hysteria that had pasted on the man's face the features of Harry Lime. That watcher had noted his visit to Anna, and the member of the ring – the penicillin ring – had been warned by telephone.

Events that night moved fast. Kurtz lived in the Russian zone, on a wide, empty, desolate street that runs down to the Prater Platz.

What happened was this: Russia, you remember, was in the chair as far as the Inner Stadt was concerned, and when Russia was in the chair you expected certain irregularities. On this occasion, halfway through the patrol, the Russian policeman pulled a fast one on his colleagues and directed the car to the street where Anna Schmidt lived. The British M.P. that night was new to his job; he didn't realize till his colleagues told him that they had entered a British zone. He spoke a little German and no French, and the Frenchman, a cynical, hard-bitten Paris *flic*, gave up the attempt to explain to him.

The American took on the job. "It's all right by me," he said, "but is it all right by you?" The British M.P. tapped the Russian's shoulder, who turned his Mongol face and launched a flood of incomprehensible Slav at him. The car drove on.

Outside Anna Schmidt's block the American took a hand in the game and

503

demanded in German what it was all about. The Frenchman leaned against the bonnet and lit a stinking cigarette. France wasn't concerned, and nothing that didn't concern France had any genuine importance to him. The Russian dug out a few words of German and flourished some papers. As far as they could tell, a Russian national wanted by the Russian police was living there without proper papers.

They went upstairs and the Russian tried Anna's door. It was flimsily bolted, but he put his shoulder to it without giving the occupant an opportunity of letting them in. Anna was in bed, though I don't suppose, after Martins's visit, that she was asleep.

While Anna was dressing, the British M.P., a Corporal Starling, phoned through to me, and I gave my instructions.

When he went back to Anna's room, a dispute was raging. Anna had told the American that she had Austrian papers (which was true) and that they were quite in order (which was rather stretching the truth). The American told the Russian in bad German that they had no right to arrest an Austrian citizen. He asked Anna for her papers, and when she produced them the Russian snatched them from her hand. "Hungarian," he said, pointing at Anna.

504

"Hungarian," and then, flourishing the papers, "Bad, bad."

The American, whose name was O'Brien, said, "Give the girl back her papers," which the Russian, naturally, didn't understand. The American put his hand on his gun, and Corporal Starling said gently, "Let it go, Pat."

"If those papers are not in order we got a right to look."

"Just let it go. We'll see the papers at H.Q."

"If we get to H.Q. You can't trust these Russian drivers. As like as not he'll drive straight through to the Russian zone."

They got back into the car with Anna, who sat in the front with the Russian, dumb with terror.

After they had gone a little way, the American touched the Russian on his shoulder. "Wrong way. H.Q. that way." The Russian chattered back in his own tongue, making a conciliatory gesture, while they drove on. "Just as I figured it," O'Brien told Starling. "They're taking her to the Russian zone." Anna stared out with terror through the windscreen. "Don't worry," O'Brien said, "I'll fix this all right." His hand was fidgeting round his gun again.

The driver put on his brakes suddenly;

505

there was a road block. You see, I knew they would have to pass this military post if they didn't make their way to the international H.Q. in the Inner City. I put my head in at the window and said to the Russian, haltingly, in his own tongue, "What are you doing in the British zone?"

He grumbled that it was "Orders."

"Whose orders? Let me see them." I noted the signature – it was useful information. I said, "This tells you to pick up a certain Hungarian national and war criminal who is living with faulty papers in the British zone. Let me see the papers."

He started on a long explanation, but I saw the papers sticking in his pocket and I pulled them out. He made a grab at his gun, and I punched his face – I felt really mean at doing so, but it's the conduct they expect from an angry officer and it brought him to reason – that and seeing three British soldiers approaching his headlights.

I said, "These papers look to me quite in order, but I'll investigate them and send a report of the result to your colonel. He can, of course, ask for the extradition of this lady at any time. All we want is proof of her criminal activities. I'm afraid we don't regard Hungarian in itself as Russian nationality."

He goggled at me (my Russian was probably half incomprehensible), and I said to Anna, "Get out of the car." She couldn't get by the Russian, so I had to pull him out first. Then I put a packet of cigarettes in his hand, said, "Have a good smoke," waved my hand to the others, gave a sigh of relief, and that incident was closed.

While Martins told me how he went back to Anna's and found her gone, I did some hard thinking. I wasn't satisfied with the ghost story or the idea that the man with Harry Lime's features had been an illusion. Keeping Martins silent with a glass of whisky, I rang up my assistant and asked him if he had located Harbin yet. He said no; he understood he'd left Klagenfurt a week ago to visit his family in the adjoining zone.

"All right," I said; "go on trying to get hold of him."

"I'm sorry, sir."

Martins was right; I had made a complete fool of myself, but remember that police work in an occupied city is not like police work at home. Everything is unfamiliar – the methods of one's foreign colleagues; the rules of evidence; even the procedure at inquests. I suppose I had got into the state of mind where one trusts too much to one's personal judgment. I had been immensely relieved by

Lime's death. I was satisfied with the accident.

I said to Martins, "Did you look inside the newspaper kiosk, or was it locked?"

"Oh, it wasn't exactly a newspaper kiosk," he said. "It was one of those solid iron kiosks you see everywhere plastered with posters."

"You'd better show me the place."

"But is Anna all right?"

"The police are watching the flat. They won't try anything else yet."

I didn't want to make a fuss and stir in the neighborhood with a police car, so we took trams – several trams – changing here and there, and came into the district on foot.

"This is the turning," Martins said, and led me down a side street. We stopped at the kiosk. "You see, he passed behind here and simply vanished – into the ground."

"That was exactly where he did vanish to," I said.

"How do you mean?"

An ordinary passer-by would never have noticed that the kiosk had a door, and of course it had been dark when the man disappeared. I pulled the door open and showed to Martins the little curling iron staircase that disappeared into the ground.

He said, "Then I didn't imagine him."

"It's one of the entrances to the main sewer."

"And anyone can go down?"

"Anyone. For some reason, the Russians object to these being locked."

"How far can one go?"

"Right across Vienna. People used them in air raids; some of our prisoners hid for two years down there. Deserters have used them – and burglars. If you know your way about you can emerge again almost anywhere in the city through a manhole or a kiosk like this one. The Austrians have to have special police for patrolling these sewers." I closed the door of the kiosk again. I said, "So that's how Harry disappeared."

"You really believe it was Harry?"

"The evidence points that way."

"Then whom did they bury?"

"I don't know yet, but we soon shall, because we're digging him up again. I've got a shrewd idea, though, that Koch wasn't the only inconvenient man they murdered."

Martins said, "What are you doing to do about it?"

"I don't know. It's no good applying to the Russians, and you can bet Lime's hiding out now in the Russian zone. We have no line now on Kurtz, for Harbin's gone."

"But it's odd, isn't it, that Koch didn't

recognize the dead man's face from the window?"

"The window was a long way up, and I expect the face had been damaged before they took the body out of the car."

Martins said thoughtfully, "I wish I could speak to him. You see there's so much I simply can't believe."

"Perhaps you're the only one who could speak to him. It's risky, though, because you do know too much."

"I still can't believe – I only saw the face for a moment." He said, "What shall I do?"

"He won't leave the Russian zone now. Perhaps that's why he tried to have the girl taken over. Because he loves her? Because he doesn't feel secure? I don't know. I do know that the only person who could persuade him to come over would be you – or her, if he still believes you are his friend. But first you've got to speak to him. I can't see the line."

"I could go and see Kurtz."

I said, "Remember. Lime may not want you to leave the Russian zone when once you're there, and I can't protect you there."

"I want to clear the whole damned thing up," Martins said, "but I'm not going to act as a decoy. I'll talk to him. That's all."

Martins gave Mr. Kurtz no warning of his visit. Better to find him out than a reception prepared for him. He was careful to carry with him all his papers, including the *laissez-passer* of the Four Powers that on the face of it allowed him to move freely through all the zones of Vienna.

He had no difficulty in finding Mr. Kurtz's block, and when he rang the bell the door was opened quickly by Mr. Kurtz himself.

"Oh," Mr. Kurtz said, "it's you, Rollo," and made a perplexed motion with his hand to the back of his head.

Martins had been wondering why he looked so different, and now he knew. Mr. Kurtz was not wearing his toupee, and yet his head was not bald. He had a perfectly normal head of hair cut close.

Kurtz said, "It would have been better to have telephoned to me. You nearly missed me – I was going out."

In the hall a cupboard door stood open, and Martins saw Mr. Kurtz's overcoat, his raincoat, a couple of soft hats, and, hanging sedately on a peg like a wrap, Mr. Kurtz's toupee. He said, "I'm glad to see your hair has grown," and was astonished to see, in the mirror on the cupboard door, the hatred flame and blush on Mr. Kurtz's face.

When Martins turned, Mr Kurtz smiled at him like a conspirator and said vaguely, "It keeps the head warm."

"Whose head?" Martins asked, for it had suddenly occurred to him how useful that toupee might have been on the day of the accident. "Never mind," he went quickly on, for his errand was not with Mr. Kurtz. "I'm here to see Harry."

"Are you mad?"

"I'm in a hurry, so let's assume that I am. Just make a note of my madness. If you should see Harry – or his ghost – let him know that I want to talk to him. I'll be waiting in the Prater by the Big Wheel for the next two hours – if you can get in touch with the dead, hurry." He added, "Remember, I was Harry's friend."

Kurtz said nothing, but somewhere, in a room off the hall, somebody cleared his throat. Martins threw open a door. He had half expected to see the dead rise yet again, but it was only Dr. Winkler, who rose from a chair in front of the kitchen stove and bowed very stiffly and correctly, with the same celluloid squeak.

Martins turned to Kurtz: "Tell the doctor about my madness. He might be able to make a diagnosis. And remember the place

512

by the Great Wheel. Or do ghosts only rise by night?" He left the flat.

For an hour he waited, walking up and down to keep warm, inside the enclosure of the Great Wheel. The smashed Prater, with its bones sticking crudely through the snow, was nearly empty. A few courting couples would be packed together in a single car of the Wheel and revolve slowly above the city surrounded by empty cars.

Martins wondered who would come for him. Was there enough friendship left in Harry for him to come alone, or would a squad of police arrive? It was obvious from the raid on Anna Schmidt's flat that he had a certain pull. And then as his watch hand passed the hours, he wondered, "Was it all an invention of my mind? Are they digging up Harry's body now in the Central Cemetery?"

Somewhere behind the cake stall a man was whistling, and Martins knew the tune. He turned and waited. Was it fear or excitement that made his heart beat – or just the memories that tune ushered in, for life had always quickened when Harry came, came just as he came now, as though nothing much had happened, nobody had been lowered into a grave or found with a cut

513

throat in a basement, came with his amused, deprecating take-it-or-leave-it manner – and of course one always took it.

"Harry."

"Hullo, Rollo."

Don't picture Harry Lime as a smooth scoundrel. He wasn't that. The picture I have of him on my files is an excellent one: he is caught by a street photographer with his stocky legs apart, big shoulders a little hunched, a belly that has known too much good food too long, and on his face a look of cheerful rascality, a geniality, a recognition that *his* happiness will make the world's day. Now he didn't make the mistake of putting out a hand – which might have been rejected – but instead just patted Martins on the elbow and said, "How are things?"

"We've got to talk, Harry."

"Of course."

He had always known the ropes, and even in the smashed pleasure park he knew them, tipping the woman in charge of the Wheel so that they might have a car to themselves.

Very slowly on one side of them the city sank; very slowly on the other the great cross girders of the Wheel rose into sight. As the horizon slid away, the Danube became visible, and the piers of the Kaiser Friedrich Brucke lifted above the houses.

514

"Well," Harry said, "It's good to see you, Rollo."

"I was at your funeral."

"That was pretty smart of me, wasn't it?"

"Not so smart for your girl. She was there, too – in tears."

"She's a good little thing," Harry said. "I'm very fond of her."

"I didn't believe the police when they told me about you."

Harry said, "I wouldn't have asked you to come if I'd known what was going to happen, but I didn't think the police were onto me."

"Were you going to cut me in on the spoils?"

"I've never kept you out of anything, old man, yet."

He stood with his back to the door as the car swung upward, and smiled back at Rollo Martins, who could remember him in just such an attitude in a secluded corner of the school quad, saying, "I've learnt the way to get out at night. It's absolutely safe. You are the only one I'm letting in on it."

For the first time Rollo Martins looked back through the years without admiration, as he thought, "He's never grown up." Evil was like Peter Pan – it carried with it the horrifying and horrible gift of eternal youth.

515

Martins said, "Have you ever visited the children's hospital? Have you seen any of your victims?"

Harry took a look at the toy landscape below and came away from the door. "I never feel quite safe in these things," he said. He felt the back of the door with his hand, as though he were afraid that it might fly open and launch him into space.

"Victims?" he asked. "Don't be melodramatic, Rollo; look down there," he went on, pointing through the window at the people moving like black flies at the base of the Wheel. "Would you realy feel any pity if one of those dots stopped moving – forever? If I said you can have twenty thousand pounds for every dot that stops, would you really, old man, tell me to keep my money – without hesitation? Or would you calculate how many dots you could afford to spare? Free of income tax, old man. Free of income tax."

"Couldn't you have stuck to tires?"

"Like Cooler? No, I've always been ambitious."

"You're finished now. The police know everything."

"But they can't catch me, Rollo – you'll see. I'll pop up again. You can't keep a good man down."

The car swung to a standstill at the highest point of the curve, and Harry turned his back and gazed out of the window.

Martins thought, One good shove and I could break the glass, and he pictured the body falling, falling, through the iron struts, a piece of carrion dropping down among the flies.

He said, "You know the police are planning to dig up your body. What will they find?"

"Harbin," Harry replied with simplicity.

"Why did the Russians try to take Anna Schmidt?" Martins asked.

"She had false papers, old man."

"Who told them?"

"The price of living in this zone, Rollo, is service. I have to give them a little information now and then."

"I thought perhaps you were just trying to get her here – because she was your girl? Because you wanted her?"

Harry smiled. "I haven't all that influence."

"What would have happened to her?"

"Nothing very serious. She'd have been sent back to Hungary. There's nothing against her, really. A year in a labor camp, perhaps. She'd be infinitely better off in her own country than being pushed around by the British police."

"She loves you."

"Well, I gave her a good time while it lasted."

"And I love her."

"That's fine, old man. Be kind to her. She's worth it. I'm glad." He gave the impression of having arranged everything to everybody's satisfaction.

"I'd like to knock you through the window."

"But you won't, old man. I'd trust you anywhere, Rollo. Kurtz tried to persuade me not to come, but I know you. Then he tried to persuade me to, well, arrange an accident. He told me it would be quite easy in this car."

"Except that I'm the stronger man."

"But I've got the gun. You don't think a bullet wound would show when you hit *that* ground?"

Again the car began to move, sailing slowly down, until the flies were midgets, were recognizable human beings.

"What fools we are, Rollo, talking like this, as if I'd do that to you – or you to me." He turned his back and leaned his face against the glass. "In these days, old man, nobody thinks in terms of human beings. Governments don't, so why should we? They talk of the people and the proletariat, and I talk of the mugs. It's the same thing." As the car reached the platform and the faces of the doomed-to-be-victims, the tired, pleasure-hoping Sunday faces, peered in at them, he said, "I could cut you in, you know. I have no one left in the Inner City."

"Except Cooler? And Winkler?"

"You really mustn't turn policeman, old man," They passed out of the car and he put his hand again on Martins's elbow. "That was a joke; I know you won't. I've got to leave you here. We'll see each other – sometime. If you're in a jam, you can always get me at Kurtz's."

He moved away and, turning, waved the hand he had the tact not to offer; it was like the whole past moving off under a cloud.

Martins called after him, "Don't trust me, Harry," but there was too great a distance now between them for the words to carry.

"Anna was at the theater," Martins told me, "for the Sunday matinee. I had to see the whole dreary comedy through a second time. About a middle-aged composer and an infatuated girl and an understanding – a terribly understanding – wife. Anna acted very badly; she wasn't much of an actress at the best of times. I saw her afterward in her dressing room.

"I told her Harry was alive – I thought she'd be glad and that I would hate to see how glad she was, but she sat in front of her makeup mirror and let the tears streak the grease paint, and I wished, after all, that she had been glad. She looked awful and I loved her. Then I told her about my interview with Harry, but she wasn't really paying much attention, because when I'd finished she said, 'I wish he was dead.'"

"He deserves to be," Martins had answered.

"I mean, he would be safe then – from everybody," Anna had said.

I asked Martins, "Did you show her the photographs I gave you – of the children?"

"Yes. I thought, it's got to be kill-or-cure this time. She's got to get Harry out of her system. I propped the pictures up among the pots of grease. She couldn't avoid seeing them. I said, 'The police can't arrest Harry unless they get him into this zone, and we've got to help do it.'

"She said, 'Thought he was your friend.' I said, 'He *was* my friend.' She said, 'I'll never help you to get Harry. I don't want to see him again, I don't want to hear his voice.

I don't want to be touched by him, but I won't do a thing to harm him.'

"I felt bitter – I don't know why, because, after all, I had done nothing for her. I just got up and left her then. Now it's your turn to work on me, Colonel. What do you want me to do?"

"I want to act quickly," I told Martins. "It was Harbin's body in the coffin, so we can pick up Winkler and Cooler right away. Kurtz is out of our reach for the time being, and so is the driver. We'll put in a formal request to the Russians for permission to arrest Kurtz and Lime. It makes our files tidy. If we're going to use you as our decoy, your message must go to Lime straight away – not after you've hung around in this zone for twenty-four hours.

"As I see it, you were brought here for a grilling almost as soon as you got back into the Inner City; you heard then from me about Harbin; you put two and two together, and you go and warn Cooler. We'll let Cooler slip for the sake of the bigger game; we have no evidence he was in on the penicillin racket. He'll escape into the Russian zone to Kurtz, and Lime will know you've played the game. Three hours later you send a message that the police are after you – you are in hiding and must see him."

"He won't come."

"I'm not so sure. We'll choose our hiding place carefully – when he'll think there's a minimum of risk. It's worth trying. It would appeal to his pride and his sense of humor if he could scoop you out. And it would stop your mouth."

He said, "I told Harry not to trust me, but he didn't hear."

"Do you agree to this plan?"

"Yes," he said, "I agree."

All the first arrangements went well. We delayed arresting Winkler, who had returned from the Russian zone, until after Cooler had been warned.

Martins enjoyed his short interview with Cooler. Cooler greeted him without embarrassment and with considerable patronage: "Why, Mr. Martins, it's good to see you. Sit down. I'm glad everything went off all right between you and Colonel Calloway. A very straight chap, Calloway."

"It didn't," Martins said.

"You don't bear any ill will, I'm sure, about my letting him know about you seeing Koch. The way I figured it was this: if you were innocent you'd clear yourself right away, and if you were guilty, well, the fact that I liked you oughtn't to stand in the way. A citizen has his duties."

"Like giving false evidence at an inquest."

Cooler said, "Oh, that old story. I'm afraid you are riled at me, Mr. Martins. Look at it this way – you as a citizen, owing allegiance to –"

"The police have dug up the body. They'll be after you and Winkler. I want you to warn Harry."

"I don't understand."

"Oh, yes, you do." And it was obvious that he did.

Martins left him abruptly. He wanted no more of that kindly, humanitarian face.

It only remained then to bait the trap. After studying the map of the sewer system, I came to the conclusion that a café anywhere near the main entrance of the great sewer, which was placed in what Martins had mistakenly called a newspaper kiosk, would be the most likely spot to tempt Lime. He had only to rise once again through the ground, walk fifty yards, bring Martins back with him, and sink again into the obscurity of the sewers.

He had no idea that his method of evasion was known to us. He probably knew that one patrol of the sewer police ended before midnight, and the next did not start till two;

and so, at midnight, Martins sat in the little cold café in sight of the kiosk drinking coffee after coffee. I had given him a revolver; I had men posted as close to the kiosk as I could; and the sewer police were ready, when zero hour struck, to close the manholes and start sweeping the sewers inward from the edge of the city.

There was no heating in the café, and Martins sat warming each hand in turn on a cup of ersatz coffee – innumerable cups. There was usually one of my men in the café with him, but I changed them every twenty minutes or so irregularly. More than an hour passed. Martins had long given up hope, and so had I where I waited at the end of a phone several streets away, with a party of the sewer police ready to do down.

My telephone rang. It was Martins. He said, "I'm perishing with cold. It's a quarter past one. Is there any point in going on with this?"

"He can't delay much longer if he's coming. He won't want to run into the two-o'clock patrol. Stick it another quarter of an hour, but keep away from the telephone."

Martins's voice said suddenly, "He's here. He's –" And then the telephone went dead.

I said to my assistant, "Give the signal to

524

guard all manholes," and to my sewer police, "We're going down."

What had happened was this: Martins was still on the telephone, still talking to me, when Harry Lime came into the café. I don't know what he heard, if he heard anything. The mere sight of a man wanted by the police and without friends in Vienna speaking on the telephone would have been enough to warn him. He was out of the café again before Martins had put down the receiver. It was one of those rare moments when none of my men were in the café. One had just left and another was about to come in.

Harry Lime brushed by him and made for the kiosk. Martins came out of the café and saw my man. If he had called out then it would have been easy to shoot, but it wasn't, I suppose, Lime, the penicillin racketeer, who was escaping down the street; it was Harry. He hesitated just long enough for Lime to put the kiosk between them, then he called out, "That's him!" but Lime had already gone to ground.

What a strange world unknown to most of us lies under our feet; we live above a cavernous land of waterfalls and rushing rivers, where tides ebb and flow as in the world above.

The main sewer, half as wide as the Thames, rushes by under a huge arch, fed by tributary streams. These streams have fallen in waterfalls from higher levels and have been purified in their fall, so that only in these side channels is the air foul. The main stream smells sweet and fresh, with a faint tang of ozone, and everywhere in the darkness is the sound of rushing water.

It was just past high tide when Martins and the policeman reached the river. First the curving iron staircase, then a short passage so low they had to stoop, and then the shallow edge of the water lapped at their feet. My man shone his light along the edge of the current and said, "He's gone that way," for just as a deep stream when it shallows at the rim leaves an accumulation of debris, so the sewer left in the quiet water against the wall a scum of orange peel, old cigarette butts, and the like, and in this scum Lime had left his trail.

My policeman shone his light ahead with his left hand and carried his gun in his right. He said to Martins, "Keep behind me, sir – he may shoot."

The water came halfway up their legs as they walked. The policeman kept his light pointing down and ahead at the disturbed trail at the sewer's edge. He said, "The silly thing is he doesn't stand a chance. The manholes are all guarded and we've cordoned off the way into the Russian zone. All our chaps have to do now is sweep inward down the side passage from the manholes."

He took a whistle out of his pocket and blew, and very far away there came the notes of the reply. He said, "They're all down here now. The sewer police, I mean."

He lifted his light for the moment to shine it ahead, and at that moment the shot came. The light flew out of his hand and fell on the stream. He said, "Dod blast it!"

"Are you hurt?" Martins asked.

"Scraped my hand, that's all. A week off work. Here, take this other flashlight, sir, while I tie my hand up. Don't shine it. He's in one of the side passages."

For a long time the sound of the shot went on reverberating. When the last echo died, a whistle blew ahead of them, and Martins's companion blew an answer.

Martins said, "Let me come in front. I don't think he'll shoot at me, and I want to talk to him."

"I had orders to look after you, sir."

"That's all right." Martins edged round, plunging a foot deeper in the stream as he went. When he was in front he called out, "Harry," and the name set up an echo,

"Harry, Harry, Harry," which traveled down the stream and woke a whole chorus of whistles in the darkness.

A voice startlingly close made them hug the wall. "Is that you, old man?" it called. "What do you want me to do?"

"Come out. And put your hands above your head."

"I haven't a light, old man. I can't see a thing."

"Be careful, sir," the policeman said.

"Get flat against the wall. He won't shoot at me," Martins said. He called, "Harry, I'm going to shine the light. Play fair and come out. You haven't got a chance."

He flashed the light on, and twenty feet away, at the edge of the light and the water, Harry stepped into view. "Hands above the head, Harry."

Harry raised his hand and fired. The shot ricocheted against the wall a foot from Martins's head, and he heard the policeman cry out. At the same moment a search light from fifty yards away lit the whole channel, caught Harry in its beams, Martins, the staring eyes of the policeman slumped at the water's edge with the sewage washing to his waist.

Martins stood above the policeman's body, with Harry Lime halfway between us. We couldn't shoot for fear of hitting Martins, and the light of the searchlight dazzled Lime. We moved slowly on, our revolvers trained for a chance, and Lime turned this way and that way, like a rabbit dazzled by headlights. Then suddenly he took a flying jump into the deep central rushing stream. When we turned the searchlight after him he was submerged, and the current of the sewer carried him rapidly on, past the body of the policeman, out of the range of the search light into the dark.

Martins stood at the outer edge of the searchlight beam, staring downstream. He had his gun in his hand now, and he was the only one of us who could fire with safety. I thought I saw a movement, and called out to him, "There. There. Shoot."

He lifted his gun and fired. A cry of pain came tearing back – a reproach, an entreaty.

"Well done!" I called.

I looked up, and Martins was out of sight in the darkness. I called his name, and it was lost in a confusion of echoes, in the rush and the roar of the underground river. Then I heard a third shot.

Martins told me later: "I walked upstream to find Harry, but I must have missed him in the dark. I was afraid to lift the torch; I didn't want to tempt him to shoot again. He must have been struck by my bullet just at the entrance of a side passage. Then I suppose he crawled up the passage to the foot of the iron stairs. Thirty feet above his head was the manhole, but he wouldn't have had the strength to lift it, and even if he had succeeded, the police were waiting above.

"He must have known all that, but he was in great pain, and just as an animal creeps into the dark to die, so I suppose a man makes for the light. He wants to die at home, and the darkness is never home to *us*. He began to pull himself up the stairs, but then the pain took him and he couldn't go on. What made him whistle that absurd scrap of a tune I'd been fool enough to believe he had written himself?

"Anyway, I heard his whistle and came back along the edge of the stream, and felt the wall end and found my way up the passage where he lay. I said, 'Harry,' and the whistling stopped, just above my head. I put my hand on an iron handrail and climbed. I was still afraid he might shoot. Then, only three steps up, my foot stamped down on his hand.

"I shone my light on him. He didn't have a gun; he must have dropped it when my bullet hit him. For a moment I thought he

530

was dead, but then he whimpered with pain. I said, 'Harry,' and he swiveled his eyes with a great effort to my face. He was trying to speak, and I bent down to listen.

"'Bloody fool,' he said – that was all: I don't know whether he meant that for himself or for me. Then he began to whimper again. I couldn't bear it any more, and I put a bullet through him."

"We'll forget that bit," I said.

Martins said, "I never shall."

A thaw set in that night, and all over Vienna the snow melted, and the ugly ruins came to light again: steel rods hanging like stalactites and rusty girders thrusting like bones through the gray slush. Burials were much simpler than they had been a week before, when electric drills had been needed to break the frozen ground. It was almost as warm as a spring day when Harry Lime had his second funeral. I was glad to get him under earth again. But it had taken two men's deaths. The group by the grave was smaller now; Kurtz wasn't there, nor Winkler – only the girl and Rollo Martins and myself. And there weren't any tears.

After it was over, the girl walked away, without a word to either of us, down the long avenue of trees that led to the main entrance and the tram stop, splashing through the melted snow.

I said to Martins, "I've got transport. Can I give you a lift?"

"No," he said, "I'll take a tram back."

"You win; you've proved me a bloody fool."

"I haven't won," he said. "I've lost."

I watched him striding off after the girl. He caught up with her and they walked side by side. I don't think he said a word to her. It was like the end of a story, except that before they turned out of my sight her hand was through his arm – which is how a story usually begins.

And Crabbin? Oh, Crabbin is still arguing with the British Council about Dexter's expenses. They say they can't pass simultaneous payments in Stockholm and Vienna. Poor Crabbin . . . Poor all of us, when you come to think of it.